Harald Meier

Detour back to Life

Honest, thoughtful, sometimes funny:
my way through cancer
via Kalimpong/Darjeeling

The German National Library lists this publication; detailed bibliographic data is available on the Internet: http//dnb.dnb.de.

The German 1st ed. in 2024 was published as:
Kalimpong *Leukämie* Ist das ansteckend? *Ist das eine Chance?*

Publisher: BoD · Books on Demand GmbH, Überseering 33, 22297 Hamburg, bod@bod.de
Print: Libri Plureos GmbH, Friedensallee 273, 22763 Hamburg

ISBN: 978-3-8192-2890-2

To my children

Fabian, Sarah-Lena and Simon

and in memory to my friends

Peter and Rainer

Page

A word beforehand ...   8

Postscript, and thank you all   10

Off to Darjeeling   Before the New Truth   **11** 31

My New Truth   **The Himalaya Highlands**   35 **42**

First Days in a new Home   Hospital Intensive Care   **58** 64

Trapped in my Body   **Lower Echhey Village Life**   83 **121**

Home away from Home   My Chemo Life Cycle   **140** 167

Follow-up Treatment   **Goodbye, and see you again**   184 **195**

Everlasting Memories   Years Follow-up Treatment   **213** 227

The Truth remains   **... Darjeeling Village Life too**   249 **259**

... and a word afterwards   286

A word beforehand ...

The idea for the book came at short notice. At the age of 61, I was diagnosed with Acute Leukaemia, also known as blood cancer. Untreated, it means to die within a few weeks. Today, after months in hospital, years follow-up treatment, weeks rehabilitation I am now considered as medically cured.

Of course, you can't let go of this break. But, there were also funny and sometimes beautiful experiences, friendships with people with a common destiny, even it was only for a few days, weeks or months. So, my attitude to life has changed from the ground up.

After I had been stabilized in the clinic intensive care unit and had overcome the initial shock, I was transferred to what I now call the normal leukaemia ward. There, despite limited physical and spatial possibilities, I then began to become active. Not only professionally, because there was a lot to organize for my students in the middle of the semester. But also for me personally, I accepted this supposedly last short period of life as an important part of my life.

At that time, I neither knew nor could I have imagined that I would be virtually isolated in a hospital for many months, followed by years follow-up treatment. Like probably most people in such a situation, I searched for information, including pseudo-knowledgeable internet blogs, where someone knows someone who knows someone who has heard from someone ... And my questions directly to my medical care were answered in a friendly but, for me, evasive manner.

Today I know, unconsciously I only was looking for a percentage of how likely it is to die or to survive. Even though most people still associate leukaemia with imminent death, unspeakable pain, fear and loss. But over time I gradually began to see more funny, positive and also interesting things.

Whether or not my impressions are published is a minor matter for the time being, it's first and foremost about my family, for myself, and for my friends. But perhaps it will also help others to understand and encourage me.

I don't want to relativize this terrible disease, nor do I wish it on people I personally don't like.

When I was able to return to India one year ago – for years I had done monitoring work in development cooperation projects – I sat over tea at a small self-sufficient mountain farm in the highlands, the so-called Lower Himalayas, for us known as Darjeeling with their famous tea. In November, the climate was very pleasant for me as a European, in contrast to the hot and humid lowlands in India.

And then there was My Room; bed, table, chair, and on a door outside a sign: Western Toilet. All this in the midst of a huge green vegetable garden with terraced rice fields and an indescribable view of the Darjeeling and Himalayan image we know. At that moment, I knew that I want to live here for a while.

After exactly one year, I am now here for three months. And in the days before my trip began, I had the idea of linking the experience of my leukaemia with diary-like impressions here. Will it be the end of leukaemia for me?

Harald Meier
Bonn/Lower Echhey, April 2024

P.S. An English friend, I asked about their punctuation: 'If you're German and think you have to put a comma, just leave it.

Postscript, and thank you all

Everyone has certainly heard 'beetroot helps with cancer' from someone who have heard it from others, etc., or as journalistic half-knowledge or esoteric self-medication. Yes, it is true that some things help, such as transcending dance as well. It helps to forget the cancer for moments and to enjoy dancing, but does not stop a biological development of cancer.

Despite a century of research, there is no evidence for the so-called Alternative Therapies. Many of my fellow patients who, in desperation, saw such pseudo-therapies as their supposedly saving straw, also lay next to me; in most cases, it was then too late for them.

Of course, medical terms overwhelm me. Even hearing them repeatedly and writing them correctly doesn't mean I understand and use them correctly. Also, with a little more knowledge now, I can only describe my perceptions. I have certainly forgotten or suppressed some things. Or I don't want to write it for personal reasons, and also to avoid embarrassing others or myself. But I try to be honest and realistic.

Please forgive me if I mislabel or misinterpret something medically from my subjective patient perspective; the same applies, for example, to the culture and religion in India, for which I have great respect.

Thank you to all of you, Fabian, Sarah-Lena and Simon, Dr Joest, Professor Dr Brossart, Dr Schwab and Ms Lerbs, Ms Martini, Sujoy with Sarah and Suniti, Mr Ziegler, Mr (†) and Ms Griem, Ms Knobel and Jutta, Torsten, Martina and Barbara, Rainer (†), Erika, Professor Muck, Professor Lemke, Judith, Peter (†) with Ute and Hannah, Anke, Petra and Andrea, Uli and Linda, Manju, Giri-Raj and Prashant, the people of Lower Echhey ... and one always forgets to thank someone; thank you to all the helping hands in the families, neighbourhood and organisations and your thinking of me even in silence.

Off to Darjeeling   Before the New Truth

You have been given a second life, never forget that.
What do you want to do with it now?

One of my specialist doctors

Off to Darjeeling

What can I expect?

For over 10 years, I have regularly travelled to India for a few days to certify start-up training. People in precarious living conditions such as SHGs (self-help groups), small farmers in rural regions, or young people as former child labourers, they learn how to stabilize and improve their income situation or to become self-employed; because they have no chance on the labour market without training or there is simply no chance of earning a decent income without training.

Exactly one year before the end of my follow-up treatment, I visited two cooperatives made up of women SHGs in the far north of West Bengal in the Lower Himalayas, known to us as Darjeeling. All of them have a kitchen garden with a cow and calf, a couple of goats or chickens, small fields as rice terraces or they work as tea pickers each day six hours for an average a bit more than 2 USD a day. Their husbands are small-scale self-sufficient farmers or sometimes also work in the tea garden, as seasonal workers or as day labourers on building sites in the surrounding area. This is how they try to earn a living and send their children to school.

In one project, where we had lunch and we sat together over tea afterwards, they had just furnished two rooms as guest rooms; bed, table and a chair. And they had already added a western WC as well as a hot shower.

I immediately realised, I wanted to spend some time here. That's what I need next year after retirement; far away from it all, surrounded by nature, reading, writing; let my mind and thoughts roam, as we say. And the climate here in the highlands is so pleasant. It is not this humid and often unbearable heat we Europeans experience in India. It is relatively dry, with a maximum temperature of 24°C. During the day there is always a cool breeze coming up from the cold valley river, pleasantly cool (for me) in the evening and at night.

I spontaneously asked if they would rent out the room for a few weeks or even months? They had not even thought about how they wanted to market it in future; and for Home Staying they would need a specific permission. So, they just invited me as a friend to stay for some time, that they learn about having such kind of guests. I took photos and kept in touch via my colleague and friend in Kolkata who had introduced SHGs in skill- and start-up training programmes here.

Then, of course, I read a lot about West Bengal with 92 million people; a mid-sized federal state with a significantly larger population than my home country Germany. And about the changing history of the Darjeeling region here in northeastern India, bordering Nepal, China and Bhutan. Also about he arbitrarily drawn borders by the British colonial rulers, their partitioning and annexation of territories and violent deportations, regardless ethnicities, religions and histo-rical regional affiliations; although Hindus, Christians, Muslims and other religions had lived together peacefully here for centuries.

Nepali is still spoken regionally today. The family ties, grown over the centuries, are more important than a national passport.

During my growing dream of spending my Time-Out there I star-ted a to-do list. Step by step, I added or deleted something during my daily afternoon coffee. And the books I was reading about the region and its history became more, as well as books I wanted to take with me to read. As a matter of principle and as a long-time author – mainly business books – I no longer want to get used to e-books. Also I wan-ted to be completely without the internet, social media & co.; that would only distract me from thinking, writing and relaxing.

I wanted to live spartanly and wasn't afraid of it, because I had already lived in North Africa during my civilian service, and later again and again, writing by the sea or in the mountains; improvising every day is a satisfying challenge for me.

Probably unconsciously – here in anticipation, as I later realised – I was somehow missing the loneliness and monotony of the hospital room during the leukaemia, which motivated me to be creative and to confront myself.

Despite two 23-kg baggage allowances on an international flight, I managed to get by with just one large travel bag and a small backpack cabin luggage. That with a gift for my Kolkata friends and my new hosts. Later, this proved to be helpful on the one hand, but also challenging. Because on the domestic flight Kolkata–Shiliguri, north of West Bengal, which had to be booked separately a few days later, only one 15-kg check-in luggage was allowed in addition to a 7-kg cabin baggage.

I think about the travelling route and time. First a short walk to the local train station, then by train along the river *Rhein* with a change to Frankfurt airport. An evening flight to Delhi with a four and a half hour shorter night as the time difference flying towards the sun. After a few hours' layover there, a two-hours connecting flight to Kolkata. No problem, I've done that before several times. And I love arriving slowly. If there was the option of a days-long train journey, I would seriously consider it. In Kolkata they will pick me up at the airport as usual, and I wouldn't have to defend a mass incessant taxi recruiters. Then another two hours through an unbelievable maze of buses and cars, rickshaws and these tuk-tuks, the 3-wheeled semi-open auto-rickshaws as taxis, to the centre of Kolkata; a mega-city with over 15 million people. My home town, the city of Bonn, with around 400,000 inhabitants would be just a small town district.

My Indian-German friends *Sujoy* & *Sarah* have already renovated an old townhouse with a roof terrace, including the traditional old ceiling fans and modern air conditioning; otherwise the hot and humid climate would be unbearable for me.

Kolkata, this city always fascinates me; it is so different from Delhi or Mumbai. Bengalis feel themselves much more people with great intellectual, cultural and political tradition. Kolkata used to be the capital of India until it became, as the name suggests in the western world, New Delhi.

After three days I will go into my solitude; a guest room at a small farm in a rural village, scattered on a mountainside without a centre. And I will not understand the language. At first I thought it is Bengali as the language of the federal state of West Bengal. But it later turned out to be a completely different language with Nepali. And who will speak English? During the short visit a year ago, we had the local project manager with us as a trip manager and of course as translators.

And finally, I think, will it feel the same there as it did five years ago during my many months in the university hospital? There, my radius was mostly limited to the nearly isolated hospital room and occasionally shuffling up and down the corridor at night when there was no other people.

A long Thursday

My flight is scheduled for the evening. Of course, I'm at the airport far too early. But why should I sit around at home for half a day? And I haven't slept half the night anyway.

While waiting at the check-in, I meet an Indian professor; she is a regular visitor to Germany and has worked in my neighbour town Cologne for some time. Check-in goes smoothly and I manage to upgrade my booked aisle seat to the last available seat in the emergency exit. Great, I have more legroom and can always stand up and stretch my feet without disturbing the person sitting next to me.

Shortly before the boarding announced on the display board, it is already very loud around me. The flight seems to be fully booked. Many Indians, and especially Bengalis, are flying to visit their parents or to go home; their days-long highest religious and social event *Durga Puja* takes place.

Indian culture generally communicates louder and always laughs a lot; I like that. Babies sleep or cry and small children whinge when they are overtired or from the chaos around them. Others happily roll their parents' suitcases back and forth, preferably far away from their parents. Nuns pray, two Buddhist monks write on their laptops, travel groups in trekking outfits discuss, young white European women and even a few men play it cool in supposedly Indian artefacts.

They probably want to go to Puna and Goa. At worst, when they arrive, they'll be wearing European-style off-the-shoulder and body-hugging leggings. No Indian woman would do something like that, my Indian friend once said on a flight together. He is very competent in Indian history and culture. Married to a German, they have been commuting between their homes in Kolkata and Stuttgart for many years. Indians make jokes about it, my friend said, these women usually don't even know what the many forehead signs mean. Even the *Tika* as a small red mark between the brows would not always and everywhere mean married. Depending on the religion, ethnicity and situation, it would also have a different meaning. Not even he knows all this for whole of India. That also applies to the traditional clothing and jewellery. Compared to Germany, he added, like we tourists here wearing *Lederhose & Dirndl,* your old-fashioned and for regions limited trousers and dresses on historic festivals.

The flight, or rather boarding, is delayed every quarter of an hour, even though the plane is already at the gangway. Business people are now on the phone, young people are excited on their social media, and parents look annoyed. A few, probably Indian students or engineers and IT professionals, quickly grab a last German beer.

Finally, the boarding call comes. A queue immediately forms for boarding. I make small talk with an Indian chemist, he just came from a conference in Germany. Suddenly it gets restless and I hear the first excited shouts. The plane can't take off, a spare part is needed, which is due to arrive here the next day on the daily scheduled flight from Delhi.

I ask myself, don't the aircraft manufacturers store spare parts in Europe for the thousands of flights every day? Or German *Lufthansa* with Frankfurt as central hub and *Air India* as the *Star Alliance* partner? Because many passengers have *Lufthansa* tickets in the shared flight as it turns out later.

Buses to hotels are reserved outside, we can download an app in our mobile phone for a food voucher with delivery service. Of course

I don't do that, I won't be stuffing my face with fast food in a hotel room at almost midnight.

Half an hour later, I arrive with many others at a so-called 4-star hotel belonging to an internationally renowned hotel group. But this doesn't mean anything. The room looks appealing on the surface, but there's many hair in the bathroom and in the shower, and the desk and side table must have been wiped clean a week ago? But never mind, it's the international book fair and Frankfurt is fully booked, so they excuse everything, as we later realise.

... and Friday, Saturday, Sunday

Now, supposed to be in Delhi changing to Kolkata, I am taking hotel breakfast still in Frankfurt. The breakfast buffet is great and everyone seems to be in a good mood. I join a table with people I know from the check-in queue and the bus to the hotel that night. We'll become a team (anticipating here). A young Indian women studying her Master in Germany, a Mexican, she is a cocoa importer, and later the Indian professor joins us as well.

The latest information was to take the same flight in the evening; our plane would then fly parallel to the daily scheduled flight. And we can leave everything in the room during the day and stay in the hotel, the food will be delivered by *Air India*. That sounds professional, and we concluded that *Air India* is not responsible for a technical defect. Our checked baggage from last night is already on the plane.

So we share a taxi to the airport to see if everything is okey. Of course, as their quasi-German host here now, I pay the almost 40 Euro and kindly reject all attempts by our team to participate.

A new check-in is now necessary at the airport. It is the same plane, but there is a new flight number for the new day; the former flight number is the daily scheduled flight. We are given the same boarding time, but with now a different gate. The normal scheduled flight is of course at the daily gate; everything sounds logical. We are told to drive to the hotel, where we will have lunch and an afternoon snack.

We hear from other passengers stranded like us that they have tried to re-book. For them business class, there had been quick rebookings to other airlines the evening before and even now. Of course, this was not the case for us in economy class. And even not the ones with a *Lufthansa* ticket, they were also asked to contact *Air India*. This is of course a trick to get rid of them as a problem in the first place; *Lufthansa* doesn't feel responsible. This confirms not only my impression, their service has become worse and worse over the years and a lot of Small Print in ticket booking excludes a lot.

Our flight is now shown on the large display board with the new flight number, but still as 'delayed' flight time; so, no right to re-book.

More and more, we realise among ourselves that there are different and contradictory statements. *Lufthansa* doesn't bother to provide information. That would be the minimum of customer friendliness, says a disgruntled passenger with a *Lufthansa* ticket. Okey, right hand in *Star Alliance* obviously doesn't know what left hand is doing.

Like me many try to contact *Air India* office Frankfurt, but we are always ending up in an announcement loop. Then someone got indirect contact via a lady form the central airport information desk. With her for sure different number she immediately got *Air India* on the line. She presses getting louder, and it is promised someone will immediately come to the airport info desk; where we are now standing with about 30 passengers.

Another group, we had split up, has gathered at the check-in, which is due to open at 5 p.m. Maybe someone will show up before then? Still after two hours, there is nobody from *Air India*. The helpful, friendly lady at the information desk tells us laconically this happens more often with them.

We discuss what this chaos means for the individual. One family had given their son a 5-day trip to visit the Taj Mahal as a graduation present; their group, which was supposed to meet in Delhi, was now gone. The same applies to two sporty-looking older men, now have missed an onward flight to Kathmandu for a Himalayas hiking tour; probably despite having already planned a buffer day, as following flights there are usually fully booked well in advance ... and so on.

Young parents with babies and small children have been unable to access their baggage, which has been on the plane since yesterday. But business class passengers were able to re-book or continue their flight on their own, they have been able to collect their luggage in a special room since yesterday evening. *Air India* and *Lufthansa*, together with other *Star Alliance* partners, boast about their so-called *CSR*, Corporate Social Responsibility, as being family- & child-friendly; but obviously not for the economy class.

I myself am relatively relaxed, as it doesn't really matter when I'll arrive. That's what I think at first, because after all I have three months ahead of me; a few days delay don't really matter for me.

In the meantime, we drive back to the hotel in a team of four to pack our cabin luggage and have something to eat. They tell us that lunch is coming soon, but it's already past noon and the food arrives shortly before 5 p.m. But hardly anyone eats anything and the four of us take a taxi back to the airport. It's starting to get expensive, I'm running out of cash, and my fellow travellers have hardly any Euro-cash left. The Indian women give me her share in Rupees, which is very practical for me. And I manage to persuade the Mexican woman to use her share for a donation in Mexico; we joke that the best thing to do is to help victims of air travellers.

Air India check-in is on time, new flight ticket, new flight number and new gate for the now hopefully repaired plane from yesterday. Some manage to re-book in a free seat on the regular flight. I have to smile, because they are pretty convincing at the check-in to appear super-stitious.

Everything now goes smoothly and boarding is announced with only an hour's delay. I hear someone saying we won't be taking off, we're late again. *Air India-* and airport staff don't seem to have coordi-nated. It gets loud again among us waiting. Despite my boarding pass, I am now asked to show my visa, even though it has already been checked twice at check-in. It is also stamped all over my passport; in previous years my passport was always enough. As a typical German in my age, I have of course printed everything out again and am now rummaging around in my backpack for the paper printout of the e-visa.

Suddenly an announcement: 'Please all line up in a row and just show your boarding pass, we'll do everything else on the plane.' Now it's on and we hurry down the stairs one after the other to a waiting room. After a short wait, we sit tightly packed in the bus for the relatively long, winding drive to our plane parked far away.

Someone jokes: 'The bus driver would be better off driving straight to the runway and asking the tower for permission for the bus to take off, cars in Germany are all in such good technical shape.' Relaxed laughers. Another, 'maybe it's better to take the bus overland, German buses are always so punctual.' It seems we're all in a good mood now.

Boarding completed, all baggage is stowed, safety instructions are shown on screens in various languages and seatbelt signs light up. Our plane is still stationary, and stands still, and ... nothing happens.

Things are slowly getting restless again. New announcement from the cockpit: 'Just a short delay in take-off, we are waiting for clearance from the tower.' Some passengers start to laugh and sarcastic remarks can be heard. Many of the Indians probably work in Germany and speak relatively good German; most with a regional southern dialect, which sounds funny for us.

New announcement: 'We had problems clearing the outside stairs, *Air Traffic Control* must confirm clearance because take-off is now after 11 p.m.'

Now it's getting even more restless. Stewardesses try to calm us down. I feel sorry for them, because they have nothing to do with it. New announcement: 'We have still no clearance from the German authorities. But we'll get the exemption authorisation from the ministry. It's just routine here, but it's the law.' The first ones shouts: 'That's a lie.' And, 'has the pilot ever seen anyone working in a government office on a Friday evening in Germany?' Many laugh. 'Civil servants only work until noon Fridays anyway,' shouts one. 'They sit in their local pub Friday evening anyway,' adds another. The atmosphere becomes more heated.

Announcement again: 'We can't get clearance, no take-off now. You can still eat the catering here on board. Then buses will come and take you to the same hotel. We are sorry, there were problems getting the outside stairs off.'

Now, the atmosphere explodes. Passengers are standing up, they start shouting, rhythmic clapping begins and the first ones chant: 'We don't leave the plane, we don't leave the plane ...'.

After what feels like five minutes, an *Air India* manager comes on board, an older, very gentlemanly-looking man, dark blue suit, grey moustache. He's got the nerve, I think. He repeats that he has spoken to the German Ministry of Transport and that the flight can no longer take off.

Now a few Germans laugh as well, asking if he really believes that there is someone in the ministry now who is clearing flights at night at all German airports? Does he even know where the Ministry of Transport is? An Indian adds: '*Air Traffic Control* is not a German authority, why do you blame the problem on Germany?' But the *Air India* manager is of course right about the departure; he and the airport cannot ignore legal regulations.

Now the mood has completely changed. A young stewardess, she might be Bengali or Tamil I assume, is typing into her phone, trembling; you can see her fear. I, too, am afraid that it might turn violent. Because some Indians are no longer complaining loudly and smiling, but shouting aggressively. And they push the manager further down the aisle to the back of the plane. But he remains steadfast and I – no longer believing the awkward *Air India* half-truths – still admire his courage to come onto the plane in the now heated up atmosphere.

The first passengers are already getting their food from the two galleys and retiring to their seats. They are tired, and I feel sorry for the children and young, stressed parents. There is no special announcement for them. Slowly the mood calms down and word gets round that there are police on board. It's true, some in dark blue police overalls with machine guns are standing at the front exit next to the cockpit; we also see some later outside next to the outside stairs and by the buses waiting for us on the tarmac. A passenger in front of me asks a policewoman whose protection they're there for? But he immediately answers himself: 'Better you protect us from *Air India* than them from us'; the policewoman nods to him imperceptibly and apologetically.

On the bus back to the terminal, the unanimous opinion is that it is not the technical problems that are decisive, but the many inaccurate and contradictory pieces of information and the unequal treatment of passengers. An Indian agrees loudly, looking for German faces: 'That's how it is, they treat us like stupid children instead of just telling us the truth. It's always other's fault, never their own. And this happens all the time with *Air India*.' 'That's why they were practically bankrupt', adds another, 'now they taken over by *Tata*, but they are not allowed to replace this incompetent lower and middle management.' And someone added: 'Because it will take years. That's why *Tata* has founded *Vistara* as second airline, which now also flies internationally.'

Great, I think, and I didn't book them because I wanted to take a flight with a stop-over. And then I remember that some people pretended to be superstitious and had re-booked on the other plane. So superstition can help after all, I smile self-deprecatingly to myself ... at least with Indians.

Of course, the announced buses outside the airport is only one bus, which cannot possibly fit everyone. First of all, it goes to another hotel, but the bus driver says it will take a while to leave. And then he wouldn't be back for at least 40 minutes. He recommends that we take a taxi. Our team is already practised at this and it is already after midnight when we arrive at the hotel.

Now, according to the Desk Manager, as his name badge shines, the hotel is fully booked due to the book fair. We can't believe it, and I realise that a bus with lots of other people is about to arrive.

He would call the Night Manager. So, exhausted, we drop into a group of seats. The young Indian student nods off immediately and the Mexican woman taps away on her social media. The desk manager is chatting to four dolled-up prostitutes, who are usually waiting for clients at trade fairs in hotels after their procession through the bars and pubs. But no sign of a call to the night manager.

I think what a night manager does all night? I come to the conclusion that he's either playing games on his phone, typing away on his social media or standing by the window smoking. Outside, I walk round to the back of the hotel to a row of doors and windows. Bingo, there's someone standing in an open doorway smoking. And when I get close, I see someone sitting very casually in front of a computer, using a phone.

'Of course, the rooms are still booked for you,' he replies. *Air India* hadn't checked us out. Another new truth? The rooms are not made up, but no matter, the main thing is to shower and sleep. The desk manager gave us a dirty look as we waited for the lift and he is told off by his superior in front of the prostitutes.

Fortunately, I have a change of toiletries with me, but at the breakfast next morning the mood of most passengers is gone. More and more dramas are opening up. It seems that everyone is now having problems with connecting flights and trains. A young couple with their baby is on their way to Kolkata for *Durga Puja* festival and to introduce their granddaughter to the family. A manager from a known agricultural machinery manufacturer was with his team at their headquarters in Germany. He set up a *WhatsApp* group last night, which has now grown to over a hundred members in a very short space of time. He wants to put pressure on *Air India* to actually pay out the legally prescribed 600 Euro in compensation to every passenger.

When lunch is delivered to the lobby on time, we are told to take it to our room and not eat in the lobby. Understandable, even if the lobby and the integrated open bar-restaurant have free tables, it just doesn't make a good impression on arriving guests if we all unpack our aluminium trays there. But we simply enter again the banqueting room, where the food was placed yesterday; there are still beverages from previous day. The hotel employee finally gives up asking us out repeatedly; a crying baby can do more than annoyed and exhausted travellers.

As soon as we have finished eating, things suddenly have to move very quickly. Room check-out, bus transfer, new tickets at a check-in reserved for us, security check and quickly off to boarding; things are steaming ahead. You get the feeling that we are to blame for everything. Of course, there is no plane to be seen outside at the new gate. Again there is anxiety, what is going on? And again the staff at the boarding counter are besieged. Almost everyone from *Air India,* who tried to make us believe their different stories yesterday, is also there.

Suddenly applause, the plane with our luggage is slowly pulled to the gate. Like almost everyone else, I take a photo.

Then chaos again, because an *Air India* manager wants us to line up in rows by seating area from the back to the front; that's logical. Another organises from the end of the queues. He wants to check all passports and boarding passes first; this also seems logical, although it has happened repeatedly. And a third person simply opens the door to the gangway at the front and lets the first passengers through.

The older *Air India* manager, who was on the plane with us yesterday, looks agonised at the new confusion that his and the airport employees are obviously creating independently of each other.

He then takes the microphone out of the hand of a member of staff at the boarding desk and makes an announcement showing his flexibility: 'Please go through here in two rows and hold up your boarding ticket and passport at your seat in the plane, we'll do it all inside.' Said and done. As the plane slowly taxis to the runaway, some people clap cautiously. And when we take off, there is a roar of applause. I think *Air India* ground staff are happy to get rid of us ... just like us them.

We arrive Delhi early Sunday morning. Applause breaks out again as we touch-down. Later we stand in small groups with our new flight folks at the baggage carousel. Applause again when the first bag was ejected. What may the many hundreds of the people on the other baggage carousels think?

Along with many others, I quickly go to the immigration control and on to check-in to get the new ticket for the supposed connecting flight. To get to the check-in hall, we have to go through a security check, which is done by soldiers. Like many other countries, India is heavily armed after many attacks in sensitive locations. Some passengers in front of me are turned away and complemented out of the queue; others get through … why?

Again, some start to grumble. The Indian chemist I know is also there, and he gets louder as well. Then I'm not allowed to check in either and first asked in a friendly manner and then, in response to my repeated question, why, I have a valid ticket, a little more firmly behind the barrier belt.

The soldiers, whether they understood my English or do not, know no mercy. Later I learn that my ticket for the onward flight is two days old; from the soldiers' point of view it is invalid.

Now I'm also in the grumbling group, which is quickly growing. The *Air India* staff at the two check-in counters in the hall, which is now inaccessible to us, keep looking over at us as they check in other passengers.

But what are a few tens of passengers compared to 160,000 passengers here every day? Delhi airport, a mega city with almost 20 million people, is one of the 10 largest airports in the world.

The group gets bigger and several passengers get louder. We are also increasingly blocking the corridor to other halls for check-ins from other air-lines. This causes additional resentment among un-involved passengers who have to go this way. Young parents among us sit demonstratively on the floor with their children and luggage. Between them are older people, some in wheelchairs; you can see their exhaustion.

Inconspicuously, several soldiers have gathered on either side of us. Is there a threat of new chaos?

Finally, someone from *Air India* check-in comes to the hall entrance close to us. I'm standing near the chemist I know. With this typical Indian head shaking, he laughingly whispers to me that I shouldn't do anything and let them do it. And it gets loud again and rhythmic comes up: 'Let us check in, let us check in …'.

Slowly at first, then faster and faster, two employees run back and forth with our passports and old tickets between us and a third, newly opened check-in desk. After more than an hour, I have a new ticket. Now from the other airline, *Vistara*, which also belongs to *Tata*, I am allowed to pass. Like others before me, everyone with a new, now valid flight ticket who gets through or hurries to another check-in hall is given a friendly farewell by the crowd, still without new tickets.

I have to hurry again, boarding for my new flight to Kolkata has already begun. A *Vistara* employee guides me past other passengers to baggage check-in. 'Please, quick, quick,' he forces me. But it's not possible. Firstly, my luggage is too heavy. For them now it is a one-way domestic flight, not an international connecting flight. Allowed now is only a 15 kg check-in baggage. How is that supposed to work now?

I manage to get my former *Air India* employee to my new *Vistara* check-in desk. There is a discussion and a manager arrives. Indian solution, just do it: 'Have a good flight, sir, and sorry for any inconvenience.'

It's the so-called Murphy's Law that now the printer for the baggage label breaks down and needs a new replacement roll first.

A young *Vistara* employee personally accompanies me to the security check. Again, 'please quickly, those at boarding are already waiting.' There are only a few people, but I am pushed past. Everything as usual, mobile phone, laptop etc. in a plastic tray, cabin luggage and plastic bag with liquids next to it, including my hotel belt, in the next plastic tray and off into the scanning tunnel. I had seen that some people go through the body scan in socks, and I asked: 'Shoes too?'

'No, no, leave your shoes on.' Great, I think, but the signal is on. 'Just come through, no problem sir.' I'm standing on the platform at the end of the security check and am also scanned with a hand-held device. It beeps at the bottom, there must be metal in the heel of my shoe. So they should have been taken off like the other clothes. What should I do?

The *Vistara* employee asks me to pack everything up quickly. He hurries back with the shoes. I wonder if they're a bit smelly by now. Then the tray with my shoes comes out of the scanner tunnel, but the belt stops. Several security guards are standing at the screen discussing. Apparently there is something unclear in the luggage of a subsequent tray.

We can't reach the bowl, there are high protective screens between us and the shoes. I see my companion shake hands with someone from the security service for a while; in India this is only usual if you've known each other for a long time or if you give a gift of money without an envelope. He then fetches the tub with my shoes, runs them through the baggage scanner again on another belt and brings them to us with a smile. 'Double check, one for the right, one for left shoe,' he laughs with the typical Indian head shaking; I smile rather agonised.

I feel like the very last passenger boarding. Two rows in front of mine the Indian chemist greets me. 'You see, our kind of communication works,' laughing with this Indian head shaking; we clap *high-five*.

Durga Puja in Kolkata

When I arrive in Kolkata, the driver I know is not there and neither is anyone else. So I'm standing outside in the sweltering morning heat and, despite my flight ticket and passport, I can't get back into the air-conditioned check-in hall. The soldiers are of course no exception; every country seems to have similar problems. And India, as a multi-ethnic nation the size of a continent with its arbitrary borders drawn by British colonial rulers, still suffers from this today. As I write this, I realise that India was still under British colonial rule 10 years before I was born.

Finally, I manage to reach my friends on the phone; I've probably rung them out of bed so early in the morning. They haven't received any message I've texted from Frankfurt or Delhi. Their offices are closed, all of them and their driver are off because of the *Durga Puja* festival.

I was told to take a taxi from the company in the blue building, on the left-hand side of the road opposite me. And I'm told to be careful when crossing the 4-lane traffic-calmed drop-off zone, as no one follows any rules there. I already know the taxi company and how to cross such roads, and I slowly and stoically cross several lanes of the road. Honking without end, but everyone stops at the last moment when they realise they are one step ahead. So I can also ignore the many taxi brokers with their scouts, 'sir, best taxi ... best price ... fastest to centre ... know best hotel.'

I'm already sweating profusely at the taxi company's little house. Everything's new. You have to download the company's app first. But it doesn't work, I can't get internet. But I can't do it without the app.

At least I can use *Google Maps* to identify the large park with lakes near my friends. Then I know the way and find the dead-end street where their house is at the very end. A boy, I guess 12 or 13 years old, speaks a good English. He does it on his phone and registers the taxi order in his name. I'm saved and I want to give him a tip, but he refuses: 'You are welcome, sir, where do you come from?'

Already after 15 minutes we are in the middle of the festival; today is the second festival and also a Sunday. The driver doesn't speak any English. We make it at least to my friend's city district in a good hour. But it's not so easy here. With my friend's help on the phone, we somehow manage to get close to my final destination in this relatively very early holy day chaos. Not without having to turn around a few times in the maze of streets somewhere in front of or behind an altar with lots of people blocking the road and looking for a diversion. Finally I see a shop I recognise on the opposite side of the street. We have to go in there, then take second left and we'll be at the dead-end street we're looking for.

But how to get across on a road with two 4-lane carriageways, separated by a barrier with gaps for pedestrians only? But that's the least of my driver's problems. He simply reverses against the 4-lane traffic, gradually backing up about 100 m, even if it takes about 10 minutes. Despite the wild honking, he remains stoically calm; it's just his daily job.

Durga Puja, the Hindu festival in honor of the mother goddess *Durga* in her most popular 6-armed manifestation of creation. This *UNESCO* intangible world cultural heritage site lasts at least 10 days, depending on region and interpretation. The highlight is the full moon at the turn of the month September–October. In Bengal in particular, but also in Assam or Nepal, for example, the celebrations often last two weeks. A speciality in West Bengal, and especially in Kolkata, it's Kali, the fierce and evil black apparition with a blood-red tongue hanging out and holding severed heads in her hands; the festival of good over evil.

In addition to religious rituals, there are social events such as concerts, gifts, festive meals and communal strolls. Celebrations range from family and neighbourhood activities to major central events. Entire streets are often closed off with oversized altars and even walk-in works of art; music and celebrations last until the next morning. With altars, religious rituals, festive decorations everywhere it is often compared to the Christian Christmas or Easter festival; but of course it has a completely different meaning in terms of content. But not even the lightful typical German *Weihnachtsmarkt* can compete with the sheer unbelievable Indian sea of lights and colours.

Now, the heat and high humidity are getting to me again. Although I've been here at least once a year for a few days for many years, I won't be able to get used to it.

I take a shower and change my sweaty clothes so that I don't catch a cold here in the house. It's pleasant here, my favourite thing is to lie under the old ceiling fan on the lowest setting and enjoy the laziness at noon and in the afternoon; it's also great protection against mosquitoes.

But I know that I'll be sweating again on the way to the restaurant, where I'll first enjoy the pleasant coolness of a new air conditioning system and then end up freezing. I know that I will catch a cold from this constant change between the air conditioning in the hotel, flights and now again. It would be strange if I didn't? But the prospect of months ahead of me in the mountains in a few days' time, in a climate that is so pleasant for me, puts this into perspective.

The days in Kolkata are as nice as ever. Mum *Suniti*, who is still sprightly, lives downstairs in the house. I've known her for so long now, since I was in India for the first time; in the meantime she has learnt a little English again after her husband passed away and she is very sprightly. She has also stayed with us in Germany before, so we are all a great community.

Still having the old flat in another part of the city, where I often stayed as well as in hotels; they are undecided whether to rent it out or sell? I'm staying up here on the roof terrace in a modernized room. Great view, and it's a good place to stay at night with a cold beer or two or three. As I knew that they had put a lot of plants on the terrace and *Suniti* also likes to be up on the roof, I put a big garden gnome in-between them as a present.

My youngest son with his girl friend had arrived the day before; staying in the old flat in the other part of the city. They both already know India and are correspondingly relaxed in the hustle and bustle of this mega-city. They came from Nepal hiking in the Himalayas at the beginning of their 1-year trip around the world; they are planning to visit Kolkata and later my home in the Darjeeling region. And *Suniti* is sad for me because my time here has now been significantly shortened due the days delay in travelling. My reply that I have known my son for 35 years doesn't count. Indians have a completely different understanding of family than we do, and if you don't speak on the phone at least once a day, something is wrong.

Sarah's mother and a colleague from her German NGO *SOCEO* are also here. *Sarah* wants to show them how they live in Kolkata, visit some of their projects in the area, and travel to Darjeeling, 'for a tea at my place,' they joke.

We spend three wonderful days together and let ourselves be carried away by the *Durga Puja* hustle and bustle. Of course, *Suniti* doesn't miss the opportunity to cook for us on this occasion in keeping with tradition.

Next day, as always when I'm here, we eat at the Calcutta Rowing Club; this over 150 years old club it's quite something, if you ignore the horrors of British colonial rule.

On my last evening, an invitation to my friends' newly opened restaurant. It's a small and, by Indian standards, exquisite restaurant that serves traditional organic cuisine with products the local women's SHG cooperatives that my friends have trained and advised. And ... the restaurant will take a special meaning for me later on, but I have no idea at the moment.

Road to Kalimpong

Now I know, only one 15 kg check-in baggage is allowed on domestic flights. I had never realised this in previous years, as we had only ever travelled with cabin luggage for a few days on projects on the Indian sub-continent.

I manage to reduce my check-in baggage to 17 kg by taking out the 30 cm-tall garden gnome made of plaster and my books. My experience was that 1 or 2 kg overweight can go with a smiling Indian head shaking. And the cabin luggage has also recently been limited to 7 kg, but my experience was that it is not weighed; size must fit and must look light. The now very heavy backpack really cuts into my shoulder.

At the first check-in counter of the low-cost airline *IndiGo*, which in my experience is always punctual and very pleasant, the employee sends me to another counter to pay for the 20 kg of excess baggage with a smile and the typical (for me at first apparently) approving head shake: 'No problem, sir.'

Crap, I think first, that's it so far with my experiences. But I tried again at the last of the five counters as far away from her as possible. While I'm waiting in the new queue, I see her leaving her counter; change of staff. Great, so maybe one more attempt. And here it works straight away and my checked baggage runs on the belt towards the plane at no extra charge; I relax with the unchecked backpack, which cuts into my shoulder, to the security check and on to boarding.

It's only a short flight of just less than an hour. Later I will learn the subtle nuances of the typical Indian head shake; it could have meant a friendly 'yes' or 'I don't know' or 'I can't decide' or ...

Last year I travelled the route by train. I was looking forward to slowly immersing myself in the countryside in the north of West Bengal up to the famous Darjeeling region. Unfortunately it was an overnight train, but it was my very first train journey in India, with its own interesting inner life. The whole journey, including the trip to the railway station and then four hours by car into the mountains, had taken a total of 16 hours.

The mountain region was their administrative summer residence for around 100 years until the end of British colonial rule in 1947 due to its wonderfully mild climate. In the anniversary brochure of a traditional German teahouse, which I found on the Internet, I read that in 1830, for example, you first had to travel up the river Ganges from Calcutta by boat, which took a week.

And then from the foot of the Himalayas for another week on foot with porters and pack mules, and later on more developed paths with ox carts.

At the end of 19th century there was a railway from Calcutta and years later a separate mountain railway for the last 80 km; it was built primarily to transport tea and soldiers. Now it is still very popular with tourists today as a way of slowly immersing themselves in this landscape.

Today, apart from an hour drive to the airport and the short flight to the foot of the Lower Himalayas, I only need less than three hours by car to reach finally.

Before the New Truth

Review

After my commercial apprenticeship, studies and a career in banking and consulting, I moved to a university in my mid-40s. Working with younger people again and again, spending more time for researching and writing independently, this interested me more than the same old projects in same old client organisations with same repeating hotel stays all over the country.

For me personally, the university was by and large a non-hierarchical organisation with a variety of types and characteristics. Coming from the so-called Free Economy and self-employment consulting partnership – where you are not really free, but totally dependent on superiors and customers, turnover and expectations of the social class – I found now new and often seemingly strange regulations, procedures and peculiarities that were not always logically comprehensible. But, there was also a lot of freedom, fun experiences and interesting people. And for me, there was no longer the usual career hysteria surrounding me. I didn't want to manage a university or a faculty, because then I would be back on the career carousel from which I had previously freed myself.

And like so many people my age, I was divorced after around 20 years of marriage, have three great grown-up children and still have lots of plans. In particular, I had already set the course for my retirement and had already channelled my international orientation and activities in this direction.

I am now 61 years old and the last five years of my regular working life at the university began in March. I feel physically exhausted and put this down to the general Spring Fatigue. I also can't bring myself to prepare the mountain bike for upcoming short tours as a kind of spring cleaning, as has become a habit in recent years. I keep getting dizzy and, for weeks in April, I have the feeling that I'm coming down with a flu. No need to worry, you know what it's like and you can deal with it.

But it lasts longer and I sweat easily at night. The sweating gets worse and I get little red pimples on my legs, which sometimes burst and bleed or when I scratch them. Of course I know that you shouldn't do this, but (at least) I can't resist it completely. I also feel weak during the day despite sleeping longer in the morning or sometimes during the day. And somehow I'm always tired. But that's just part and parcel of the flu, I think to myself.

I can work at my desk without any problems, but as soon as I get up and go down to the basement or make my bed in the morning, I'm exhausted and have to sit down. As soon as I sit down, I can think clearly again, read the newspaper or work. But every walk is some-how too heavy for me.

I seem to give lectures as normal at the start of term. However, I no longer walk around the lecture theatre or from one group to the next in the seminar as I usually do during a lecture or seminar, but I stay seated at the front; I've never done that before.

The dizziness gets worse, after a few steps I feel unsteady and sway. What will the people around me think? That he's drunk in the morning?

So I sit down again briefly every few steps. I pick up a CD from a table in front of a bookshop and sit down again in the shop, preten-ding to read the contents with interest. Outside, halfway to my bike, I do the same thing again, reading the CD cover on a little wall around a flower bed in the small pedestrian zone of my neighbourhood.

I finally make it to the bike; I can manage on the bike. Pushing it stabilises my gait. And I can get on and cycle the five minutes home without problems.

And as soon as I get home, I have what feels like a never-ending coughing fit.

The green Miracle Juice

The slight flu-like feeling, sweating at night, dizziness during the day and repeated long bouts of coughing like bronchitis, I know that from a few years ago. At the time, I had caught bronchitis, developed a fever and passed out at some point. At the ENT doctor's practice, it turned out to be hidden pneumonia on both sides and I had to go to hospital immediately.

That's why I think of flu and bronchitis first and buy the green miracle juice (a chemical medical high-end cocktail) at the local phar-macy; the 200 m I have to drive by car. Take a small portion cup with the cap on 3-times in a row at night and you sleep well and sweat out the flu. It tastes disgusting, but it helped when I couldn't afford the flu at work.

I wake up at night and am literally soaking wet in bed. Everything is wet, not just my T-shirt, shorts, sheet and quilt, but right through to the mattress. I dry off, put on fresh clothes and lie down on a sauna towel on the edge of the mattress next to the wetness in case it happens again. Two hours later I wake up again. Everything is soaking wet again, as if someone had watered me with a watering can. Dry off again and change into fresh clothes. I'm freezing and put another bathrobe on over it; I lie down in the guest room. Early in the morning I wake up freezing, everything is soaking wet again.

After a hot bath I feel better, but also weak. During the day, I take one of these capsules as a day miracle juice equivalent and no longer feel feverish; and I drink fast-dissolving anti-cough pills to cough up. I hardly notice any dizziness as I have already unconsciously got into the habit of sitting a lot and using the bike as a support.

In the evening, I make provisions. After a unit of the miracle juice, I prepare the guest room with a bath towel and dry laundry, as well as the sofa in the living room.

Again I have to change sleeping places during the night, an now across all the rooms. So is pneumonia coming? Or is it already one? And as if on order, I get a coughing fit. It takes a long time for my throat to calm down. Then, changing my clothes is unusually strenuous and I have to sit down again immediately afterwards. After a few minutes I stand up, but the dizziness is so bad that I'm really afraid of falling over. I immediately sit back down.

Things around me are somehow different. I croak self-ironically, wow dude, full on drugs, the juice has it in it; which is kind of true. There's a book on the floor in front of me. I bend down to pick it up. But I reach into the void and think, but it's right in front of my feet, isn't it? I bend down further and further. But again I reach into the void. It all looks distorted somehow; like Salvador Dali paintings, it goes through my head. Even my feet are some-how so far away.

At some point I wake up shivering from the cold. Was it a faint? Why am I lying on the floor? What's happening here right now?

Do not despair, even in the face of great suffering;
Perhaps misfortune is the source of happiness.

Menander, Greek poet 341-290 BC

My New Truth

The day of the truth

The next morning, I went to the lung doctor I knew who had diagnosed the hidden pneumonia years ago. On the 200 m or so from the parked car to the surgery, I was glad be able to sit down at a tram stop halfway there.

The receptionist probably realises that I am somehow acutely unwell and I am immediately taken to a treatment room; the doctor remembers me. After I've told him everything, including that I was in India and the US at the beginning of the year and in the DR Congo before Christmas, and that I wasn't any worse afterwards. Then, his usual routine begins: blood pressure, blood sample, lung function test in a chamber that looks like an old tele-phone box, and an X-ray was taken.

According to the doctor, it's just the beginnings of pneumonia, 'but that's not a problem, we can get it under control with antibiotics,' he said and continued: 'I quickly make an appointment with a cardiologist today,' and he sends me directly. 'You shouldn't drive', he adds.

I wonder why? It works better than taking the train or walking ... and I'm also thinking about a possible parking fine. But I don't have a ticket, yeah. So I take the car; again no parking fine at the cardiologist in the city centre.

I sit with him again in the afternoon. According to the cardiologist every-thing is okey, he mumbles as he looks through the report. 'There's just one more blood value that needs to be checked. Don't worry, I'll send you to a haematologist to be on the safe side.' I've heard the term before, but I don't know what they do. He's already made an appointment; strange. But it's convenient, the practice is in my neighbourhood and not far from my flat. I could go straight away, he knew the doctor. I would be seen straight away. But I should go by train or taxi, never by car. Outside, I think about the parking, where my car is again. No parking fine again, so off I go; I'm as happy as a child.

In the haematology practice they're already waiting for me. I was examined immediately and the doctor, she was friendly but firm, took another blood sample. After what felt like five minutes, she comes back and directly clarifies that everything now has to be done quickly. She already has reserved a bed for me at the university hospital. They would wait for me, because a acute leukaemia was suspected.

Apart from the changes I had previously noticed myself, I consciously had not noticed the other typical symptoms such as pallor, nose and gum bleeding or bleeding that was difficult to stop, uncharacteristic back or headaches until then; I only realised this later when I read about them. Swollen lymph nodes, the typical slightly enlarged liver, and spleen were only diagnosed later in the hospital.

I know the term leukaemia, but I only know that it has something to do with blood. At school, at the age of 12 or 13, a classmate had this disease and died in hospital a few weeks later.

Then, my first thoughts were to wash my still wet clothes? And in between, I pack a small trolley. I have to sit down again and again for two minutes; I function like a machine, completely without emotion.

Emergency admission and escape

I take a taxi, it's already dark when I arrive at the hospital. The haematologist had said, a doctor would pick me up in the emergency room. When I report there and say so, I am told in a friendly but clear manner: 'We are doing the programme here. please take a seat back there.'

I'm sitting in the middle of what I see as real or less real emergencies. Finally someone takes me to a treatment room to take blood samples. They have trouble finding a good vein. I've known this all my life and I immediately feel better and more confident, when I said, 'it's best to go straight to the abdominal vein.'

I once heard this saying from a venereology specialist during my studies when a colleague couldn't find a vein. And he confidently, almost like a mate in her presence, told her about his professor during his year at the hospital. The both look horrified, so do they here now. Then they call in someone else and it works. And I should drink.

Sitting outside again I see the full emergency programme here with drunks, people ranting and complaining. I feel sorry for the young nurses and doctors or trainee doctors. Gods in white, I think, they have to put up with everything from everyone here, and they remain calm about it. I'm told twice more that I have to drink water. Good, at least they know I'm here.

Now, I've been waiting for two hours, enough is enough. I go to the admissions desk: 'May I leave my things here? They've been telling me to drink for hours. But nobody shows me where a tap is. I now look for a vending machine where I can get something to drink.' Within two minutes, they give me wo large bottles of water.

Finally, shortly after 11 p.m., a young doctor takes me to another admission room. She looks over me at some papers and repeatedly palpates the lymph nodes in my neck. She looks at me seriously and asks a few questions. Basically what I had already answered at the lung doctor and the haematologist. And she then asks just as seriously whether I know that I have leukaemia? I answer, probably a bit too flippant: 'Yes, I've heard that before today, something about blood or something?' 'IT's a very serious matter now,' she immediately replies. 'You must know, blood cancer, as it is popularly known, doesn't take a break,' ... and she adds after a pause for breath and holding my arm ... 'and no jokes either.' A clear message ... and I wonder if I would be here now if I had *googled* it beforehand.

With the doctor, a hospital paramedic pushed me in a wheelchair (why actually?) through the night to a nearby building. They took the lift to the 4th floor reception area of a ward with four corridors, each protected with closed large double milky-white glass doors.

As the haematology practice, here they're already waiting for me as well. I slowly get an idea how serious the situation is, but I remain supposedly relaxed. The night nurse leads me into a hospital room. I am told to lie down on the free bed by the window and not to undress yet, the doctor will be back in a minute.

I knew as a child that cancer is very dangerous and it is often equated with death. I remember hearing the word cancer for the first time in the late 1960s. My mother had for a long time a non-specific allergy and there was on TV something like the movie Cancer Hospital, based on a novel by *Alexander Solzhenitsyn*.

At some point my mother jumped up from the sofa, now I know what I have, that's why the doctor doesn't tell me anything? Of course she didn't have cancer and later got her allergy under control. But what kind of fears did she have for a long time and at night? And I knew about my classmate who had died of leukaemia during this time, which I didn't think had anything to do with cancer at the time.

Later, I often hear from friends that he or she had cancer or had died of cancer. But it was always far away. For me, it was always like someone else's illness. It was only when it hit two colleagues in the last few years that it was suddenly very close. And now me?

I would later learn that there are very different types of cancer, and it is actually just a kind of collective term for the so-called Malignant Tumours, which can occur and act differently even within one organ. Even though, a cancer diagnosis was practically the 'death sentence' some decades ago; there are now many relatively successful cures. Of around half a million cases of cancer every year, slightly more than half survive.

Rapidly developing molecular biology has made it possible to understand cancer on an individual patient-centred basis. As a result, differentiated therapies that are customised to the individual patient now have a high probability of survival in some cases. In children, for example, it is around 80%. It is therefore very helpful for patients to find a hospital that specialises in their specific cancer.

I'm in luck, this university hospital is part of a leukaemia research network, nationally and worldwide.

I'm lying on a fresh hospital bed, still foil-covered. At that moment, all I could think about was dying, and I never imagined that it would be my shared 2-bed room apartment (or quarantine cell !?) for the next few months.

I wonder what some-one was lying here with before? Surely cancer too, the building it's obviously the hospital's cancer department. I can't get the film out of my head, which I had only seen a short clip of at the time and my parents had then sent me to bed.

It's unpleasantly warm in the room and it smells of urine. I try to open the window a little, but the window handles are blocked and the panes seem smudged. In the bed facing the door, an elderly man is snoring and gasping. There are two open urine bottles hanging from his bed and he is connected to an infusion stand with a few bags.

I lie down again and think, if I have to die, then please in the Swiss Alps or at a nice coastal seaside spa? I don't actually know any specific place, I just remember pictures of the beautiful panoramic terraces at health resorts.

Spontaneously, I get up quietly and just as carefully pull the suit-case, which is not yet unpacked, past the first bed to the door of the room. I think to myself that I want a single room anyway. Slowly and silently, I open the door and leave the room. It's right in front of the milky-white glass double doors, which I open just as carefully.

The night nurse at the ward reception – later we patients ironically call it the checkpoint – looks up. I can see her sheer horror; she literally blurts out: 'Where do you want to go now?' Then she sees my bag, 'you can't leave here now.' She becomes frantic: 'It's life-threatening, you don't know what's wrong with you, do you?' I reply supposedly clear conscious: 'Of course I do. May I call a taxi, or should I just go outside to the taxi stand?'

She keeps trying to convince me to stay. She obviously has a distress signal, because suddenly the doctor is standing next to me, just as agitated. She also persuades me to at least wait until the next morning for to meet the professor in their daily's doctors' ward routines. 'No, I want to go now. I also need to speak to someone else,' I reply. She: 'Whom you want to ask?' 'Another doctor or professor, of course,' is my somewhat arrogantly comment. She looks at me in astonishment: 'Which professor do you want to ask?' 'There must be one in the *Rotary Club*, or someone who knows one,' I lie, because I'm not in such – seen in my eyes – useless See-and-be-seen Clubs.

After a few more attempts to keep me there, she gives up. I have to sign something, at my own request and risk, and the night nurse issues me a taxi voucher.

I'm home after midnight. During the night I sweat like ... again, but I'm prepared. And there's still a portion of this green miracle juice.

Next morning I drive to the haematologist's surgery before the regular consultation time. The doctor's assistant from yesterday is there again and recognises me. 'We've just tried to reach you by phone, please wait a few minutes, the doctor will be with you shortly.'

I ask for the doctor from yesterday. 'Today is her hospital duty, but her colleague is there, he's also a haematologist and already knows about it.' It's a joint practice, which I wasn't aware of. He arrives after a short time and takes me to a kind room one floor up with cosy designer chairs. It looks more like a private reading room or where people are invited for a tea.

I apologise, but he rebuffs me friendly smiling. 'Tell me how you experienced the day yesterday. The hospital contacted me this morning at breakfast. They're looking for you,' he begins the conversation.

It bubbles out of me, the sweating, the dizziness and these hallucinations, coughing, lungs, etc., and in-between he adds further – later I know the right – keywords. 'And what was wrong with you, why did you leave the hospital in the mid of the night? I'll tell you right away, that's completely normal,' ... and after a short pause for breath, he adds that I don't need to apologise to anyone for anything.

Then I realised what I had been missing. No one had sat down next to me and asked me how I was doing, how I was feeling? Nobody knew how I was living, what I was doing, what I was afraid of?

He confirms: 'Yes, I can well imagine that. But also look at the other side. They are also there for you and feel responsible for you. They want to help you. And I'm telling you, it's very tight. The chemotherapy has to start as soon as possible. I am honest, you have a very, very serious illness that is guaranteed to be fatal within a few weeks if chemotherapy is not started as soon as possible. Give the hospital a chance. As soon as the chemotherapy starts, you will stay alive for the time being. And you, and we doctors, have time to talk to you. But right now, your lifespan is being shortened because the blasts, as the non-functioning and malformed blood cells are called, are increasing exponentially. Above a certain level, there is nothing more medicine can do for you.'

It's a conversation that lasts more than an hour and includes a lot of private information about my previous life, my current life situation, my children, etc.

I realise he is serious and ask him where he would go in my condition? 'To our university hospital, which works in a network and is one of the leading treatment and research centres here in Germany and in the world for acute leukaemia, or *AML* for short.'

Now I feel calmer and more at ease and ask: 'How quickly does it have to go?' 'If you manage to get back to the hospital ward by 11 a.m., they can start straight away, they're already waiting for you. I've already told you, you don't need to apologise to anyone. This is all perfectly normal.'

So I decide to go, because I still have the packed trolley. 'Can you please call the hospital, so that I can set off and try to be there before 11 a.m.?'

Leukaemia

Acute myeloid leukaemia (ED 05/2018) ... it says under the headline Diagnosis at the beginning of the medical report I later received ... WHO: AML with recurrent genetic abnormalities (inv16) initial blood count: L 21.8 G/l, Hb 9.8 g/dl, TZ 97 G/l, 31% blasts, cytology KM: 40% monocytic blasts ... And so it goes on for half a page with the following tables of measured values, probably up and down, criss-crossing my body. There are 10 pages in total and I don't understand a thing. Dictated, I wouldn't even have been able to spell most of the terms correctly, let alone understand the context.

In the moment of this terrible truth, or rather only really realising it after the initial shock – for me it took longer than I had come to terms with the intensive care unit and all the beeping and glowing LED readings connected to me – I actually think of all the (supposedly) so important appointments first.

And how should I tell my children? And what will happen to the street children in Africa that I have been supporting for years? And how should I continue my commitment there? My own children have been out of the house for a long time now and are enjoying their own interesting lives. Until now, the street children's home has only recei-ved individual donations when something was needed. And what needs to be done here now? And what I hope I can still manage some-how? And a will? And the foundation I've been planning instead individual donations for the street children? And, and, and ...

Death as such, which is more than likely given the relatively high proportion of blasts in the blood and bone marrow, remains strangely abstract for me and supposedly without fear. The focus is on my self-organisation. This goes so far that I make a Whom to inform and how? What needs to be done? What text do I want in an obituary, and, and, and ... as a to-do list for me and then for my children.

The Himalaya Highlands

Off to the mountains

Leaving the airport near Shiliguri at the foot of the Lower Himalayas, I immediately recognise the driver booked for me. We also had him last year on our 3-day tour of projects in the mountains. We laugh and greet each other like old friends. He often drives the tours here in the mountains to the cooperatives' projects for my friends or for their employees.

Talking about the Lower Himalayas here, it's about the Darjeeling highlands, known to us only for the famous tea. It stretches up to an altitude of 2,000 m; my final destination is a village in the area around the town of Kalimpong, which lies at an altitude up to 1,700 m.

Parts of the famous highest peaks in the world can be seen as an imposing range in the distance. And *Kanchenjunga*, the world's 3rd highest mountain at almost 8,600 m, which is located here in India, stands out; Mount Everest is to the north-west behind it in Nepal.

The border with Nepal is relatively porous. My future hosts, their neighbours and actually all the people in the Darjeeling region have relatives in Nepal, as I find out later. It is historically a common area and people. The borders here were drawn arbitrarily by the British occupying power. People from here travelled back and forth without a visa. You wouldn't need a pass-port or be checked on certain routes, they later remarked with a grin. Italy's *South Tyrol* spontaneously I've in mind, where I was many years ago practically hiking one day up a mountain through three countries (Switzerland, Austria, and Italy) without realising it.

The journey into the highlands to my destination takes well over three hours on the increasingly narrow roads that wind their way, over the first passes into valleys and up another mountain.

All the small houses by or near the roadside are becoming more and more colourful, and I see also more of them with colourful Buddhist prayer flags. The proportion of people of the Buddhist religion is relatively high here, as many refugees from Tibet have settled here in the past.

It's sometimes so narrow that two vehicles can only pass each other step by step. And the one or two steps from a house or small shops, which are more like kiosks in size, lead straight onto the road.

People mostly live from their big kitchen gardens with a cow, a goat or a few chickens and trade their produce with each other. And some run a small kiosk, the room by the road or a wood or stone hut. Why almost all of them always offer the same snacks, sweets, drinks etc. remains a mystery to me at first. It seems to be like here: if there are three hairdressers or in the same kebab stands, someone else opens something like this in the hope that something will come off for them. But then it's spread across more providers and sales fall for everyone. This explains why so many close down again after a year or two; that is often the case here too.

Many men are also day labourers for harvests, on building sites or in road construction; I often hear later that the men work in Arabia or women in households, for example in Singapore. The Indian government's major infra-structure construction projects – impressive and wage labour for one or two years – also lead to mountainsides sliding down, destroying people's homes. Or there is a catastrophic flood, like the one at some weeks shortly before I left here, which washes everything away.

For years, climate change has been causing snow to melt earlier and faster in the Himalayas. A dam burst and the flood swept everything away for 100 km through the narrow gorges; half of the villages on the banks were washed away, countless bridges destroyed and more than 100 people lost their lives; many are still missing. Later I learn that a barracks was also washed away. My hosts' son's college was a little higher up and only the ground floor was flooded; the students were able to help rescue a few of the soldiers. Now the campus is closed until next spring. And now, many km downstream there is ammunition from the barracks that has been washed away. A parallel tragedy, as it were, when I think of the river *Ahr* valley flood in my home country Germany two years ago.

It takes us almost an hour through an area by the river where you can see the clearing work and where they are trying to make the road passable again somehow; the only reasonably passable road for supplies and trade to and from the north. I can also see the houses that have slipped down and been destroyed on the lower slope or half in the river; pictures of the destruction, shown weeks ago in our news.

There is no compensation or help for the homeless from the state. The reason is simple. The owners of the original huts, converted into houses from generation to generation, do not have a building licence. This did not exist in the past. And if they had registered, they would have had to pay immeasurably high fees. In a country as large as India, three and a half times the size of the EU, just as in Russia, or China with in the same around 15% of the world's population, individual destiny does not count.

The son of my future hosts, who is studying engineering, will later tell me that it is a kind of swarm intelligence. An uncountable number of flexible little ideas emerge, but often at the expense of individuals as a kind of collateral damage.

I've noticed this before in Kolkata. An ambulance with blue lights stands in the queue of cars just like everyone else. No one thinks of making way; it's usually not even possible because the cars are bumper to bumper and hand-wide apart or moving forwards.

I arrive in the late afternoon. We recognise each other again and of course start with a *Ciyâ;* the traditional hot tea here, boiled with equal parts water and milk and very sweetened. This is accompanied by a spicy snack, like we have at a side snack roasted peanuts or so. And to celebrate the day, a box of chocolates is opened, creamy milk chocolates decorated with roasted almonds, walnuts and pistachios.

My host, *Giri-Raj,* is retired from the army; you can retire from the army after just 20 years with an age under 40. He can speak some English. And I can also communicate with his wife *Manju,* who I already know from my last visit, using key words and body language. Then son *Prashant* joins us, currently home on holiday from his college. Like all young people here and even school pupils, I will find out later, they speak relatively good English.

More people come. The neighbours from across the road, who saw me here last year. *Giri's* older brother and his wife, who live next door next door below. He is also Ex-army, like many in the family or neighbourhood, as I find out later. I realise that I am something special.

After I have orientated myself in my room and freshened up a bit, I have my first evening meal. *Roti,* freshly baked in the pan, the size of the palm of your hand, which is toasted again over an open flame. Served with typical *Dal* soup, available every morning and evening in many variations. Served with wonderfully spiced green beans, a reddish-brown, spicy-hot paste for seasoning or dipped in *Roti*, a bowl of freshly made yoghurt, some pickles and then pieces of apple and banana. All wonderfully simple and organic from their own kitchen garden and fields.

I eat immediately, not using spoon or fork, with my right hand, just like everyone else here. Thanks to my many visits to India, I've got the technique down to a certain extent; at least that's what I think ... and very often to the amusement of the Indians. Because at the latest when I'm tearing off pieces of *Roti* with one hand and picking up some very soft vegetables, my repeated failed attempts seem quite funny to them.

Of course, I always forget not to use my left hand later on; it is for the personal hygiene and is usually in my lap or held behind my back when eating. So of course I often unconsciously touch door handles, chair backs etc. with my right hand again. But I'll be fine, I think to myself. I'll soon need charcoal pills again, that's for sure.

I was asked what I would like for dinner and what I still need in my guest room? 'Please don't bother me, I just want to run along in your life. Just tell me what time you want me to be in the kitchen?' And it means 9 a.m. breakfast, 1 p.m. light snack, and dinner at 7 p.m., but Indian Time.

That fits for me very good; an extremely flexible concept of time I will later realise again and again. And there's always tea in all forms, I'm simply supposed to help myself with fruit, snacks etc. The only thing that will later turn out to be completely different from ours is the distribution of meals.

In Kolkata, I had bought a small kettle, the kind you usually find in hotels, for freeze-dried ready-made coffee (which is frowned upon at home), which I had taken with me, including milk powder, for the 80 days here. I knew they had a cow – now with offspring – and therefore fresh milk. But I didn't want to disturb them early in the morning, I thought.

Of course, the coffee only lasted for two months, as I often had a cup in the afternoon too. Fortunately, there was a kind of kiosk shop with ready-to-drink sachets of coffee within walking distance. That's where I bought more later on. That must be the talk of the town, I always thought.

In Germany, I don't think I'm a typical German, but abroad you somehow realise how typically German you are.

After the hustle and bustle of the all reception, I have to take a rest on my bed. Exhausted my tears are running, but with happiness. I really have made it; in more ways than one.

Now, five years after spending several months in hospital, I am considered medically cured. And my dream of taking a longer break from my family after my retirement – to write – has come true.

And I am now here in the Lower Himalayas. The word cannot be repeated often enough. Despite acute criticism of the nature-destroying summit euphoria of mountaineers from Western countries, it still has a mystical ring to it for us. Far away and lonely, I think at first, on a house farm of an organic cooperative that has set up a guest room for the first time.

It had long been a plan for the beginning of my retirement to relax and write for a while.

Initially, I wanted to go to an old mountain farm in *South Tyrol* in Italy, where I had already been twice before for one or two weeks to write, but the owners had separated in old age and sold the farm.

Then a picturesque village at the Belgian Atlantic coast was an alter-native; I've also been there a few times in the past few years for a few days to write. But at weekends there are much to many German visitors from the around 3-hours drive German-Belgium border area. The harbour town of Ostend with its galleries etc. is also too close to be a danger for work escapes.

Alternatively, also a picturesque village near San Francisco, where Chaplin made his first films. My eldest son lived in nearby Silicon

Valley. I had already looked on *Google* for flats to rent and was about to write to him when I got a photo and, 'we did it.' They had just bought a house in this village. Even if there is enough space, at some point the question of proximity and distance comes up; true to my father-in-law's motto, 'after four days, the fish starts stinking'.

Now I had arrived here, as a European city dweller at the – from our point of view – end of the world; even if it is only the far north-east of India, Nepal, China, and Bhutan are just a stone's throw away – with little and often poorly developed infrastructure.

I realise that this is not the case within the first few days. Together with my hosts' son *Prashant*, I start by tracing my way to Germany on a map of the globe; centuries ago, this would have meant months of climbing up and down, walking and riding, maybe swimming ... and then, just for fun, we continue around the globe. He has never heard many of the names of countries, but I realise that I have heard many of them, but would not have been able to place them geographically; the many federal states alone are often larger than Germany. And after all the virtual walking, scrambling, swimming and rowing, driving etc., we arrive right here again.

It sounds childishly simple, but it is. This is not the end of the world, but the centre of it, with just as much life as here. And later I often realise that there is even more life. Because there is much, much more and more intensive communication and cohesion; but it doesn't mean everything is better, it's just different and beautiful.

People know all their neighbours personally, even many km away, are related across generations and communicate more and with many on a daily basis. And living in the here and now, which we often describe today as visionary life goal, such as the desire to live in harmony with nature, to have less stress, and, and, and ...

It reminds me of a short story *Anecdote to lower morale* by *Heinrich Böll* (got literature Nobel Price), which I am reproducing somewhat freely from my memory:

A tourist goes for a walk by the sea after lunch and sees someone in a worn straw hat lying on the beach, obviously looking for a light with a cigarette in his hand. The tourist quickly approaches and offers him a light. They strike up a conversation and the tourist hears that it is a fisherman. The tourist asks him, if he has fished anything today? 'Yes, I did,', says the fisherman. The tourist looks out to sea and after a while asks, if the man could go out fishing again, then he would earn more per day. 'Yes,' replies the fisherman, he could. And so the one-sided conversation continues. The tourist now calculates to the fisherman that if he did this regularly, he could soon buy a second boat, then another, and another, and ... until one day he would be rich enough to use his helicopter to direct his fishing fleet to where the big schools of fish are. And then he would be so rich that he could lie on the beach every day and no longer have to work. The fisherman looks at the tourist thoughtful, ... 'but that's what I'm right now doing here.'

Thursday, the first night and day 1

I go out again into the now cool night. At least for a few minutes in the darkness under the glowing starry sky and all the lights of the houses on the mountain opposite; it feels like the starry sky extends all the way down. A full moon announces itself.

I'm enjoying the coolness after the hot and humid days in Kolkata. But I also realise a cold is coming on. My throat hurts slightly when I swallow, my eyes water a little and I feel a slight pressure in my head. The typical accompanying circumstance of constantly switching from outside to inside between the air conditioning in trains, cars, airports, aeroplanes. And now an enormous difference in altitude from Kolkata onto sea level too quickly ... I don't know exactly.

Darjeeling town lies at 2,000 m altitude, Kalimpong a little lower at up to 1,700 m. From there it is around 15 km, a good half hour drive, to our village, always up and down in many serpentine-like curves.

I wake up at past midnight and feel a bit cold, marvellous. I've had a lot of mixed-up dreams and now realise where I am.

Instead of the simple room downstairs on the terrace, that what I had previously imagined, I now have a room on the first floor with a veranda and balcony as well as a western-style WC and shower on the same level. It's good that I don't have to feel my way down the narrow steps in the dark or light up my mobile phone.

It's been raining since the evening. What a beautiful and calming sound. Together with the rustling of the trees, the occasional animal sounds from the neighbouring forest, the mountain stream flowing past the edge of the property. Dressed warmly, I sit on the covered balcony and listen to this concert of nature for a while.

Early in the morning, I'm already awake at half past 5 a.m., and the rising sun can be seen in the morning mist behind the mountain ridge opposite. My hosts are already working on and around the house, in the stable and garden; first the cattle and then breakfast. Every morning and evening, *Giri-Raj* – we later agreed on *Giri* – prepares a large pot of pounded maize with additions such as leftovers from the mustard oil press as concentrated feed for the cattle, which then simmers at night or during the day on the traditional clay stove in the half-open shelter.

While the cow calf slurp up their concentrated feed, he can milk in peace. The calf is otherwise too excited hearing the milking noise, but in the end it is also allowed to join its mum.

Giri also has to cut huge stretchers of fresh green twice a day as day and night rations for the cattle. When he comes up or down the mountain with around 40 kg of greenery in the huge, overfilled stretcher on his back and held with a headband, just like the pictures we know from the Himalayas highlands; unbelievable for me. And *Manju* fetches fresh vegetables and fruit from the kitchen garden, cooks a big pot of rice and vegetables and makes the *Roti* dough for the day.

Later, they tell me, they want to be quieter now so as not to disturb me early in the morning. They usually talk louder to each other from the house to the garden or to the neighbour's garden. But I refuse, it doesn't bother me. I want to experience normal everyday life and not a tourist customised backdrop.

After a short time, my own daily rhythm adapts; I'm up at 6 a.m. and therefore I sleep much earlier in the evening.

On the way to the shower, I wonder if I can manage to only take cold showers for the next few days. The whole atmosphere around me somehow seems to demand it if you really want to belong. But even my still half-true ideas about this country are set straight – at the latest when I'm standing under the hot shower. Even though everything around me looks spartan and rustic, almost everyone has a water tank on the roof that heats up in the sun during the day and an instantaneous water heater for the colder months of the year.

Then I make my hot morning coffee in my room. My room kitchen is a corner next to the desk by the window with a stool with a kettle, a plastic tin with instant coffee and powdered milk, a coffee pot with a teaspoon, a glass, a few bags of bronchial tea and a large bottle of boiled water, which is re-filled every day. Later, I will add a second cup for my early morning tea with honey and black pepper.

Breakfast is served in the neighbouring house, the parents' former traditional *Gurkha* house, which is now used as a huge kitchen-cum-living room, surrounded by a covered veranda. As it is situated on the mountainside, the basement houses a half-open stable (closed overnight) with a cow with a calf, two male goats and two kids.

On the same level as the kitchen house is the basement of the newer main house, with three rooms; one *Giri* uses for office-work and store, the daughter's former room – planned as second guest room – and a prayer room for the Sunday school, singing circle, for religious rituals.

In-between, covered by the ground floor of the main house above, there is an open terrace and an extension with storage and sanitary facilities. From the terrace, a staircase leads up to the ground floor of the main house, to a large covered terrace; it is the official and beautifully designed entrance area from the narrow street that runs along here.

On the right, above the sanitary facilities from below, there are also sanitary facilities with western WC, traditional Indian toilet, shower and to the left above the rooms from below, a long veranda with living rooms and at the end my guest room.

The beautiful large entrance terrace at the top, as I experience it later, is also often used for meetings of the cooperative, neighbourhood or their joint music evenings. The covered terrace below, next to the kitchen house, is for daily tea and small talk, for kitchen work or simply for a little rest in between the strenuous field and garden work.

At the very top of the main house there is a large open, roofed attic, which has not yet been further developed. Two weeks later, *Giri* hangs a large 2-seater swing on the roof scaffolding; this will be my favourite place to read in the afternoon or just to look around near and far.

Often houses here have an open attic that looks as if it is still under construction. I know from many southern countries in Europe, where load-bearing concrete pillars are already exposed on the provisional roof level or re-enforcing bars are sticking out. It can take many years, *Giri* explains to me later with a smile, because as long as the house is not finished, fewer fees are due.

And everything is full of flowers in all shapes and colours: terraces and stairs, veranda, balcony; I forgot, my guest room has a balcony on the other sunset side in addition to the veranda, it's *Manju*'s hobby. Women often come and she gives them cuttings and advice on individual special flowers.

Cabbage is also grown in plastic bags on the terrace downstairs in front of the kitchen and the basement of the main house, as if on a 2-tiered low shelf; in my time I see cauliflower and broccoli, white cabbage and kohlrabi. I will learn the reason for this type of cultivation later; and later my German gift, the big garden gnome will watch over this still life.

After my first breakfast, rice, *Dal,* kale and potato vegetables, sour and spicy pickle and a plate of raw vegetables with tomato, cucumber and onion, I talk to *Manju.* What do I need to do about the house, garden, field, animals, etc.? She also wants to know what I'm missing from my first impression of the room. She has already provided a large bottle of boiled water that I can fill up in the kitchen. But I should also help myself with everything.

All I can think of at first is a wastepaper basket, an extension cable and a lamp at the table to work with, because it gets dark here very quickly when the sun disappears behind the mountain.

I doze off until noon with a slight cold and a little cough, and I organise my guest room as my new living space. I see parallels with my stay in the hospital; for a long time now, this will once again be my living space, limited in the truest sense of the word, but this time voluntarily chosen.

The table is my new workplace – if you can call my writing work – I see it more as a leisure activity. And, in contrast to the hospital with its view of a tower under construction with its helicopter landing pad, I now have an indescribable view of the valley and the mountains. Next to it is the stool as my coffee kitchen compared to the hot and cold drinks trolley on the ward corridor in front of the ward kitchen in the hospital. And I have the luxury of a balcony and a veranda here, for the morning sun facing south-east and the evening sun facing south-west; what more could you want? The bed is the bedroom, the flat side table next to it is used as a shelf; books, a plant, a few medicines. My unfolded travelling bag in front of the large purple wall opposite the bed is the wardrobe. And the wall will become my pinboard for the book concept and other things; with countless *Post-it* notes, pages and sheets from a cartoon tear-off calendar, you can stick dynamically changing shapes on it again and again.

Was I unconsciously looking for a repeat of the long hospitalisation? In any case, in the years after the hospital and apart from the rehabilitation centres, I often missed the seclusion to which I had become accustomed during the many months in hospital. Of course, there was often a lot going on, with hospital staff coming in all the time, regular meals, countless examinations and a limited amount of time out in the corridor between chemotherapy cycles. And later, after my stabilisation, I went to the patients' lounge room; here on my farm it's the garden or downstairs in front of the kitchen house. In the hospital from time to time a visit directly at the bedside or at a distance in the lounge room, as well as the few days of short stays at home after the chemotherapy and aplasia phases for re-immunisation. And that's almost how it's going to be here, I realise later. People regularly come to fetch milk or for tea, we are invited somewhere for dinner, and we go on a few excursions. But I want to be able to focus on myself here, to be as free and self-responsible as possible for my day; and always with a view of the vast mountain world and in concert with the nature of Darjeeling.

That's what I think at the beginning, until I get to know the social and unofficial rules of living together here, such as attending weddings and funerals, religious festivals, visiting neighbours and meetings of their SHG or the cooperative chairwomen, or the efforts to achieve political independence in the region, in whose geographical and spiritual centre I find myself here; but I only experience or learn about all this over time.

At first, the large kitchen garden and a few smaller terraced fields with rice cultivation look like my run-out area, comparable to the three corridors of the hospital ward; that should be enough. I also have to improvise a lot, which is fun.

More than forty years ago, during my civilian service in a *Kibbutz* (farm cooperative) in Israel with short stays in neighbour country Lebanon and north African Egypt, I had already learned to live under much more simpler circumstances. With the so-called Swiss Army Knife, a gift from my parents, I had managed almost everything, right down to the spartan bookshelf or writing desk. Or on rail journeys across Europe. Since then, I don't see every problem as a burden, but rather as a challenge to find a solution.

And it was the same in the hospital, not just physically, but also psycho-logically, when I learnt (for myself again) that life time is one life; it makes no difference whether it's just days or weeks, months or years. It is life time that should not be denied, but used ... even within a limited framework.

On the first Sunday, my hosts *Manju* and *Giri* are away during the day. In the morning, the niece comes from the neighbouring brother-in-law's house to see if I need anything. She fetches me for a snack at lunchtime and we eat *Roti* with egg, banana and grapes. The 80-year-old grandmother, who traditionally lives in the eldest son's house, wants to know everything: 'Married, children, grandchildren?' Those are always the first questions in India. And then, of course, what I do for a living, why I'm here, why for so long? And what does my family say? They don't want to believe that I'm already 66 years old.

The granddaughter translates; she is working on her PhD thesis at a university in the about more than 700 km away federal state Assam and is visiting on the occasion of *Durga Puja* holidays. And as always, as I will also experience here, someone from the neighbourhood often joins us for a *Ciyâ* tea during the day. Grandma is obviously happy about the change. When she hears that my son and his partner are coming to visit me for a few days, she invites them for tea as a precaution.

I probably won't be able to avoid to stop by almost every house here on the mountain for tea or a meal, or they'll just drop by, as I'm about to do.

Of course they are curious, also because I offer their children an additional new perspective, alongside organic gardening with product sales that is now up and running. This means that some of them can now not only send their children to school, but also to a college or university in neighbouring Nepal, for example. Education is now also seen as the key to their future here; many live almost spartanly and sometimes go into debt so that a child can study. This frees up a room for weeks or months, or permanently if the daughter marries and in tradition moves in with her husband's family.

This is also the case here. The daughter has been married for two years in her husband's home in the hundreds of km away state Assam. Her former room, which is now vacant, is to be adapted and rented out for Home-staying. This is currently an important step for *Manju* and to her SHG (about women's self-help groups more in the chapter *Everlasting Memories*). My long-term visit is also quasi a pilot project for her and the entire cooperative with 55 SHGs in terms of Home-staying as a new service for their tourism development and income opportunities.

But experience also shows that in such large groups or organisations, envy and conflicts also arise over time. The fact that they, *Manju* as the SHG chairwoman, with a key role in the cooperative and otherwise very socially and culturally committed and networked, have two rooms available from the studying son and married daughter already available; I am quasi now as their friend the first external guest, is still accepted.

In this way, others learn vividly what effort such a guest means, what changes have to be made? This is particularly important here, where everyone in the family has to work full-time during the rice harvest season, for example.

But such a long visit? Even if it's very cheap for me due to the difference in purchasing power here, it's a lot of money for the people here. I discussed this with my friends in Kolkata who know the area. In the end, I will also make a donation to the community, the cooperative or the village. I'll say it here in advance, to the village community centre, which is currently under construction, has turned out to be a useful project for everyone.

Around 4 p.m., the sun sinks behind a higher mountain, then shortly afterwards dusk sets in, by 5:30 p.m. it is dark.

An hour later, *Giri* and *Manju* are back and call me into the large kitchen. Son *Prashant* is also there; he's studying Mechanical Engineering at a college an hour's drive away in the neighbouring federal state Sikkim, on whose border we are located.

Like almost all the young people here, he fluently speaks English; later I realise that this is true even for primary school children; they start speaking it at the age of three in pre-school. Otherwise, he speaks Nepali, the official regional language here, and like almost everyone else, no Bengali; nor Hindi, the formal Indian official language.

He naturally wants to know about famous German Engineering. We drink the flavoured *Ciyâ* and pepper each other with questions. In an emergency, the *Google* translator helps, which I have downloaded English–Nepali as a precaution, as I can't get a net here and don't want to. He is at home until next summer as his college was badly damaged by the big flood.

The food: freshly baked *Roti* with ghee, traditional hand-churned butter, served with vegetable mix, potato, onion, ginger, and a flavour-some omelette. And I'm asked if I want pickles? Of course; it's like chips and vinegar in England, which at first you don't like the intense vinegar flavour, but then you get hooked. And in addition to the obligatory glass of warm water, something between kephir and yoghurt and a banana. I later got out of the habit of drinking warm water; it's certainly healthy, but just not my thing.

Of course, as far as possible, everything is home-grown or bartered from neighbours. The cow gives around 8 litres of milk a day when milked in the morning and evening, 3 litres are used by the family, the rest is sold to neighbours or exchanged for eggs, for example. *Manju* and *Giri* no longer want chickens, they make too much mess and they need to be let out. The last ones were taken by the fox. He has a family to look after too, they laugh. The goats are all bucks, which are fattened up and then sold at around 60 kg weight.

And of course not forgetting house cat *Mr Tiger*; probably the only vegetarian cat in the world. He actually only likes rice stirred into milk.

Here, I have also secretly placed a large German garden gnome around the kitchen as a gift; it can only be recognised at second glance ... and then: 'Oh, what is that?'

Always remember that there is only one important time:
Today. Here. Now.

Tolstoy

First Days in a New Home

Day 2, Friday

I go to bed early, but I can't sleep through the night; the full moon is high. It shines almost dazzlingly bright over the whole valley and the mountainside opposite. I wake up every two hours.

I've never actually had any problems sleeping under a full moon. Some people sow seeds in the fields according to the lunar cycle and others have spiritual experiences. I smile, that would fit with India and the Himalayas, when so many people in my school and student days in the 1970/80s aimed to find the supposedly correct truth here.

Of course, I was also looking for such 'mind-expanding experiences' back then. Starting with Yoga – it was more about getting a better grade; my English teacher led a Yoga course at the German *Volkshochschule* (state supported evening adult education). Later and up to (for sure, not state supported) independent extreme spiritual experiences with beer, wine etc. and even smoking these forbidden plants; or was it more the red wine drunk too much at the same time?

Then, just like today, many tried to expand their consciousness with esotericism, accompanied by aroma therapy, light showers and the like. What, if they knew that 90% of aromatic oils and fragrances are chemically pro-duced? There are the corresponding breathing techniques. But you don't need an Indian, Ashram or Guru for this – the drop-out hit in the 1980s – all you need to do is pant long enough or use massage techniques to change the oxygen supply to the brain, or even smoke relevant plants in the form of tea, baked into biscuits or smoked. And this is best combined with repetitive rhythmic citations and dance movements.

I realise that the moon does have an effect, at least for these now pointless thoughts in the middle of the night. So, I keep going out and looking into the pleasantly cool night. What will it be like when I soon feel like part of the inventory here?

Next day I realise, some of the (supposed) forest and garden noise is a mountain stream that flows past the garden and small terraced rice fields below. It is our water source, not only in the household, but also with a variable tube system for watering the gar-den and fields. For example, a tube is clamped into the top of a forked branch and the water jet hits the bottom of an upturned tin canister. This sprays the water onto the vegetables in the surrounding area. Every hour, someone simply moves the branch fork and canister a little further.

Two nieces are visiting for three days. Like almost all young people in the world, they are all about social media. On the other hand, they are very respectful towards older people, regardless of whether they are parents, grandparents or neighbours; I'll leave out the topic of puberty for a moment, as the parents here also smile in agony. On the other hand, the old people here – as I notice again and again later – are very open-minded towards young people with the new media. And of course they are also very interested in how young people see their future and how they hope to shape it here in their home country.

In the afternoon, together with another related family with a child and baby, who have travelled overnight by bus from Kathmandu, Nepal, we take a trip to our mountain's top. There is a large park around a Science Centre with lots of experimental equipment to try out, as well as explanations of knowledge. From a viewing platform you can see the paragliders taking off from here against the imposing high mountain backdrop of the Himalayas.

Even on the excursion, everyone invites me to try this and that without fail; I'm sure I'll burst at some point. But eating together is a traditionally and important gesture of friendship, especially among mountain peoples, where the paths to each other were often long and arduous. And they drink a lot of hot water and offer this to me as well; but even is seems to be un-friendly, I hate to drink warm or hot water.

Day 3, Saturday

The evening before and at night it was correspondingly loud. The brother-in-law with family joined us and of course there was plenty to eat and laugh; and some pray together in-between. Children romp around into the night and the teenagers sit together talking and on social media. It bothers me a bit, the stress of travelling, the difference in altitude, some of the unfamiliar food are still weighing on me. But I have managed to fit in at the important relatives' meeting. I ask my-self sarcastically, is the mix of loud music, this drowning out loud talking and parallel social media already Acoustic Pollution or E-smog 2.0? It has nothing to do with the silence of a secluded mountain village in the singsong of nature and perhaps a little spiritual tinkling of bells, according to the generally Western Bias projected idea.

People talk loudly between house and gardens. In this way, people take part in everything and everyone as neighbours; and it is then passed on. The kiosk shop has a similar role to the one we have in the villages. Why should it be any different? I had already realised that spiritual chants and meditative bells don't ring all day long here.

Over time, I also hear music competing with chain saws and axe blows from forestry work. And of course, especially late afternoon until dark, cool young men on scooters or motorbikes trying to impress the young ladies. That's probably village life all over the world for generations, why should it here be different?

During the day, you can hear the famous Indian honking. I know the short honking from the big Indian cities, be careful, I'm here too. And here in a less frequented area, people honk for safety reasons on the narrow, often hairpin-winding and often steep roads. At some point, you don't even notice it any more, and when it gets dark, it stops. On the one hand, a scooter or motorbike doesn't look any better, and on the other, you can see the light cones of oncoming vehicles a few serpentine-like ahead in the mountain.

My usual diarrhoea seems to be over. Somehow it's a part of learning to eat with your right hand or savouring a delicacy in a street kitchen. Next will be sunburn despite the cool altitude. After all, 'you're closer to the sun here at altitude than in the valley,' *Prashant* laughs.

At breakfast, *Manju* told me that around 20 children will be coming here tomorrow morning for Sunday school in the room below me to pray and sing. She runs the school voluntarily; at this point I have no idea that I will once play a central role in this school.

After breakfast, we go on an excursion to the river bridge far down in the valley. As everyone dresses more solemnly and polishes their shoes – usually everyone walks around in the garden and on the terraced fields in flip-flops during the day – I do the same; but I always have a shirt, trousers and shoes 'for good' as we say in Germany. On the way, I learn that *Giri,* now in the *Durga Pura* following the astrological calendar, gets a traditional *Tika* at his uncle's house. 'Don't need to be afraid,' he laughs, 'they won't paint you.'

In the end, there are five households on this outing, as we are also visiting *Manju*'s close relatives for the same reason. And of course I also have to take part in the traditional ritual everywhere. Hinduism, which is thousands of years old, sees itself as the 'mother of all religions' and is very tolerant, they say open-minded.

I repeatedly sit in front of the elder of each house, who mixes a paste of crushed rice and flour coloured red for my *Tika,* a larger red mark in the centre of my forehead. Then, accompanied by prayer-like chants in Sanskrit, rice and yellow-green leaves of a medicinal plant are sprinkled on my head and in my hands. For the people here, this is followed by mutual spiritual bows in Sanskrit, but I am exempt from this.

Sanskrit, the ancient Indian language of the *Vedas* as a collection of Hindu religious oral traditions – comparable Latin as traditional Christian church language – dates back to 3,500 years. Today, it is primarily used for cultural and religious ceremonies as well as weddings and funerals. Many borrowed terms can also be found in the German language in same writing or spelling, for example: *Bambus, Bungalow, Yoga, Guru, Orange, Ginger, Zucker.*

Afterwards there is small talk, water, sweet and spicy snacks and, of course, *Ciyâ,* which is pronounced as *ci-yâ* in two syllables. For me, it is the same as Indian *Chai,* here you are Indian on principle, but ethnically Nepali.

Giri and *Manju* have a bag of their own harvested rice, some juice and snacks for each house, and we as the blessed receive a small envelope from the elder at the end; blessing and money is this festival tradition here.

From my point of view, the households range from rich to rather poor, and I know I must not turn it down under any circumstances. The total will be 1,700 Rupees, varying from 200–500 per envelope.

On the one hand, it shames me, but on the other hand, for the people here this is a very important gesture on this special holiday, as I learn later on other occasions. The equivalent of in total around 20 Euro is more than a week's salary for a tea picker; I will later donate it to an aid project for eye cataract surgeries for destitute women to protect them from blindness.

In the river valley it was relatively very warm for me throughout the day. When we get back around 6 p.m. under a full moon, it's noticeably cooler further up the mountain: finally my weather again, I'm pleased to say. And because of all the snacks during the day, we all skip dinner.

Day 4, Sunday

At breakfast, *Giri* announces that we are going to the market in Kalimpong tomorrow. I remember the travel last year and days ago. A town on the steep hill-side of a mountain, constant traffic jams, cars travelling through narrow streets, scooters, motorbikes and pedestrians meandering between them.

The scooters are perfect for the mountains here, often carrying up to three people with shopping bags, sometimes also a small child inbetween them. People often step straight out of a shop into the queue of vehicles. But there are hardly any accidents, as I find out later. Everyone is looking for an ad-vantage in what we perceive to be chaos. But there is a system behind it, nobody complains and honking is as usual. At the last moment, the one who is a tick behind always stops and you laughingly give way to the other.

We know it professionally as a dynamically Self-organising Chaos; one of the many management fashions today in our western world.

The many supposedly stray dogs and cats also find their way around. They usually belong to some household or business and are fed regularly; it is not common here to keep animals indoors. And they serve as natural enemies against mice and rats; and in the mountains also against monkeys (this I will learn by own examples later).

But our *Mr Tiger* still doesn't know that, because as a vegetarian cat he does not care about small animals. I wonder if there are now pets that go against nature and eat a purely the new western fashion 'vegan'? My hosts have once again tried to get him used to meat: 'Maybe he'll get the idea that hunting mice is somehow part of his nature? But he continues to disdain both meat and hunting and actually prefers milk with rice without any exception, and only Basmati quality, of course.'

Sundays are a kind of rest days like ours; only the necessary things are done. For example, in the mornings and evenings we boil the pots of concentrated feed in the barn for the day and night respectively, milk and feed the animals in the mornings and evenings – *Giri* collects the two green feed rations for Sunday on Saturdays – and fetch fresh vegetables from the garden; today a pumpkin, few carrots and small cucumbers and freshly picked some guava fruits. *Manju* later waters the many cabbages growing in half pot-shaped plastic bags on the edge of the large terrace.

On the mountainside, the garden and rice fields can only be cultivated in terraces, otherwise too much irrigation would run off above ground; topsoil would also be washed away, especially in the rainy season. Plastic bags or buckets can therefore be used sensibly and directly next to the kitchen.

In addition to Sunday school, people from the near and far neigh-bourhood come by for tea during the day. They are naturally curious about me, I have to greet them and again almost everyone invites med for tea or a meal. And the same old questions: am I married and how many children do I have? But also about other things. Strangely enough, *Hitler* has a good reputation here.

I experienced this years ago in India. At that time, I sat as a guest speaker on the podium of the Chamber of Chartered Accountants of West Bengal together with representatives of Indian NGO, mainly small regional and local grass root initiatives.

It was about start-up initiatives by people in precarious living conditions, such as the poorer rural population. In his opening address, the Chairman then emphasised Germany. Using brief historical references, he spoke more intensively about *Hitler*, according to the motto that there were of course also critical things, but the achievements should also be recognised. This was followed by the examples we are already familiar with: motorways for the infrastructure, a people's car for everyone, jobs in the steel and armament industries. And India should also take this as an example: this was before the election of Modi as Indian Prime Minister 10 years ago.

I had real problems holding myself back and avoiding a scandal. The German wife of my Indian business partner and friend was sitting in the front row. She imperceptibly gestured to me to remain calm at all costs. I later learnt that Germany is not only so popular here because of its economic and technical achievements, but also because of its attack on India's former colonial ruler England.

Hospital Intensive Care

Return to hospital and KMP

My return to hospital after what I consider to be a minor 'first night escape' – from the hospital's point of view, it was probably 'life-threatening' for me, I learn later – is unspectacular. On the way back, I let the taxi driver stop, and I to buy some apology pralines for the night nurse and doctor.

When I arrive, everything is already prepared and I start immediately. First a large blood sample – later I often count 12 collection tubes in different sizes and colour coding – a trolley with a laptop at the table and a doctor who needs the results promptly.

Shortly afterwards, the cutlery table that I had already seen outside the hospital room rolls in. I call it medical cutlery, because the equipment speaks for itself. I start to feel a bit queasy, it's still really serious. I don't have the self-confidence to make my stupid comments now.

I have to lie on my side and am given a local anaesthetic injection. 'The anaesthetic works all the way to the bone,' the doctor says, 'but then you have to endure a bit of pain, the anaesthetic doesn't work in the bone and bone marrow,' he adds and gives me a kind of hard bone to bite on. 'But feel free to shout, we're used to that.' I'm not thrilled, but I also know that I can develop a stoic calm in situations like this, at least that's what I've always managed at the dentist.

A slight, dull ache as the needle penetrates the pelvic bone. Easy to bear, I think. And playing the strong man, I drop the bite bone from my mouth. Then I am told that they are already in the bone marrow and that it will only take a few seconds to take the fresh blood. A second later I have to let out a loud groan. I have never felt such an intense, strange pain in my whole body; it's like an imploding bone marrow. I just noticed that someone was holding my pelvis that I wouldn't move.

'It's almost done,' the doctor said, 'we'll just take a few more bone marrow samples.' Later I realised that it's a relatively thick needle through which various other needles etc. can be passed. Taking the marrow samples it's a rather funny feeling – I call it bone marrow snapping – and without pain I twitch 3- or 4-times, just like muscles relax when you fall asleep. The doctor asks me: 'Does it hurt?' I deny and think, do they practise this on themselves at university?

The samples are sent to our inhouse own laboratory and to another university hospital for an independent testing in order to prepare a weakened chemotherapy for the first tolerance test, I am told. Their plan is to start directly after the weekend on Monday.

Then I have to lie on a sandbag that the pressure helps to close the puncture. Must be a borehole and they're looking for oil, it occurred to me?

At some point in the afternoon, I am woken up. A doctor and a young female doctor are standing by my bed with a new, still covered cutlery trolley and a mobile computer. Oh my god, not again, I think.

But it was a different, and no less challenging remoteness for me. They are about to insert a central venous catheter for all the infusions and blood samplings. 'This is so that you don't always have to be pricked, because we need your blood every day now,' one says.

I was expecting a permanent venous cannula on my hand and yet I don't think so much medical technology ...; but it's going to be a bigger deal again. I have to lie on my side and a tarpaulin is placed over my head and neck. I still don't realise that there is an opening in my neck. I realise it when they disinfect it repeatedly and it runs cold down my neck and shoulders. The disinfectant vapour makes me cough under the tarpaulin. Someone lifts it slightly above my face so that I can breathe better. The doctor turns the computer screen slightly into my field of vision, saying: 'If you want to watch what we are doing now.' And he would keep asking me in-between if I was still awake. I should just hum or something, but please don't try to move my head, which is now pressed firmly against the mattress. He shows me the large pumping carotid artery on the screen. My supposedly stoic composure is gone again. He continuous, 'and that next to it, that's your neck vein. We're going to push a very small tube into it up to about 20 cm from your heart. We can then use this to regulate and combine the various infusions. I'll show you how this works later, if you're interested?'

What if they accidentally miss and get stuck in the pulsating carotid artery? I close my eyes, the strong man inside me is far away.

I can't feel anything due to the local anaesthetic. At some point I hear: 'Be careful, back again ... yes, forward again.' Something warm runs down my neck and suddenly presses firmly on the puncture site in my neck. Everything is spinning. Oh my God, it's the artery, goes through my mind.

Or was I dreaming? A hand shakes me gently: 'Please stay awake. Stay awake, we're almost finished.' I grumble. 'Done,' he says, and I can still hear him whispering, 'wipe everything away first.' I don't actually feel anything on or in my throat. Then the puncture site is disinfected again and covered with a thick layer of adhesive.

Now I have a slightly oversized button with short tubes sticking out of one side of my neck, it's like a multiple adapter. I must look like this monster in the horror movie *Frankenstein*, I try to be self-ironic. They smile and I think, well, it's easy to make jokes when it's over.

In rotation, the computer and cutlery trolley are pushed out, an infusion stand with bags already attached arrives, some of which are now connected.

Over time, watching the infusion bags dripping empty at varying speeds to extremely slowly became a great way to fall asleep. After just a few days, I call him *Emil*, my ever-faithful infusion stand. But in time I will realise that I am the one who is loyal to him.

It feels like the venous catheter in my neck is placed every fortnight, alternating between left and right. Later, the doctor explained to me what had happened the first time. The port tube that had been pushed into the neck vein had moved back a little when the catheter needle was pulled out, it could not be pushed forwards again easily.

When the nurse pulls out the port during the next change – quickly and painlessly, so that I don't even notice it – I want to know from her how it works? She comes back later with the disinfected super-thin port. Creamy white, like an extremely thin power cable with (I think) five wires inside and with openings at different distances. This allows the individual infusion solutions to be combined in a targeted manner, one after the other. It looks fascinatingly simple. But behind it is a highly developed system to avoid the complications that used to occur time and again with the necessary quasi multiple infusions. 'Some hospitals also apply the catheter to the chest,' she explains and concludes her explanations, 'would you like to keep this as a souvenir?' I shake my head, pained smiling I think myself, no, thank you.

My cough gets worse over the weekend. I try to suppress it and am afraid that the port will be pushed out. All I can think about is a port about 20 cm long, which is a plastic tube inserted into the central neck vein just before my ventricle, right next to the carotid artery. This is supposedly the most dangerous in the event of an injury, according to my childhood fears, which have never been relativised or questioned since then.

I get a high fever. Every 10 minutes they come to check on me and take my blood pressure and temperature. The bed next to me isn't occupied, I'm alone. I ask if it will stay that way because I would like a single room. The nurse – later I find out and see it as increasingly positive that she is the senior charge nurse and literally has everything under control – explains to me that there are no single rooms for us. At some point I would be glad not to have to lie alone all the time. I reply: 'Yes, if I'm still alive then?' My sarcasm was back. 'Oh, young man,' – I was definitely older than her, 'let's wait and see, you'll manage,' was her motherly reply. I'm getting calmer and for the first time, given the circumstances, I feel like I'm in the right place.

My first roommate

I estimate my first roommate to be 10 years younger than me. With recurrent malignant lymphoma cancer he has had to lie here regularly for one or two weeks for years now.

Next day, a doctor comes to see him. She wants to tell him about the possibility of bone marrow transplant as a final perspective instead of recurring relapses and hospital stays. She asks if I can listen to this? 'Yes, of course,' he says, 'there are no secrets here anyway.' And she asks me if I would like to listen or perhaps go outside?

Looking at my *Emil,* we both decide to stay. What could possibly shock me now? I find out how a bone marrow transplant works; but only if a suitable donor marrow can be found worldwide. 'Basically, it looks like a blood transfusion,' she explains and continues, 'but it means total isolation for weeks in a hermetically sealed room on the special corridor here, you know the one I mean.'

Even I now know this always locked corridor on our floor with *KMT* sign (German abbreviation for bone marrow transplant); only allowed to enter with authorisation and completely disinfected with protective clothing.

'We then see whether the body accepts the donor bone marrow,' she goes on, and explains possible side effects and complications and how high the risk is that it won't help. Afterwards, total isolation at home. The flat must be germ-free beforehand. Carpets and upholstered furniture out. No plants, because plant soil is a jungle of germs. This is vital for the plant's survival, but it could be life-threatening for you at first. Many also use the situation for renovation. And who buys the food for them?

Later, my roommate tells me that he collects orchids. His biggest worry now is what will he do with the orchids? And who will he leave them to if things turn out badly for him?

Weeks later, my roommate left the hospital a week or two before and I was back from hell at the intensive care unit, I lose whole tufts of hair due to hemotherapy, which looks kind of stupid with the remaining hair. And I asked for a hairdresser to remove all my last hair from my head. 'No, we don't have a hairdresser here, too dangerous. And, you're not allowed to do it yourself with a razor because of the risk of infection, even with a tiny cut. A carer in training does that here,' I was advised. A young carer then has shaved the last hair off my head.

When I've just rubbed some cream on my head after shaving and come out of the room's bathroom there's a knock on the door. In comes the orchid man, whom I haven't seen for around three weeks. He asks me if I know where I am? I laugh and only then does he recognise me. I'm still scarred from the intensive care unit phase, and what a difference a bald head makes.

He is in outpatient follow-up treatment here and has decided to wait with the bone marrow transplant. But he has already found a solution for his orchids as a precaution; a flower shop would take care of them.

My first chemotherapy cycle

'Don't worry, we have a lot under control, medicine is much more advanced here than what you hear on the street about chemotherapy and side effects of cancer treatment, they explained to me.

I have to fill in a long questionnaire, tick or cross out boxes and sign it. It also says something about freezing sperm donation. I'm probably looking at my medical counsellor too dumbfounded. 'Yes, that's just in case. It's sometimes necessary if you still want to have children. Chemotherapy can have an effect on fertility in rare cases,' he answered my questioning look.

What does he think? He knows how old I am and I've already stated my marital status, children etc.; this is all in my patient file that he has tucked under his arm. After all, there was also an admission interview. So, I ask: 'Do you have children?' He replies that he doesn't have any yet, and is now surprised. 'You see, when you've raised three children, you don't want to have any more children, and especially in my age. What are they supposed to do with a father who looks like their grandfather? I decided to have a vasectomy after my third child.' 'Oh, yes, sorry, but that's just in the questionnaire,' he replies and seems happy that the issue has been resolved. Then I think, well, he's right, it's great to know for young potential fathers and possibly mothers.

Monday morning is a restless day at my bedside. *Emil* has a box with digital displays screwed on at bed height and an infusion tube is fed through it. Then the data from the infusion bag is compared with the medical records and I have to say my name and date of birth again to be sure.

The infusion bag is opened by a cap in the infusion tube. Slowly, to the beat of the strange box with an intrusive green digital display, the chemo, which looks like clear water, drips into me. It would take about an hour, the doctor in duty advised me, and I was given the call button in my hand in case anything happened. Also he reassures me:

'If you got scared, just press it. Better call once too often than not at all.' My first chemotherapy was on.

After a while I feel warm and my whole body tingles, as if ants are crawling through my veins. Is it my imagination, because I'm now sensitised to side effects, or is it really real? And I'm sweating. What should I do? So the call button, better one too many than too few, they said. A nurse arrives immediately, followed seconds later by the doctor. 'That's normal' the doctors say, and he continued, 'the sweating is caused by the developing small lung infection. A common side effect of acute leukaemia. Tingling too, your body is defending itself, it is reacting. And that's a good thing.'

And then, I can no longer suppress the constant coughing fits. It's getting exhausting. The port in my throat, the infusions, I feel bloated and heavy, it's all too much. I have no chance to act and feel like I'm trapped in a box. And I'm always supposed to drink, and drink again. How do I tell my children now? Is it already too late? I'm in tears. Unjustly I tell the young carer who brings me a meal to leave me alone.

I wake up, it's late in the afternoon. The professor is there, tall, slim, younger than me. After a bit of small talk he comes to the point: 'We have to take you to another ward two floors below. The chemotherapy will continue there, but we also have to take care of your lungs. I've seen from our file that you already had severe bilateral pneumonia few years ago. Just a precautionary measure,' he takes my hand, 'don't worry, we'll meet again.'

Intensive care unit

As soon as he has left the room, two paramedics are already next to me with a wheeled and bed-high transport stretcher. I have a feeling it was all set up while I was sleeping. And that I now have no time to think about it and make another escape?

Not allowed to stand up I'm lifted over. The upper part of the infusion stand – *Emil* and I are not yet an inseparable couple – is pulled out and plugged into the transport stretcher. A carer packs my things into a large white plastic bag and places it on my feet. I feel queasy again, I get scared; the im-pacts are not getting any closer, as they say, they are there. I didn't expect to die so quickly.

I have to inform the children. But when and how? Where is the lap-top, where is the cell phone? I can't get out of bed. Tubes on my neck. Wired to flashing machines. Where is the patient phone? I want to sit up. I can't. The bladder catheter is poking. No patient phone at the bed. I remember. No connection here. Everything is going too fast for me again.

The pneumonia has progressed too far, it' is becoming a dangerous complication (I'll find out later). My body has becoming really fluid.

A lung puncture is immediately performed down here, now two floors below at the intensive care ward. The medication is changed on the infusion stand, which is now in a permanently installed tube on the new bed. No more talk of chemo, a misunderstanding? Nobody answers me, the room is half open, I can hear rhythmic pumping, bee-ping and ticking, and not just from the equipment at my bedside.

I realise that there are other cases in my immediate vicinity. Or am I now also a serious case? My trolley case is against the wall opposite, next to it is the white plastic bag with my things. I read 'patien...' and think '...stuff'. It's probably not worth unpacking it any more. I take a closer look around. Yes, no wardrobe. Will the relatives get the stuff in the bag afterwards? I'm getting scared and cold. Although it's warm here, I crawl under the light duvet like a baby and cry, shivering.

When I wake up, my side cabinet with the fold-out table is next to me. I feel for my old *iPod* out of the drawer, and then press the pillow to my face while listen to Joe Cocker's hard-rocking music at maximum volume. Then I'll just suffocate myself, I think theatrically, this is not what I want.

This time I get a real crying fit, I don't want to cry, but my whole body is twitching uncontrollably. I can't stop it. Choking myself is not an option, of course. I don't really want to, I think when I've calmed down a bit. I'm sweating profusely and coughing without end. An infusion is added.

Waking up again, I am dressed only in a half-length patient gown, open at the back. Tubes and cables are connected to devices behind me, which are now pumping, beeping and ticking in chorus with the others. I was probably left alone to deal with the shock while a sleep aids slowly trickled into me. They know this, and certainly worse, every day here.

No windows, artificial light. Is it day or night? I am exhausted. No mobile phone reception and internet; later I know it's for security reasons because of all the electronics. I try to sit up and feel a slight twinge in my abdomen.

That moment, an intensive carer arrives. 'Careful, stay lying down, we had to insert a urinary catheter. The anaesthetic will wear off and you will feel it a little more strongly. It's best not to move at first,' he explains, and that I have too much water in my body, which absolutely has to come out.

I tell him that my right arm hurts because every few minutes the blood pressure cuff around my upper arm inflates to the point of pain. He nods, 'unfortunately that's the way it has to be now. You will be monitored around the clock. Don't worry, I'm always there for you. I also have you and your device readings on my screen next door.'

Exhausted, I lie in a daze. Again and again, again and again, the blood pressure cuff brings me briefly and painfully back to reality. I can only lift my head slightly and carefully turn onto my right side, a quarter turn so to speak. That's all I can do because of the bladder catheter and the cables and infusion tubes. But what gets me most is the ticking and the digital screen, which I can still just make out with my head turned halfway to the side behind me with all possible numbers and curves.

A fairy tale from my childhood comes in my mind. I see the picture from the storybook in front of me. Father Death, with scythe and life clock in his hand; the clock had run out. Is this here now my life clock?

'Hello, hello, ... wake up,' I hear coming out of the dream through the fog. I see a people in white and blue. Thank God, my carer in his blue protective gown is one of them; I am immediately reassured. All sense of time is gone.

Later I will realise that some time, was it minutes, or hours, or ... I don't know, must have passed without me and that they must have gone to great lengths to bring me back to consciousness.

At some point during the night, I can't manage to lie any more and can't sit up either. In sheer desperation, I try to carefully pull out the bladder catheter. It doesn't work. I pull harder, doesn't work. Then I realise that there is negative pressure. The harder I pull, the stronger the resistance becomes.

Now I can also physically feel my loss of control, I'm not only lokked up but also chained up. So far it has occurred to me repeatedly, but something always happened and I was distracted. But now, in the middle of the night, or is it daytime, I feel completely alone and am part of the ticking, glowing, buzzing and pumping devices; I freeze and keep twitching uncontrollably with my whole body.

I had this as a child when I was playing hide and seek in a concrete tube and other children held both halves of the tube shut to tease me. I dreamt about it for years afterwards.

I ring for the carer, but a nurse arrives with 'it's the middle of the night.' I ask her to remove the catheter, but of course she refuses and an exchange of words ensues. 'Please get a doctor, please,' I beg. 'It can't be done that quickly,' she replies. 'But this is an intensive care unit, surely there must be a doctor around', I'm getting more aggressive and louder. 'Can you please calm down? Please, you're not the only patient here. I'll see if I can get the doctor. Please understand,' she tries to calm me down.

Finally a doctor arrives, or more? In any case, there are three people in white coats. The doctor, he is Korean. I ask him where he buys his *Kimchi* – traditional spicy cabbage and radish side dish with almost any meal – in this city, and I hadn't found it really good yet. He laughs and responds that they make it themselves at home. He wants to know why I'm asking this and we talk a bit about Korea, where I worked at a university in a summer school some years ago. That impresses him, at least that's what I think, and I ask him to let me try without catheter. We make a deal. The catheter should be removed the next morning and I should try to urinate normally again. If I can't, I promise him I'll have the catheter put back in.

My carer comes to remove the urinary catheter, 'how did you manage that?' I tell him about my deal with the Korean doctor. 'Yes, he's nice,' he says, 'but he's always far too understanding with the patients. We have got the work and we are then the bad guys. Well, let's do it then.'

I had lost all my shame by then. Somehow you're always naked in front of people. 'No wonder,' he says, 'it's much too big. Next time we'll go down a size. It'll be a bit shorter in the bladder and it won't poke you when you move.' Then he raises the top of the bed a little to a semi-sitting position for me, I'm relieved.

I can no longer hear all the mechanical and electronic noises all around me, and even this stupid automatic blood pressure cuff can make me ...

'Here we go,' says the carer, and places a urine bottle on my bed at my feet. 'Do you think you can get up carefully, but very carefully, please? But first just sit up and stay seated.' He lifts the half-height side rail of the bed slightly, folds it down and moves the back section of the bed further into a sitting position. 'Now try sitting freely without leaning against it.' He holds my shoulder firmly, 'and now get your legs out of bed, but remain seated and supported.'

What a freedom, I can let my legs dangle with pleasure. 'But don't get too cocky,' the carer laughs. 'How many do you think thought you could stand and then just toppled off? I'm sure you can imagine the annoyance I get.'

I obey. He lowers the bed a little so that my feet are on the floor. 'Now slowly get up,' he holds me with both arms, even when I'm already standing. 'And now let all the weight rest on my feet, I'll hold you,' he adds. Wonderful, I'm standing by myself. 'You can move on maximum of your arm length on, that's how far the infusion tubes reach.' I've forgotten again that the infusions and cables on me are firmly attached to the bed. 'So it's not that easy to run away,' I joke.

'Even if you try that again, you won't get past me,' he replies smiling. So that's what he knows about me. I'll close the subject. 'Do you think I'm going to walk around naked in this shirt? And then you'll be taking me straight to the loony bin.' 'I'll put it this way,' he laughs, 'even those psychiatric in such as your condition are more likely to come here.'

With the urine bottle I stand next to my bed ... nothing happens. It doesn't work. When I tried to push a bit it still hurts a little because of the former catheter; I realise it won't work that way either. And I keep turning around to see if anyone is there. Because after all, I'm standing there in my open-backed mini, half naked just above my bum.

After a while, the carer comes back and asks, 'well, what's been done?' He answers his question himself straight away: 'Well, there are already a few drops in there.' He puts a hand on my shoulder, 'take your time and look at the picture on the wall.' Then he leaves again. I do as I'm advised. What a stupid picture here in this place, you're supposed to be able to die with it? That's what goes through my mind, and at some point I feel my wet hand. The urine bottle is overflowing and I can't stop the flow of urine; I call out.

He comes straight away with a second bottle in his hand. 'No problem, that happens regularly here. We're even glad, then we don't need to insert a catheter. Just lie down and pretend you're asleep. Someone will come and wipe up in a minute.'

I'm slowly getting used to the truly intense situation here. In any case, there's less going on here than at the previous ward upstairs, I think sarcastically.

In thought, I now officially welcome my side cabinet: Hello, that's handy, we already know each other. *Emil* Infusion stand is here too ... well, at least half. But he's got new drugs with him, and we've got new equipment here too. The blood pressure monitor sighs as if in response and squeezes my upper arm to the point of pain, while behind me – as I twist my head and eyes until I can't see any more – other measuring devices flash and draw strange diagrams on small monitors. I should actually sigh as I look at the cuff on my upper arm. And back at the side cabinet, do you see how it flashes and beeps here? They all work together here just for us. And now, whether you like it or not, I'm going to tell you all the joke, when _two planets meet together_.

> _Just be happy with me that we, you, Emil, and because of me, you stupid blood pressure cuff, are allowed to be here. I look expressly at the group and say, you're probably wondering why? Well, in these times I mean now. Oh, now the joke, before I forget._
>
> _So, two planets meet again by chance. One says to the other, hi, how are you? The other one, well, to be honest, not so good at the moment. What's wrong with you? I'm not missing anything, I just have Homo Sapiens. Oh well, don't worry about it. I've had that too. But it'll go away and then you'll feel better again._

After that, my sarcasm is gone again. I feel so helplessly alone and I realise again what situation I'm actually in here. Everything is so sterile and I feel like I'm locked away.

I take some writing materials from the drawer and, looking at the stupid picture on the wall, write to-do at the top of the page.

Without a catheter and pressure in my bladder, I relax and then I'm completely absorbed in the list. I draft the text for an obituary, make key-words for a letter to my children and my ex-wife. And also one for very close friends and to _Anke_, the woman I separated from a few months ago when I started to feel tired. She had written me a long letter afterwards, but I had always put off replying; now it's too late. And I realise why, months before the terrible diagnosis, I had always unconsciously tried to avoid not only physical but also emotional stress. And I write down who all needs to be informed, what needs to be done, insurance, bank and many other things.

At some point I'm interrupted, there's food. I didn't even realise that I hadn't eaten for a long time. Even now I don't feel hungry. But the carer asks me to eat something: 'I know, it looks terrible and certainly tastes like nothing,' he says, 'but please eat, we really need your bowel movement.' 'Great,' I reply, 'so it's not about me at all?' He laughs ...

'and if it doesn't work, then we'll help out. But then you don't really want to, because that's embarrassing for patients again.'

I put on a good face, eat stoically the to the point of no return overcooked yellowish-green gruel. I realise that my taste buds are suffering as I start chemotherapy and everything will somehow taste the same, no matter what it is. In future, I will only be able to taste sweet intensely. And that all our food will be cooked again to make sure it's germ-free, and fresh fruit and salad will no longer be an option anyway.

A commode chair on wheels is pushed next to the bed. They unplug me from all the IVs and other cables and help me onto this strange chair that looks like it's from a previous century.

I'm talking to myself. Is there an instruction manual? Where is the seal of the technical quality test – after all, we are in Germany – and what are the test criteria, process or result? Does this thing have its own cost centre number in the administration? What if an accident happens, and can an accident happen when you're sitting here and ... What can you do in such a situation apart from making stupid jokes about yourself? But that doesn't help me either, I wait and wait ... I feel like a very old person about to have his bum wiped. Well, I'm already close to that here, my sarcasm continues. Or even beyond that tomorrow; is it cynical to think like that?

I don't know how long I've been sitting on this strange vehicle. In the end, there are just some small comparably bunny droppings. That should be enough, I think, and say more loudly, 'mow, mow'. I know the carer can hear and possibly see me on the screen.

But the blood bothers me. He tells me: 'It's normal, the leukaemia is still there, so don't panic.' That's right, I'd forgotten all about it. I ask him: 'But what about the chemotherapy?' 'I'm not a doctor, I'm not allowed to give you any information.' I understand that, but it doesn't help me now, I just think; this time without saying it as a stupid thing.

I wake up, the professor is standing by my bed. 'I told you we'd meet again,' he greets me. 'Great', it escapes me, 'you say we'll meet again and send me down here. And then you come here and say, look, we'll meet again.' He smiles, 'don't be impatient, we're glad to have you back with us for now.' Now I realised the meaning of the sentence I have heard before.

He explains that they first have to get the pneumonia under control and the water out of my body before they can continue. They had to cancel the chemotherapy cycle, which is critical because time is running out. But things were looking relatively good now. They would now alternate as necessary. If the blasts were to multiply too much, chemotherapy would be started immediately ... *et vice versa*. Treating both at once would be too dangerous. And I should drink, drink and drink.

Later, while I'm filling another urine bottle – by now there are always two empty ones hanging on my bed – I notice a chair behind the bed at the foot end. Like an acrobat, with my tubes and cables on one side and one leg stretched out on the other, I manage to pull the chair towards me with my toes, utilising its entire length. Only afterwards, lying back in bed, do I realise how stupidly dangerous that was. What if I had fallen? And ripped the port out of the neck vein? Surely I could have just asked the carer?

But now I have a bed, chair and side cabinet with a fold-out table. Under the given circumstances, chained or rather attached – a very strange word – and wired, this gives me a relatively large amount of freedom of movement. I can lie or sit in bed, sit on the edge of the bed and let my legs dangle out, and I can stand next to the bed and take two small steps in any direction I want. I can also sit on the chair and, as a luxury, put my legs up on the bed. Doing handstands is no longer necessary with so many options, I think to myself ironically; then I realise that I couldn't do it before anyway. I have to smile, what if they could see me here in fast motion?

And so they do, but contradictory. The Korean doctor comes back in the evening. He sees the chair and open table with my laptop. 'You're working,' he asks? 'Yes, of course, I'm still alive and this is my home office now.' 'We could have come up with that idea,' he laughs.

Then he asks a few questions, looks at my various medical meters and screens, and says goodbye. On the way out, he advises me: 'Please, don't overdo it, always rest in between.' This is the more pleasant comment on my now regained little freedom; that I will remember next day.

Physiotherapy, the first

Next day after breakfast, which could have been made into a porridge, a physiotherapist is at my bedside. First I have to do breathing exercises. With two bubble tubes, I feel like I'm in a nursery school. One has three vertical transparent cylinders, each with a coloured plastic ball and different size, which I have to hold at the same height for as long as possible after taking a long, deep breath. The other has a kind of turbine that whistles when I breathe in and makes an inner gyroscope hum when I breathe out.

I'm quite weak in the lungs, as they say; that's why I do breathing exercises. If you do not become like the children ... I think; she is Greek, and I will meet her more often.

Somehow I had got into the habit of reacting sarcastically, sometimes even cynically, to everything that happened to me or was about to happen to me. Especially when my life here is severely restricted and possibly only short, complaining makes the least sense. I would be taking a part of my life away from myself, even if it was only for a short time. That was my motto ... at least in theory and as long as I wasn't overcome by direct fear.

After successfully completing the breathing exercises, I have to stand next to the bed; again slowly and carefully. Then a few exercises with my feet and legs to improve circulation and train my muscles. I now have to do this 5-times a day, about every two hours.

'Are you crazy, this is an intensive care unit and not a gym,' someone yells from behind me as I do my prescribed exercises standing next to the bed a few hours later. This is the more unpleasant comment on my little freedom.

But I am able to respond immediately: 'Good afternoon, there should still be time for that. Shouldn't I do my prescribed exercises now? Should I also switch off the equipment and tubes here? Or do you want to consult with your colleagues first before being impolite criticising me?'

Ha, that did it. She turns around and leaves without saying hello or good bey, just as she came. Later, in bed, I realise I'm obviously in fight mode. But her revenge could hit me at some point. Some pill or infusion bag with some-thing in it? But I never saw her again.

Intensive care daily routine

My day is now routine and I feel better. I can urinate well, my bloated body is stabilised, I am losing weight slowly but steadily; still at a very high level. I later realised that the water had made me weigh well over 100 kg, which was of course also due to the huge amounts of cortisone I had to take.

We get chatting during daily personal hygiene, and once I even get my hair washed. 'That's soon a thing of the past,' laughs my carer. I realise what he means.

He talks about his daily routine, the many hours of overtime, night shifts and weekends to supplement his salary. His wife is a nurse in the neighbouring town and does a lot of night shifts. So there is always someone at home for the two children. 'As a whole family, we only really see each other every fortnight,' he says and continuous ... ,'if we didn't have the allowances, we wouldn't be able to afford the flat. And the children should get a better job one day, where they don't have to work so hard.'

I can really understand that now. Of course, other people also work full time. But their mental strain, what they have to see and experience here, who actually pays for it? He wants to study so that he can take on a management position. Again, I know my way around and explain to him the different types of part-time degree programmes. I would also ask my daughter, who is more specialised in the healthcare sector and knows about the various possibilities and training courses on offer in the region. And that further education, especially in this sector, is being subsidised by the state.

He wants to know what I meant when I said, while I was practically out of my mind, 'they satisfy themselves on their share index before breakfast?' I didn't realise that I had spoken at some point. But this sentence was definitely my creation, because I had cynically referred to it as such in a discussion with good friends; we had then indirectly rephrased it 'indexing them-selves' for these young aspiring investment bankers, consultants & co.

I explain: 'Throughout my professional life, I have seen so many people see their purpose in life as increasing their income and investment figures and developing egomaniacal character traits in the process.' He then adds: 'So it's a compensation for inferiority complexes, like a car, the bigger, the smaller?' I laugh: 'Yes, I know that saying.' 'You often only realise the real value of life in situations like here,' he adds. I'm sure, these words will make the rounds during the coffee breaks here in the building.

I enjoy my new multi-functional mini workstation. The personal to-do items now take more of a back seat. I start working on a new edition of a book I've already started; after all, the publisher is waiting.

This will stabilise me mentally, as I know later from the notes about myself in the patient file and in the reflection in the first consultation hour of follow-up treatment after discharge from hospital.

Trapped in my Body　　Lower Echhey Village Life

Laughter sustains and is more sensible than annoyance.

Lessing, in: Minna Von Barnhelm; Or, the Soldiers' Fortune

Trapped in my Body

Back to earth, and the research study

I don't know how long I've been in the intensive care unit. And I keep asking myself how much longer? I feel better and I don't have any of the horror chemotherapy side effects that everyone talks about; and they had not yet continued the chemotherapy cycle. The automatic blood pressure cuff is particularly annoying. Day and night, it squeezes my right upper arm every few minutes to the point of pain.

When the carer comes to me, I ask how long he thinks it will take for the arm to be completely crushed or fall off? He laughs: 'Yes, of course that's a problem.' An then he turns off all the machines, then removes the blood pressure cuff from my upper arm, stops all the infusions, and removes the catheter from my neck. They want to get rid of me now, yeah. 'Let's pack, but you stay put.' And he thanks for advising him for part-time university programs. Both, he and his wife had already searched and found interesting possibilities for them both. As goodbye he says: 'I hope we won't see each other here again.' Tears come into my eyes; is it melancholy or happiness?

As I am pushed out of the lift on the transport stretcher past to our floor at the ward checkpoint, they clap hands. Later I realise that it was – as we say – 'at the very last minute'.

Everything is already prepared again. First the new bone marrow extrac-tion, and I have to lie down again for over half an hour with the puncture site pressed onto a sandbag. Then, immediately afterwards, a new port in the neck vein, this time on the other side of the neck. The change will now become routine over the next few months.

But I don't know that yet at this point. For me, chemotherapy is one therapy, through and done, or not.

I am alone and have some quiet. It seems that *Emil* is always following me, or is he a double or a twin? In thought I speak to him: Hello my dear friend, even if it's not you, it's then you now. You probably tell each other what you're experiencing here during your breaks. I've seen you standing together out there in the equipment room as I drove past.

'Good morning, hello ..., good morning.' The professor's visit morning ward round is lined up at the end of the bed. Had I slept so long? Was there an infusion in there to help me sleep? Is it still the same day? 'You see,' the professor said, 'I told you we'll meet again, ... here,' he added after a second and emphasised this in particular, 'how do you feel?'

The bone marrow procedure just before and the intensive care unit time before that had done me in. But of course, I was glad to have escaped the intensive ward down there. 'Good morning, yes, ... it's a university hospital, aren't most people here to study?' I tried to make a joke again.

Even though sarcasm, and occasionally a pinch of cynicism, is like the crowning glory of humour for me, I know that other people see it differently.

I realise immediately that this didn't come across. 'Sorry,' I apologised immediately, 'but I'm a bit exhausted, it's all been too much for me the last few days.' I'm trying to salvage the situation.

The research study

During the preparation of the first chemotherapy test cycle, which was cancelled and is now being repeated, so to speak the second attempt, I am asked to take part in a study with a new concomitant pill from the US; the third and last study before authorisation. I would also not be a clinical Guinea Pig, but would receive more extensive and detailed support, as my data for the study would be continuously recorded. And so it goes on for what feels like half an hour.

Then the doctor asks me to read through a pile of papers again, he'll be back later. *Randomised phase III for the evaluation of intensive chemotherapy with/without ... in adult patients with newly diagnosed care-binding factor acute myeloid leukaemia CBF-AML / AMLSG ...* plus *patient information, consent form* and *insurance;* in total there are almost 20 pages and signatures on various sheets of paper.

Even despite my reading glasses, I can no longer read. After just one paragraph I've forgotten what I've just read, let alone understood most of it. All I can see are drips of infusion bags dripping into me. Because of my university job and my own scientific work, I can't really say I don't want ... and somehow I'm no longer interested in my cancer – at least at the moment.

At some point, the doctor returns with a colleague. After he sees my signatures on the various papers, he points out to me again in the presence of the colleague: 'There is no obligation, you can withdraw your consent at any time;' the other doctor also signs the instruction.

I would later realise that the trial with this new treatment-accompanying pill – an inconspicuous white pill costing 200 Euro each, financed by the US pharmaceutical company *Bristol Myers* – required me to take it not only during the months in the hospital, but for two years after that. What I didn't realise at the time was that this would involve regular, extensive blood tests and bone marrow extraction for the whole time.

If only I hadn't signed up for this stupid study, I often thought later on during the years of repeated extractions in search of a haemato-poietic vein and the more or less painful extraction that usually followed.

What won't you do for progress? I try to be self-deprecating with this well-worn saying when I'm gritting my teeth against the pain again. Because I had decided against an anaesthetic and also against a bite block. Did I want to play the Cool Man? I don't know.

Only once in all the months I spent in hospital, I did complain and seriously demand that I am no longer going to let this (future?) doctor extract my marrow. Either she was a beginner or didn't have time, or she didn't like men; I had never seen her before. The pain was unbearable, I screamed several times. She didn't stop to try another place like others or to change sides of her body at the pelvic bone. She kept trying to force her way through the bone. You can anaesthetise tissue, but not bone. And I couldn't move. If the needle had broken off, it would have been unthinkable. I never saw the doctor again.

First impressions

My bloated body requires me to keep a consistent record of how much I drink. A chart is stuck to the cupboard next to me at eye level as I lie in bed so that I don't forget. Probably because of the huge amounts of cortisone that are being pumped into me under the intensive care and even now in a race against the leukaemia-induced blast formation in the bone marrow so that they can finally start the regular chemotherapy.

I get reprimanded pretty harshly if I only write down a glass or cup and not 100 or 200 ml. At first I felt patronised, but later I understood.

Once again I am asked quite seriously why it says so much to drink? That wouldn't fit in with the urine collection. I remarked that a full urine bottle had already been collected twice today. Then a care assistant is chewed out for not noting this down.

As a private insured patient, I naturally enjoy advantages, even if I find this kind of differentiated treatment ethically very questionable. The cutlery is in pastel green napkins in matching colours with the cup covers. There is original world famous *Nutella* chocolate spread in miniature jars instead of the *no-name* one available to patients by statuary health insurance on the other corridor. In addition to direct care from the professor – patients with state insurance only have a senior doctor – we also have a fridge by the bed, the internet is free and we get a personalised daily newspaper. And we are in a twin room. Are there still any multi-bed rooms? Do we have any other advantages? I don't know. Is that the reason for the significantly higher daily rate and the higher rates charged by doctors and laboratories? They're piling up faster than I can get them paid.

Later, a doctor explains to me that the private health insurance system can certainly be questioned in terms of health policy. But she sees it as purely practical, it also has advantages. For example, very expensive equipment could be purchased, which would then also benefit patients covered by the statuary insurance.

I notice the (supposedly) badly cleaned windows. As if they were smudged, you can't see outside clearly. Even if, sitting in bed on the fourth floor, all you can see is the sky and a towering outbuilding under construction with a helicopter landing pad. But what at first seems to be a technically interesting change by watching a helicopter landing and taking off again turns into pity in the next moment at the sight of the first transport couch.

At some point, together with *Emil* and one of the many handy bottles of disinfectant and paper tissues, I manage to wipe a wide strip above the windowsill clearer for us. 'That way, even my *Billy Goat* – *Peter*'s mascot in red-white club colours from his favourite first division football club – can have a look outside,' he says; *Peter* is from now on my favourite roommate. Later, we realise that the supposedly smudged windows are the result of disinfecting the room when we move in.

Our Little Freedom is from the bed to the bathroom integrated into the room and back and we always say: 'I'm going for a little freedom.' More freedom is, when we can walk up and down the corridor when it's quiet, for example, when there are no daily's doctors' ward routines, food trolleys or at night and we're not in a shielded aplasia phase after a chemotherapy cycle. It feels like it's 25 m to the end of the corridor. And you can look through the window on grounds with lawns and trees.

Of course, these are also special experiences for *Emil*, he sometimes meets someone from his family in passing, dressed with other infusion bags. Or we pass the storage room, which is always open, where many of *Emil's* relatives are still standing and waiting for a job.

Of course, there are also handrails and a chair halfway down our ward corridors. When you meet another patient, you have different experiences; from looking away and shuffling past to a never-ending torrent of moaning. Everything has to be accepted, because you don't know the individual ill-ness situation and personal background.

Someone thinks it's funny that I named my infusion stand *Emil*. Then we juggle with keywords like immune system supplier, out-sourced, artificial, company branch, network system ... finally we agree on Project-outsourced Immune System.

But the more freedom after my second chemotherapy cycle will be Grand Freedom tour. Out to the left to the end of the corridor, look out and half the way back, then across a short cross corridor, left again to the end and look out, then all the way back to the this corridor door. Directly behind it is our patients' lounge room, where you can see if anything new has happened – of course, nothing ever really changes – or look longingly down at the city or into the sky. Next to the entrance is a trolley with coffee, hot water for tea and crates of – medium carbonized (!) – water. I have no idea yet that the coffee and water will become special experiences for me. And then I look into the glazed kitchen behind it and wave hello; the staff there are always in a good mood. This is also where the four ward corridors with lifts, visitor WCs and the reception meet.

One is the always closed *KMT*-corridor, everyone here is afraid of it, even though the bone marrow transplant behind it may also be our very last hope.

Behind the reception – we say checkpoint – are a small laboratory and a staff room. Despite the fact that the staff are always noticeably stressed, they are always friendly and helpful. A greeting, in my case usually more of a silly saying or in best case a joke, and then back to the room.

The Grand Tour becomes, according to the inventor *Peter* as my dearest roommate patient, our Fitness Mile. A lot of the activities that we develop ourselves, I later realise, are noticed by the staff and noted positively in their meetings with the doctors and our patient files, in the sense that one activate themselves.

At first, I could hardly manage such a big lap, but later I got better; *Peter* held the unofficial record of four laps in a row. 'As a football club fan, therefore somehow obliged to set standards,' he once said laconically. When I asked him whether he was setting the standard for you or his preferred club – which by the way is not that successful in this time – he just said, 'watch out, *Billy Goat* has horns too.'

But my first room neighbour after the intensive care unit is the *Nutella-boy*, as I later call him. I am asked, if a patient with statutory health insurance can stay in my room for a few days, the ward opposite is overcrowded. What a derogatory term, especially in this hospital building; I say, 'yes, sure.'

He tells me – I realise immediately that he is in total shock – that he had only just started his vocational training a few days ago and now the illness. He doesn't really understand everything yet. Later, his girlfriend comes and sits with him for hours, holding his hand; that's closer to me than my own truth at that moment.

Next morning at breakfast, he is surprised: 'Oh, *Nutella* in a jar. Over there, there's only a no-name chocolate cream.' A day later he is transferred back to his corridor. I hoarded two jars with me in case I ever see him.

Two weeks later, during the World Cup, he is sitting with friends in the patient's lounge room watching football, all wearing German national team shirts. They all have a full load *McDonalds* with them ... which all together continue to tuck into, even after a carer points out the danger to the patient, and laugh cautiously and uncertainly when the carer has left the room. Then I fetch the *Nutella* glasses and put them on the table for him; his friends look puzzled. 'Drugs, folks, he gets them for free, for you I'll make a good price.'

After all, we patients should feel good psychologically. A football match with his friends is at least something like everyday life again for two hours.

The first person I meet in the patients' lounge room – I'm was allowed out in the corridor to inspect the surroundings before the next chemo-therapy cycle – is on the phone to a colleague about the session he's just had to cancel. It seems familiar somehow. We have a chat; he's a IT project manager.

Weeks later, after the chemotherapy cycle and a following aplasia phase, I meet him again in the corridor; this time walking: 'Two small children I have, now walking in a support vehicle, in a fortnight from a hundred to ...', he says in a broken voice and looks at me. 'Oh sorry, I don't want to whinge all over you, you're here for a reason too,' he interrupts an emerging conversation. I realise he's struggling to sup-press his tears.

And there are a lot of very individual fates; naturally among many other people. For example, the one who always talks about his friend with the horse ranch in Texas. The young man from Afghanistan who can't speak a word of German or English and doesn't know what's happening to him. And Mr Müller and his wife, who somehow, you get the impression, is always with him, and, and ... then there's the journalist, who knows everything and of course knows what's going wrong here too. You should know that I work for TV, he explains. I search the internet, but there are only two or three short reports from some private portal that did a short piece on a construction project for a regional TV programme with his name on it years ago.

How do I tell my children?

Admission to hospital and transfer to the intensive care unit happen so un-expectedly quickly that there is no time to inform my children. And there was absolute e-communication silence in the intensive care unit, which also helps me with my internal excuse to protect them from this shock for the time being. Because at first I think it will only be a few days.

A mistake that will probably never be rectified, as it turns out later.

Now I'm in what appears to be a normal-looking hospital room, apart from the infusion stand, access regulations etc., virtually shielded from the world. I can no longer put it off. I'm afraid of making a phone call. So I write an e-mail, which I re-write several times and which takes me half a day. Again and again I re-write it and probably unconsciously look for reasons to post-pone it. But the word leukaemia has to come out somehow.

I try to tone it down in the sense that the first thing is over, and that my body accepted the first chemotherapy cycle well – a lie, because it was cancelled and I don't yet know the results of the new chemotherapy cycle I've had – and they shouldn't worry. Of course I won't write anything about the intensive care unit and what happened there. For me, it was at the end an e-mail that took several hours to compose, and it was sent at some point with a simple keystroke; I feel relieved of an unspeakable pressure.

And for them, this keystroke is a shock of a lifetime, as I learn later. Of course, they immediately *googled* leukaemia and my *AML* version in particular, and got in touch with each other.

Until now, their relationship has been characterised by mutual isolation; *Fabian* has just turned 32 old and lives in California, *Sarah* (30) works in Cologne and *Simon* (28) in Luxembourg.

Everyone wants to come straight away, of course, but I resist. I won't be able to do that, I don't know enough myself, apart from what *Google* more or less tells me is right and wrong. I also had to be considerate of the room-mate, who is in an equally difficult situation.

We agreed that my daughter would come to me first to bring me things. I only found out later that *Simon* also wanted to make the 2-hour journey regularly, but they came to an agreement between themselves. And *Fabian* wanted to fly over from California straight away. But what then is the point? At a some-meter distance from the room door during my chemotherapy cycle or the aplasia phase?

Firstly, I no longer feel like I'm dying, after all I've already won the battle with the intensive care unit. And all the children at once or at daily intervals is too much. And it's not fair to you either, because I'll hardly be able to concentrate.

Theoretically, everything is easy to explain, but ethically it's a minor evil to weigh up. It's better for just one person to look after me at first until I've found my rhythm, am more relaxed and can then really enjoy myself.

Sarah Lena – she doesn't like her second given name, as it was always for her associated with seriousness and strictness as a child – then provides me with everything. She does this very self-sacrificingly to the point of exhaustion. *THANK YOU* my dear. I wish I'd known how great her own professional and private burdens were during this time.

I write a short e-mail to my friends, diagnosis, hospital, no visit, I get in touch, motto, 'it is what it is', but I am confident and get in touch. Later on, after two months, I'm doing well so far.

Uli is a friend of mine who I grew up with and we both did two Laps of Honor at secondary school; as we mean in German when failing and repeat a class. For 35 years now I've been bringing him a box of our regional German beer to Wales in the UK. And we call each other twice a year, while then drinking our *Fernbier* as a remote beer on phone.

Later he will sum it up, probably for others too: 'It's a shame you don't use *WhatsApp*. With so little contact, it's such a hassle to send a photo. We would love to let you share more of our lives here. Conversely, that would have been particularly important for us with your leukaemia. We didn't know how you were doing for months, whether you were still alive at all?'

Of course I've thought about it, but how should I organise? I'm probably also unconsciously trying to justify my inner resistance to the Social Media. What is actually social about these little screens that send around pointless photos of all kinds of fast-food waste, because nobody knows whether it then tastes good or whether you get stomach problems anyway?

And are there different *WhatsApp* groups and message intervals depending on the degree of the friendship's closeness? How detailed, not too personal and medical-technical; and really describe the examinations and the side effects to your body? Should they or do they even want to read this? They have their own problems; I don't need to be the centre of attention.

In any case, I don't like the fact that some people tell me everything and anything about themselves without being asked. It seems to me that this has become the main purpose of social media for many people with their quasi-implanted phones. Or does such a turning point in life also mean having the right to know more? Surely you're worried about me too?

Later, after my hospital time, I came to the conclusion that I will continue to reject this for myself. But in future I will consider whether I should be a little more open in such extreme cases?

Surprises

I get a guardian angel from a neighbour's friend I once had exchanged a few words with. Together with a little wooden duck that I got from a friend on our card and cooking team, they are now protecting me.

A first and completely unprepared visit overwhelms me. First time since the intensive care unit, that I'm allowed to stand up for a few hours without infusion tubes attached to my neck and walk down the corridor to the day room. I'm probably pretty quiet and unapproachable, I'm sorry.

The head nurse, who seemed very strict to me at first, had given me just an hour before clear instructions. 'Keep always distance! Don't touch anything outside the room! Never pick anything up from the floor! Never let a towel touch the floor, leave it there! Sanitise your hands immediately if you have accidentally touched something! And always inform us before you take a shower! The port for the neck vein must be thickly taped! Don't let it get wet, always wrap a towel around your neck! Don't use a toothbrush! You may have infections from canker sores in your mouth, even if you don't feel them yet. Better to use mouthwash; I hate the taste now. Don't shave either! And, and, and ... don't, don't, don't ...!' Just one germ could take me floors down again. Hopefully she meant the intensive care unit; because further down in the building's basement would only be the cold store, I cynically thought.

After returning from the intensive care unit initially felt it like a small victory, but now I'm getting scared again. So, this is still a very, very serious matter for me. Do I even want to leave this room for two days at home?

Peter ☦

Peter, a typical *Rheinländer*, one from the river *Rhine* region here, as we say, is not just openly communicative. With a typical white moustache and golden necklace, he is of course a fan of the regional first division football club. When we were put in the same room for the first time, he immediately places the club's *Billy Goat* mascot demonstratively on the window-sill.

His beloved wife, *Ute*, is an excellent cook and often brings him a little something extra as a change from the general and, for us, often overcooked hospital food, and then for both of us together. We don't even dare to say that we occasionally have to dispose of something later; we are not allowed to eat from outside. Of course, we like to sin from time to time, for example with the deliciously pickled rolled herring or her home-made jam.

And his daughter *Hannah* is always cheerful, at least outwardly, despite the incomprehensible burden of her father's sudden and dangerous illness. He even has her bring him his stylish bright red trainers when his order is delivered. And he demonstratively puts them on for his first short holiday at home. *Peter*, although much older than me, is daring.

At some point he jokes, 'we'd both like a *Kölsch*, please' (our local beer). The staff member from the ward kitchen laughs, 'she could imagine that.' And she returns the joke, 'bottle, from the tap, or straight into the vein?'

In the evening there are two bottles of beer for us. We are amazed … until we recognize 'non-alcohol'. After the first sip, we agree, that we will never order a beer in this pub again … but it's certainly better than rosehip tea.

Once, very early in the morning before wake-up time, panic … blood, blood everywhere on the floor in front of his bed. It's already light from outside. *Peter* sits in his bed, pale in the face like a bed sheet. It must have just been shift change, the new day nurse comes running. 'Oh my God,' ... but then the all-clear. 'It's just a broken infusion tube, don't panic, it happens from time to time. It's mixed with the potassium water, it looks like more blood than it is.'

We talk about everything, about family and everyday things, but also about art and of course about the hospital, medicine, care etc. around us. About the food, the laps in the corridor, our hospital room and the patients' lounge room; 'about God and the world', as they say.

I stay out of football, I don't know anything about it. For *Peter*, and also his daughter, he once added, there is only this one club in the neighbouring town. Then, tears in his eyes, he said that *Ute*, his wife – she was younger than him and he was a 'late father' – and his daughter *Hannah* were the best thing that had happened to him in life.

Peter has been my longest and favourite roommate here the whole time. Here, they always try to put us both back in the same room when we have to move. And if it's possible, they finish their daily rounds with our room, they look forward to it because we're always so funny.

After I was discharged from hospital, I was able to visit *Peter*, once at his bedside and once some distance away at the door of his room. And I also called him from time to time. I realised that he was getting worse. *Peter* has passed away year later.

Later, when I felt up to it, I was at the grave with his wife *Ute*. I also got in touch on the first anniversary and we were at the grave together again shortly afterwards; she and *Hannah* invited me to their place for dinner.

And what a surprise, there was little *Sami*, who now ruled their lives. Unfortunately, *Peter* was no longer able to experience his grandson as his third happiness.

Everyday life in hospital ... Good morning, please wake up

The day is clearly structured here, as long as there are no special interventions such as a chemotherapy cycle that postpone everything or you no longer experience everyday life due to the side effects.

Relatively early, around 6 a.m. – we are often the first or second room at this ward corridor – fever, pulse and oxygen measurements etc. are announced as well as weighing.

It's always fun with our usual silly sayings, such as when we do the scales test; which one actually weighs correctly? Both of the digital scales available to us at the moment show different weights for each of us, even when we weigh us repeatedly, as does a third scale we have brought in. We then agree on which looks better for the patient file; we are equally very ill anyway, but at least this way the doctors have some positive impressions.

Then there is a little time for the morning toilet and the blood sample is taken. Until breakfast *Emil* and his colleague next bed are hung with the new daily infusions. I don't usually notice this because I often doze off again.

And of course our personal pill dispenser as well as drops and gargling liquid, ointments & co. for the day. Our Medical Orchestra we say, for the short concerts in the morning, mid-morning, at lunch and dinner and at night, as well as a serenade meanwhile with new infusion bag artists coming from outside. Then instructions from the conductor, such as 'before-during-after food, with water …,' it's some-times a bit complex with this amount of instruments such as pills and capsules, mouthwashes, drops and ointments, plus the infusions as guest performers. In any case, almost everything comes in different shapes, colours and sizes. And let's not forget the colourful physio-therapy toys that are always on hand for us, the audience, encou-raging us to join in interactively with movement and breathing exer-cises.

It seems funny now, and our jokes make it seem so, after getting used to the amount of medication we have to take all the time. But you do wonder whether over 20 different medications a day won't start to fight with each other at some point. A large family or like the Euro-pean Union with all their laws and regulations can't manage that with the same mission.

But over time you get an eye for it and it helps me, for example, to recognise a wrong pill. At first they said, no problem, it's just from a different company. I'm unsure and ask another member of staff, I'm scared because we're supposed to be so careful and sterile with everything. After just two or three minutes, the pill is replaced.

Later, as I shuffle up and down the corridor at night, I often see how a night nurse sorts tens of medications for each patient into pill dispensers between her assignments; from a trolley with a quantity of medications that is confusing to me. It's more than understandable that mistakes happen in such a stressful job with the simultaneous responsibility for so many seriously life-threatening patients.

The breakfast buffet trolley between 8 and 9 a.m. leaves nothing to be desired. You shuffle to the corridor with or without an infusion stand; those who can't go out are served their wishes on a tray at their bedside. Of course, there is also a daily newspaper for us with private insurance.

Sometimes a quick glance into the neighbour room, which may already be open. Just a friendly nod or an apathetic look with a slightly raised hand is often the only way to communicate.

Back here after the intensive care unit, I still weigh almost 100 kg due to the water in my body. Lots of cortisone and antibiotics to get the pneumonia controlled and prevent further infection are also having an effect. I could hardly get into my normal trousers. Later, after two rounds of chemotherapy cycles, my weight is less than 80 kg and my trousers practically fall off my body.

When, in the daily's doctors' ward visiting routine they ask me: 'Why do you eat so little?' I realise the kitchen team also keeps records of how much I eat and drink; the water has to be removed from my body, but you should not lose weight during chemotherapy under any circumstances.

Of course, many things are understandably sterilely packaged. I have clear instructions what not to eat or drink. In any case, I ate more varied food than at home, even with nearly no flavour experience.

I am alone in a room and they move me to another room after breakfast. This is normal so that a room can now be occupied by women or an infected high-risk patient alone, for example.

Apart from a name tag at the end of the bed Mr *von* ... I don't really notice my new roommate as they move my bed to the free side of the window; he's sitting up in bed and has probably had a coffee brought in with his news-paper. The curtain between the two beds as a half-height privacy screen is still drawn forward – as it is at night or during the day for examinations. I realise later that this is for him still the case during the day.

In the Middle Ages, a (German) *von* in a name was a sign of – at least the lowest rank – nobility; today it no longer has any meaning. However, some people still use it to distinguish themselves.

I can hear him turning the pages of the newspaper when a young female carer comes in. She greets him in broken German and asks him to take his blood pressure again, the entry from earlier in the morning is missing from his patient file. And, without saying hello, he barks at her, asking what this is all about. And that he can't even drink his coffee and reading the newspaper here undisturbed, and besides, he would be a privately insured patient.

The young carer, she has obviously an Asian migrant background, she stammers something like, 'sorry, excuse me' ... and bows and walks backwards out of the door. Unconsciously, she is probably making her usual cultural gesture of humility to an older person. I am shocked. What is this now? What am I supposed to do? We haven't even really seen each other, spoken to each other and introduced ourselves. I'm insecure and I don't want a fight. Who knows how long I'll be sharing a room with him?

Then comes the head nurse, whose expertise I have come to appreciate very much. The seasoned woman with life experience from the rural-village region rounds him off in the truest sense of this word. 'Title, profession and private live will not apply here, it's all about friendly cooperation. That also means duties for the patient. Would you like to try your tone for me as well? Or to the medical doctor, or the professor. If you like, you can complain to the professor? The ward organisation here is in our hands. And you should know, even not a professor would talk into it. I wish you a nice day anyway, Mr *von* ...', and she leaves the room.

On the same day, I get a surprise, they move me again to a room that's free again; what's this all about? A short time later they push in a second bed and *Peter*, my now favourite roommate, follows the bed.

The next day, this young carer is with us. I apologise to her for the behaviour of 'the *von* gentleman' from yesterday. Then, she briefly explains, her English is better than mine, how she and her sister did a training programme in Malaysia to prepare for the hospital here. They share a room in the hospital's dormitory and study German diligently at night, practising new technical terms for the activities they know practically. Both are proud to transfer their salary home to help their grandparents, parents and siblings. These are, of course, living conditions that 'Mr *von* ...' private insured patient is unable to imagine or represses.

The time between breakfast and lunch is determined by the daily doctors' ward routine with the professor, and is followed by a senior doctor, a doctor, a nurse and carer, doctor in training and sometimes a nursing assistant. How do you feel? Any aphthae in the mouth, petechiae – punctiform haemorrhages – on the legs, palpation of the lymph nodes? Followed by a little small talk. My attempted joke a few days ago back from the intensive care unit about here practising in a university hospital seems to have been forgotten.

Our personal relationship gets better and better over time, the professor is interested in my family and what I'm writing and reading currently? In response to my counter-question, he talks about upcoming holidays and his children, for example.

Even meanwhile, such as routine interviews for the study, application of chemotherapy, or blood transfusion, all doctors are always friendly. When we ask them questions, they also tell us about themselves, why they are here on this leukaemia ward, about their future career plans such as further training to become a specialist or about their private interests.

For example, the doctor who first studied in a homoeopathic orientated medical university hospital; now doing his haematology specific studies in this hospital here. It came out, that he lives in the neighbour town, when he mentioned, nodding to *Peter* and pointing at *Billy Goat*, the football mascot at the window: 'I think I'm in the right room,' the three of us are going to be a team for a long time. Even without medical reasons, from time to time he comes in for a small talk; I understandably stay out of any football discussion.

Once again, a port is inserted into my neck vein. *Peter* leaves the room, he doesn't want to see it; he always let it done under anaesthetic. Again I see the pulsating carotid artery on the screen. Once again, huge amounts of disinfectant running down my shoulders and back. Although it's always warm in the room, especially in this extremely hot summer that even the air conditioning can't cope, but you suddenly feel cold in situations like this.

A young trainee doctor performs the procedure. Our trainee specialist is with her. 'I hope you're a fan of our football club now,' he says. 'If you're not, I'll just say Attention Carotid Artery; and after an artificial respite,' ... and he adds, 'but then you won't notice.' Great, I pick up on his marvellous sarcasm that has developed between me, *Peter* and him. 'From now on I'm with your team, were can I sign?' I get the local anaesthetic injection and he continues ..., 'but then I have a problem here, why did you leave us so suddenly? So don't worry, I also like other clubs ... as long as we don't lose.' Conversations between doctor and patient that I like.

Students, beetroot & co.

As we have agreed, from time to time students, accompanied by the professor or a senior doctor, come to practise an anamnesis interview with us. Of course, I also ask them questions. At first the professor is surprised, but later he seems to like it, because the young students are still a bit shy with real patients ... and someone sarcastic like me comes along?

Of course, I know how to get students out of the usual standard rhetorical formulae and encourage them to speak freely. 'Why medicine? Is it a family tradition or your personal wish? Where and what do you want to be later? What would you do differently when studying medicine?' After their initial amazement that one patient is also asking questions, they accept. Later I have the impression that word has already spread to the next group. The answers come faster and more confidently; just as prepared?

And then comes the friendly Greek physiotherapist, I already know her from the intensive care unit. In addition with a new in-and-out breathing pipe-like tube, she's now also doing balance and stretching exercises with a gymnastic band. We make jokes like old friends, but she pays attention and corrects me. Not so fast, it is best to count to four slowly until the next movement, try to keep straight ...

Another day, I've just opened an organic spinach smoothie in my hand and our training specialist doctor and football club fan comes to ask how we're doing? He sees my smoothie and smiles: 'Well, you're drinking something that won't do any harm. Always remember, drink it up and don't leave it overnight, otherwise germs will develop. But you already know.' I nod in agreement and add, 'thanks God no beetroot juice, I don't like it, even if it helps against cancer.' He laughs 'yes, you discuss superstitions with almost every new patient.' 'Can you tell us what is true and what is not,' *Peter* asks. 'Well, it's true that there is evidence of blood formation from beetroot. However, this also applies to other vegetables, but it is slightly more pronounced with beetroot. But you would have to eat at least 2 kg per day over a long period of time before there is any evidence of haematopoiesis. But you won't be able to do that, because before then you will have irreparable organic damage from this one-sided diet ... and about the spinach juice,' he turns to me again, 'I would put it this way, it doesn't help but doesn't harm either. There's not much left in it for a healthy diet anyway. How do you think it is preserved and what happens to the nutrients?' 'Then let's talk about our football club,' *Peter* objects, 'durability is somehow more important there at the moment.'

Cancer diets are often so-called Alternative Methods for prevent or treating cancer; usually based on non-scientific evidence they suggest effects against cancer. They are simply recommended as a mixed, low-fat, varied diet rich in vitamins and trace elements ... and sometimes even mixed with esoteric exercises.

However, these recommendations often contradict each other. Contrary, unbalanced diets, for example vegan or macrobiotic, have been proven to lead to deficiency symptoms. Some advertised diets also have side effects; for example, severe weight loss in the case of cancer is dangerous. These are often fasting or bulking diets as low carb or *Keto* no/low carbohydrate, iso-pathic or macrobiotic ... there is until now no scientifically proven success. Most cancer diets were developed up to more than 100 years ago, without any real experience of cancer and its development.

Today, **the** World Cancer Research Fund generally recommends preventive and supportive treatments that are scientifically proven to be successful:
- Stay within your normal body weight range, get daily physical activity and exercise.
- Avoid sugary drinks, a predominantly vegetarian diet, little salt, little alcohol, as well as
- avoid energy-dense food supplements or foods wherever possible.

Many teams ... and the admin challenge

The collaboration between the teams, which sometimes even work at cross purposes, as is often the case in such large organizations, is initially opaque for us. There's the team around the professor with doctors (or those in training) from different hierarchies and specialisms and sometimes medical students. Then there are the medical nurses and nursing assistants, and also (for us not recognizable) they are in different levels of training and hierarchy. Then the cleaning and disinfection staff and a ward kitchen team. And if required, physiotherapy, psychological services and a hospital priest, in-house paramedics for transporting patients around the hospital, as well as the administration with its tradesmen, house messengers etc. and all its offices and laboratories – more in the background for us.

I had already noticed in the intensive care unit – when I first did my prescribed physiotherapy exercises standing next to the bed – that sometimes one hand doesn't always know what the other is doing.

This happens when processes are differentiated too strongly in terms of division of labour or outsourced to external departments or service companies. After all, it's the same everywhere, who hasn't experienced it?

A little anecdote that I was given as a working copy in a seminar on teamwork in my first years at work is something I've carried around with me all my working life on a pinboard in my different offices. And it always comes back to me when I am connected back and forth in the administration or in an endless complexity of new waiting loops of hotlines; I even saw it once in English in an office in Ireland, the _Story of Everyone, ...:_

> _There were four people with the names Everybody, Somebody, Anybody and Nobody. They got an important job to be done. Everybody was sure that Somebody would do it. Anybody could have done it, but Nobody did it. Somebody got angry about that because it was Everybody's job. But Everybody thought that Anybody could do it, but Nobody realized that Everybody wouldn't do it. It ended up that Everybody blamed Somebody when Nobody did what Anybody could have done._

This, we also realise sometimes, or example when it comes to a new bathrobe that has fallen down in the bath. As we are not allowed to pick anything up from the floor; it will be removed during room cleaning. However, no new bathrobe arrives and when we ask the next day, we are told that the care assistants are responsible for this. But the room cleaners didn't tell them that, and they are so stressed anyway that we don't necessarily want to bother them with every little thing. So at some point we each ordered two bathrobes in stock, as well as disinfectant bottles, which we keep in the cupboard.

The rooms are cleaned twice a day by one team. And, all surfaces that could be touched, such as door handles, table and chair, handrails on the bed and the side cabinet, the windowsill etc. are disinfected by another team. The water filters in the washbasin and shower are also replaced regularly by a, in-house craftsmen team. You get the impression that we can see with the naked eye if there are still bacteria, viruses and the like somewhere.

There's always something going on in a hospital room like this; and from *Peter's* and my point of view, everyone here is, even in their mostly stressful work, always friendly and helpful to us.

Although the hospital management here talks about process management like in the industry now for many years. But, this is more likely to be reduced to a printed mission statement and quality certificates hanging everywhere here in the corridors.

For us, it remains old-fashioned product management (as service); everyone does exactly what's in the job description ... they do it really well here. However, needs that deviate from this are not included. For example, I always have to go to the administration for a formal re-admission for the upcoming new chemotherapy; sometimes right from my hospital bed. At least I can organise it so that *Emil* isn't there every time. Otherwise he would certainly have had to fill in a form too.

Now that I think about it as I write, why didn't I just take him with me on a full infusion run? That would have been fun and would have demonstrated the absurdity to the administration. Or could the administration clerk could not simply have come into the building next door on the fourth floor; then he would have experienced reality, that would have been a first approach to process management.

So, I sit with my number drawn, waiting with other patients and possibly new patients to be admitted? I wonder if this is in the interest of the doctors looking after me? In the cramped registration office, it's more like a cubicle, countless forms are printed out for me to sign, even though they already have all my details. They also (supposedly?) don't know that there is no single room occupancy for us. It was simply charged additionally until I consistently crossed it out in the form ... and suddenly the bill is 60 Euro less per day.

Everyday life in hospital, the second

On Thursdays after lunch we're asked to choose the meals for the following week. There is a daily choice of normal and light meals as well as vegetarian or alternatively a hot soup. The food is varied, even if I can nearly not taste the flavours because of the chemotherapy. Our ward kitchen team is always in a good mood and we make jokes when we are asked for the food choices and maybe some extra wishes.

Since I can only really taste sweet, I get addicted to *Fanta* beverage; cold and sparkling, refreshing and unhealthily high in sugar; sometimes I drink two ice-cold half-litre bottles at once. And for a while I ate like crazy the same highly sugar-enriched chocolate bars like *Kinderschokolade*, and even *Nutella* spread out of the single-serving jars; all things which we tried to avoid with my children.

It wasn't until many weeks after the last chemotherapy cycle that my sense of taste gradually developed again. Just as my hair slowly began to grow at my final time in hospital ... at least where there had been hair before.

In the ward kitchen, where our food is re-cooked until it is 110% germ-free and fresh fruit and salad are removed, they are also always ready to cater for our special requests, such as hot soup in the evening.

And we do deals. As private insured, I get two half-litre sparkling soft drinks a day. When I once saw cocoa in the ward kitchen, I asked for it. 'Sorry, it's not for you, it's only for *KMT* bone marrow transplant ones,' one says. My, 'but I don't want to go there now,' broke the ice. 'But also, we don't want to let it get that far,' one of the team winks at me. So we swap one *Fanta* for cocoa from time to time. Shortly before I left, I also saw buttermilk. I would even have given two beverages for one cold buttermilk.

It's quieter after lunch, time to sleep, doze or have a walk with *Emil* in the corridor. There's brief small talk at a distance with some of the other neigh-bours, and over time you get to know each other as everyone has been here for a while ... or are suddenly no longer here.

After a chemotherapy cycle, you have virtually no immunity due to the reduced haematopoiesis. During the aplasia phase, which lasts about 10 to 14 days and allows the body to rebuild its immunity, even the slightest infection is extremely dangerous.

Nevertheless, I start my personal daily rhythm. After the daily's doctors' ward routine before lunch-time I work in bed or our patients' lounge room away from others. Meanwhile our ward marathon develops; walking the Ultra Freedom with three rounds in one go. Later *Peter* becomes the champion with four laps without stopping.

And fortunately, I can take a breather in-between and sit on a chair or just watch; still better than just being in my hospital room. At some point, I manage to activate one of the exercise bikes at the end of the corridor by the window and pedal – of course without resistance – first time the wheel for five, later up to 10 minutes a day, if I can.

Later I see handwritten comments in the patient file, 'activates himself'. The file is placed in my lap for some examinations in another hospital when I am pushed there in a wheelchair and have to wait.

On the exercise bike, I always secretly open a narrow window directly in front of me – unlike my hospital room and patients' lounge room, they are not locked. The fresh air, we say 'infinite freedom', that is out of reach for us; even ice-cold *Fanta* and *Nutella* together can't compete with that.

It's not so easy to cycle with *Emil* next to me without having an accident; we both feel very personally connected with all his tubes.

Once, on a big Freedom Tour, I greet them at our checkpoint friendly. They ask me where I want to put the infusion stand? I look puzzled. *Emil* is unplugged, I unconsciously have him by the hand automatically. 'We experience this regularly,' they laugh. And *Peter* laughs later, 'I've already seen it when you left the room.' He'd thought to himself, that I have to go through this now, 'it happened to me as well' he says. And it happens more often. You're sitting in the bathroom and suddenly think, why are you holding on to the infusion stand? Once I come to the patient café in our lounge room and someone says – *Emil*'s name has got around – even if you bring him with you, he won't get an extra piece of cake.

After lunch, new medication is often given based on the laboratory results of the blood sample taken in the morning and the daily's doctors' ward routine. In addition, it is often impossible to get out of bed during the chemotherapy cycle or even in the aplasia phase if there are noticeable side effects.

Not to forget negotiations for an extra germ-free, shrink-wrapped small cake slice or second biscuit if the coffee trolley finds you awake and responsive. I can't really taste, but it seems to be a hamster instinct before for the winter time? Or is it sub-conscious *Darwinian* struggle of survival when you can handle two biscuits as opposed to the other?

I experience that visitors come straight after lunch; some even come in the morning and are surprised that they are asked to leave during doctors' ward routine or bedside treatment. Or they step in without knocking or even any greeting or showing consideration for other patients.

The staff remain remarkably calm and friendly, which is understandable given the severity of their relatives' illnesses. What I find incomprehensible, however, is that some visitors only leave the room when expressly asked to do so, if it involves a very personal conversation with the roommate or a direct treatment at the bedside.

However, disrespect for staff, the routine medical procedures and fellow patients now seems to be a contemporary phenomenon. Even large notices in the lifts asking patients not to bring flowers or children onto the ward, or to use the hand sanitisers at each corridor entrance and in- and outside each room door, are ignored.

I only reacted directly, I think, 3-times. At the beginning, when *Nutella* boy's girl-friend lay down next to him on the bed, street clothes and trainers. I held back, it wasn't my bed after all. When she then used our inner bathroom, I later asked her outside in the corridor to use the visitors' WC by the lifts in future. It would be very dangerous for me and her boyfriend to come into contact with germs from outside. The next day, she took her shoes off when she lay down next to him and hugged him.

Another time, when a roommate's wife and daughter without paying attention to me, clucked around my roommate like chickens, telling him what to do and not to do. And, when in our patients' lounge room there was a group of overly loud visitors who stuffed themselves with cake and blasphemed about everything on the ward.

In the beginning, my daughter *Sarah* tries to come every two days. But over time, I manage to slow her down to only once a week; it always takes her an hour one way by car. I suspect her stress at work and at home; she and her partner are constructing and renovate an extra loft in their flat. And then the hours of travelling to work, to my home and to the hospital, plus laundry, the bank and my special requests. I also don't want her to see me with some of the side effects of the chemotherapy. But she has a strong will of her own.

My younger son *Simon* also comes a few times. He lives farer away and working in Luxembourg. Of course, he also offers to come more often. But I know he also has a stressful job and then the two hours journey; that doesn't make sense for me for a relatively short visit. We postponed the visits until after my hospital time.

My eldest son *Fabian* came over from the USA after I had stabilised; it wouldn't have made much sense beforehand. The father-son trip we took around two months before my illness suddenly came – a whole night and day by train from San Francisco through snow-covered, lonely Oregon up to Seattle on the Canadian border and a few days there – was also an issue. At the time, there was nothing to suggest that leukaemia was imminent. Both our beloved sarcasm lightens the queasy mood here; no wonder, the beer in black cans. Or was it the old and rare whisky that we found in the largest selection in a bar up to that point?

Would you like a pastor from your parish or from the house? I could only answer in the negative and added sarcastically: 'I would rather do what I had to say to God directly myself if necessary.' That was the end of the matter, but of course it still bothered me later on.

Why does *God, Allah, Jehovah, Manitou, Shiva ...*, allow, for example, children to be abused by his representatives or preachers on earth or abortions of pastors' children to be covered up by his own church? Or that in other countries street children are forced as child soldiers and prostitutes? Or as a *Hare Krishna* follower, as even a controversial sect in India too, says to me in one of their centres that the street children did something bad in their previous lives for which they now have to atone. I had to restrain my-self from answering with the term sadist; it is not my place to criticise this kind of religious practice.

I realise how my thoughts are getting stuck on the subject. Does it deal with my own situation, which is currently still close to death? But the thoughts criticising the church don't go away. Do I need a scape-goat for my own situation at the moment? And why does God give me my own sense of morality and allow representatives, some of whom contradict each other or confront each other with violence, to guide me in my thoughts and actions? Who made this so complex that its proclaimers need years of study and strange, contrived spiritual exercises? Or are they simply organisations competing in the faith market with tax exemption, donations etc. for the purpose of self-sufficiency? Social greenwashing as a cover for their secure income?

And in my case here, why a religion that is supposedly 2,000 years old, if you ignore the sometimes contradictory evidence? Why not one thousands of years older – from which Christianity, for example, drew – or in another place in the world where even greater miracles took place; if miracles can be quantified and differentiated in a qualified manner at all?

Even more interesting for me is the question of why not a newer religion, right up to a designer religion created in my own lifetime?

Something from the 18th century French philosopher *Rousseau* fits with it. During my studies, I had read his fascinating socially critical novel Émile – perhaps I unknowingly named my infusion stand in the hospital after it – which was immediately banned at the time and has stayed with me ever since. He wrote in the sense of, what do those who preach in the many different religions and interpret them, who they are, believe that they are above the human knowledge given to us by God?

When I tell *Peter* about it and get upset, he says: I should be careful today. It sounds like you want to fight God and the world today.'

One day, one doctor comes in during dinner, saying directly: 'I am the Chief Senior Doctor and have heard that we would have students at our bedside to practise diagnostic questions.' *Peter* and I look at each other. We decline, and the Chief Senior leaves without saying good-bye. 'Just for that reason alone,' *Peter* says, 'he should at least have knocked or said, may I come in, hello, how are you, or something like that.' However, we can't find him on the hospital's website in such a medical role. Later, when we ask someone, we learn that there is no such one or function; if there were, it would always be the professor.

Then, a few months later, during my follow-up treatment I was able to hit back. While a young doctor examines me with the sonogram, the door opens without any knocking or a greeting. Mr. Chief Senior Doctor enters the room and saying to a visitor in street clothes: 'That's our room for ...'. I interrupt very clearly: 'I am being examined here, a knock or a, may we come in, would be polite.' The young doctor examining me, she winces a little; I'd hit him properly. 'I can come in here when and how I want,' he replies, turning back to the door and saying to the visitor, 'well, just a patient.' Before he closes the door behind him, I add: 'My students learn respectful behave.' The young doctor smiles imperceptibly, which shows me that I've met the right person. Later I learn that others think he's an arrogant snob. I'm sure that will also make the rounds here again.

But there is another way. One late afternoon, I'm sitting at the table without an infusion attached and being lost in thought. The door to the corridor is open and the professor greets me as he walks past, and then stopped and asks how I am and if he can sit down for a moment. He wants to know what my family is doing and how they are coping with my situation. Being me, I also inquire about his family and find out that he is a so-called Late Father and will be hiking in the mountains with his family for a few days next week.

The small talk quickly turns professional. We realise, we both work in completely different disciplines, we are struggling with the same problems. More and more this administrative tasks on the computer instead of being able to take care of our students and research, our staff as well as the patients for him like the projects for me. Then he has to say goodbye, the family would be waiting for him. He is very optimistic about my recovery.

Later, during the years follow-up treatment, we always talk a bit about the family and these time-consuming administrative tasks. I realise that he's also happy just to have some small talk with outsiders during work.

At some point, an elderly new patient is transferred to my room. He tells me about his job and that he has now come from a hospital where they tried alternative treatments, but now his cancer is more advanced. We both had a quiet night and even a good chat at breakfast the next morning.

After lunch, I'm dozing in my tracksuit; this is how I try to motivate my work rhythm when I wake up. My new roommate is asleep; it's the usual time for patients to recover. His wife and daughter enter our room without knocking - they at least give me a brief nod - and then they wake him up.

Like clucking chickens, they loudly talk at him non-stop, and also with-out regard for other patients; in this case me. I can see he is really stressed. Even when he turns to the side, one of the both immediately enters to this side, talking again on and on.

When one said: 'Why don't you try to sleep like the others,' I kindly note 'then please let him rest for a while. Why don't you just go outside for a while, for example downstairs is a café at the neighbouring building? He won't calm down if you talk at him non-stop.' 'What do you think,' his wife shouts at me, 'I have very ill husband here and my daughter her father.' I slowly get up, take *Emil* by my hand and carefully push him towards the door. As I leave the room, I simply reply: 'And why do you think I'm here?'

Outside, I realise that *Emil* and I are not connected to any infusions. So I leave him outside in view of the room and sit down by the window at the end of the corridor, later in the patient's lounge room and read.

In the evening, my room neighbour is completely out of his mind. He talks crazy and keeps calling his wife and the professor. I keep waking up at night from his calls.

The next day, I'm hooked up to numerous infusions again, *Emil* and I go to our lounge to work and I don't go back to my room until dinner. Now it's getting worse with my roommate. He's hallucinating, sometimes shouting: 'What are you doing out there?' He yells that his wife and daughter talk to the doctors about him. I get up, open the door and tell him: 'Look, there's nobody here, it's the middle of the night.' But he won't shut up.

At some point it gets too much for me. Luckily, I am unplugged from my dear companion *Emil,* so I easily can go to our lounge room. After looking at the city lights in the valley for a while, I feel that I have to sleep on. At first I sit sunken at the table with my head on my arms, but I can't fall asleep, it's too uncomfortable. Then I place three chairs next to each other and lie down on the seats. It's very uncomfortable, but somehow I'm still half asleep.

I am brought back to reality by a question from a night nurse. She knows immediately why I'm lying here and takes me to the end of another corridor to an empty room. 'You can lie down here, the room is free till noon tomorrow.' Now I'm lying on a bed that's still covered in foil. What must have happened in this bed before? Someone discharged? Transferred to the *KMT* corridor, which is always locked, or even ...?

I wake up in daylight. I carefully leave the room without touching anything and pass our checkpoint. 'Where have you been? We were looking for you?' Obviously the night nurse's thankful action had been lost in the hustle and bustle of the morning handover. Were they afraid I'd run away again?

The night

In the evening at the buffet trolley, there is always something special in addition to cold cuts and the like, such as pickles or a preserved fish paste.

After that, the night shift nurses make their rounds, checking or giving new infusions, and if needed, a little red sleeping pill; until now I still refuse these little red pills consequently. It is getting quieter on the ward now. But the stress of the day and the situation here don't let you go, the thoughts circle endlessly ... I toss and turn as much as I can with the tubes at my neck and monitoring cables. Eventually you fall asleep, completely exhausted.

Sometime around 10 p.m., the night doctor quickly checks our pill dispensers and infusions; more thoroughly and frequently, of course, during an ongoing chemotherapy cycle.

I'm one of those people who often walk up and down the corridor at night or sit by the window in the patients' lounge room and look longingly down at the city in the distance. I often can't sleep properly and wake up every now and then. Or is it just too warm in this particular summer? And, of course, the constant alarm signals from some room or other. Quick steps, and then often several following another critical situation ... and then there's my own situation here; will I be one of them soon?

Suddenly I'm crying, freezing despite the heat, shivering all over. I can't get a grip on myself. *Peter*, once again for weeks my dear roommate, has woken up and presses the emergency call button. They hold me tight, calm me down. I get a new infusion ...

I wake up next day very late and everything passes me by as if behind a veil, my perception and movements are mechanically rehearsed. My thoughts about the situation here come back and won't let me go.

There was a suicide in my family long time ago. Even if the reasons were understandable, the free will and courage in particular are to be admired, you are not alone. The, if not economic, then emotional responsibility for others. But what about others' responsibility to allow someone's free will?

Again I fall asleep and wake up two or three hours later. Now, of course, I've been dreaming about suicide attempts. Why did I have to think about it for so long, I reproach myself now. Everything was somehow mixed up in the dream, it never worked out. And I had to justify myself to a committee; strangely enough, a former teacher from secondary school was there, but also an unfriendly neighbour from a long time ago.

Over a coffee, which really brings me back to consciousness, I wonder about myself; the father of psycho-analysis *Sigmund Freud* greets me in my thoughts. But I continue to spin my thoughts, this time abstractly and indendently of myself. Is it possible here, as in Switzerland – and, as I now know in other European countries – to die accompanied by your own will? *Google* shows blogs that say that despite the judgement on self-determined dying; the German politics has repeatedly rejected draft legislation. The church and the pharmaceutical industry in particular are probably lobbying quite hard, otherwise they would lose sales during such extremely expensive medical treatment phases, it occurs to me. Can you decide this on your own or only after one or more independent medical consultations? How quickly can this decision be made? Who can decide and why force me to stay alive? Who can prevent someone from cancelling everything like this and going home? After all, I've done it before, I think ironically to myself. And then you just let the leukaemia do its thing. Or does the emergency doctor come and you end up again back here?

For two month, I have avoided taking the little red pills to help me fall asleep quickly and happily. Now I take half a pill in the evening and stick to it for a while. I don't get any happier, but now I can sleep through the night.

Such a chemotherapy cycle starts hours beforehand. Additional blood samples are taken, blood pressure and oxygen measured, *Emil* gets this strange box with the green digital display screwed on, through which the infusion tube will later run, etc., and then you wait for the first chemo infusion bag. In the hours waiting I'm under constant stress, I can't sleep or concentrate to read.

At some point a doctor comes in, checks all the data in the patient file, on the chemo infusion bag and other parallel infusions such as for the stomach etc. and asks me who I am. It's like at the immigration desk when you enter the US: 'What's your name, date of birth, ...?'

Five infusion bags in one chemotherapy cycle are then repeated at half-day intervals. This means that I sometimes receive a chemo infusion during the night. The doctors on duty at night, most of whom I don't know, have to wake me up and do the usual safety checks, although I usually only doze off in short, alternating phases because I'm far too nervous when the chemo is dropping into my neck vein.

It is also oppressively warm despite the room door being open. Not all night staff like it when we leave the door open; otherwise we hear too much about crisis situations during the night. But of course we also know immediately when the door is closed, because that's how it was with us.

As the chemo slowly and steadily drips into me, I am magically drawn to the digital flow indicator. The device is attached to *Emil* at eye level. It often beeps even when the chemo unit is not yet finished; some devices show their venerable age. Who is supposed to sleep through it? And which side effects will strike that night or tomorrow? And above all, how?

I won't find out the medical results for a few days after the lab tests, the morning blood tests and the usual bone marrow extraction. While I still had the feeling during the first chemotherapy treatment, which was initially cancelled due to the transfer to the intensive care unit and the subsequent resumption of chemotherapy up here, that it wasn't that bad, I am now being taught otherwise.

For once I ask what happens if the tube breaks? Because it happened to my roommate *Peter,* but without chemo. That mustn't happen, definitely make an emergency call, turn away and breathe on the other side. It corrodes the whole floor. I look down at the blue-grey linoleum? Slightly agonised and yet ironically meant: 'That runs into my vein?' 'What do you think your veins can take? Don't worry about it,' is her short unemotional answer. Then the doctor is gone again. No jokes today, she's in a hurry.

Of course, chemotherapy is not a cure-all, it's quite the opposite. It is highly dangerous and nobody can predict its risks, you must know, every human body reacts individually ... but what is the alternative?

The success is demonstrated by the enormous increase in cure rates and, in the case of most cancers, also by constantly improving forms of chemotherapy. Chemotherapy is then a useful approach to prolonging life. In any case, risks of chemotherapy are lower than the otherwise certain death, according to an oncologist who has repeatedly suffered himself from a very rare cancer himself.

Acute myeloid leukaemia (AML)

> <u>Note:</u> *All information on AML is taken from the Internet in 2024 and accessible brochures from the hospital, and – due to its unverifiable accuracy for laypeople like me – should not be taken as medical information. Current research and continuously improved and new therapies absolutely require the advice of experienced medical professionals.*

Leukaemia, or as we say Blood Cancer, is not a single type of disease, but refers to various types of cancer of the blood-forming system in the body. My form *AML* is fatal without treatment in a few weeks.

The regular process of haematopoiesis of myeloid cells in the bone marrow – red blood cells, platelets and a proportion white blood cells – virtually gets out of control. Suddenly, white blood cells divide and multiply unchecked in the middle of the development process and are therefore unable to complete their development. The resulting immature, functionless precursor cells are then called 'myeloid blasts.' The rapid spread in the bone marrow hinders the formation of healthy blood cells. They disable the body's own immune system, so to speak, and the body can no longer defend itself against even the smallest infection. There is an additional risk that the blasts will then spread through the body via the blood and infect other organs.

There are three to four cases per 100,000 people annually, mostly the elderly. The risk increases with age, and men are affected slightly more often than women. And there are many *AML* <u>forms</u>; the most simple differentiation (with further subtypes in each case):
- *primary AML* without prior cancer or bone marrow disease, or
- *secondary AML*, which occurs after a disease in the bone marrow or as a result of radio- or chemotherapy for another cancer treatment.

I ask the professor to explain *AML* to me like to a child; biology used to be one of my weak subjects at school, along with many others. He laughs, then he explains: 'It's like a machine that produces *Lego* toy plastic bricks. At some point, a brick suddenly appears where a stud is missing. Then sometimes two or a stud is crooked, or a corner is missing at the bottom. As if not yet fully moulded or slightly deformed. If there are only a few bricks, then the brick house holds together. But with more and more incorrectly shaped bricks, it becomes so wobbly that it eventually collapses.' I interrupted him: 'Yes, I've already wobbled a lot when I got so dizzy.' He smiles and continues, 'and that's what we're going to save the house from, now you know.' I'm happy; biology can be quite simple after all.

Genetic changes are thought to be <u>causes</u>, but the triggers are still unknown. Possible risk factors include genetic predisposition, previous cancer, heavy exposure to environmental toxins and chemical substances such as herbicides, pesticides, benzene or chemotherapy for another cancer, smoking in old age, high radiation exposure and previous blood disorders.

<u>Symptoms</u> develop differently in different individuals within a short period of time due lack of normal blood cells. The lack of red blood cells erythrocytes, responsible for transporting oxygen in the body) leads to anaemia with paleness, weakness, dizziness, general malaise,

reduced performance (tiredness, low resilience, fatigue, shortness of breath, palpitations).

The lack of white blood cells (leukocytes are important for defence against pathogens) causes increased susceptibility to infection, fever and swelling of the lymph nodes. And a lack of blood platelets, the thrombocytes important for wound healing, causes unusually prolonged bleeding such as prolonged nosebleeds, poor wound healing or so-called Petechiae as small, punctiform haemorrhages, often on the legs and arms or in the oral mucosa. Those affected often have bone pain or pain in the upper abdomen due to enlargement of the liver and spleen as well as loss of appetite, which then leads to nutritional disorders and weight loss.

The <u>diagnosis</u> usually comes as a complete surprise, as you hardly have any pronounced symptoms or interpret them differently, as I did. *AML* leukaemia is often only discovered by chance – like mine, shall I say, 'with good fortune?' – during a blood test. For example, 20% myeloid cells in the bone marrow, specific gene mutations and an increased number of leukocytes and their immature precursor cells in the blood count are suspected. Once the diagnosis is clear, it is no longer a matter of months and weeks, sometimes only days or even hours

During a consultation it's usually first established whether organs are enlarged. Then the blood is analysed in detail, followed by the blood in the bone and the bone marrow itself. This is removed by a bone marrow extrac-tion under local anaesthetic with a special needle for laboratory microscopic analysis. Imaging procedures like X-rays, computer tomography, sonogram can be used to analyse the organs for infestation.

Thanks to the recognised and successfully proven <u>treatment options</u>, which are constantly improving in line with the latest research, *AML* leukaemia has been transformed from a previously fatal disease into a disease that is more often treatable today; the pre-requisite is that it is detected at an early stage with subsequent immediate individual therapy depending on the many *AML* sub-groups. A patient's general condition and age also are important:

- <u>Chemotherapy</u> usually takes place in five cycles: As a preliminary phase, a mild chemotherapy plus cortisone to prepare the body for the highly stressful next phase. This is followed by intensive induction therapy – as a combination of different active substances – in several cycles to completely eliminate (remission) the leukaemia cells. The subsequent drug consolidation with a milder combination of active substances for several months is intended to destroy the remaining cancer cells and prevent a relapse. Longer maintenance therapy over several years with less intensive chemotherapy inhibits cell division.

- <u>Stem cell transplantation</u>: If there is still a high risk of relapse after the chemotherapy consolidation phase, bone marrow- or stem cell transplantation is possible instead of a maintenance therapy. The patient's own healthy blood stem cells or those of a donor are transferred, from which healthy blood cells are then to be formed.

- <u>Radiotherapy</u> if cancer cells also colonise the brain and central nervous system as part of acute leukaemia.

- Relatively new, <u>Targeted Therapies</u> can support aforementioned approaches. For example, monoclonal antibodies recognise certain molecules on the surface of cancer cells and can therefore target the malignant cell. Surrounding tissue is largely spared with correspondingly fewer side effects.

Today, more than 80% patients achieve remission, provided that the proportion of blasts is still low enough when the disease is recognised and treatment is started. However, around 30% patients suffer a recurrence, in which case the previous treatment is repeated.

Administration challenge, the third

I feel isolated from the world and receive a bill 18,000 Euro; probably including the intensive care unit, with a payment deadline impossible for me to meet. The administration doesn't seem to realise that I'm tied to a hospital room in their own building. Although my daughter has been able to transfer some smaller lab bills in meantime, this amount is too high; even an *ATM* machine doesn't give out that much at once. Authorisation by the bank is only possible in person.

I call the administration office on my house phone at my bedside to explain my situation. 'Yes, but you can go to the bank branch, it's only 300 m outside the hospital. Or use the automatic transfer machine there as well,' the office clerk said. I repeat, 'but I've just explained that I'm here in chemotherapy. Or is it allowed to walk there with an infusion stand and despite the upcoming two weeks isolation due to the aplasia phase without my body's own immune system?'

Now I find the conversation funny. I imagine myself in a hospital shirt with the infusions; should I say, with my love *Emil* hand in hand on street, like the horror movie monster *Frankenstein*. Would I even be able to manage the distance or would I not be stopped beforehand by police for being men-tally unstable? Or in the darkness, especially at a cash machine?

They don't accept my suggestion to extend the payment deadline or to split the bills up so that my daughter can transfer the money in stages. 'Don't you have anyone who can transfer the money?' 'Okey,' I reply, 'I'll ask one of my sons who works abroad to transfer the money if they have that much cash, but minus the international transfer fee.' 'No, that's not possible,' comes back immediately. I end this conversation, it's getting too stupid. And before I say goodbye and thank him for the helpless information, I sarcastically remark: 'I will try to scrape together the amount of banknotes somehow and send it in an envelope by post.'

How many times would I have had to shuffle back and forth, without breaking the machine, to get the many thousands of cash? Even then, how would the administration clerk have looked if I had put a plastic bag full of banknotes on his desk? Of course, it wouldn't work, would be his answer.

What I didn't realise at the time was that it wouldn't be the last conversation of this kind. And I came up with the idea of writing down all these peculiarities in keywords.

Lower Echhey Village Life

Manju and Giri, my hosts

My new (temporary) home is located at a narrow serpentine roadside around 15 km north-east of the town Kalimpong with an altitude from around 1,300 up to 1,700 m. The village Lower Echhey is spread over several sqkm on the hillside with altitude difference of around 200 m.

I quickly say My Village, because after a few days I feel I'm part of it's society; people know me, invite me around or drop in for a cup of tea. All houses have huge so-called Kitchen & Farm Gardens and often more or less terrace rice fields in this mid mountain area. They usually have a cow, a few goats or even chickens; some now also have one or two bee boxes.

My view from the room with veranda is over the terraced farm garden below the house and the rice terrace fields, as well as the vast and indescribably beautiful mid-sized mountains opposite, called Lower Himalayas; the locals say Little Himalaya. From our mountain at the top, which is around 15 minutes by car, you can see in north-west the imposing snow-capped peaks, a part of the central Himalayas with *Kanchenjunga,* a mountain in the triangle-region with Nepal and China belongs to India.

Like his brother, our neighbour, and many others here, *Giri* retired from the army after 20 years. With a small pension as a basic income, they can sell products on the market in addition to their large kitchen garden and rice cultivation for their own use; economically, they are doing relatively well.

In addition to TV, instantaneous water heater and scooter, they now can afford a small car. With a solar cell, they are almost energy-independent and the water comes from the stream and is boiled. The sale of individual pro-ducts from their cooperative here is quite new, but already reaches as far as the market Shiliguri, two and a half by car away in the lowlands. And even now to 650 km far away Kolkata for organic spices, honey or ghee.

They are almost self-sufficient; growing rice as their daily staple food, garden vegetables and fruit as well as milk. They trade the rest with others, for example eggs, flour for the daily baked *Roti,* and garden products.

Giri is also part of a kind of a local committee and he manages the village community centre warehouse on a voluntary basis; they are renting out for example musical instruments and village community equipment (like tables and chairs or catering utensils) for family celebrations for a small fee to the village treasury. Whether religious or cultural, celebrations here quickly involve a hundred, often several hundred people; I will soon realise that.

Manju is not only in charge of the household – fresh food is cooked at least twice a day – and the production of household products such as honey, chutney, spices, etc. But she is also head of her SHG, leads the singing and dancing group in the village, does Nepalese expressive dance with friends, and she runs the Sunday school for children from the village in the prayer room here in the house. Therefore she is invited to many events such as the yearly last day at neighbouring schools, at anniversaries and openings.

The road

The narrow street here is The Road to work and home, road to school and visits, processional and monks' road, transportation and trading road, a shopping and meeting people road, and a road to the peak and to the river valley, a road to other rural villages or into the wide world.

Along - often with a hundred or more meters distance and serpentines – there are kiosks, a cookshop or café desk with only three, four plastic chairs under a tree; 400 m from us is for me the smallest restaurant in the world with just a table and integrated kitchen; like a garage for a small car.

There are also shelters for regular shared taxis, which are also a neighbourhood meeting point for old (during the day) and young (in the evening), as well as the primary school with brand new pre-school room as extension, currently with one or two children. And adjacent to this is the village community centre, which is currently under construction.

You can already hear the street vendors in the distance. Shouting loudly or singing on foot, balancing a large transport net on their heads, or on a scooter or flatbed lorry with a loudspeaker, they offer their wares. For example, carpets and mattresses, clothes, drugstore items or house-hold appliances.

It reminds me of my youth, we recognised the scrap dealer or coal man, the egg man or coffee dealer, potato farmer etc. from far by the sound of the flute, the bell or the horn; whereby the bell from the ice cream van was the most important thing for us children.

As if on a secret signal, a street vendor stands in the courtyard. He deals in cups, vases, plates and bowls made of copper and brass. His first price for a hammered copper bowl is 5,000 Rupees (55 Euro). The traditional haggling seems to begin very emotionally. They break off, he can freshen up and gets tea and fruit. The new price is now 3,700 Rupees, they wave goodbye and turn away, pack up and open again … they agree on 1,500 Rupees.

My hosts know the market price. In Kalimpong market it will be 1,200 Rupees and another 100 or 200 Rupees for both of them, as a return fare, a tea etc.; the price is okey.

Two weeks later the same street vendor comes again, this time for selling house-hold goods. The same procedure like before with the brother next to us; the large wok-like pan changes hands for around a third of the initial asking price.

You can also tell from distance whether it's a school or city taxi; I can't, of course. A minibus, an SUV or a real off-roader with official six or eight seats may carry up to 12 passengers plus luggage on the roof.

On one trip to the market in Kalimpong, there were 14 of us, three adults in the front and two rows of four, plus three children. On the return journey there were only 3-times three adults, but there were three large suitcases, lots of shopping bags and a carton containing 250 fresh eggs, which someone at the front took on his lap. Taxis also take parcels or whatever else needs to be transported on their way. A 2-seater scooter also often carry three plus bags and a child or two.

You simply sit down in the bus shelter, and several times an hour a lift or a friend comes by. Apart from a few private cars, there are more scooters. Flexible and fast, they are simply more suitable for the mostly dirt tracks from the road to the houses. Only occasionally does a small lorry squeeze through the tight serpentine-like curves on the mountain. Normal buses do only travel between towns on the main roads, however that is defined here.

According to *Giri*, our little narrow street has only existed for two years. We both are now friends and always talk to each other with light irony, because Indians like to laugh a lot with ironic undertones. After years of pressure from the regional administration, the people in the valley and the mountain dwellers around it have all come together under the motto No Road, No Vote. It works, we would say, and they already have the demand for the next election in mind.

My new daily routine

After the first few days of familiarisation, my daily routine is on now. I wake up in the morning with a view of the almost daily clear sunrise behind the mountains opposite. *Giri* and *Manju* are up and about from 5 a.m. in and around the kitchen house, with the animals or in the garden.

At first I get up at 7. a.m., later mostly an hour earlier. First I drink a hot ready-made coffee from my Room Kitchen' (the little stool with kettle by my desk) on the balcony and look out at the world. 'Good morning sir, welcome to the new day,' comes cheerfully from downstairs. In addition to the busy birdlife, the sound of the stream and animal noises from the forest, I can also hear people in the far neighbourhood. Hammering, someone has been building their house for days, a dark horn, someone has passed away or it is from the nearby Buddhist monastery, or the bells from the Hindu temple 2–3 km away, and the cattle; I wonder if they are also talking from house to house with 'moo' or 'mow'? And of course our *Mr Tiger* meows now loudly all the time. He knows that he will get his first milk as soon as the milking is finished. Only the dogs are remarkably calm; given the noise they often make at night, they probably need to sleep in now.

Giri and his brother are standing a few terraces below me, chopping dead branches from trees. *Manju* is chatting with her sister-in-law, who has just picked up fresh milk from us, on the terrace in front of the kitchen while she does her morning chores, and the early morning washing is already hanging on the lines. And not forgetting my morning fitness exercises for my back & co., which I also do during the day and in the evening; I've planned a lot.

Around 9 a.m. it's time for breakfast and small talk. We would call it a hearty farmer's breakfast. Rice, always in Basmati quality, or in rotation freshly baked *Roti,* the typical thin pure flatbread in the east and south-east Asia. This is always accompanied by two well-seasoned vegetables – some of which are unknown to me – and *Dal,* the traditional lentil soup, or made from other pulses, in different variations. Plus raw food and fruit from the garden; currently carrots, radish, cucumber, banana, guava, oranges, or sometimes apples or grapes from the market. And of course our own honey, home-made kefir and yoghurt; and when it is warm, it is diluted with cold water and salted which reminds me of Turkish or Arabic *Ayran.*

Everything is great, especially the variety of spices. I just have to get used to these huge portions. Or do they have to be smaller for me? That's going to be a fun fight later.

In the mornings, I write or hang out, as they say. This includes snoozing, visiting the stable with fresh treats from the garden. Or I go for a walk on the large terraced property and the neighbourhood, where I always discover something new. For example, how a banana tree grows and banana children ripen. I photograph this in phases and a children's story emerges, *Mini-Monkey and the Banana Babies* (chapter *Goodbye, and see you again*).

And of course, greeting neighbours, waving or with few Nepalese words I already know. Many adults know some broken English, especially the men those who have retired from the army. But, especially the children; they start learning English at pre-school.

Passing by here does not mean along the road, but across properties; there is a widely woven public network of more or less stone and natural steps criss-crossing the properties and past the houses on the hill. These are still the main traffic routes here.

Giri's 84-year-old mother is sitting on the terrace a little below us with his older brother, and the neighbour's old father across the road is sitting in the shade in front of the house. They are always happy to see me and return my greetings with a smile.

I can already hear the familiar sounds of lunch at 1 p.m. coming from the kitchen. Today, for example, it's a guava, a small bowl of dried, spiced chick-peas and, of course, a hot *Ciyâ* with small talk.

Afterwards I try some relaxation exercises; I usually then fall asleep briefly. Exercise and a coffee then bring me back from my afternoon sluggishness. And then it's like the mornings again. *Manju* and *Giri* look after the house and farm, plant vegetables, make yoghurt, dry spices, sow and harvest, cut huge baskets of fresh green fodder for the animals; now I also know how much green fodder a full-grown dairy cow needs during the day and at night in addition to the two large pots of concentrated feed mixture.

And many other activities, but all without the hustle and bustle. Time is different here. Small talk with visitors is always important, or you go over to your neighbour for a quick chat. Members of the cooperative also come and you swap seeds, discuss things or just say, hello. From time to time the project manager *Gobin* comes along to various cooperatives, pay out money from the market yields. This was part of a pilot project that was previously subsidised and has since become successful and financially self-sufficient. Of course, always the *Ciyâ* is served at every opportunity everywhere.

I ask if the milk in the tea comes from the British in colonial times? No, from the cow below us, they laugh. They grew up that way. They also like to drink plain black tea flavoured with pepper in the morning. Of course, every tea is drunk with four teaspoons of sugar, a tradition. With their typical Indian head shaking they laugh: 'You must know, in India we don't drink tea with sugar, but sugar with tea.'

Sometimes I go up or down the road on the mountain, or over the footpath network and on trails criss-crossing through nature. There aren't really any dangerous animals left, apart from monkeys, but I don't fall into their prey category. A baboon monkey will only attack humans if they feel directly threatened, but then in groups and it becomes dangerous.

GPS works even without a phone signal; I had downloaded the map of the region from Google Maps. But it only knows the official roads and paths, not the traditional trails. But the direction is relatively clear. Downhill means uphill at some point. And when I hit the road, the direction up or down is clear. If necessary, I ask for *Manju*. They laugh and point me in the right direction, five minutes; but I already know Indian Time, it could be around the next two bends or half an hour.

In the late afternoon, from half past 4 p.m. it is dusk and an hour later it is dark, the twinkling lights of the houses on the opposite mountains together with the stars create an immeasurable night sky. I read, write or sit outside. Cows are mooing, waiting to be milked, crickets are chirping like in South France, the cries of monkeys and peacocks can be heard from the forest.

Dusk and dawn is the time of the monkey gangs and the peacocks, which usually appear as a pair of thieves. They invade a rice field or garden; when the house owners are away and a window is open, the monkeys also take what the house has to offer. They are a protected species. Chasing them away with a slingshot at dusk is difficult, but the people here are practised. Later I will experience, when the fields are harvested, they also come during the day because they are simply hungry.

During the day it was usually sunny with 20–25°C and always a slightly refreshing breeze up the mountain from the cold river in the below valley. In the evenings after sunset it gets much cooler, 12–16°C until mid-November and then sometimes below 10°C; then I put on a jumper; lovely, just my kind of weather.

Dinner at 7 p.m. is similar to breakfast with *Roti* variations (I will describe later). Hot milk with honey and hot spices, chutney and pickles are always included. I now love chilli peppers, which I pick in the garden from time to time and then (first) eat them without, later including their seeds. I did learn very fast, never touch your eyes, when you've worked with a chilli pepper.

And there is small talk with the latest news from the neighbourhood and the valley. Yesterday evening, while I was still eating, three women came with torches – there are no street lights – to practise a dance. In the next few days there will be a performance at the Cooperative Market in Kalimpong.

Together with a neighbouring cooperative, they sell their products and always do something traditional, which goes down well with the people here.

The aim is to maintain the regional and historical tradition of the famous *Gurkha* hill tribes and strive for partial independence of the whole Darjeeling region as a separate federal state or at least the status of tribal people with their own district, like the ethnic indigenous peoples.

When they started a cooperative market to distinguish themselves from the mass-produced goods of the traders from city of Shiliguri a good two hours away, they were kept out of the market. The local market mafia is happy with the municipal allocation of licences, says *Giri* with a smile. In the meantime, however, they have pushed it through politically and the market is developing now. It started on the public football pitch and now has its own section next to the usual market. And two other smaller towns now also have it once a week.

As there is at least one early retired soldier in almost every family, and every young man dreams becoming a soldier before pursuing a degree as alternative, they now have political power. This is because the central government has an interest in their presence in the mountains here. The China border is only 80 km away; armed skirmishes occur time and again.

Tribal People

Before the today so-called Modern Civilisation, indigenous natives lived in groups, at greater distances from one another. This made the utilisation of natural resources more diverse and sustainable, as these were their only source of livelihood. India's population growth with the advance of the cities and industrial agriculture then pushed the communities to the margins of society. They mostly live in the rural areas as impoverished day labourers.

In addition to the aid projects of many national and international NGOs, there are now also numerous state and regional socio-political and economic support programmes. If they have not already done so, they don't want to repeat the mistakes made in Australia, for example, with the *Aborigines* or the native American Indian population.

However, it is important to realise that India is many times the size of the USA. Many of the tribal communities are also sometimes critical of such programmes because they believe – and often not without justification – that they have to give up their original culture.

Adapting to each other

At the end of November, halfway through my time, I summarise that I have already unconsciously adopted a lot here. The folding of the hands with a slight nod of the head when greeting someone: I always get up earlier in the morning because I also sleep by 9 p.m. at the latest in the evening. Like *Manju* and *Giri*, the first thing in the morning is a black tea with pepper. And then they wear a woolly hat and jumper if it's below 20°C. Later, I stand on the veranda with my self-made hot coffee and look out over the garden and the terraced fields. Of course, without hat and jumper and coffee with-out pepper ... although why not pepper in a coffee, should I try?

I can eat with my right hand without any accidents and, like everyone here, I also walk in the garden and fields in flip-flops. This makes it easier to just leave them outside the door when entering a room and slip them back in afterwards. I also like the hot *Ciyâ* now.

However, we have agreed on just two teaspoons of sugar for me instead of the usual four; they won't accept any less for me.

I now always eat a chilli in the evening for oral hygiene, feel that one or more portions of rice – half the size of hers, but still a lot for me – a day is normal, as are at least two bowls of *Dal*.

I always take a break at lunchtime, and I now always wash my hands thoroughly before and after eating, as well as between meals. And I no longer understand why I've never put pepper in black tea before? But, the only thing I can't manage is a typical friendly Indian head shaking.

My hosts also like some of the things I have tried. For example, the special *Sel Roti*, deep-fried in oil can be also eaten lightly salted instead of sweetened; for me at least, they also go well with spicy *Dal*. Honey on the freshly baked plain *Roti* or dipped in hot milk is also delicious in her opinion. They find an omelette with *Roti* as a sandwich, or raw vegetables cut into small pieces as a mixed salad dressed with salt & pepper, oil & vinegar sounds interesting, but somehow also too elaborate; you could just enjoy each on its own, they say.

And laughingly, they tell visitors about misunderstandings in our body language, as well as the garden gnome legend of course. Only her grand-mother understands me. Whenever I'm down at the neighbour's, she makes a black tea for us; she also thinks four teaspoons of sugar is too much. But I know from *Giri* that she is trying to save money, sugar was an expensive luxury in her youth. It seems somehow familiar to me when I think of my grandparents, traditional sugar pots with locks.

A few days ago, at dusk, *Manju* planted very small eatable cactus in halved tin canisters. They will take a year to grow up to four portions, she laughed. Then she invited me for this upcoming dish next year.

In the evening, son *Prashant* brought a small creamy cake with the words 29th wedding anniversary, a surprise. Now I know what *Manju* meant with invitation; they are celebrating their 30th next year.

My breakfast today in December – it's now winter here with 12-14°C
at night and 20-24°C during the day – consists of
- freshly baked four to five *Roti,*
- *Dal* with, this time, yellow lentils,
- spicy cauliflower and pumpkin-potato mix,
- liquid yoghurt,
- tomato and chilli paste, and
- flavoured, wafer-thin crackers made from yellow peas (like potato
  crisps);
- and there is always honey, ghee, pickle, salt for the yoghurt and,
  of course, black pepper on the table.

Here in the mountain region, characterised by kitchen gardens, small-
scale farming and self-sufficiency, a large substantial meal is eaten
warm in the morning and evening; at lunchtime there is only a small
snack. There is always rice or *Roti* and *Dal.* Known to us as Indian
lentil soup or stew, it varies from a fairly thin hot soup to a solid
vegetable. There are significantly more varieties of lentils than we are
used to and all other pulses such as beans and peas; and everything is
always well flavoured and very different.

Rice, flour and pulses are not usually sold in shops in small packs
like we do, but in shops or markets in the countryside and even in
supermarkets in Kolkata they are available to buy openly in bins or
sacks or as ready-made 5-kg bags.

Roti – actually you have to eat a few, otherwise you'll soon be asked:
'They're no good?' – are thin, palm-sized patties of bread dough that
are baked fresh for every meal in a very flat pan. They are traditionally
used instead of a fork, torn into pieces with the right hand, to pick up
the food. It can also be baked in fat or you can use ghee as home-made
butter. There is always a slightly spicy chilli-tomato paste, chutney or
pickles. Or the *Roti* dough is enriched with pieces of spiced potato or
vegetables; soft and doughy, similar a small pancake, it is then also
called *Roti Pizza.* Another variation is a thicker *Batura Roti;* the dough

is enriched with baking powder and yoghurt and is left to rest for around three hours.

There are always two differently flavoured vegetables with the rice or *Roti*. Potatoes are considered vegetables here, as are carrots, radish and other root vegetables that I'm not familiar with. There are different types of beans, tomatoes, cabbage too – here we grow white cabbage, broccoli, cauliflower and turnip cabbage – and, of course, vegetables that I don't know.

This is decided early in the morning when *Manju* walks through the garden to see what is ripe for harvesting or preserving. And pumpkins come in all shapes and colours from white to black; they can be stored in the shade until the rainy season in six months' time, I learn. And that means that it rains here in June and July practically in one go.

Some vegetables are also varied into pastes, for example boiled potatoes enriched with onions and flavoured as cold mashed potatoes. Or a banana blossom instead of potatoes; this is enough for three people as one of the side dishes in the morning and evening; it is as big as a bottle gourd, because a whole bunch of bananas she leaves at her end. On special days, it is served with a boiled egg or an omelette, or sometimes fried noodles.

Salad here means a plate of raw vegetables, a mix of slices of cucumber, carrot, onion, radish etc.; only sometimes tomato because of me, but *Giri* doesn't like it and always gives it away to children or the day labourer.

I always have home-made yoghurt, which I drink diluted with water and slightly salted like kefir; I can get addicted to. I may also have hot milk, but *Dal* or vegetable soup and drinking yoghurt are enough for me.

And always are spicy pickles on the table, as well as our own honey and, I can't believe, a huge bottle *Maggi* ketchup; the student son is currently here.

At lunchtime there is only a small light snack, like raw vegetables or a fruit, and for example home-made unsweetened popcorn or a roasted *Papal,* like crisps, and of course *Bhujia.* I now know the name of the roasted spicy-hot snack, which comes in many combinations and spicy flavours; I measure by chilli heat; here, normally the food is a bit less spicy than I prefer. *Bhujia* is made with a potato, bean or lentil base and eaten on its own or mixed with peanuts, almonds or peas, for example. And served with whatever fruit is hanging on the bush or tree in the garden; we grow banana, guava, papaya, and the brother next door also orange; apple or grapes we buy from market.

As something special, there is also occasional packet soups; *Knorr, Unilever, Nestle & Co.* are also on the rise here with their ready-made products in the kitchen. *Nescafé* is replacing what I consider to be the tastier Indian coffee *Bru,* which is also much cheaper; as it is in our western world, the brand is everything. Even the innovative Indian cola version *Thumbs-up,* which was launched many years ago, is now part of *Coca-Cola.*

As a sweet variation, the traditional *Roti* or small dough-soft pancakes are spread with honey. On special occasions, the handful of *Roti* dough runs thickly from the circling hand to form a ring or spiral from the outside in-wards for deep-frying in hot oil; it then tastes a little firmer to the bite, similar to our lard pastry. There are certainly regional *Roti* variations. As foreigner, who is supposed to know their way around here? I don't even know at home the many regional or baker-to-baker roll names.

Today we had at dinner:
- classic *Roti* (dough from morning, yesterday it was rice),
- vegetable-enriched *Dal* with yellow lentils (from morning),
- sweet and savoury pumpkin puree,
- light salted yoghurt drink,
- spiced tomato and chilli paste, and
- as always on the table, honey, ghee, pickle ... and ketchup.

In earlier years in India I had seen onions as an important part of daily food, and I knew the discussions about the price of onions; it is something of a perceived cost of living index. In Ireland, I had once seen on the evening news how the price of a pint *Guinness* beer was being discussed in the Irish parliament that day. Onions are now so expensive that the first people here going back to growing their own. *Giri* and *Manju* are also considering it; there is still potential growing space in the garden.

It is also interesting to note, for example, that all cabbage varieties are grown in plastic bags and pots on the terrace by the house. The advantages are less watering – on the slope, water runs off too much above ground and washes out the topsoil at the same time. 'And there are no snails,' *Manju* says, looking around to see if son *Prashant* is listening and laughs, 'they can eat even faster and more than this young man.'

But here too, the eating culture is changing. We're sitting down to dinner. When I asked him what his favourite food was, his son said it was actually from the garden here. But at college, out and about with his friends or in the city, he prefers to go to *KFC* ... it kind of reminds me of my time with the *Currywurst & Pommes* (sliced roasted sausages and French fries).

Now and again they also buy noodles – making their own rice noodles would be an obvious choice, but they don't want to go to the trouble – or other types of rice such as black rice. However, this is more of a speciality, as their own and regional cultivation takes precedence. *Manju* says: 'That it's boring if you always have everything available from the shop. So you look forward to the next harvest, planted and experienced growing yourself.'

Singing, dancing and the village community

Singing and dancing together is also part of everyday life. In my time there are many public holidays and the rice harvest. People from the neighbour-hood or cooperative come at least twice a week, and there are easily 20 of them. I always want to stay in the back, just listen and take a photo. But I can't escape it so easily and have to join in.

Quickly I realise, I'm not used to sitting cross-legged on the floor; they always put a chair for me. So, I sit together with the old people, for example next to grandpa from across the street, like me he has back pain. We under-stand each other really well through body language, and we clap to the beat and sing the chorus; I'm listening in, he by decades of experience.

There are always children from babies to teenagers ... and mobile phones. It seems natural that even those who are playing an instrument get up and talk on their mobile phones from time to time. I later learned to accept and understand this behaviour, which I saw strange at first. Here on a mountain, people live further apart and communication is the 'be-all and end-all' of living far apart.

It is important, for example, what is currently happening in Nepal, where the people have chased the government out of office because of corruption and are calling for the king. They all have relatives, their families are all of Nepalese background. The border was drawn by the UK colonial power without regard for history, former kingdoms or the ethnic indigenous population. So, naturally, they continue to cultivate their old traditions and have enforced them politically. Their first language at school is both Nepali and English. Hindi can be learnt, but if you want to, you won't get far here, they laugh. And even though they officially belong to the federal state West Bengal, they distinguish themselves from the culture and Bengali language; nevertheless they are proud Indians, but from the *Gurkha* people.

So far, joint meetings such as choir and dance, village community or SHG, have been held at our house because it is relatively central for everyone else and has a large covered terrace. Later, the meeting place will be on the neighbouring property at the pre- and primary school; *Giri*'s father donated the ground to the village in 1960.

The building is next to the school and has the same ground floor as the school. This allows the school to use it for activities in addition to the larger village gatherings. The basement is the community store-room with tables and chairs, cooking utensils etc. which can be hired out for events.

The roof is a simple bamboo construction with foil; it has been badly damaged by the months of rain, birds and the monkeys with their claws. The plan is to build a solid roof made of corrugated iron and to erect bamboo walls and windows in the traditional style on one side facing the hillside. And to provide the other sides with proper railings. This will also allow it to serve as a school-, gymnastics- and dance hall, and they will receive a small fee from the school administration.

It still needs around 4 Lakh (1 Lakh: 100,000 Rupees; around 1,100 Euro), including the upcoming renovation work. That's an enormous amount of money, around 6–times to our relative purchasing power here. The people are mostly self-sufficient without a regular monthly income, so cash has an even higher value for them.

Mid-December, the Kalimpong district administration comes to the village for a day with representatives from important offices or such as passport or veterinary documents; they therefore use the school 3-times a year.

Suddenly the electricity goes off. Men from the village unceremoniously throw a power anchor into the public power line. The officials look away, they are happy to have electricity. 'But more important,' *Giri* laughs, 'their food is cooked by our women,' and he adds after a short pause, 'they only come anyway to escape their dusty offices.'

When this started, he bought a copy machine and is then busy all day. People have come from all over the mountain on foot or by scooter, and they need copies of their IDs, other certificates or applications.

In the evening, you can see that even the civil servants leave everything lying around and simply throw their cups, plastic bottles etc. around the school into the forest. How can people here from this bad example?

Giri has already installed the first waste bins on his own initiative, at the taxi stop and stairs to school for example. But, but what good is it if there is no central regular waste collection? This, too, becomes a topic among many others in the village community that meets regularly. In the meantime, they have decided on a village fee for households for tasks that the regional community does not fulfil. Anyone who is newly admitted must first pay a large amount. The official village community is growing slowly, but it is growing. 'And so does our cohesion for the independence movement,' *Giri* smiles.

I receive visitors

The visit of my son *Simon* and his girl-friend on their one-year trip around the world had already been planned before my trip. After their Himalayas tour in Nepal, they had visited Kolkata for a few days – there I met them for three days on my way up here - and are now making an own stop-over here for a few days before travelling on to India. After the strenuous high mountain tours and then Kolkata high humid, they are enjoying simply here to hang out.

Of course, this visit is not only exciting for my hosts, but for the neighbours as well; so many Germans at once. One evening, we all-together with a neighbour family we make *Momos;* dumplings like in many other cultures, here traditional Himalayan a handmade version.

The *Momo* dough – wheat powder, not rice powder, a mistake I made later at home first time – kneaded thoroughly and left to rest for minimum two hours. Then a good spoonful of dough is rolled out with a traditional thin rolling pin to the size of the palm of your hand. A teaspoon of filling is placed on top and the whole thing is moulded closed (for us a bit similar to Italian ravioli); each region has its own design. Our filling is a mixture of chopped onions, white cabbage, some carrots, seasoned with green spring onion, garlic, some green chilli, coriander, ghee, salt, pepper.

Here, the women mould them into semi-circular shells with over-lapping folds of dough that look like ornaments, surprisingly quickly and almost without looking. After a few attempts, we Germans give up, we create our own shapes as a way out; there's a lot to laugh about.

*Momo*s are then placed in a multi-tiered steamer and are ready in a few minutes. You don't really need anything else, they simply taste heavenly and you can hardly stop eating. If you like, you can dip them in a chilli and tomato paste. They are served with a clear, hot vegetable soup with leftover *Momo* filling and fresh coriander, with soya sauce to flavour. To everyone's amazement, I like to drizzle it into the *Momo* when it's bitten into. I can also imagine this traditional vegetarian dish with other pastes and fillings.

Two days after my visitors' departure, my Kolkata friend's German wife *Sarah*, her mother and a women, an employee of her German organisation, come by for a day visit. For them, too, it is of course an experience, although they had already been to India and Nepal years ago. Now it's mainly about visiting a few projects in the area.

'We've never seen so many Germans here in one week, if ever,' they say later at a dinner with friends in the wider neighbourhood. I add and look around: 'And I've never seen so many *Gurkhas* at once.' We're all laughing; and better German tourists than them as warriors, is my sarcastic thought.

One day they said we were going uphill to have dinner with friends, it's not far, we'll take a shortcut. I already suspected it wouldn't be that easy, and so it was. We set off in the dark with a torch and mobile phone light; and we really need the light. We start off on a long, ascending stepped path that feels like it was concreted 100 years ago and is correspondingly battered, with large holes or pieces of concrete that have slipped apart.

Further up in natural rocky climbs and trails. At one point, there is a steep descent of many steps one side to our mountain stream. *Manju* and I lead the way, *Giri* and his son *Prashant* follow a little later. So we wait from time to time; I need the breaks too. There's a very steep section at the end and I'm really out of breath. So much for a short walk; perhaps for the people here.

Later I hear that the woman usually makes this walk twice a day, and in the evening she comes to get milk from us in the dark. She saved that once today, because *Giri* brings a full milk jug.

The friends are, like everyone here, very nice. They run a small fish pond alongside field and garden work, and the husband also has a part-time job as vet for artificial insemination. His wife is native Mongolian. Their grown-up son has two pennants on the wall; one Indian and one German. He is fan of the German football team. The only thing he finds more interesting is cricket, India's national sport. The game that we Germans will never under-stand. It can last for days and has more fans worldwide than football.

Weeks later, it is a special, informal national day of mourning; India has lost in the final of the Cricket World Cup. My question as to whether second place isn't also great is not well received by anyone. And when I say as a joke that second is the first loser, they nod sadly in agreement.

The way back is then almost an adventure, because going down such paths is more dangerous than going up, and it is also hard on the knees. It is also not without danger, as monkeys feel disturbed and sometimes attack in hordes, especially if there are many newborns in the herd.

As we climbed up, we saw large areas of ruined rice paddies in the light of our torches. Are they watching us?

Home away from Home   My Chemo Life Cycle

... is reserved for the convalescent: eternally builds his house of being anew.

Nietzsche, in: Zarathustra

Home away from Home

The surroundings

The village Lower Echhey lies below the main road from Kalimpong north-east to Algarah; and to the neighbouring federal state Sikkim it needs about one and a half hour by car or scooter. My new home for the next time is some minutes by car below the main road; above the main road is logically Upper Echhey.

Down in the valley is the icy cold river Relli, tributary of the big Teesta river coming down from Upper Himalayas; the one with the devastating flood wave at the beginning of October 2023.

No matter the weather, the view of the mountains opposite and behind is breathtaking day and night. It's not just the sunrise and sunset that change colour, but also the whole valley.

Down, in Relli river is a small natural swimming pool; only real *Gurkha* fighters, or those who want to become one, go in this ice-cold water there voluntarily. A small kiosk-café in traditional bamboo design is currently being built on the river-bank. The large rounded rocks in the river give an idea of the masses of water that come down here when the snow melts.

At top of the mountain there is a huge park with walking paths, small food stalls in front – here in Darjeeling a must wherever people want to feel at home – and offers tandem paragliding. There is also a scientific centre, where in addition to seminar rooms for schools, you can experience in- and outside the laws of physics. Indescribable views in all directions with the overwhelming Himalayas Panorama is not only a magical visual attraction. It also leads, at least for me, to a deep inner humility that regularly brings tears to my eyes.

In the Kingdom Bhutan, a neighbouring country 130 km away by car, on all the mountains above 6,000 m is taboo zone. There, everything is reserved for the gods; what a sensible and also sustainable decision.

After a few walks in the neighbourhood, I take my first short hike halfway down the mountain. First through our garden and the terraced fields below, then along trails between arm-thick bamboo trunks over 20 m high, mostly further down the mountain. I was always discovering new things, plants unknown to me, huge flowers in all colours or another stream with decorated ritual sites. Here, something was sacrificed to one of the gods; in Hinduism, the 'one creation' appears variously as an animal, divine figure etc. and has a role similar to that of archangels or the Trinity, for example.

I know that I can't get lost; in the end, it's just uphill again until I reach the road. At some point I realise that going downhill also means going uphill again. It's already half past 3 p.m. and the sun is still blazing. But as I'm mostly in the shade and there's always a slight cooling breeze uphill, I don't notice it that much. But from 5 p.m. onwards, it very quickly gets dark as the sun sinks behind a nearby higher mountains.

So I turn around and look for the next trail upwards; the same path criss-crossing back seems too long. I feel like I'm going in the right direction and have to climb in places. I see people carrying huge baskets of cut grass on their backs to feed their cattle up the mountain to their houses without stop-ping. But it feels like I have to take a short breather every 100 short steps. Is it my lack of fitness, the altitude or my prestressed lungs? Probably all of the above as my personal tribute to having survived leukaemia.

But, where now is the path, what to do? At the same moment, a man calls me to come to his house. His gestures are clear, the path continues between the house and the traditional kitchen and stable. When I mention the name *Manju*, he laughs and continues with me up the hill to the road. Every now and then I have to take a breather, as if I'm interested in the view; I can't walk uphill as fast as he does.

At the road, I thank him and he points down the road; great, up the hill and straight back down again, I think. But I'm glad, because it's almost dark by now. 'Its just 15 minutes to walk,' he laughs with the typical Indian head shaking.

One of the few times in India it is exact time according my own cultural habits; here time is due traffic in cities or mountain geology very relative.

My next neighbourhood excursions are shorter. Sometimes I climb up the bed of the mountain stream or along the edge of our property, or I visit a Hindu temple about 2 km away. Or I make various detours to the next kiosk or the one after that.

Or I take a portion of these addictive *Momos* in the world's smallest restaurant with the single table, bench and three plastic stools in the hallway. In the opposite corner is a small table with two bowls (dough and filling), a wooden board for rolling out the dough and a two-flame gas cooker with a four-tiered pot and a gas cylinder underneath. Next to it is a shelf of spices, a few plates and soup bowls, and some snacks and sweets for sale. Once again, I get puzzled looks when I drizzle soy sauce over the *Momos* - this is sure to be the talk of the village again - because it's actually for the broth that will be added later.

But what I enjoy most is just being here in my temporary home and changing places. Next to my desk there is my bed, the veranda in front or my balcony the other side, sitting on a bench on the terrace upstairs, in a chair down-stairs in front of the kitchen house, a shady spot in the garden at a banana palm, at the edge of a rice terrace or a stone by the murmuring stream. That's enough, because a stream is a stream is a ... the sound of the forest is the sound of the forest, and the monkeys and peacocks here in the forest call in the same way all over the world.

Almost a third of my time here is now over. People not only know me in the neighbourhood, but also in the villages around the mountain, at least from hearsay or from the regional media about the special reception at the trade fair event. Conversely, I also recognise a lot of faces, but often can't recognise them, but that doesn't matter, I just belong. My Nepali vocabulary is slowly expanding, and it's enough for one, two, three, yes, no, please, thank you, tea, rice, potatoes and flatbread as well as greetings and gestures depending on the occasion or person. But I can forget about any writing; from my point of view it's more drawing art: 1, 2, 3 is एक दुई तीन, *ēka, du'ī, tīna.*, pronounced *ek, du-i, tin.*

They can't believe that I also had to take a Lap of Honor twice – two years to repeat secondary school – also because of English class; I explain the term they find funny, when I speak English so well for them.

All here know, English is more than important for the children alongside the regional language Nepali. Both come before their official formal federal state language Bengali or national Hindi – I have long had the impression that it is spoken relatively little or not at all in the areas I have been to.

They actually always bring or pick up their children that they can speak English with me; also they then act as translators for the parents. Once again, I have a really good conversation in English with a girl aged 7- and a 5-year old boy. Their parents look puzzled and the kids shrug their shoulders, as if to apologise to their parents. Smiling, and with their culturally typical head shaking, they say goodbye with the usual international gesture *high-five.*

Shopping in Kalimpong

I visit Kalimpong town with *Giri* only 3-times in the entire quarter year here. At the very beginning he buys, among other things, a table lamp for me and the pink children's umbrella for the garden gnome. I buy a typical Indian cotton scarf, which I only use two or three times, and we eat *Momos* there.

Twice his son *Prashant* takes us by car and has to drive a long way out again; parking a private car in the streets seems to be from my point of view nearly impossible or it is incredible expensive.

Kalimpong town is situated on a steep slope with winding narrow streets and alleyways; a typical hustle and bustle of cars and scooters; virtually in a permanent traffic jam.

I then invited them both for tea and biscuits and bought some biscuits for *Manju*. I travelled to Kalimpong a third time together with *Giri*, because I wouldn't have been able to figure out the shared taxi system, just before Christmas.

A few days later, *Manju* and a neighbour go for shopping in Kalimpong. *Giri* is supposed to make at home a small lunch snack, which for him means we go for our small *Momo*-restaurant. On the way, we meet others with the same destination; they joke: 'Today is national women shopping day.' Of course, I get a place of honor on the bench, others spread out on the three plastic stools in the aisle, the entrance step and on a small wall next to it; a great atmosphere, the owner has a lot to do. But she is prepared with the amount of dough and filling on hand; days like this are her business.

On the way back, a minibus from the *Don Bosco* school stops. *Giri* and the driver know each other, so they make small talk. The last little girl in her school uniform on the bus looks at me shyly at first. I ask her something in English and she starts babbling. We exchange ideas about which subjects she likes at school and which she doesn't. Of course, she wants to know that from me too; she is five years old, we clap *high-five*.

Two weeks later, *Prashant* drives *Manju* and me and the neighbour with her daughter to Kalimpong town. There are queues at the cash machines; maybe it's payday? We have to go into the bank on the first floor with lots of desks and counters. Many of the customers go back and forth several times between the counters and desks with forms, a procedure I can't understand.

Most shops now also accept payment by phone. Even with all the poverty you see, India is simply much more digitally advanced than we are. You only really need cash at old street vendors and at the market ... 'and if you need something cheaper,' *Manju* laughs.

I buy me new flip-flops, the most important type of shoe here. You only really wear sturdy shoes for official occasions such as weddings, travelling or shopping in the city today. Then we buy also some spices for me; *Manju* will show me how to make the typical spice mixture for 'tea masala.'

On the way back, she buys a lot of things from a shop, including different types of lentils and vegetables that we don't have in the garden, 4 kg sugar, two huge sacks of maize and oil mill mustard seed waste, concentrated feed for the cows. We'll stop here later on the way back and to load everything.

I see a café diagonally opposite and this time I invite everyone in for a coffee, which is something rather special here. What I then learn is that it's *Nescafé* vending machine latte ... and already pre-sugared in Indian style.

Social Engineering, the big trade fair

It's a big day in Kalimpong, the Social Engineering fair in the football stadium and 3-hours opening ceremony in the morning in the town hall. Hundreds of festively dressed visitors, most of the men wearing the *Dhaka Topi*, the traditional cap of their *Gurkha* tribe. This is about their historical Nepalese culture – much more older than the neighbouring Nepal – in what is now the Darjeeling region in West Bengal, as well as in the neighbouring Indian state of Sikkim and the kingdom of Bhutan.

As guest of honor and speaker, the governor of Sikkim – similar to our federal state prime minister – arrives traditionally with pompous escort and music. The people are thrilled. There is a reason for this, of course, because like Sikkim, they want to become a small state of their own and independent of West Bengal. Also, beside the here officially spoken Nepali, people prefer to send children to study in Sikkim or in Nepal; but everyone is proud to be Indian.

Later in his speech, the governor supports, among other things, greater independence for the Darjeeling region. Politically, he is seen as a critic of the current Indian government, which is trying to give the India a more national-conservative Hinduism. And, of course, he emphasises Social Engineering, the theme of the event, as do other speakers, including a scientist, entrepreneur and regional politician. It's about organic farming, cooperatives that focus not only on profit but also on culture, green tourism, etc., which reminds me a little of the policies of neighbouring kingdom of Bhutan.

We have such kind of concepts as well, for example Social Entrepreneurship and a relatively new term Social Business; this is actually a tradition that is well over a hundred years old and which was increasingly pushed into the background as part of the so-called Economic Miracle after World War II. Today's public saving- or the cooperative banks, which are committed to the society, have anymore little to do with their founding ideas; unfortunately, this development is also known in India.

But we are already further ahead than the rest of the world in some areas. Every school now has mandatory environmental projects, universities have entire subjects and degree programmes on the subject, and CSR (Corporate social responsibility, which is in Germany only voluntary as national guide-line), has been the law here in India now for around 10 years.

But you also have to see the dimensions here. Such tasks are relatively autocratic. Germany has 1% of the world population, but the sub-continent India is almost 4-times the size of the entire EU and accounts for around 15% of the world population with over 100 different independent languages and ethnic groups.

The term Social Engineering in their socio-political understanding is not yet familiar to us; for us it is more seen in the negative sense of interpersonal manipulation like purchase manipulation or via password phishing. We use the term Capacity Building. Through social and technical skills, organisations such as cooperatives, villages and an entire region should become economically independent through crafts and trade; this also includes cultural activities that promote the community.

When welcoming and introducing important guests, surprisingly I hear my name from the loudspeakers. In the audience, sitting in one of the front rows next to *Giri*, I am mentioned as a special guest from Germany. And as well as *Giri* and some other seemingly important people, I am also given the traditional silk-like guest of honor sash.

Later, some people want to take a photo with me: I wanted to be here privately, but this seems to be very important to the people, so I comply.

My hosts must have been pulling the strings, because they are involved or mentioned several times, including as an economic co-operative, successful on the road to economic independence, in building a community in their spread out over the mountain and as a traditional chorus and dancing group on stage at this opening event as well as open air in the evening at the fair in the stadium.

Later I find out, a neighbour's son is one of the organisers; I meet up with him several times to exchange experiences; and I also wanted to find out more about the socio-political and -cultural environment here in the area.

After sunset, we drive to the exhibition centre again in the evening; the municipal football stadium. All around are cookshops with regional cuisine, handicrafts, jewellery and clothing etc., an art exhibition and a stage with speeches and local artists with music and dance.

Manju and three neighbour women perform a traditional dance with a neighbours' daughters singing duo, and balancing burning oil bowls on their heads. They had practised this repeatedly in the kitchen-living room above the stable, in the old *Gurkha* house; I emphasise, on the wooden floor and under the relatively low wooden ceiling.

Gurkha House

The traditional house – in the plains it is often built on stilts, as ours – has a wooden floor and a half-open stable underneath, which is covered with a tarpaulin in the evening. In *Giri*'s childhood, the roof of the house was made of bamboo and thatched; today it has a weatherproof corrugated iron roof. The house is a dark timber frame and the (our) green spaces in-between, formerly bamboo wickerwork with clay, are now sealed or plastered with cement. But more and more people in the area are following tradition and renovating back to their historical state. And it's all about colour, colour, and colour.

I'm thinking of my childhood home region, where the preservation order traditionally prescribes black and white, green shutters, black slate roof; but here, always in a different colour to the neighbours.

Today, at most new buildings, the *Gurkha* house of their parents and grandparents can be seen as an extended kitchen. In this often impassable area, they usually have a 2-burner gas cooker with a gas tank underneath. In this way, the risk of fire is sensibly limited to the kitchen house. But tradition takes centre stage, even if see more and more a satellite-TV.

The *Gurkha* tradition does not refer to a specific ethnic group, but in general as the mountain tribes in the former kingdom of *Gorkha Rajya* – kingdom until the beginning of 20th century – which once stretched around 2,000 km from present-day Nepal across the north of West Bengal to Bhutan.

Their people were considered frugal, persistent, tough and were known for never giving up in battle. For this reason, they were also recognised as separate *Gurkha* units by the British colonial power. Even today, they are still thousands in service with both the British and Indian armies worldwide, for example with the *UN Blue Helmets* or as paratroopers *(Gurkha Rifles)*, who are feared as jungle fighters due to their mountain tradition.

This is another reason why India is heavily developing the Darjeeling region militarily as a deterrent to China. Here in the near and far neighbourhood, every second farmer was in the Indian army. And in every family, the first thing the boys dream of when it comes to their professional future is to join the Indian army. The motivation behind this, especially for the first-born son, is of course to take early retirement after just 17 years in his mid-30s and return to live here in the mountains, so that he can later take over the ancestral home with its garden and farm.

Due to an arm injury as a child, *Prashant*, the son of my hosts, had no chance in the Indian army; so he is studying mechanical engineering, which he is not really enthusiastic about.

An excursion ... and a mental challenge

Today, we set off early after breakfast to a higher mountain in the distance, we were told. From there you could see our house with a telescope; that's all I knew. Of course, that turned out to be a crazy winding route up and down the hairpin-like curves; there were two other mountains in-between, which you can only partially see from our house. We stop at a few places along the way for the views, including these incredible Himalayas high mountain panoramas with the 8,000 m peaks, as we know them from pictures in Europe.

Because the European *Alps* and the Himalayas have the same geological history, the Himalayas are considered the *Alps'* big brother. Three times as large in area and almost twice as high with its mountains, it stretches in a west-east direction over 2,500 km from Pakistan via India, China and Nepal to Bhutan. I can't see Mount Everest, but I can see the *Kanchenjunga.*

At a viewpoint, a very small village on a mountain-top plateau, we drink coffee and eat chocolate. Then we continue on to an old suspension bridge. I felt a little queasy when I thought about the mostly functioning, but often old and improvised technology here.

A German engineer would not even bother with this jumble of self-made, improvised power distributors and lines, as well as the water pipes from streams with simple tubes like a power line across roads, or bypasses of slipped road sections ... as a joke, it occurs to me that in Germany the whole mountain would first be cordoned off and evacuated. But of course you can't say that out loud, improvisation is important for survival here.

On the way to our final destination, the Hanging Bridge, my impression is confirmed. Although parts of the roads up there have already been up-graded like a future 4-lane motorway, but the former car park is not existing anymore, and the ticket office slowly decays, we park on the unpaved roadside. After a good quarter of an hour's walk through the forest – I'm not interested in the otherwise unfamiliar plants and trees – we reach the Hanging Bridge. And it's a tough one. Even the first planks are loose, and further in, some are hanging halfway out of the fastening or are missing completely.

Prashant, who is driving us, hugs his mother and says succinctly, great setting for a horror movie. *Manju* shakes herself, stop. She tells us, a little sadly, that they used to come here a lot as children and would race to see who was faster up and down the Hanging Bridge.

Because it is not, or was not, a hanging bridge over a valley or a river, as I had feared, but used to be an excursion attraction. It hangs at a height of a 2–3 m, criss-crossing the forest for around 300 m and is already mystically overgrown with plants in places; I am saved.

As we drive on, it quickly becomes clear why the road is already so well developed. We keep seeing Indian army lorries and we have to fight our way through two huge construction sites where bridge pillars are being built on the slopes on both sides of the valley.

Giri explains that India is greatly expanding its military presence up here in the north near the border with China and also with its direct neighbour Nepal; the border is just one valley away. There is also a fear that China will overrun Nepal up here in order to have an easier target than in the high mountains. This is because Nepal is not really politically serious here, it is always flitting back and forth between India and China. 'Always straight to where they get something from,' *Giri* says laconically.

Unfortunately, we can't use the telescope at the actual excursion destination. The site has been dismantled because a viewing terrace and a hotel are being built there; another huge building site. *Giri* followed the roofs of the houses as coloured dots along a road and then showed us a red dot, below it another red one and next to it a blue house roof. This should be our house with that of the brother-in-law and the family who were involved in the trade fair event.

Afterwards, we stop for tea and a snack in the valley with one of *Manju*'s sisters. And as we drive on, we realise that I was here exactly 1 year ago to the day and had the idea of spending some time here.

I think, we're driving back now. But then it was told going to stop by a funeral; the father of one from our neighbourhood has passed away. But I'm not prepared for that. And it's also too personal for me, as I don't know the people directly. I'm also writing – that's one of the reasons I'm here – about my own experiences so close to death and about my deceased friends *Peter* and *Rainer*. I ask that I stay by the car. And they shouldn't ask me to come with them, I would explain later. This is accepted and I walk around for a good hour on this other and very lonely mountain.

Later, the young man from our village stands by the car for to say goodbye. I offer him my condolences and apologise to him for not being able to go to a funeral I don't know so easily; I hope he understood.

A different route back, we pass another large construction site for extension of the main road to the north. *Giri* explains: 'This road is not only important for military purposes, but also economically. It's the main transport route to Sikkim and then hundreds of km on to Assam.' Then it becomes military again, after all he is a retired soldier and at his age – he is 12 years younger to me – he is of course still part of the army in terms of status.

If China were to conquer this geographical bottleneck – narrowest point a little south of us between Nepal and Bangladesh is just 40 km as the crow flies – eight other Indian states such as Sikkim, Assam, Manipur with a combined population of around 280 million people would be cut off in addition to the northern part of West Bengal.

'But we are not that afraid of China,' he laughs, 'the *Gurkha* people have already experienced something completely different.' He also sees the jobs in road construction, for the barracks and in tourism. And all this despite the recurring border violations and exchanges of fire between India and China. 'And, very importantly he,' he laughs and points to *Prashant*, 'he would definitely save at least an hour's travel time to his college in neighbouring state Sikkim thanks to a new main road. And we, we will save even more time travelling further hundreds of km to our daughter in Assam.'

I am thinking of the current Russian invasion of Ukraine. How is an army supposed to take control of this huge, often steeply rugged territory, criss-crossing up and down over hundreds or thousands of sqkm, far-flung and remote villages and farms?

And that, when on the roads to villages here in the mountains, two cars cannot just usually pass each other? You can't overtake buses and lorries here anyway, except on the main road. You should know that dis-placement, flight, migration etc. have a centuries-old tradition among these mountain peoples and that they will not be impressed by new occupiers? Or do you want to end up with unmanaged mountain farms?

Indian funeral

In my time, *Manju* and *Giri* often had to attend a funeral together or alone. Families here in the mountains are very large networks. But the humour here is sometimes borderline even for me. At breakfast, when we briefly discuss the day, we realise that weddings only happen once, but funerals happen twice a few decades later. 'But that would be *Prashant's* job at some point,' laughs *Giri* sarcastically; I realise that he sometimes finds the many invitations to weddings and funerals annoying.

He explains me the funeral process. Because Hinduism is a very complex, interdependent the caste and religious system, funeral and mourning rituals are also different. What they all have in common are personal funeral services, spiritual mantras as prayers and chants by relatives and the priest (usually from the neighbourhood or family) and the laying out of the deceased in the home. In tradition, the eldest son shaves the head, washes, dresses and decorates the deceased.

New to me, there is no outward display of grief, which is reserved for immediate family members in the house. The cremation is only carried out by men from more distant relatives or neighbours; it takes place on the same day or the day after. There is often a public place near a river, cleaned, decorated and blessed beforehand by relatives or neighbours. The ashes are then returned to nature on one of the following days. Traditionally, mourning lasts for 13 days, during which time the family members wear white clothing and have virtually no further social contact; they are not allowed to go to a wedding or other celebration, for example.

However, funerals, like weddings, are also meetings of the cooperative, village gatherings, religious festivals, regardless of the occasion, as well as social gatherings. You meet people you often never or only rarely see and talk about everything and everyone. If you're close relative, you attend funeral service for several days. Distant relatives and neighbours attend for half a day, for example.

'In the end,' *Giri* laughs, 'financially it is the same, you spend more on weddings than on funerals.' When you see the immense effort involved in decorating and cremating, monks for the prayers and the funeral chants, a funeral feast lasting many days, cooking and catering for all the visitors, shopping and employing day labourers, because hundreds of close and distant relatives come along, just like at weddings. Often a large bamboo roof shelter is erected on the property or in the neighbourhood for eating, providing shade, etc.; the relatives need a considerable amount of money to pay for all this. A guideline for visitors is to give at least the same amount for the food as you would in a restaurant plus a personal gift according to your financial means.

I remember mourning ceremonies at home, where people traditionally get together after the funeral at the home of the deceased or at a nearby pub to enjoy coffee and cake and later sandwiches and alcoholic drinks. While in Hinduism, the food here is purely vegetarian and alcohol-free.

Diwali, the festival

In the afternoon before *Diwali*, the highest traditional festival lasting several days, *Manju* takes me to her sister-in-law's house next door. *Giri*'s brother had already fired up the old clay oven in an equally old shed next to the stable behind his house.

Manju sits down on a footstool and pushes a large long piece of wood on the floor further into the open fire hole. On the clay oven stands a cast-iron cauldron with hot oil. And for the dough, her sister-in-law had previously ground rice with the old stone mill on the floor next the oven and prepared it with a little soda, water and sugar. *Manju*'s now will fry the huge dough as *Sel Roti;* traditionally the first one goes into the fire for creation. The sister-in-law brings spicy *Ciyâ* for all of us, and we taste the first freshly baked *Sel Rotis*. It tastes delicious, especially in the quasi-archaic ambience, in keeping with tradition. In the end, it is a huge tray full of *Sel Rotis* that will be later distributed in the village community for poorer people and children.

In the evening, I am invited under our kitchen house into the half-open stable. *Manju* is now sitting at our clay oven, which *Giri* uses twice a day to cook the concentrated feed for the animals – and makes again *Sel Roti* for us for the festive days now. Next to us, the goats, always eager for a treat, and the cow and calf moo behind the wooden wall, because they realise that something is happening next door.

We sit in the stable and eat a spicy vegetable soup with the *Sel Roti*. What a view into the night with the lights of the houses on the mountain opposite and the starry sky. For my sake, *Manju* has also made some dough without sugar and lightly salted it. They tasted good to everyone, including some who came around later ... or are they just being kind to me? In any case, they were the first time everyone had had them without sugar. Let's see what the rest of the neighbourhood has to say. After I had already attracted attention with my unconventional *Momo* design, now this; will they chase me out of the village?

Diwali, the 5-day festival of lights and the highest festival for Hindus, is two weeks after the October full moon. Outwardly, it resembles our holy night with religious rituals in front of small, colourfully decorated altars on streets or at house entrances, decorated with candle-like, countless small clay bowls with mustard oil a burning wick, accompanied by visits from close relatives, mutual gifts and festive meals.

And above all with light, with lots and lots of light. Of course, artificial garlands and LED lights have also found their way into the festivities; in our case, an LED rain curtain around half the house. The joy of colour defines the festival of light and we keep up with the times in terms of technology.

In the days leading up to the festival, the house is repaired, painted and decorated with wreaths and garlands of flowers that have been put up over many hours, as well as colourful ornaments scattered around the entrance. All this for the various manifestations of the divine in Hinduism, including nature. Ritual plates of offerings are set up for this purpose and important animals such as dogs or cows are also painted a *Tika* and given something extra tasty to eat.

As the sun rises in the early day, still half asleep I can hear the long, low, half-high notes of horns singing somewhere in the mountain; just as you would imagine from here. Everyone celebrates in their own way, the majority of people here have a Nepalese Hinduism background, but the Buddhists, the Christians or Muslims and others also celebrate; just as they all celebrate Christmas Day here, for example, right up to the Christmas tree.

For example, a Christian can be a Hindu at the same time. Here, creation only manifests itself in different forms, whether human, animal or in mixed forms; first and foremost, it means respect for nature and the life of humans, animals and plants in this purely agricultural region.

What counts here in the mountains is the community, and not individual demarcation; everyone chooses the form of spirituality for themselves. But the outward appearance is of course same as here, alongside religious-spiritual ceremonies, decorations, gifts, visits and dancing. I am literally asked to photograph the celebrants during their prayer chants or other rituals.

However, they find it absolutely incomprehensible, for example, when passing tourists take ritual Hindu artefacts or Buddhist prayer flags from the roadside as souvenirs.

The small, colourful and often printed garland-like prayer or pole flags at monasteries or public prayer places, for example, have their origins in the Tibetan Buddhism. They are widespread throughout the whole Himalayas region. Place, occasion and order of the colours have different meanings. Their main characteristic is that the wind carries the prayers. This makes them popular souvenirs for tourists. What will they say? Am they pretending to be Buddhists or have stolen something personal and religious from someone? I imagine someone with a very dark skin would take intercessions or something else for example as a souvenir from our cemeteries, or from a wayside cross or a church.

The first festive highlight is in the evening, starting in the dark. I am taken into the stable for the ritual for the animals. *Manju* brings from upstairs a decorated tray made of bamboo fibres with rice, flowers, bananas for the animals, a few rupee coins, some small bowls with mixed colours and in-cense. After this ritual thanksgiving, *Giri* and I dab cow and calf with flowers dipped in colour, while *Manju* waves the incense sticks in a ritual Sanskrit chant. The cow is then given a string of flowers and a banana as a treat. Interestingly, the calf, the goats don't get anything, although they look curiously at what's going on around them. My question receives the simple answer that they are not giving milk either. I decide to give them treats the next day too.

Later, the festively and traditionally dressed women from the singing group meet with us on the reception terrace. They sing to house-lord *Giri* under the motto, 'good luck and blessings on your house, your family and you, it's all in your hands.' And of course he had already prepared this and at the end he ritually presented them with a large tray of flower blossoms, burning oil lamps, rice and banknotes.

The women then move on from house to house, repeating this ritual over and over again. We men stand outside making small talk and listen to their direct neighbours. Later, as I fall asleep, I can still hear their songs from houses further away; *Manju* tells next day, she was back home at 2 o'clock in the night.

Next day, the neighbourhood singing and dancing group and others meet up and we drive in overcrowded cars and scooters, some walk cross-country, to a house a little lower down the mountain. Other neighbours, near and far, are already there. There is traditional singing and dancing.

At the end, the eldest family member sits on a chair with a beautifully decorated tray, surrounded by visitors dancing with music and singing. Someone from each household briefly joins the circle and places a small envelope on the tray. At the end, the donations are counted and the total is announced to applause. The current donation target is the completion of the village community centre. Beside there is *Ciyâ & Sel Roti* served. By late afternoon, we visit three houses, each with well over 100 visitors.

At the second event, I was seated next to a British woman with whom I chatted in-between. Visiting from Australia, she has been supporting a school here for many years. Young women in front of us – they had previously performed a traditional dance – giggle and keep looking at us. I slowly realise that we are supposed to dance too; completely unprepared in front of more than 100 spectators. But it's also clear that we can't get out of this number now. As I stand up and point ironically at the dancers in front of us, their laughter breaks the ice. We dance somewhat awkwardly to traditional rhythmic Nepalese music and the spectators clap along happily and take endless photos. Luckily few small children come running up to us and we include them in our dance to the laughter of the audience.

Afterwards we are given a typical scarf of honor and I, as a man, am given the *Dhaka Topi,* the cap of the *Gurkha* men. Whether the visitors – at least my awkward movements – clapped along out of politeness or joy, I'll leave it at that. Later I hear that someone has circulated a video on social media ... please don't let it reach Germany, I think.

As soon as we arrived home at the beginning of dusk, *Giri* told us that we had to go to the neighbours' house an hour later, as the grandfather there had invited us. I get on particularly well with him in mind and with body language.

Of course, it's another party with lots of people from the neighbourhood. Again there is singing and dancing and sweet *Sel Roti & Ciyâ* passed around. First the daughter performs a modern Nepalese dance with a friend, then a neighbour and his young sons perform their own creation.

Suddenly the music stops and the first lights are switched off. In a house in a walking distance nearby, a very close relative of the family has just passed away. Tradition dictates that all celebrations, including decorations, should be can-celled immediately for a set period of time. So, I experience the whole cultural spectrum here and empathise with the family.

Visit the sister

On last day of *Diwali*, the brother visits the married sister – following their tradition she lives in the husband's family – with a gift for her. So basically, brothers all over India are travelling to visit their sister on this day.

Son *Prashant* had already travelled the hundreds of km on to his married sister in Assam the day before. He stays there for a few days, travelling there and back overnight for a day and a half.

Right after breakfast, *Giri* dresses up, he and his brother are going to visit their sisters. And his sister-in-law's brother has even travelled overnight by bus from Nepal to visit them. *Manju* has also dressed up in the traditional way and happily packs up the flower necklaces she put on early in the morning. This year, everyone is meeting at a sister's house in the valley, where the brothers will then come. One brother will take us by car around 10:30 a.m.; he lives a little higher up here on the mountain. That's the plan, but of course that's Indian Time; in the end it will be around noon.

On our way, as usual, a mountain slope has slipped a little further on and trees are lying across the small road. People help each other and clear a gap so that they can pass with even a cm-precision. It takes time for an excavator to get up here, and I haven't seen any tractors here yet; it doesn't make sense to use them for farming on the slopes.

The ceremony is another experience for me; of course I'm involved again. I now realise that the terms children, siblings etc. are relative; as a housemate, I am of course part of their extended family. So I also receive the traditional flower necklace and the ritual tray with rice and spices, coloured bowls, flowers and snacks, and the women paint a large *Tika* on the fore-heads of their brothers and me. Here, too, I get on with the 84-year-old grandfather sitting on a bench outside the door straight away; our gestures are completely sufficient. And I learn that nieces and nephews are regarded and protected just like my own children.

In this mountain region, almost all families have only two or maximum three children; this is for one reason due to poverty in history. Today, the birth rates throughout India have fallen sharply in recent years and population growth is levelling off. One of the reasons for this is also that there is no housing for larger families in cities. The now steadily improving and stable income situation also automatically effects on lower birth rates; a worldwide phenomenon.

The current population increase in India is due to the large number of young women now being born as a result of the many girls born in the past, despite the current increase of births.

When we return in the late afternoon, *Manju*'s niece and nephew stay with us over night. They immediately discover the garden gnome and the niece quickly makes a little flower necklace for him for *Diwali*, as the big festival ends tomorrow.

A day in December ... coffee, hairdresser and banana knowledge

The day could also be in November or January. At night, it's quite cold here at 13–16°C. Early in the morning I go down to the kitchen to get some fresh milk for my early morning coffee. *Giri* has already finished feeding all the animals and milking the cow, *Manju* has potted plants.

I ask if they would also like a coffee. *Manju* immediately nods in agreement, *Giri* agrees somewhat more cautiously and sceptically. I have made the coffee for the three of us the same way I did for myself; two tea-spoons of milk and no sugar.

After tasting it for the first time, *Giri* says, interesting, but have you forgotten the sugar? It had to be four teaspoons for him, as usual with tea, and then he took another one after the next sip. Friendly, but still sceptical, he can't imagine that this is the main drink for a whole nation? There's nothing like hot and sweet *Ciyâ* or black tea with pepper.

Manju sweetens her coffee too, of course, she also wants to learn more about coffee. Her daughter and son-in-law in Assam would also drink coffee more often, but of course with lots of sugar, which is stirred into the hot milk first; sounds like a *Coffee latte* to me. She knows, young people in the cities today drink more coffee. And in Kalimpong there are more and more coffee machines as well as tea. I once tried this pre-sweetened brew, but I no longer need to have it. However, sweet and flavoured coffee variations in junk food cafés a la *Starbucks* and *McCafé* are also common here. I agree with *Giri*, they're not my cup either.

Below us, the cow has been mooing unusually often for the last two days. The season of daily fresh green is over and she is now gradually being acclimatised to the straw left over from the rice harvest as supplementary feed, which of course she doesn't like. 'Now her diet begins,' laughs *Giri*, 'she will give less milk. 'And,' I add, '... probably, then it is diet milk,' which *Manju* supplements in turn, 'so then we have low-fat ghee, which is supposed to be healthier.'

After a good breakfast, the sun is slowly fighting its way through the usual morning mist on my makeshift desk, it's getting again impressive. I look out over the garden and the fields below, where a contractor is ploughing under the remaining rice stumps with a motorised hand plough. The monotonous noise, which will no doubt continue all day long due to the terraced fields still to be worked, even by our immediate neighbours, has a calming effect.

I don't know what's going on in the world, what's happening with the war between Israel and Palestine or Russia and Ukraine, but at the moment I don't care. I keep realising how my secluded time here helps me. And I also achieve what I set out to do; I happily enjoy the warming rays of sunshine through the open window in front of me.

The hairdresser has been ordered for this morning, a relative, a house call; who is not a relative here? He is unusually punctual by Indian standards, and by my standards too.

Giri is up first and sits on a plastic chair that is brought outside from the kitchen. Next to her on a plastic stool is the hairdresser's cutlery, and it goes quickly. I'm already unsure that the communication won't work and that I'll end up with the currently regionally fashionable cut.

'I'm from a different culture,' I say. 'No problem, sir, no problem,' he replies and the scissor flit on and around my head. Everyone is having fun, a neighbour joins in and *Prashant* laughingly takes photos. After a while, the hairdresser hands me a pocket mirror. Wow, better than at home, I think. When I want to give him the 100 Rupees (1.10 Euro, 50 Rupees for haircut, 50 for driving up here), he laughs, 'no, no, sir, it was a pleasure for me, you don`t have to pay.' But I insisted, he accepted only the 50 Rupees. *Giri* al-ready had paid the fare.

Then it's *Prashant*'s turn and *Giri* pays another 50 Rupees for his son. But the hairdresser quickly gives it to *Prashant* for the internship in Kolkata that he is travelling to tomorrow, 'the tea there is not only worse, but is also more expensive,' he laughs.

Afterwards, we sit together with a *Ciyâ* and he and a neighbour, who know each other, want to know everything about the EU. Both collect coins from other countries. Thank God, I still have 50-Eurocent coins. The hairdresser laughs, you see, now I have in total 100 Rupees.

Later, *Prashant* shows me that the hairdresser is using me as an advert and I see myself on his *Instagram* sitting in the chair getting my hair cut; titled, my first German customer and friend.

Afterwards I watch *Manju* prepare banana blossom vegetables. The outer, already unfolded, beautiful purple-oval leaves, the size is bigger than an adult hand, are removed first. 'The cows will get them,' says *Manju*.

I immediately think of the Slow Food hype in my country. It could be a slow spiritual rumination of rice, tofu & co. fried in ghee and served in these large bowl-like leaves. All organic, of course, with equally spiritual sounds from their banana blossom home culture ... topped with a mystic Certified Quality label of course, including hand-sown under a full moon, etc.

She opens the inner leaves, removes the many thin stalks, which look like thin matchsticks, from around the inside of the flower and everything goes into a pot with the inner flower cut into pieces. Then it is seasoned and cooked, spicy in this case, of course. Alternatively, it can also be steamed in mustard oil, for example, she explains, which then gives it its own flavour. When cooled and mixed with fresh onion, it makes a cold side dish with *Roti* and rice or as a lunchtime snack with *Papal* crackers.

Meanwhile, in the garden, *Giri* cuts large leaves from banana palms, some of which are bigger than me. A favourite food for our animals. Later on, it looks funny at the top of a banana palm, as the large blossom slowly grows downwards due to its weight. The bush with finger-sized bananas develops out of her; slow banana multiple birth, so to speak. And after two to three months there are easily up to a hundred bananas. The flower continues to grow downwards, hanging from a tube-like stem, and can then be cut off. The bush automatically grows larger as the bananas ripen and can be harvested when growth stops; the bananas that are still green continue to ripen in dark storage. This is also advisable because of the monkeys, which are known to be addicted to banana drugs.

I also now know that not all banana varieties are edible for us. Unfortunately, not even the ones on the just ripe bush that I can see from my desk. The next edible ones for us, and from which my *Story of Mini-Monkey* emerges (see chapter *Goodbye, and see you again*), are unfortunately not ripe for another three months or so.

Later, the brother-in-law fertilises his banana palms naturally – nature can be quite difficult to accept from a human-ecological point of view – with fire. He cuts off withered and dried palm leaves and sets them alight at the foot of the banana palms together with other dry residues from the garden. Initially, a large cloud of smoke is created, which envelops large parts of the garden and is very slow to dissipate. At the end, the ashes, which are still smoking, are mixed with water into the soil as fertiliser.

I can think of bushfires as a fertilisation form in other parts of the world. Or certain tree species in Australia or North America, for example, which ensure their survival as a species in this way. When they burn down, they release their fireproof cones, which only burst open after the heat wave of the fire and their seeds are spread in the ashes in the surrounding area. After the next rain, the seeds take root in the ground and grow into a new tree.

You can also recognise whether banana plants look the same to us by their palm leaves, and whether they are only edible for animals; so to me, they all still look the same here in the garden.

Indian wedding

We're going to a wedding. I'd rather avoid it, because crowds and celebrations haven't been my thing for a long time. Especially not seeing and being seen. But I've been specifically invited.

I know, an Indian wedding is very different to ours. And I have literally seen entire wedding tent cities in Delhi or Kolkata; completely organised by agencies. It's a real business and up to 2,000 guests or even more there are completely normal; at least a few hundred in a poor village, I will find out. Many families go into debt for years for such a big multi-day festival. But, it should not be judged by our standards. In my country too, people go into debt for holidays, cars, house building etc., which in turn meets with a lack of understanding in India.

It is different here in the mountains, but no less elaborate and colourful. According to *Manju*, around 600 guests have been invited. We will also meet neighbours who have travelled there a day earlier and are staying overnight because they are closer relatives. We will be back home the same evening. The outward journey will take more than two hours, the return journey in the dark will be a little quicker because you can get through small villages or rough places more quickly without traffic jams.

Right after breakfast, we set off; *Manju*, me and the neighbour's daughter – it's the first Indian wedding for her too. She's been living with her grandmother in Nepal for many years – and *Prashant*, he's driving. *Giri* laughs, or would you like to milk the cow here, muck out the barn, cut the green twice ... and he pats me on my shoulder. Weddings aren't his thing either. He sees it as an unloved chore and is happy for any reason to stay at home.

Manju is of course dressed traditionally. On the way, we stop for tea and small talk with her mother, who according to tradition lives in the house of the eldest son, *Manju*'s brother. Then, a little further on, we met for a small talk her youngest sister, who teaches at a higher secondary school; comparable to our school system up to year 12. The rest of the journey is all up and down winding roads, of course with fabulous views.

The wedding is in a small, somewhat remote and rather poor-looking village. It lies in the middle of the tea gardens of well-known western brand companies, where many people have only work to cover basic needs. But a wedding is unique, and it is celebrated with all the ceremonies that go with it; and I get a different concept of a small wedding.

There are several tents in two houses with different functions. After being greeted by a festively decorated entrance portal – where in front or behind is a decorated wall to be photographed – you are led to the reception area with refreshments and snacks. You can already hear and see other stations. For example, a 5-men music band with traditional costumes and instruments plays. There is a 'veg' food tent and one 'non-veg,' one for tea and the main tent for the pompous ceremony. Of course, everything is very colourful and the women in particular are dressed up. But it is also an event for visitors to get to know each other. In the widely dispersed village communities here in the mountains, young people often only see each other at school or such celebrations. Married or widowed women can be recognised by their forehead painting. Following their tradition, the ceremony is held at the bride's parents' home and paid for by them and their relatives. It is the daughter's final farewell from her parents' home; according to tradition, she moves into her in-laws' house.

Of course, I ask myself should it be so expensive and elaborate. But there's no point in scrutinising cultures, otherwise you quickly find yourself in need of an explanation. We also have dowries, balls for unmarried so-called Blue-blooded Nobles, Rotary Club members and the like. I remember, in a town in Northern Germany I used to live, a

200-year-old Club For The Good End for dignified citizens; it really exists, but I won't reveal the town. They were all nice people who invited me to become a member. But I thought my children were too young at the time and that it wasn't my place to make decisions for them like joining such a sheltered social class.

Tea garden

At another wedding, two hours by car to the village where I've spent some hours at a cooperative last year, everything is of course decorated magnificently and traditionally again. It's in a small village inside a tea garden.

The tea garden manager, to whom I am immediately introduced – at first I think he is part of the family, later it becomes clear that he is the boss of all the residents here – showed me around as 'his' German guest. It is of course interesting for me to be able to look behind the scenes of a wedding. For example the mobile kitchens working in the background, the music technology and the (naturally closed) women's room for dressing and decorating the bride. He also explains to me that the decoration, and including the marquee, inventory, music and cooking team, is ordered from a wedding agency by catalogue. I spontaneously realise that this has become a booming market in our country in recent years as well; even nowadays a kid's birthday party has become a management-like event project.

It is up to the bride parents to decide whether to contribute something special with friends and neighbours; here a miniature pagoda-like temple made of bamboo in the large main tent. This is where the bride and groom sit and receive blessings, say prayers, etc.

In large cities, weddings with several thousand guests need to be booked one to two years in advance for suitable venues - there are, for example, complete wedding venues the size of a football field. Now, I understand what it means when a wedding is cancelled for whatever reason.

This also reminds me of today's tradition in our country, where wedding tables with wish lists of the bride and groom are set up in a so-called Brand Shopping Centre, and everyone can finance something from crockery to household appliances etc.

Giri, son *Prashant* and two other neighbours, distant relatives of the wedding family, are happy as we head back after lunch and the bride's subsequent ritual of unveiling herself in public outside the main tent. It's all a bit much at this cooler time of year for them with weddings, but you have to be seen to be believed. Each visiting household adds an amount, noted and monitored by a member of each family; after all, it's a huge amount of money for individuals to secure; and not forgetting their farm duty.

The tea garden manager had taken me under his wings. Right after the wedding tour he showed me around 'his' village, introducing me as 'his' guest from Germany. I get introduced, that he oversees more than only this tea garden; there are several tea gardens, on the plain here in the valley and additional further up on the mountain slopes.

Many of the men work in the city or abroad for a better life. However, some also work here in areas such as planting or tending crops, pest control and fertilisation, a small fact-Cory for mechanical tea sorting or in logistics.

The women here and seasonal workers are almost tea pickers. In addition to the three annual picking seasons – First Flush in spring with the traditional pick of 'two-leaves-and-a-bud' (top quality), then Second Flush in summer and later the Autumn Flush – they work in the garden maintenance and deal with pruning, weeding, cleaning irrigation ditches and more.

For the prescribed 18 kg a day, they pick for around six hours early in the morning until late in the afternoon for 2 Euro a day; and 1 kg above adds 10–20 Rupees (22 Eurocents) for them depending on the quality.

The small houses with an allotment and shelter for a cow or goat belong to the tea company, which makes them available to the working families permanent or seasonal.

Although I would prefer to have a conversation about the colonial era and its wage slavery, I will comment on it here as a modern corporate concept for employee retention. Any other comment would probably be an irreparable insult on this day and wedding occasion. But, also we still have concepts like this. In business personnel management we call it Retention Management, which ranges from contractual penalties and employee loans to so-called Feelgood Concepts such as 'we are a big family'. Or Outsourcing, when we think of completely underpaid lorry drivers from eastern Europe who drive goods for all well-known western companies.

The Indian company here is a subsidiary, which in turn belongs to one of the global leading western multi-national beverage company. Tea gardens are also often sublet, for example to the local village community.

He then proudly showed me his available house with a modern off-road SUV, which is certainly necessary in the area with mostly agricultural roads and in the mountains.

What is also new for me is that they also grow Assam tea varieties in the Darjeeling region; Assam tea is therefore not automatically linked to Assam, the federal state, where tea is also grown in even larger quantities.

On the way back, *Prashant* and I manage to take a photo of a warning sign that we had seen as we drove past on the way there. This time we are prepared: After whisky, Driving Risky.

My Chemo Life Cycle

Chemotherapy side effects and Aplasia phase

Even terms like Chemotherapy, Side Effects, Aplasia Phase ... unsettle me, I'm no longer as confident as I think or show on the outside. It's like a dark cave, you do not know what to expect inside. Of course I read brochures and also *googled* a lot.

For me, I notice <u>side effects</u> during or after the chemotherapy cycle.

- In the weeks leading up to my second chemotherapy cycle, my sense of flavour gradually drops off. Everything is bland, no matter what shape, consistency or colour it is. However, I suddenly feel sweet more strongly, but not sour, salty or otherwise flavoured. So I start drinking ice-cold sparkling *Fanta* and eating *Nutella* for breakfast and often also in-between; who would have thought it? And I have a bag of chocolate bars and *Kinderschokolade* brought to me. Later, at breakfast, I take at an extra roll for my afternoon *Nutella*-pastry.

- I'm shivering in this decade's hottest summer. The sun is beating down on the large window front; the air extraction system for the hermetically sealing the room and the air conditioning are reaching their limits. I have to put on more and more clothes, including a thermal jacket and bath-robe, have a second duvet and a blanket brought in and still shiver.

- Rashes and pimples all over my body, endless itching. I should not scratch under any circumstances, but, I often rub my back unconsciously on the mattress, it must stop somehow; pain is easier to bear, and I yearn for a scratchy brush. It doesn't matter, the main thing is that it stops itching.

- My hands are shaking, my fingertips are tingling; I can no longer control it. I hold the cup with both hands so as not to spill anything because my fingers can't feel it. I can only hold the knife and fork with my fist; and ... I realise this with full awareness.

- The stomach rebels, it resists the unfamiliar chemo toxins. I can't talk him out of it. With this constant gagging feeling, I would prefer to sit in the bathroom unobserved. I have piles of strange but sensibly shaped card-board bowls and paper towels by the bed.

- I feel bloated and am afraid of the pain when I have a bowel movement. I often sit on the WC for a long time, my room calls how I'm doing? Once, he presses the emergency button, I don't answer immediately because of the pain. Or *Emil* crashes loudly to the floor because I'm trying to hold on; thank God nothing happened to the neck infusion port. Every bowel movement is an endless ordeal; it would be more sensible to wear adult nappies, but that's too much for me.

When I think about, I'm, as we say, caught between a rock and a hard place. On the one hand, I'm glad that something in my body is now going into battle against the cancer cells. On the other hand, it is often unbearable. I disregard the warning not to scratch and work on my back with a rough towel. So, that the pimples tear open and bleed, and I use the disinfectant atomiser as a shower; it burns wonderfully.

Of course, this doesn't go unnoticed because the sheets are covered in blood afterwards. I am literally told off by the head nurse and then again by a doctor; they are right, but ...

The worst thing of all is the loss of control, which I experienced physically and mentally for the first time in the intensive care unit. This powerlessness instead of self-determination It won't let go of me, even without the infusion tube on the port of the neck vein. This port alone, which I can't see and I know I won't be able to remove – which is a good thing, I'll reassure myself later – and the knowledge of having to take all the medication and never knowing whether new unfinished leukaemia cells aren't forming as blasts in the bone marrow again? After all, the regular blood tests only tell me my condition until the blood sample is taken ... I don't know what has happened since then.

And sleepless nights without end. Some of the night staff allow the door to be left open so that the air can supposedly circulate a little; the ward is also connected to the suction system. And there is always a beeping from a room somewhere and you can hear the hurried footsteps of the night shift. Will he or she survive? Who could it be? Is it someone you once saw in the corridor and talked to? Or will a bed be quietly pushed out in the night to the lift at the bottom; the lift with also the bone marrow transplant door. This possible last stop for us? I don't know whether I'm thinking or dreaming.

The chemotherapy destroys the blasts as cancer cells in the blood and bone marrow. It is now important that no new blasts form in the bone marrow. The body's own immune system is completely destroyed and it takes time for it to rebuild itself. In this aplasia phase; every little cold or infection can be fatal. My progress is monitored daily, I am virtually isolated, feel correspondingly weak, am constantly tired and the side effects are a rollercoaster.

I'm not supposed to leave the room and I have to disinfect my hands before and after touching anything. How long can my skin actually with-stand this constant disinfecting? Above all, I'm not allowed to touch my mouth, which is the main gateway for possible infections.

It can quite take a while, sometimes my immune system builds up in a good week, another time it takes three weeks. Then, I get additional blood transfusions as well as leucocytes, the white blood cells. Intra-venously, it looks like a bag of orange juice hanging from *Emil*. It gives him a colour effect, I remark to him; like me, he's usually so monotonously dressed. But *Emil,* he remains calm and lets it drip stoically. Nothing can upset you either, isn't it, I remark again. Are my conversations with him another side effect of the leukaemia?

But I also realise how quickly the side effects of the chemo cycle are wearing off and how I am slowly recovering physically and mentally from the permanent tiredness and lethargy. So I wait every day for the doctors' ward routine, how far along are the crucial values? It's always a new disappointment, of course, because they can't decide. After all, my body sets the pace. It also happens that values deteriorate again from time to time, and then I need additional infusions.

But then, completely unexpectedly you are told, 'you can leave home for a few days now.' After the second chemotherapy cycle it was three days; in reality, it's two days from noon to noon, so only one full day at home. On the first day it took until noon to get all the paper-work etc. ready, and on the third day you just pack your things and wait, you can't do anything else than in the hospital anyway. First instruction: 'Behave as you would in hospital. You will be given your medication right away with a plan, and be careful with the sun. It is better to stay in the shade, as the skin on your face and scalp is particu-larly at risk during cancer treatment. It is best to always wear a hat or a baseball cap.' When I ask what I can and can't eat, the professor replies: 'Eat what you like, you should be fine.' Behind him stands the senior doctor, who freezes at the statement and then gestures to me behind the professor's back with a lecturing index finger, No, No, No!

First home leave

Of course, later I also get again instructions from the head nurse on how to behave. A lot of it, like not picking anything up off the floor, I already know from my first chemotherapy cycle. And the thing about plants, I learned from my former roommate's bone marrow transplant information: 'Best, to remove all plants from the home beforehand, potting soil is a kind of infection temple, how else are the plants supposed to get natural nutrients? And never put a finger on your lips or in your mouth, but you know that. So don't eat anything uncooked, certainly not lettuce, always wash and peel fruit thoroughly. There are dangerous germs in the smallest corners of the skin or on the stem.'

'Okey,' I remark, 'I would always peel bananas anyway, if at all, they're not my thing anyway, I prefer apples.' She ignores my flat joke and says, 'just buy apple sauce in a jar.' And, as she always sanitises her hands, so she gives me one of the sanitiser bottles from our cupboard. How does she know that we store certain things here?

Then I get my Medical Orchestra, the pill dispenser with these many notes – on an empty stomach one hour before breakfast, for and after breakfast etc. – and medicines to gargle if necessary; it feels like half a pharmacy.

And, and, and ... by the time all the paperwork is done and it's lunch time again, I can leave.

I ask the taxi to stop one house away that I can enter my home out of sight behind the neighbour's hedge. I am so pale and emaciated and have a typical chemotherapy baldness that I am embarrassed, I don't want to be talked to.

Now, I don't even know what to do at home. Nobody's there, the children live and work far away; I smiled, they don't even know I've got a short holiday. At first I sit around a bit indecisive. But then my activism starts. First two machines of laundry, in-between sorting dry laundry from before I was ad-mitted to hospital and folding things for the next hospital phase. I don't feel like working like I did in the hospital. Unconsciously, to distract myself, I think later as I lie down on the sofa, relatively exhausted, to rest.

It's suddenly boring, no nursing staff, doctors etc., and above all no food. My daughter had emptied the fridge and switched it off to defrost it. Well, after years, it had to be done. As I'm not allowed to eat anything fresh any-way, I end up with tinned spaghetti, tomatoes and tuna; it's like being at university, three tins can be a diner. But despite a lot of spices and garlic, it doesn't taste good at home either.

I do the test, spice by spice, half a teaspoon or the tip of a knife. I taste nothing but sugar, I knew that beforehand. I'm thirsty now and my face is burning up, as I see in the mirror ... and above all my chemotherapy bald head, like a lighthouse. Chemo and chilli, that works, I tell myself and grin agonised in the mirror; a rather stupid self-experiment. My scalp is definitely well supplied with blood; an interesting change from her hair loss.

I keep waking up at night after short, confused dreams and sweating slightly. It's probably the spices, I reassure myself.

The coffee in the morning tastes strange, but still better than a hospital's brown hot water; the change alone is a deep exciting experience. Now I'm sitting around again, undecided. I go down to the cellar. I wonder if the washing is dry yet. Then I check my almost newly packed trolley; what nonsensical activities? I start to have my first doubts. What is happening in my body now? As long as chemo is dripping into me, nothing can happen. But now, what if cancer blasts form in the bone marrow again right now? And I've also been sweating at night, haven't I?

When I see dust on a box in the storeroom and want to get a cloth to wipe it away, I realise that I'm about to tidy it up. It felt like I hadn't done that for 10 years. Another rather stupid and dangerous activity.

So, I sit outside on the sheltered and covered terrace. But it's far too hot this summer, even in the shade. And I don't want anyone to see me. I don't want any curious looks, I don't want to hear any pity and I don't want to answer any questions.

In the hospital, it's the other way around if you still have hair on your head. I still recognise these chemotherapy heads long after my time in the hospital. Even if someone is wearing a baseball cap, or for women, no matter how fashionable it is.

There are piles of brochures for such headgear, including wigs, in the hospital. It feels like 90% of the offers are for women; like shoe shops, we men on the ward make a joke about it. But we also admit to each other that it's important for our self-esteem and that we men prefer to hide, like me.

Yes, I do wear a baseball cap from time to time when I have to go to the *ATM* to pay bills. I do this late at night or on the taxi journey back to the hospital, where nobody knows me; *sic.*

I have to be back at the hospital before noon the next day. So these three days were actually only two days by hours, or just one whole full day in-between.

Strangely enough, I'm happy to be able to return to the hospital. In the taxi, I remember the *Story of the Polar Bear* I once heard in a team training seminar:

The new, young director takes an annual tour of an ageing zoo with the organisation's board of directors. They look for necessary changes and also look for new ideas. They all notice the polar bear's old and cramped enclosure, which is actually just a large cage with a few steps up and down and a large water hole. The big, strong polar bear in his prime walked along the wall at one end of his cage, turned around and went back again, and again and again. And at every turn, he let out his terrifyingly beautiful polar bear roll. It was quickly decided to have a larger, species-appropriate outdoor enclosure built, with indoor and outdoor areas, rocks for climbing and sunbathing, and a large pool with a waterfall, etc. Finally, after a slightly delayed construction period, the big opening day arrived. Many visitors from near and far, the city leaders, representatives of the political parties, the media, even regional TV. They all waited for the opening of the gate into the now greater freedom for the polar bear. Hours earlier, the polar bear had been given an anaesthetic injection. A camera was installed in his old cage, which also transmitted the images to a huge screen outside, so large was the crowd at this joyous event for everyone. The polar bear woke up from his stupor and, after stretching and stretching and taking a few uncertain first clumsy steps, he walked the few meters up and down his old path again. He ignored the large open fence into the enclosure. And every time he turned round, his terrifyingly beautiful growl rang out.

Caught

After three months, I'm physically reasonably stabilised. The chemotherapy is looking relatively promising. I'm allowed to leave the ward before the next chemotherapy cycle with the aplasia phase, protected by a face mask, with or without *Emil*, depending on how I feel on the day.

Once I'm outside in front of the building. No Smoking signs everywhere, especially on a long bench under the fresh air intake system, but people still smoke there; and not only patients and visitors.

Whenever possible, I like to go to a hospital café on Thursdays to get a newspaper and a chocolate croissant. I then take the elevator down two floors, turn left over a floor bridge into the ENT building next door and take the elevator down another floor. I walk about 30–40 m to the kiosk in the café. It's always an exciting little adventure for me. And probably also for patients from outside waiting for their treatment, or visitors, when they see me like the horror movie monster *Frankenstein* with tubes around his neck, coming in with an *Emil* infusion stand and a bald head.

Once, on the way back, I took the lift to the ward below us for stopover. There is also still water there. Of course, back at my ward I was caught in passing at our checkpoint. We are only supposed to drink carbonated water because of its anti-bacterial effect.

Later I remembered that my dear friend *Rainer* (who have passed away in the meantime) told me on one of our many hikes in the neighbouring German-Belgium *Eifel* highlands at a spring that the Romans had used the water from carbonated springs here as drinking water for this reason in addition to growing wine.

First the nurse and later the professor were of course right in explaining to me why I should only drink carbonated water during this time. But still, I feel like I'm getting sick of all the (also) medium carbonated water here, as well as peppermint tea, chamomile tea, fennel tea, herbal tea, fruit tea ..., 'grrr.'

Where is Mr Müller?

I'm too lazy to get up; a new infusion bag is now hanging high up on my faithful friend and helper *Emil*. I can only vaguely recognise the patient's name. A short name ... *M* is the first letter. But somehow there is a bump in the centre of the letters in the name; it doesn't feel like mine. I stay calm for the time being, because I will be checked repeatedly before the chemo broth flows into me. But then I realise that if a doctor checks it and is wrong, then someone on the ward is in big trouble. So I ask my roommate *Peter* if he can look up the name when he gets a chance. Of course he gets up immediately. '*Meier* or *Müller* doesn't really matter' (very common German names), he says ironically as he looks. But then he pushes the emergency button.

The infusion is quickly replaced. The doctor carrying out the final examination doesn't let on in any case. Someone may have been lucky, I think. But it wouldn't have been an emergency. I am asked for my name, date of birth, etc. before it is connected to the neck vein port and drips into me.

At the time, it was clear that *Mr Müller* was still on our ward. He is a quiet, introverted person and his wife visits him regularly. At some point we realised she is always there when the local NGO *Leukämie-Initiative* offers especially baked cake for us; her cake addiction cannot be hidden physically either. But after all, it's her husband who is ill, so it's okey for us. Sometimes we put a few pieces of cake on the side for patients who come later or have to stay in the room.

But then it's just her without her husband. His chemotherapy is not really working and he has been referred for a bone marrow transplant. This is of course a shock for us, as she tells us over cake.

Our lounge room, which is very important to us long-term patients, was initiated by a local initiative: Volunteers take care of the room, which has a wall of books and a regular coffee table with leukaemia-friendly cakes two times a week. Sometimes a psychotherapist is also present.

At first I don't fancy it when they invite me. But eventually I do go. Later, I'm happy every time I wake up in the morning and know that we're having coffee & cake today with some other together; only if I'm able to, of course.

There we sit, man and woman, young and old, private or cashier, with or without a bald head, regardless of nationality; a community of destiny.

It's always funny. During my time, a running gag develops, the infusion bag championship. Who has the most hanging on the infusion stand? Empty ones and those not actively dripping don't count; that was a really important discussion at the table. I won twice in my time, and once with a tie.

And there are other rules too, for example the two seats closest to the door are reserved for those with *Dr Lasix* infusions, for example, who need to go somewhere quickly. Although we are not allowed to use the visitors' WC next to the lifts, it is sometimes a lifesaver. The term *Dr Lasix* comes from an elderly fellow patient. He was a general medical doctor him-self before he retired. Alternately cheerful and communicative or more introverted and reserved, as we all are at times, he colours mandalas for hours on end. He does this for himself, but he also has them brought to bedridden fellow patients. At first I think, nice colourful pictures, but in the long run it's kind of boring. Only later do I find out that it's an overcoming stress technique.

Once, when I was physically and therefore mentally unwell and couldn't or didn't want to go to the patient café – they probably knew from *Peter* that I wasn't doing so well – the psychotherapist came and asked if he should sit with me. But I don't want to. Shortly afterwards, he brings me a piece of cake and a coffee to my bedside. On the way

out, he says: 'It's a good thing, you need to be on your own sometimes.' Then I saw a coloured mandala by the cake. It really touches
me and I eat the cake crying. Afterwards I feel a bit better again.

The *Leukämie-Initiative* has organised a TV for this summer's Football
World Cup. We let off the same jokes as in a corner pub, only somehow quieter and less emotional. I manage to watch a whole half-time
in a row three times, including two ice-cold *Fanta*; otherwise I go to
my room to rest in-between.

During the games, someone from the below ward regularly comes
by with his walking frame for two to three minutes. He wants to know
how the game is going. We call those from below The Organs. Ironically we hold our noses higher, because we on the upper fourth ward
are The Systems after all; and feel better because we (think we) have
more dangerous cancer; what a nonsense I learn later when I know
more about cancer. We call him *Bronco* – most of us elderly remember
as a typical name in US Wild West films in the 1960s - because he's
coughing all the time and his speech is slow, croaky and choppy. We
suspect bronchial tubes, lungs or both. And he smells, no, he smells
for miles against the wind, as we say, of tobacco, which he also carries
with him in various packets in his rollator. We later learn, he only sits
downstairs in the entrance area during the day and alternates between
inside and outside to smoke.

During my follow-up treatment, I initially see when entering our
hospital building in the lounge a white bed cushion in a corner sofa
and packets of tobacco on the side table. The lady at the building
reception, who of course knows me, says: 'He has now made himself
more comfortable,' and we both have to smile.

Unfortunately, our lounge room at the ward is also often used by visitors who bring heaps of things from outside that we are not supposed
to eat. For example, full fast food bags, or once even a bottle of wine
is opened in a bag under the table.

A ward trolley with coffee, tea and water for us is at the entrance
to the room. 'I'm going to get myself a coffee, shall I get you one too?'

An important sentence, you immediately feel a bit more at ease with such normal everyday gestures.

One time, I have to react, because I simply can't remain calm and understanding any longer. Two other patients are sitting in the room with me, one engrossed in a magazine, the other colouring a mandala. Without saying hello, three visitors loudly push a patient to a free table and immediately un-pack a huge tray of cakes. One of them leaves, continuing to talk loudly with the others at the table. 'Why don't they have any pots here? You can't run back and forth for every cup of coffee,' when he returns the maybe 10–12 steps with plates and cutlery.

At first I think they're in a good mood, the patient likes that. But, it stays so loud that I decided to go back to my room. I close my laptop, which I'm working on and get up. The cutlery holder comes in again, this time balancing four cups on a plate. 'Well, there's nothing else. I've already tried it, they still have to learn how to make real coffee here.' He's obviously playing *the cock* being with the two ladies.

Should ... or shouldn't I? But shouldn't we have fun here too? As I pass their table, I say: 'Hello, well, this is the extra coffee for us cancer patients,' ... and after two seconds for breath, 'special, of course, so that we men don't get any ideas from the nice nurses.' The Mandala-painting doctor can't help but smile. On my way out, I hear one of the women ask: 'How much have you had to drink so far?'

The story about the special coffee for patients is going round, of course. What you used to often hear in the past, that you put something in the food of male patients in hospital to stimulate them, doesn't really matter here. People think about everything but that.

However, small talk with the staff reveals that it is an important topic in the hospital. For example in the emergency or in the surgery department. There it can also be abusive. Patients, for example, still drunken after a fight, smuggling alcohol into the room or generally letting their macho behaviour hang out, etc., they don't always have themselves under control.

Who hasn't experienced, in large organizations one hand often doesn't know what the other is doing. This university hospital is a large (regional) state owned organisation as corporate by public law. Dear employees here and also at my university, it is not your fault if politicians and managers – like this *Mr Moses* in the Christian Holy Bible coming down the mountain with God's advice – decide on organisation, profit orientation, efficiency ... always with ultimate wisdom and without real relevant professional experience; they say Clinic Management.

Incidentally, a manager probably does legally not require any qualified training. Today, management is always confused with business administration. Who of us would get on a plane when the pilot has no ... or lie down on an operating table with a doctor has no ... certified vocational education and -experience?

How am I supposed to transfer these many invoices that I receive from the hospital administration in my isolation separately and on time? I receive separate invoices for every examination in another hospital building – it seems that they are all own profit centres – here, such as *MRI* and *CT* scans or from various laboratories. Sometimes there are 10 invoices at the same time. Apart from my own professor's, I've never seen any of the other professors or doctors which are named on the invoices' letterhead.

My question: 'Is it not possible to bundle them?' 'No, that's not possible,' was answered. My second question: 'Why, as a university hospital, I can't simply forward it internally to the university's financial aid department? That's where I would send the invoices for partial reimbursement,' motto, from left pocket into right pocket, supposedly doesn't work either.

I end the conversation by saying: 'You could at least save on postage by using the in-house mail.' Strangely enough, however they do direct billing with a private cost bearer such as health insurance, as my roommate *Peter* tells me after the phone call. I see, one public administration probably doesn't trust the other public administration including their own university?

I'm sitting in the administration waiting area with *Emil* by the hand and my neck wired up with tubes ... or is it tubed up? And with cancer baldness; still without a cancer cap. I've decided for myself, cancer is just a part of my life, but I'm not going to let it define me all by itself. Of course, with a medical protective mask over my nose and mouth; pure *Frankenstein* horror movie monster look and virtually veiled too ... and hair that's gone can't be covered up either, I smile to myself.

That was before *Covid* time, I just remembered as I was writing. Back then, no one had any idea that everyone would walk around partially veiled in the following year. That put the otherwise public fuss about a few veiled Muslims into perspective.

Back to the administration. Other waiting people look curiously and then they quickly look away when I look back at them. Of course, I look dangerous or pitifully interesting to some. But it is a hospital after all, so others on the wards look quite different too, I think.

Each new chemotherapy cycle is to be seen as a new hospital admission. So I wait and wonder about the very strict hygiene and contact regulations at my ward and this relatively relaxed approach here.

Finally it's my turn and I have to fill in and sign lots of forms again. When I ask, 'why you don't automatically copy everything from last time and ask for changes, or why not paperless,' the friendly young employee shrugs his shoulders and the printer spits out new forms again. The young office staff here are probably up-to-date with IT technology in their private home.

On the second invoice, I notice, the single room supplement of 60 Euro a day is always shown on the invoice. Now I make sure that it is not ticked. The employee looks at me in astonishment. 'There are no single rooms up there, there are always two of us,' I tell him. He does not even know that; the item was no longer included in the next bill.

Of course, the presumption of innocence applies, because of course the employees and also the in-house business controlling do not know this, and in addition they only ever charge it erroneously in favour of the hospital for a service that was not provided.

At some point, I received a handwritten invitation from my neighbours, an elderly couple. We often had tea together and talked about development projects, as they themselves were involved in helping *Chernobyl* kids, and one daughter had worked in development aid in Africa for a long time.

Now, I'm sitting with them for tea on my second short holiday at home. He has prostate cancer, so we have our shared topic to talk. The meeting and the subsequent ones are very good for me; for him probably in the same. And, this tea times gives me a feeling of normal life outside the hospital.

He has since passed away, but shortly before I went to have tea with them again. He's lying in a healthcare bed in the living room's corner and is weak. But he can't resist a joke when his wife puts a piece of cake on my plate, 'but he doesn't get my piece of cake.'

Another neighbour also invites me over. We also used to have tea time from time to time with appropriate conversation; nice, constructive conversations, because with her immense knowledge of Christian history, we can always argue about things in a wonderfully friendly way. And once her friend who had sent me a guardian angel to the hospital joined us.

From the second time onwards, I enjoy the small hospital breaks. I am now prepared and my daughter has done the shopping. Or I go shopping myself to make jams and chutneys for the future, work and do small repairs that were always meant to be done. As I'm supposed to avoid direct sunlight on my skin and it's far too hot for me this summer anyway, I prefer to stay in the cooler flat anyway. But in the evening at dusk, I go for a walk along our river *Rhein* or sit on a bench and enjoy looking out over the big river.

I now also realise why my mother, following my father's profession all her life, wanted to return to 'her river *Rhein*'. Growing up there, she had always enjoyed spending time there, and then when my father has retired.

E-mail from Erika

Erika is a faculty colleague, but we don't have that much to do with each other professionally, so we rarely see each other. She herself survived the whole ordeal of cancer, hospital, rehabilitation centres etc. years ago.

At some point I get a message from her telling me to hang in there and a photo. It shows her and her husband on a weeks-long cycle tour. I can't imagine how that's possible again. But it also motivates me to have life again with its dreams for my life afterwards. For me, it will be a new camper-van that has just come onto the market, which makes me a little euphoric. But like so many dreams in life, I haven't realised it yet; but dreaming was still nice for a few days at that moment.

Many months later, freshly discharged from hospital and about to go for additional follow-up treatment to a rehabilitation centre, I visit them for a coffee. She gives me valuable tips and also for returning to work afterwards. She and her husband also become friends and we meet up on our bikes in the beer garden, for coffee or their traditional Christmas barbecue.

I feel a little guilty that I don't invite people around sometimes. I actually like cooking for people, but I shy away from being in the same room with lots of people. I have to make up for it, because now that my five years of hospital follow-up treatment are over, there are no more internal excuses.

Clinical study, the second

Our favourite doctor comes in at some point with blood transfusion for me. After the usual brief small talk, especially with *Peter* about their famous football club, he turns to me. As he hooks next to up the infusion bag and does the usual test strip comparison with my blood etc., he asks me: 'The study you're in, how are you doing with it, and have you noticed any side effects?' What should I answer? I look at my pill orchestra, pointing to all different shapes and sizes. Some are so big that I can't swallow them and have to split them. 'I think there are 16 pills currently,' I reply and add: 'How am I supposed to know what I'm feeling? And then there's the gargle, drops and all these infusion bags,' I look theatrically up at *Emil's* infusion bag ring. And I add sarcastically: 'I advice you to buy shares from this chemical company.' He laughs approvingly: 'Yes, that's quite a lot. But maybe you felt something else when you started taking the study pill?' 'I really don't know,' I say. 'But we,' he replied. We can see your blood values are steadily improving, and we're going to help you a little more, and points to the new red blood transfusion bag.'

And after a short break, he points at the blood infusion bag, holds up my pill orchestra and shows it to my roommate *Peter*, '... red and white today, that's how we make new fans for our preferred football club.' I hadn't even realised that all the pills were white. And *Peter* picks up on it, 'I've always been a fan. With him here,' he nods over to me, 'you just have to give him a helping hand.' The doctor laughs, 'goodbye, keep on rockin boys.'

Follow-up Treatment   Goodbye, and see you again

Before you 'actually live', you always have something else to
to do, one more requirement to fulfil, one more important
wish to satisfy for the time being, one more bill to settle.
And to this 'again, again and again' arises that indirect
structure of postponement and indirect life ...

Sloterdijk, in: Critique of Cynical Reason

Follow-up Treatment

Rehabilitation or what?

After more than half a year in hospital, one from the social services team came to my bedside. He told me that I should go to a rehabilitation centre as soon as possible for physical and psychological aftercare after the final phase of my aplasia, which was just beginning. They would make me fit for everyday life again. Whatever that is, I think to myself, somewhat arrogantly and satirically in the euphoria of my imminent discharge.

He briefly explains the general course of a rehabilitation follow-up treatment, answers my questions as far as possible and gives me a brochure. Pick out three or four rehabilitation centres you like, he says and continues, as not all have places available at short notice.

Too many rehabilitation centres in brochures and via *Google*. Sometimes exaggerated and false advertising claims, as I compare between web-information and brochures; and later I'll realise this by myself. One seems more suitable, then immediately another, depending on my mood at the time. Finally, I write down five requirements that seem important to me. At first, of course, the oncological focus, then the sea or at least brine inhalation because of my lung history. And then I rate each of the rehabilitation centres that come into question from my point of view. It will then be the second one on my list that can take me for the three rehabilitation weeks.

While I was in this rehabilitation centre, I came to the conclusion for anyone else, if one ever seed the sign Historical Town ... at the motorway south of the (German) *Harz* mountain region, continue straight on without stopping there.

After all, the rehabilitation centre is beautifully situated slightly above the edge of a park with a large lake. It also has a beautiful large open foyer, but unfortunately the information I've got was not correct; although at least a website could be changed immediately. It now belongs to a different private operator than it was stated on the website and the downloadable brochure, and now also without the designated oncological focus. Also, one part of the building is temporarily a nursing home, and the old people eat separately from us in another layer; this stigmatises them and us. I see the suitability for everyday life and the isolation of the older quasi-residents of the home more as an integrative task.

But I only realise all this after a few days, because my therapy consultation starts a week later; the head doctor is ill and there is probably no deputy; nothing specific to oncology is actually discussed. But I'm still too weak to travel and I'm not mentally up to travelling all over Germany in search of a new rehabilitation centre at short notice.

At least I have travelled here by car, so I can take some nice trips in this mountain region on my some free afternoons and weekends. I also read the recently published biography of *Michele Obama*, and I repeatedly meet up with a former colleague and one co-author – over a quarter of a century ago – who retired and now lives not far from here. So, at least I'm doing my bit socially to make myself fit for everyday life.

Pensioners at war

I am no longer afraid of death. I can let go and I'm not looking for an endless succession of experiences. I have always been able to enjoy being alone, and now I enjoy it even more intensely than being in life.

Looking into the garden or at the neighbour large river, watching birds or insects, enjoying the silence ... and even the noise of children playing in the neighbourhood children's day-care is nice. Or the ringing of bells in a nearby church, which reminds me of my childhood and makes me feel calm. It all becomes an inner peace.

Well, not everything. The growing squadron of combat pensioners is annoying with its relevant full weapon system, with a edge cutter, a lawn-mower, edge cutter, weed burner, leaf blower, high-pressure steam cleaner, drills, jigsaws and chainsaws, flex & co.; and I'm sure I've forgotten one to two other handgun-like devices. But I know that they are a close-knit com-munity who, regardless of their personal animosities, coordinate with each other because they are brothers in arms in spirit, regardless of which side of the street they live on. So they don't attack with their weapons as a group, but they are finely highly coordinated volleys of attacks one after the other.

Then at some point I started building insect hotels on the patio my-self, initially during the *Covid* period with the small desk escapes. But at some point, I build them – I don't want becoming be part of the combat pensioner squadron – on a workbench in the basement that has now been set up for this purpose. Since then I give them away to neighbours, friends and people up and down the country, whether they want them or not.

In search for self-help, books & co.

It is said, there are many leukaemia support groups, especially where there is an specialized oncology hospital. Sharing information and ex-periences with other sufferers is a great psychological help.

To cut a long story short, I still haven't found a self-help group. And that's despite the fact that I'm in one of the centres for cancer research and support organisations and associations in my town.

In the meantime, however, I have also realised that there are not that many people affected by my type of cancer, they are widely spread in terms of age and region. And because at my age it more often affects men, who often don't dare to join such a group to talk openly about their problems and fears. You quickly notice this in such rehabilitation centres; it's mainly the women who actively communi-cate at the information evenings and in group therapies.

'You may have to take action yourself,' says a lady from an association here. She hands me a bunch of brochures, all of which I already know from the hospital. Shortly before I leave for my now self-imposed retreat, I hear that there is a virtual group for leukaemia; I will look for it when I get back.

Of course I have and still do read about experiences with leukaemia. I'm interested, or is it an unconscious fear of a relapse? Beside medical broschures I found during my time in hospital, the first really very personal experiences I read a year later during my second rehabilitation follow-up treatment: From the Heart – About the Gift of My Life and the Power of Music, by the world-famous tenor *Jose Carreras*. Later I found others written by well-known people, probably together with journalistic advice. But what helped me the most were the testimonials from different perspectives; from sufferers, their partners, children or friends. They reaffirmed what I had unfortunately admitted to myself much too late: Cancer is always a psychological burden for family and friends, and in the worst cases it can be overwhelming.

Personally, I strongly advise against internet blogs and social-media advices, where people, are not themselves affected and have half-knowledge or no knowledge at all, give advice along the lines, 'I have heard ..., I know of someone who knows of someone' or countless alternative and often esoterically based promises of salvation; as a rule, it is all about showmanship and profiteering.

Even if such a terrible illness and situation takes place as a tragedy in one's own body, it can also challenge and purify the spirit like any other misfortune; just as I have perceived it in myself and have experienced it anew as not only holding on to life, but also in life. I remember a passage in the novel Monsieur Renè which I searched for and found again while writing; it was a tragic incident, but like any tragedy, it cleanses the mind and only over time brings out the positive ... (by *Peter Ustinov*).

That's how I experienced it too, only with different memories, after my then obvious shock had slowly subsided after a few weeks; more precisely, after intensive care and the first chemotherapy cycle. Supposedly because I didn't know about the following more chemotherapy cycles and the long months in the hospital room. Even then, I searched for a long time for the source, but I still haven't found it today. I only remembered, in every mis-fortune there is also a seed for new happiness.

And I immediately put this into practice and drew up a to-do list, not only about the supposedly imminent death, but also about what I wanted to experience – or rather, what I wanted to have said – for myself before then.

At that time, it was initially art and history books, among other things, that had been piling up at my place for years, waiting to be looked at and read when I retired. Then I had to write down stories that I had told my children in their childhood. And also science books; I still wanted to know what there was on, in and around the earth that I didn't yet know. And, and and, ... I still had a lot of plans.

Fatigue, or how much fatigue ... that's the question

Sometimes, I suddenly wake up while reading and then realise, for example, that I have fallen asleep halfway off the sofa onto the floor. I also can't concentrate for as long at a time and often find myself searching for words. Is this Fatigue or is it currently in the form of Long Covid?

Why do so many people blame doctors, treatments or vaccinations when they are the ones who fall ill and have decided in favour of or against treatment? Unlike in many other countries, nobody here in Germany is forced to be vaccinated or receive treatment.

Anyway, tired is tired. I often don't manage to watch full-length feature films in one go; I also feel I'm wasting time unnecessarily with the largely unnecessary distraction of mass media. In contrast, I can now enjoy books and concerts as much as I used to, perhaps because they activate my imagination?

My physical performance improved, at least during the follow-up treatment, which was disappointing overall at first, but later with the following two rehabilitation follow-up treatments. And I now regularly use physiotherapy equipment again, as I used to, to prevent consequential damage from my mostly sedentary work. After five years, I am now back to my former level of fitness, minus presumably age-related restrictions? And I haven't dreamed of a full head of hair for a decade now.

Fatigue, also called as Exhaustion Syndrome, is a collective term for long-lasting tiredness, lack of energy and lack of motivation; not to be confused with CSF (Chronic Fatigue Syndrome).

Even weeks after treatment, up to 90% of the cancer patients experience fatigue as a typical after-effect that they are often unable to explain to themselves or others. After four to six months, this is known as Chronic Fatigue, which affects up to 50% of patients.

Fatigue is particularly common after chemo- or radiation therapy, especially in leukaemia. This is because healthy body cells and cell formation processes are disrupted alongside the affected cells, and which can lead to metabolic changes. In addition, anaemia occurs because the lack of red blood cells no longer supplies organs with sufficient oxygen. Lack of exercise due to the sickbed, perceived physical and psychological weakness further exacerbate this. Beside to the medical history, it is also important to diagnose the blood values, for example to rule out diabetes, hypothyroidism, anaemia or other mental illnesses. In addition to raising awareness, therapeutic measures include a regular sleep rhythm, learning to prioritise and manage your energy levels.

I didn't take this seriously at first during my first rehabilitation follow-up treatment because we were asked to calculate a percentage using a questionnaire. The psychologist avoided answering my subsequent question about the difference between 60–90% fatigue, is this a grade of tiredness or so, and what this meant for the therapy? I then let it go so as not to disrupt the group session with one-sided behaviour. But at least with a fatigue diary I learnt to see when the fatigue occurs and how to counteract it a little with regular light (!) endurance training and a healthy, balanced diet. In the end, I took on the subject for myself and I feel much better as a result.

When I was allowed to be visited after the first regular chemotherapy cycle and the sub-sequent aplasia phase, *Rainer* regularly hiked all the way up the mountain to the hospital. And this is despite the fact that he has developed severe anaemia over the last two years, which requires regular blood trans-fusions. Hiking was one of his passions, and I often accompanied him and got to know the neighbouring *Eifel* highlands little better through him.

Rainer always brings me something to read, healthy smoothies and news from his academy and his US colleagues. My teaching at his academy, which organises study visits to Germany for US students, led me to my many years annual temporary visits and presentations at the university in Los Angeles, California. But, what us really connected, was a weekly regulars' table (German: *Stammtisch* with friends) in a traditional *Kölsch* (local beer) pub, alone or together with other German- and accompanying US colleagues.

These were always very stimulating and also amusing discussions, when a Catholic professor of theology known for his critical stance and a US professor, who also had a function as a Jewish rabbi, argued about passages in the wills. Or *Rainer*, as a German Scholar PhD, talked about his passion for the *Rheinromantik* (river Rhine Romanticism) and his friendly arguments with his brother, who as a geographer had a different perspectives.

And if there were no other colleagues around, then it was just the two of us at our regulars' pub table. He was great at arguing about things and always had a mischievous side; that's also my thing. And that's how we used to have wonderful chats about studying and universities, international studying, administrative nonsense etc. in the hospital at the bedside or in the patient's lounge room ... or our favourite topics; mine Child Labour in novels of *Charles Dickens* and *Rainer's* Rhine Romanticism.

A brief look back: When I met him, we both supposedly already knew each other as a prejudice. We'd had a brief chat at a book stall at a flea market a few weeks earlier. He was leafing through books I had put aside to look at later. I said: 'Sorry, I've put them aside, but you're welcome to look at them.' He replied casually: 'I'm not really interested in *Dickens*, I read some as a child.' I didn't want to explain to him that I was researching child labour and that *Dickens* was a pioneer in Anglo-Saxon literature.

He was looking for Rhine Romanticism in particular. 'If you see anything there, please shout loudly,' he turned away. To which I returned his irony, 'I didn't get that far, only as a child as far as to the *Drachenfels*' (medieval castle tower ruin in the neighbourhood with mystic tales). 'Well, that's something, that can maybe still develop,' he continued. I didn't realise at the time how right he was.

An international oriented academy that supports US students who are here for a semester abroad is looking for colleagues, an older colleague told me a few weeks later. He could only do half of a course there, the other half would be more my subject. So we made an appointment with the academy and then *Rainer* stood in front of us. 'Oh, *Dickens*, well, at least he can speak English,' he greeted us. The chemistry between us was right straight away and we became great friends over time.

Our favourite thing to do was to lecture and ironically annoy each other at the bar over a beer or on hikes in the neighbouring *Eifel* highlands. On a hike, if I were to say, for example, 'one of the strange scientific researches of a German Scholar,' he would reply, 'better than those strange Economists, let's see where we can get a cool, freshly draft beer soon to fight on.'

It is a shock when he tells me towards the end of my slowly approaching hospital stay that he will probably have to lie here soon too. The blood transfusions for his anaemia would not lead to the desired result and he might have to undergo a bone marrow transplant. And all this in my ward, behind this *KMT* door that was closed to us too, with the patient completely isolated behind glass panes. Shortly after my discharge, the time has come for him to enter this very special corridor at our ward.

On my first follow-up treatment appointment, I go up to my old ward and ask to see him. As most of the doctors and nursing staff here know me, I'm allowed in for a few minutes. *Rainer* has just been admitted and we are both unsure about the roles we have now reversed; although I see his situation as significantly more dangerous than my previous one.

Rainer passed away months after I left the hospital for good. At his funeral, the large church is overcrowded and many have to stand outside.

And for the first time I have the feeling of being watched by those who know about me. Why our friend and acquaintance? Why is he not surviving? Absolutely subjective and imaginary for me, which I later experienced and learnt to work through in psychotherapy – which I had previously viewed in a mostly patronising way. *Rainer*, thank you for that too.

I often, at his grave I read to him from the novel Rollo on the Rhine, a travelogue along the river in the 19th century, with a lot of the European historic Rhine Romanticism time. He used to dismiss this small booklet as nonsense. 'They have no idea about what they talk ...,' was his dry comment once; our friendly argument continues in my mind.

The first big trip again

In spring, a few weeks after my follow-up treatment, I set off on my first big trip again. What could be more obvious than the US west coast? I've often worked there at this university in Los Angeles for a week or two in February for years; knowing my way around there and the area, and always a day trip north to San Francisco to visit my son.

Now, after again lecturing in a seminar, I feel without melancholy that it will be probably the last time here in Los Angeles. My attitude to life has changed considerably.

We are now planning another father-son trip afterwards. And after a few days at their home – I've known his partner Khin for a long time, she's also stayed with us in Germany – we're off. As they live just outside the famous Golden Gate Bridge on the mainland in Silicon Valley, it's practically right next to where the famous *Amtrak* train stops; the train already has vintage character. This time, it's first three days non-stop on the train east to Chicago with a restaurant-car, sleeping compartment, sightseeing carriages with swivelling club chairs.

We set off at noon, on the third day we reach Chicago in the evening, crossing the US from west to east, retracing the immigrant trail, so to speak. I have a book with me to read about the *Amtrak* travelogue – on which the migrants travelled west until the 1960s – about this route; this time in the opposite direction. It's funny because there were always incidents from the area where our train was travelling.

Back then, the trails led along the water, and lake to lake water for people and animals. Railway existed long before cars. Chicago, more than New York, was the gateway for migration because it was the most accessible harbour from the sea to the west via the lakes on the (now) Canadian-American border.

The US had around 32 million European migrants in the 19th century, including around 6 million Germans alone; this makes the fear of migration that is fuelled in our country fade. Especially if you look at it in relation to the population already living there and the gigantic development of the US; of course with all the social and cultural challenges, success stories and also injustices.

My son shows me, using himself as an example, the famous historical migration term Go West is in fashion even today. He – as well of his former German fellow students – works in one of these global leading IT companies. The founder has a migrant background, and my son has more foreigners on his team than native US Americans, as well as in most of the departments around him. 'The economic and also the cultural development of California,' he says, and goes on, 'and in fact, whole North America and Canada would be inconceivable without migrants.' We do a quiz, A for *Amazon*, B for *Bezos,* C for ... to X (formerly *Twitter*), Y for *YouTube,* and Z for ..., 'hm, I'll find something there too' he laughs.'

I had cooked together with my children from an early age; we then did it again before we left for our trip. We can have a much more relaxed conversation – because since childhood it's been clear that one of us is the chef, the other is the Gofer, go for this and go for that; of course, here that's me.

And where can you experience more culinary delights than in a city like Chicago that has been interculturally characterised for well over 100 years? My typical prejudices about fast food have also long since disappeared. 'The cultural diversity of the people is particularly evident in the food,' says my son, adding that a shopping weekend in New York is not the US. In the same like *Oktoberfest* and *Dirndl* (traditional tivoli and skirt) in southern Germany) is not Germany. In Chicago, we will then start with their famous Deep Pizza; a kind of Italian casserole in a high pizza pie tin.

An *Amtrak* train is relatively slow by our standards, but it struggles steadily and with only a few stops, for example over snow-covered mountain passes in Nevada, with two locomotives at the front and two at the back. Or for hours along lonely, winding river valleys in Colorado or through the endless expanses of the American Midwest, crossing *Mississippi* river, until it reaches Chicago on *Lake Michigan*.

It's *Saint Patrick's Day*. I didn't even have on my radar, as they say. And following all our preconceptions, it's typically American – with about 2.6 million inhabitants, Chicago is as big as half of Ireland – with the *Chicago* river coloured green, the Irish Colour for the day.

I can see my face in photos, scarred by the long illness. I remember crying in my bunk on the train at night. I realise that I am more and more 'built close to the water' ... out of happiness.

Of course, there are also the usual father-son conversations; sometimes the other way round. I have to go on about hospitalisation, follow-up treatment and the initial period afterwards. Of course, he reproaches me for informing them far too late. My excuses – no time and everything too quickly, no phone or internet at the beginning, wait and see what happens so as not to frighten her, etc. – don't count for him. He holds up a mirror to me: 'What if it had happened to him and he hadn't informed me straight away?' He's right, but he also understands my insecurity.

'But there are limits,' he says, 'understanding and accepting are two different things.' My children have obviously discussed me and demand I have to inform them of every absence from home in future, even it's only a short trip, and also from now on, to inform them of every upcoming examination and the results. Now I feel patronised and disagree. But of course he doesn't accept that in the interests of the siblings either, after such a bad time for them too. They see it as a kind of breach of trust. 'How are we supposed to believe you if you tell us now that you're fine?' I realise that I have to atone ... and they are right.

Goodbye, and see you again

Sunday school ... and I get two jobs

Sunday morning; I hear singing, chanting and children laughing from the room below me from *Manju*'s Sunday school for the village. I now know, beside praying they're also painting and listen to stories from their shared historical Nepalese culture. I wanted to take a photo of the class for some time, but I have respect for the sacred space, even though I don't belong to any religious community myself.

During my breakfast, one child was send to invite me spontaneously to join them. The most younger children, they range in the age from 3–14, first are a little shy. But almost all of them, even the little ones, understand basic English. At some point, the spell is broken and we ask each other questions. Of course, they have particular fun with my pronunciation of my around 20 Nepali words I know by now.

We then take outside a group photo, which I will show them next time – and that will be a very special day for all of us. Because, at the end *Manju* laughingly invited me to do the next Sunday school; next week would be cancelled and then I could stand in for her on December 25; she will be at a religious workshop in South India ... who can say no in front of so many children? Actually, I just wanted to be here privately, hang out and write, experience the solitude and nature. But now I have a job ahead of me.

I would prefer a lecture or workshop in my profession, but a for such a group of children of different age? Luckily, the eldest is good at English, so she has to assist. Then, making notes with ideas it starts to be fun. In any case, I have to buy sweets beforehand, because it's a special date ... for my culture; the explanation will be part of 'my' Sunday school. And I randomly write down many ideas, I need biscuits and sweets, my *Mini Monkey* story (next paragraph *The Monkeys ...*), playing the game Silent Mail, what is your greatest wish, Christmas traditions of children in Germany, the interactive Moose Choir (from my laptop), colouring Christmas Tree hangings, and, and, and ... after two days I realise this is turning into an all-day workshop; so far too much.

Can it be also be a sensitive topic? 90% of them are Hindus, only some of the kids come from Christian, Buddhist or Muslim homes. I ask *Giri* and simply show him and a neighbour the interactive moose choir with a Father Christmas in the evening. They are immediately enthusiastic and play with it themselves.

Of course they also talk to the children about other religions, after all everything in the world is one; which is true, because all the monotheistic religions have developed from Asia into the many different cultural interpretations over thousands of years in Europe. It is not the children but the adults who are the problem when they stir up rifts and conflicts between religions.

I ask *Manju* before she leaves for the religious event in Bangalore, South India, for a good three weeks if I should water her potted plants during that time. Of course, she refuses, saying that her neighbour would do it. But I insist, and now have a second job.

'The ones in the sun every two days, the ones in the shade and on the side of the house twice a week, the ones on the roof again in a fortnight, then they would be back again after another two weeks, the ones in front of the house not at all, they would be standing in water, and ...,' she advised me.

So, the very next day after she leaves, I start watering the potted plants after breakfast. Of course, the water that she usually uses for most of the pots is in use at the neighbour's to water the newly planted potato terrace. I don't want to disturb them now, they have visitors. So I take a large watering can, enough for 15–20 plants, depending on their size. I reckon there are about 150 plants, so I have to run back and forth to the large water tank between 10- and 15-times. But there are far more than I expected and the sun is suddenly blazing as if it had been waiting to see me working here. Because walking back and forth from the water butt with a full watering can, preferably watering the plants next to and behind each other in a slightly stooped position, is exhausting in the long run. And there are considerably more pots than expected. On three floors plus on steps with hanging plants and the religious mark next to the house.

One day later, during a desk escape for fun, I count 382; including 44 of which are cabbage plants that need 3-times as much water. I then give some of the flowers the Stinky Finger, because the water from above immediately runs out again at the bottom.

In the afternoon, I made an appointment with the son of a neighbour further down the road; he was one of the initiators of the Social Engineering fair at the beginning of my stay. He wanted to find out more about our start-up projects in other parts of India, and he want explain the Social Engineering approach to me, which I had never heard of before. 10 minutes late, I was of course still too punctual, he was painting something on the house; Indian Time, he laughs and, no problem, no problem, he could paint later or so on.

First of course a *Ciyâ* tea, then he briefly explains a kind of general Indian social aid. People below the Poverty Line – defined by the *UN* as having less than 2 USD a day at their disposal – receive 500 Rupees per month. And for every household in rural areas, such as structurally weak rural regions, there is a legal entitlement to subsidised basic foodstuffs. For example, for each person in the household is entitled to 5 kg of grain or rice per month; there are also different entitlement quantities for pulses, oil and sugar, for example. The quantities vary according to urban or rural populations and the federal states. An electronic food card is used to pay the personal contribution of around 20% of the market price. All children up to the age of 14 in state-funded pre-school and schools are also entitled to a free hot meal, as are all expectant and breastfeeding mothers.

He thinks ahead politically; later I realise that he also works as a journalist and is politically active and well connected. 'Help for Self-help' is to be implemented step by step in a locally and regionally coordinated manner in coordination with existing aid programmes and supplemented with training, machinery, seeds and financial start-up aid to make villages economically self-sufficient.

Here, the Social Engineering approach comes into play. For example, it sees the region or a village as an organisational system like a machine with many small parts and cogs. And in addition to agricultural start-up aid, for example, also craftsmen and logistics to the markets. And very importantly, not to forget, 'social' as cultural maintenance.

We plan to arrange interviews with each other as soon as I'm back home in Germany; he for his monthly magazine including an internet blog and possibly on local radio, and I for a planned book contribution in our social business approach.

Here, Social Engineering actually refers to the inclusion of people's social needs in the planning of jobs, products and markets or in social structures. Unfortunately, in the western industrialised countries, the term has negative connotations as social manipulation in the sense of influencing potential customers to disclose confidential personal information, such as through phishing, or to unconsciously buy certain products or services.

But since India alone is already much, much bigger than our entire so-called Western World put together, which, as we know, always likes to think of itself ethno-centrically at the centre as world standard, I'm not so worried about the term.

The Monkeys are on the loose

They have repeatedly told me, the biggest enemies here are monkeys and peacocks. 'The Chinese too, of course, but don't worry, they won't be able to do anything against them here in the mountains when even *Google Maps* gives up,' they laugh. They are *Gurkhas*; I've never met a group of people anywhere in the world that cultivates such their distinct historical ethnic traditions across all social classes and age groups right up today; although *Gurkhas* do not actually refer to an ethnic group, but only to the traditional mountain peoples here in general.

A whole herd of monkeys suddenly appears, I estimate there are around 20 of them in the plot shared with the brother next door, and there are also some in the next neighbour's house. Men and teenagers from the neighbour-hood come with long sticks and sometimes sling-shots to chase them away. The children scream excitedly: 'Monkeys, monkeys.'

Even if it sounds funny or interesting to us, monkeys are wild animals and can destroy a harvest in the blink of an eye. Most of the people here live directly from their gardens and fields. And if the monkeys plunder banana palms or a rice terrace, although most of them are trampled down, the harvest is gone. Rice only comes back after a year and a banana plant on a palm tree grows for about six months.

So we drive the herd back through the neighbouring gardens and into the forest. But they will come back, everyone knows that. Because monkeys, like humans, are collective beings who live in groups and send out individual scouts to find out where something is ripe and to eat; they also want to feed their families.

Their intelligence is strikingly similar to ours. As soon as a house is unoccupied for a few days, they set off in the twilight hours of the morning or evening to break into the houses. Locks don't help, they know how to get under the roof, through ventilator openings or chimneys. And they also raid stables and shelters with animal feed. Hence the many dogs that often dis-turb me with their barking, but they are good guards early in the morning and in the evening and attack immediately.

Afterwards, however, there is a lot laughing: 'We are used to it, monkeys are protected. 'They're part of creation, for some they are re-incarnations or ancestors,' our neighbour smiled, 'their habitats and those of other wildlife are increasingly being taken away by us.' It goes so far that we are considering where a Monkey School could be? Do they train their youngsters with subjects such as spying, plunder planning, logistics? And with what learning methods? We agreed on Action Learning. So, my gift, the garden gnome loses the myth as a monkey scare.

Two weeks later, Monkey Alarm at the brother's house next door. But it's only one, young and rather timid. The sister-in-law thinks he is probably ill or excluded from the herd: 'But he has to go anyway, I have enough monkeys here in the house,' and she looks at her husband with a laugh.

But it is hard to get rid of monkeys. Even with our now combined strength, we don't actually manage it. Up, down, around the house, onto the roof, etc. again and again, despite the military experience of the two brothers and my support. If they knew, I think myself, I was a conscientious objector.

Later, as we sit over tea, he slowly, very slowly trolls across a small field and keeps looking around at us towards the forest. If he were to provocatively give us the finger, it would be clear that our ancestor is in puberty.

Mini-Monkey

Whilst I'm writing, I'm looking at the large garden on the slope below with a currently large banana tree directly in my field of vision. I've already taken my first photos, as I've never seen a banana palm in rea-lity and the emergence of a perennial before. Over the next weeks, I take photos of the stages of development, which I also compile from other banana palms. So, I see how a bud around 25 cm long first, the size of a bottle gourd, then gradually develops and hangs downwards due to weight. Step by step, the inflorescence lengthens and one after the other and growing slowly, many small green bananas appear.

The one in my field of vision will need a few more months before you can eat the bananas as a human; a pity. I'm starting with ideas and scenes, and ten finish a children's story _Mini-Monkey and the banana babies_:

'I want bananas,' whines Mini-Monkey once again. 'I've already told you once, they're still green and so they don't taste good. We'll only eat them when they're yellow,' replies Mum-Monkey and annoyed about always this nagging. 'I can eat them green too,' Mini-Monkey tries again. 'It's enough now. For the last time, we'll only have bananas when they're ripe. Do you think I want to listen to you whingeing when you're lying in bed at night with a tummy ache,' becomes Mum-Monkey more strict, turns around and climbs another branch. And she calls out to him that she's bringing him an avocado for dinner. But Mini-Monkey doesn't like them, 'eh, they taste like soap, eh,' he says quietly to himself. In the evening before going to sleep, Mum-Monkey explains it to Mini-Monkey once again: 'It's like mummy. First the belly slowly gets big and round. And then at some point the baby comes out. And it's the same with bananas. First, a very large blossom grows on the banana palm, hanging down like this. After a while, it opens and you can see lots of little green banana babies. They then have to grow. And when they are yellow, we can pick them.' But by then, Mini-Monkey has already fallen asleep and he dreams of a banana palm that looks like a big yellow giant banana. The next morning, Mum-Monkey shows him such a banana palm in her neighbourhood. Mini-Monkey sees the large banana blossom hanging down from the banana tree. And all around it are lots of little green bananas. 'And why can't you eat them,' asks Mini-Monkey? 'I wanted to explain that to you last night in bed. But you were already asleep by then. It's like the babies at home. The little banana babies are still sukking on the banana blossom, that's their mum. You can't play with the very small monkey babies yet either. They first have to grow up and have their own fur. And they have to learn to climb on their own.' Mum-Monkey swings on to the next branch again. From there she calls out to Mini-Monkey: 'You should finally finish the avocado from last night.' He only ate half of it, he doesn't like avocados. But I want bananas now, thinks Mini Monkey. He swings a few branches over to *his mate Boy-Monkey, who also had a conversation with his mum when he saw the little green bananas on the new banana tree. And the two of them have an idea. They tell their mums that they have to go back to the monkey school because they've forgotten something. After a quarter of an hour, they meet in a dense tree in their secret hiding place, where they cannot be seen by others. They talk it over and off they go. Mini-Monkey and Boy-Monkey pretend they have to go to school and call out loudly to each other: 'Oh, I forgot the picture I drew, will you come with me?' 'Yes, okey,' shouts Mini-Monkey extra loud. But secretly they quickly climb up the back of the banana palm and hide behind the large palm leaves. They each quickly pick a handful of small green bananas and swing over to their secret hiding place. They each open a banana and take a bite. Ieeeh ... thinks Mini-Monkey, that's disgusting. But he doesn't let on and pretends to like it. Boy-Monkey thinks the same thing, but he doesn't want to let on either and munches down the banana, which still tastes disgusting. Then they hear their mums calling, worried because they haven't seen them for so long. And Mini-Monkey and Boy-Monkey are glad that they have a reason to stop eating the little green bananas. In the evening, Mini-Monkey feels sick to his stomach. He doesn't want to eat anything and wants to go to sleep straight away. But Mum-Monkey can see that he has something wrong with his tummy. He is very pale and has to retch from time to time. Then his friend's mum comes over: 'Boy is in a very bad way, his tummy hurts so much,' she says. The two mums look at Mini. He is so sick that he confesses that they have eaten the little green bananas. Both Mum-Monkeys laugh: 'Yes, yes, that happens to every little monkey when he can't wait until the bananas are ripe.' Mum-Monkey gives her an avocado: 'Here, I've still got this one left, squashed in coconut water it helps with a tummy ache.' Now Mini-Monkey is happy that there is still half the avocado from yesterday, and they always have coconut water anyway. Later, for over two months, Mini-Monkey and his friend were able to see how the small green bananas turned into larger bananas, which finally also turned yellow. Mini-Monkey resolved to listen to his parents more. Mini-Monkey never wanted to have a tummy ache like that again.*

Over time, I learn to get an eye for monkeys. They actually live among us; in this case I mean the animals too. With their limited habitat parcelled out and interrupted by houses and gardens, they cannot move on. After all, there are other groups of monkeys and people who are defending their habitat, their gardens and fields. You can tell from the movement of the tree branches whether the movement is caused by the wind or an animal. If a branch only moves once, then it is probably a bird or a squirrel. If there are repeated, asynchronous movements of larger and smaller branches, you can quickly recognise monkeys like moving shadows.

Today, after the spy a couple of days ago, four of them have infiltrated the neighbour's house as a sort of raiding party right into the kitchen. They manage to bite into a few pieces of fruit and vegetables and probably take or two each. So the others are sitting somewhere nearby.

In the late afternoon, during my daily walk in the area below our rice terraces, there is another monkey alarm in the gardens. I see the 'Pasha', the highest-ranking monkey of the group, strutting leisurely as well as other male monkeys looking cool; provocatively ignoring the screaming people and thrown stones? The mothers with their little ones in their fur on their stomachs or backs are a little more worried and look around nervously; normal family stories?

And for the next few weeks, the monkey alarm goes off again and again. Apparently there has been a wave of births, the collective need for food is increasing. Or is it the first training sessions in the fields and gardens?

I obviously see nothing of the peacocks, which also invade the fields and gardens, in my time; but I do hear their cries from the forest ... and it is not my immediate intention to write something about the Ashrams in a moment.

At the very end of my stay on the penultimate day, I sit with *Giri* in the afternoon having tea with his brother and the old mother. She remembers how I sat with her and the granddaughter in the kitchen for tea three months ago on the second day. We see the monkeys hopping over rice terraces in the distance and hear neighbours chasing them away.

Afterwards, I'm sitting writing and see something moving on a lower rice terrace near us. From outside on the balcony I recognise a huge pheasant. I go down into the garden and slowly walk closer to take a photo, and then I see another pair of pheasants. There you go, I think to myself, thank you for the farewell visit. But they are no longer dangerous, the rice has been harvested and stored safely.

Ashram … or self discovery?

Friends and acquaintances ask me, 'why three months in India, and why so far away?' And they immediately had other suggestions, from others who had heard from others … yes, why actually?

I've already been to *South Tyrol* region in North Italy twice to write on a remote mountain farm and several times to the Belgian coast. So, why not just rent a holiday flat somewhere?

I was still able to explain India because I have often worked there for a few days on development projects for years. Then, of course, I immediately thought, why not go to an Ashram, where you can do something good for yourself mentally and physically? A keyword, that I had somehow unconsciously been waiting for, because I knew some people who had already done something like this; unfortunately also with bad experiences or after their return to their (supposedly) old world.

Who hasn't dreamed of replacing their own way of life, an unsatisfactory repetition of the same old thing, with a better one? Whether through Indian Asanas yoga exercises, Christian spiritual retreats, movement and singing in sects such as gospel or Sufism Dervish dancing, or Asketeria in a monastery or monk's hermitage as a Greek tradition of an absolute time of silence for days or even weeks.

In the 1980s, the Ashram – a place of endeavour to discard the impure and attain the pure – was a spiritual high point for young adults in western industrial societies who had grown up in a saturated environment. In the extreme to Sannyasin, shedding everything, naked-ness as the highest form of self-knowledge. And the easiest way to do this is in a group of like-minded people for mutual self-affirmation, as one of them once explained to me in his initial euphoria.

Then back in Germany, the pride of special experience in orange robes and hung with – or is it not on? – the chain in front of him (as visible as possible to everyone) with the picture of Master Bhagwan Shree Rajneesh, who later gave himself the (Japanese) honorary title *Osho*.

I remember the vegetarian restaurant with an alternative touch, the first one they opened in my university town; I liked it. They eventually closed down again and no longer fought so harmoniously among themselves with lawyers. Group dynamics such as striving for power and envy were not so easy to overcome after all.

Today it is forgotten, their master amassed the world's largest *Rolls Royce* car collection at same time. Later he turned away from his own teaching, self-confessing that he had only served the mainstream.

Even back then, psychologists, including from India, criticised the fact that the psycho-techniques commonly used there led to new depenencies and repetitions. For the most part, life is seen as mainly unconsciously and consciously repetitive physical and mental habits. You can only get out by imagining that you are different from others. And the easiest way to do this is with saints, masters etc.; but who questions their values and world view, some of which are tens or hun-dreds of years old?

Mirages of the so-called New Truth as social mechanism can already be found in Greek history. People differ in terms of skin colour due to their climate etc., but not in terms of the rhythm of their habits; from sowing to harvest, from holy day to holy day ... or today in such boring administrative jobs or for the really hard working, from holi-day to holiday ... fitting to a generation, truth is leisure, feelgood and event-like celebrations as the new holy days.

However, the majority of those minorities who are searching for the new-old meaning, the supposedly pure, have or currently are taking precautions to be able to return to the bosom of social security if necessary. Often unconsciously, they almost cynically provoke their own social environment, which gave birth to and supported them, that they are living wrongly; based on *Peter Sloterdijk's* Critique of Repetition, who himself lived in an Ashram for a long time at the time.

Today, Ashrams are increasingly under public control. With the Tantra Massage, for example, as a covert (illegal) hotel or hospitality business, they have been systematically evading taxes for decades. And nowadays the crime rate of the so-called Dropout Scene has risen enormously, so as still illegal drug use.

Yearnings to learn or pick up a new attitude to life somewhere around the globe are repeated for generations. Whether Ashram or Zen Yoga, living in a Kibbutz cooperative in Israel, Flower Power scene in California, a Silent Monastery or being transferred abroad for a while after a life crisis. Unfortunately, afterwards problems are not solved, but at best attitudes are. And this requires practice in order to make lasting changes, but in a world that continues to exist around you (see as well following paragraph on Mindfulness).

This should not be rejected out of hand. Many people have always been looking for a supposedly better world or a time out. You can always change it personally, but not by escaping from reality to become a 'better person' somewhere else. When you return to the old world, you are confronted with the same reality again ... just as it began for me over 45 years ago with a Kibbutz, and just as I will soon return from here?

Mindfulness, the new trend

For some years now, a (supposedly new) term Mindfulness has been around; a new hype. *Friedrich Nietzsche,* 1886 in his work Thus Spoke Zarathustra – still performed today as an opera, play or concert – and many other philosophers and psychologists before him and later, they mocked meditation as real wakefulness or realisation. Thus to turn away from the world in a calm and contemplative way, in contrast to the active person who turns towards the world and the truth.

I don't know if you can call it meditation if you relax on a mountain hike despite the physical exertion? Or sitting by a stream listening to its murmur and forgetting everything around you? Personally, I find my reading and writing totally relaxing and at least in my head; after hours I can already feel my back and tense shoulders.

Why is there suddenly so much hype about exercises as a means of dealing with problems, dissatisfaction, negative energy or ability to make complex decisions? Did people here in India (and Tibet, Nepal, Bhutan ...) not know this either, when it has been considered the centre of all meditation for thousands of years? To this day, these societies are run very autocratically, formally and informally. Think of the caste system, marriage ... anyone who breaks out of this system is ostracized by their social environment; and this applies not only to the rural population but also to a more highly educated urban population. Why do we see life here from the outside in such a socially romantic way? Conversely, people here prefer our modernity, social security and opportunities, environment protection ... as a dream.

I ask a Brahmin priest: 'Do you have a term for mindfulness?' 'Yes,' he says, 'in ancient Indian Sanskrit it is known like Calmness of Mind or Contentment, Hindi knows Awareness, and in Nepali it's Alertness. So, you would say the Perception of Body, Mind, Soul.' He is aware of the recurring and marketed fashions of forms of meditation in our western industrialized countries. Then he criticizes the marketing of such, which originates from Buddhism, in the sense of New Spirituality in our individualistic world. In this way, social change is actually prevented if one withdraws into an individual space of happiness with Yoga or Tai Chi; its a kind of escape from necessary individual and social developments: stress at work, in the private sphere or dissatisfaction in society cannot be solved individually. Irrespective of this, he makes it clear that meditation is not a panacea, it also has disadvantages, even dangers. It is also disrespectful to take spiritual-religious actions out of context ..., 'but that's probably true everywhere in the world,' he laughs, 'here, its often chic, youngsters wearing a necklace with the Jesus cross, even though they don't know what it means.'

I have read studies that regular meditation can lead to serenity and a light and pleasant physical calm. I know it myself, Progressive Muscle Relaxation in the rehabilitation centre did me good. But, regularly and when problems arise, however, it also leads to inertia and, in the worst case to a depression; and it often prevents necessary decisions or spontaneity. And that reminds me of all the self-proclaimed motivational trainers who offer not only yoga and the like, but also walking barefoot over broken glass or glowing coals. Any doctor can explain how to do it without causing physical harm. But do I want to walk like this, do I want to get rich, do I want to overcome my fear of spiders at all costs ... or is it their necessary business model?

My personal conclusion: as with everything that has to do with mind and soul, whether religion, positive thinking and other esotericism, but also competitive sport etc.; too much of a good thing is too much at some point and turns negative. So there is no panacea, you also have to be prepared to face reality. Because when you come out of your happy place, the problems, the environment etc. are still there.

Caste system

Castes refer to a social system based on religious hierarchy thousands of years old. In practice, it is about social status, the type of work one aspires to and marriage too; comparable to our (today) informal social classes.

In India, a caste affiliation can be recognised by the family name; if it was traditionally continued. A distinction between castes that is still common today:

- Brahmins as the intellectual elite, they were regarded as interpreters of the holy scriptures *Veda,* they were often priests or large landowners in the tradition.
- Kshatriyas were the princes, soldiers and officials.
- Vaishyas were traders, landowners and moneylenders as well as landlords with their own land.
- Shudras, trained craftsmen, tenant farmers, farm- and day labourers and village employees, for example, policemen.

- Among them, untouchable casteless Harijans, such as untrained helpers and labourers or street cleaners.

Another special feature was the obligation to provide mutual social support within a caste, for example in cases of poverty and illness. The cast system only plays a role among the rural population alongside self-appointed elites; here too, it is increasingly disappearing with participation in education. There are also impoverished people in upper castes, and conversely, extremely rich people in the lower castes or among the casteless.

Critics from the outside is out of the question, because our society also thinks (often unconsciously) in this way. Who is not familiar with the admission rituals of the Rotarians Club or the family of lawyers, in which at least one child (or at least the partner) should be a lawyer. Or academics looking down on craftsmen, even though they usually earn more than the average bachelor. Or the greed for titles and even dubious ways to get there?

In India too, you can rise through compensation, so to speak. Behaviours shaped by castes and religions have unconsciously become part of normal interaction, just like in our country. I experience how the men are cooked for and served by the women first at invitations, then the women and children eat together. And even in my childhood, men and women sat separately with the children in church, and which is still traditionally common in some parts of our country today.

Mr Tiger is back

Bengal tigers have not existed here for a long time. There are a few protected populations in reserves, for example in the *Sundarbans* on protected islands in the river *Ganges* delta east of Kolkata at the border with Bangladesh.

Our tiger is definitely the king of the household. He is very picky, he feeds, no, he takes his Basmati rice in milk slowly, and in-between, he almost struts around the kitchen every now and then. In *Manju's* absence, a neigh-bour cooks yellow rice; for two days he ignores him and meows provocatively in self-pity.

And then *Mr Tiger* is gone. The first few days are not unusual, he's done this before. But after two weeks it's clear that he's gone for good.

Exactly three weeks later, I wake up to a loud 'meow' half past 4 a.m. in he morning. I know this meowing and immediately go down to the kitchen. *Giri* is also there and makes him a big bowl of rice with milk before milking. 'He can't survive without my special milky rice,' he laughs, 'hopefully he'll remember that in future.' *Giri* is really happy.

In the meantime, we have already considered that, apart from an accident, he could only have fallen victim to a fox. There have been, beside the always hungry monkeys, no other dangerous wild animals up here for two generations; a brown bear was last seen 20 years ago. But, there are still cobra snakes; they will flee at the slightest shaking of the ground. You can walk through the forest or across fields without fear, they only come late in the evening and enjoy the warmth of the pavement. A torch is advisable in the dark on the road; and with a few firm steps they are already up and away into the undergrowth.

In the following days, *Mr Tiger* naturally gets lot attention. Even neighbours come along to cuddle him. I build him a cat toy during one of my desk escapes; a small cloth ball on a leash on a stick. Of course he spurns his toy – or is it rather my toy – and then run away.

Giri thinks he may have been beaten with a stick during his long excursion. *Manju* then ironically holds up the wooden *Roti* roller; as in my culture as well, an ironic gesture towards men.

I must fast

The food quantities are far too much for me; already various plates around at breakfast. *Dal*, a huge portion of rice or freshly baked *Rotis*, two cooked vegetables and some raw (they say salad), yoghurt, snack ..., and always repeated requests, 'one more, sir.' If I refuse or say less, they ask me if I don't like it? In the evening the same, but of course, everything is delicious.

Currently, a neighbour is cooking for us, as *Manju* is at a religious work-shop in South India; a journey of more than 48 hours by bus and train day and night. Like *Manju* at the beginning of my time here, I have explain to the neighbour that I can't eat as much in the morning and evening as the men, who work hard all day. And they are traditional mountain people and mostly work without the use of machinery. Of course *Manju* told her this, but it's simply unconsciously women's behave that men have to eat a lot.

An not everything they eat here is nearly as healthy. Despite their organic gardening, they love snacks and sweets, high-sweetened *Ciyâ* tea, and hand greasy crackers are very popular.

Each house has a washing place outside, not only for clothing, pots etc., also for feet when coming from the fields or the stables. Adults usually walk without socks in flip-flops or sandals. And everyone is first given a glass of hot or cold water. This warms in the cold and cools in the heat. That's how it used to be with us before the cars and carriages; after long, exhausting, dusty walks, guests were first given water and their feet washed as a gesture of hospitality.

I have decided to fast on our Christian holy days in my time here, St. Nicholas Day, Christmas Eve and the Epiphany. I know people in Germany who do this in protest against church abuses and donate the 3-day equivalent value of the food to an open kitchen for the homeless; so I will do as well.

They accepted – sometimes religion helps in a very practical way – but suggested a solution on their part. I should wat something just before midnight and the next day after midnight; they would provide me with something ... but every religion has its little ways out as well.

Last shopping in Kalimpong

After breakfast, I take a shared taxi with *Giri* to Kalimpong, including to see the Cooperative Market. It's now successful and has become politically accepted that it is held twice a week in one of the open market halls; and it is now also in two other small towns nearby.

We had a shopping list, and I also got everything, starting with rice flour and of course more than I had planned ... when you're in a shopping frenzy. In-between, we deposited a few bags in a shop that *Giri* knows near the taxis for our village. And people greet me. Some recognise me from the trade fair opening event, the shop owner where we bought my table lamp at the beginning calls over to us, and the bakery with the over-sugared *Nescafé* vending machine already knows me. And of course, Christas stuff everywhere, mainly colourful glittering. A large decorated Christmas tree stands at a main junction. Whether Hindu, Buddhist, Christian ... it doesn't matter, the main thing is that it's colourful and you can celebrate; it's just like the German *Oktoberfest*, the US tradition of *Halloween* or Indian *Holi* etc. here.

The journeys with a shared taxi minibus, authorised for 2+3+3, are more exciting for me. On the outward journey with 11 adults and 3 children; 3 at the front, then 4+1 plus 4+1+1. On the return journey we are then just 10 adults +4 travel bags and some shopping bags as well as a large carton with 200 fresh eggs, which someone at the front naturally takes on their lap.

We got off at the smallest restaurant in the world. Now I also have the sweets and a few extra crayons for my Christmas Sunday school. On the way here via another road, I realised that the Hindu temple is not far away, it felt like half an hour's walk for me. I'm going to ask if I can enter it as a non-Hindu and take a photo inside. They'll probably say yes and think it's fine, Hindus are very tolerant in my experience.

Tomorrow marks the start of winter season, here these days with blue skies and 20°C during the day. So tomorrow I'll have another washing day as a small gesture for the upcoming festive season in my home country; here it will be normal working days.

Everlasting Memories   Years Follow-up Treatment

Everlasting Memories

Anything but loneliness

Like sitting nearly every morning at my desk, now it's again 8 a.m., breakfast is coming up. Outside, *Giri* and his brother are cutting bamboo with their *Kukri*, the Gurkha fighters' traditional machete-like short weapon for close combat; the bamboo is as thick as my forearm and they can cut it with three or four strokes as if with an axe. They are probably building a roof for a shelter or trellises for vegetable plants. And from the kitchen I hear the overpressure hiss of the steaming pot for the daily rice.

The predominant rice cultivation on terraces on the mountain was new to me. I hadn't realised this during my short visit last year, I only had images of tea gardens in my head. But the many colourful prayer flags, the spiritual chanting and the warmth of the people were right. And I learnt to appreciate something in particular. Where there are fewer people and, as here, people live further apart, there is much more socialising. There is lot more talking and doing together, and people are mutually responsible instead of individually separating themselves from one another as is the case in our society.

The region here is known to us only as Darjeeling, like me before, to most people because of its famous highland tea. So, Darjeeling town, three hours from here by car and bus, is naturally the hotspot for visits. Accordingly, it is totally commercialised and less pristine.

Historically, this region never belonged to India. The British occupiers, above all their royal family, the military and the *East India Company*, later rich merchants, built up this region as a summer residence because of the more pleasant climate; the capital of India at this time was today's Kolkata.

Up here in the highlands, for example, the first electricity and the first railway existed long before India; even today, around 40% of the economic output of the federal state of West Bengal comes from the Darjeeling region. Like the neighbouring small federal state of Sikkim, they would also like to become a federal state or be part of neighbouring Sikkim and independent of West Bengal, but of course still belong to India.

Here, as in Sikkim, the main language is Nepali; the Bengali language plays no role. For centuries, they shared a common territory with the pre-sent-day nation of Nepal, which did not exist at the time. Everyone here has relatives there. Cultural similarities are not only evident in culture, cuisine or religion. It is also evident – as common among the mountain peoples all over the world – in daily communication, in singing and dancing together, in small talk over tea, in daily neighbourly help and much more.

Around 10 years ago, under the new Prime Minister Modi, the national Indian government promised to treat the region as a kind of special zone directly from the centre of the capital. This is because it has a very special geopolitical location for the national government, as a kind of a bottle neck with its four borders to Nepal, China, Bhutan and Bangladesh. However, not much is happening apart from a few small infrastructure projects in the sense of, 'we are doing something'. Road construction is of course happening everywhere on the rapidly growing continent; in just a few years, the aim is to be the third largest economic power and thus overtake the EU.

People communicate with each other much more here than in the cities or in our until today so-called Industrialised Countries. And this is despite the fact that houses are often far apart. Generally, three generations live in one house or on one property, and they also have their daily network of neigh-bours and relatives. It's a 'big family' here in the truest sense of the word, and it's also a neighbourhood with mutual responsibility. Then there are the SHGs which are grouped together in a cooperative.

And neighbours come every day to fetch milk, swap vegetables and help each other or just have a cup of tea for small talk between work. People also meet on the street in the covered taxi shelter – the sun shines even when it's cooler – which is also a meeting place for old people during the day and young people in the evening.

Those with mobile phone reception make calls several times a day across the entire continent, to Nepal or to distant foreign countries. Some men work as seasonal labourers, for example on road construction projects or abroad in the Gulf States, while women work in households in Kolkata, for example, or abroad like in Singapore or Saudi Arabia. The children, who then live with just one parent and grandparents, absolutely need daily contact; that's what social media is good for.

I remember one morning in my early days here, when *Prashant* showed me a message from my youngest son and his partner, who had just been here for a short visit. I reply via *Prashant's* mobile phone, everything is fine here, no mobile phone reception and internet for me, Merry Christmas, Happy New Year and birthdays in the family, please forward. Immediately comes back from about thousands km, done, as a Thumbs-up emoji.

How could humanity have developed over tens of thousands of years to the present day without social media? Can young people today still imagine that personal meetings, letters and calls were real social media and that the whole of humanity has also developed with them?

But on the one hand I'm happy to know that the children are doing well, but on the other hand I'm also a little proud that I've managed to go three months without TV, phone and internet; it feels like a sustained diet with weight loss ... I hope without the so-called Ping-pong Effect.

It always feels great for me when people practise in a choir in the early evening or simply come to sing and make music together. First of all, I sit at the walking table or look into the twilight and listen to their old songs and rhythms, often accompanied by instruments that are sometimes unfamiliar to me. Of course, there is a discussion about accentuation, entries etc. and new entries again and again until it fits. And there is always a lot of laughter.

I often have to suppress a tear regardless of whether I like this music or not, it's simply the cross-generational cultivation of culture, that's touching. Often 20 or more people sit on the floor in a traditional cross-legged position, old and young, mothers and grandparents with small children for playing instruments an d singing together. At some point, I joined in and initially stayed in the background to just listen and take a photo. And immediately I was included in the circle. Everyone has fun when I clap along to the beat and sometimes even sing some words along to the chorus.

But real life today also includes Nepali rock music. When *Manju* and *Giri* are out visiting the sick one lunchtime, their son *Prashant* has, as we say 'free hand' and blasts the songs that are currently popular with young people loudly into the garden. 'Plants and animals in the forest should be culturally aware of the future,' he says with a smile.

But then he sits in the singing group again in the evening and claps along rhythmically to the traditional songs. Does he have his eye on the young woman who is currently staying with her parents in the house next door? Usually she is studying and living with her grandmother in Nepal.

Relatively at the beginning of my time here and first singing meeting, *Manju* says goodbye after breakfast. She has to go to a temple to sing with our choir.

And she has a surprise for the group. The appearance at the Social Engineering fair has consequences. The office of the governor of the neighbouring federal state Sikkim has invited them. He was not only impressed by the cooperative's interim economic independence, but also by its socio-cultural coexistence and commitment.

Beggar monks

During night, I was woken up by chanting with deep and long horn sounds, it sounded very ritualistic. And so, the next day at lunchtime, a monk from Nepal sits with us. In keeping with local tradition, he is given refreshments, food and offerings; a small bag of rice, a guava, turmeric, onions and chilli as well as some money on a tray woven from bamboo fibres. He then prays for the house and the family, for a good harvest and to drive away evil spirits. It reminds me of our carol singers today or mendicant monks in former centuries used to pray in the countryside and bless the house and farm to keep the devil away.

When we were waiting for *Manju*'s brothers for the *Diwali* festival visits, two mendicant monks also came. I asked *Manju* because they were dressed differently and there was a new Buddhist monastery down the hill; but they were also Hindus. She explained to me that even the poorest give a small contribution so that they too can maintain their self-confidence at eye level.

It immediately thought of how rather elitist sects or orders such as the Jesuits or Mormons – I worked with both (individually nice) people for years at a US university (founded by Jesuits) – protect themselves with their social network. Here, on the other hand, it is a socio-economic cycle. The system was explained to me years ago by a beggar monk who I had picked up as a hitchhiker on the ferry to England from a highway service station in Belgium; he was a German from a not entirely unknown industrialist family in my area, from which he had broken away. At midnight I dropped him off in a London suburb area at an address in a normal huge apartment complex.

Here, they move across the country, some of them are married, and ask for donations, or they live in the village for a season as teachers in exchange for board and lodging. Their network is all over the world, and they also have contact addresses of monasteries or temples where they can stay overnight and pay with the donations; this creates an economic cycle at eye level.

In Germany, priests have regular salaries and retirement benefits, as well as titles. Unfortunately, they often present themselves as the 'better people'. Church organizations – political parties, trade unions and unfortunately often also NGOs too – are also business models for their own sake with pronounced power structures. Their believers or members often used as volunteers or poorly paid auxiliaries; not to mention scandals such as abuse of dependents or personal enrichment financially or titles and power. It can be found similarly worldwide, often sponsored by a financially strong diaspora from abroad.

Compared to the churches in Germany, relatively few temples are here. The Hare Krishna center in Delhi, for example, lives from worldwide donations and sponsors. New for me is, the here and worldwide dancing, singing and orange-clad Krishna disciples – hip in the 1980s in Germany as well – are fundraisers and not real religious monks as we know them here.

The horn blowing that I sometimes hear at night, in the morning or even during the day can mean different things. The locals can tell the difference, but not me, of course. It certainly sounds spiritual, especially in this area with a purely Nepalese culture. It can come from a Buddhist monastery or be a Hindu ritual or even serve as a sign to announce that someone has died.

Kalimpong, present and future

I haven't actually been to the town of Kalimpong that often, even though it's not far away. At the very beginning, on the way here to my hosts, I drove through. This reminded me of the previous year, when I made a short visit to my hosts' cooperative, where I had already experienced narrow winding streets, cars lined up in a row and huge traffic jams. And it was the same a few days after my arrival when I went to the Social Engineering festival with *Manju* and *Giri*.

I went shopping in Kalimpong three more times with *Giri* and once with *Manju*. And I have to admit that I didn't actively endeavour to get to know the town and its sights, as I later learned from visitors. I deliberately chose to come here to write, I wanted to live with the locals in the countryside and not wander around as a tourist.

The district of Kalimpong has existed independently since 2017 after splitting off from the district of Darjeeling. Kalimpong town, a population of around 50,000, lies at an altitude of over 1,700 m (on average around 1,300) on the mountainside on the eastern flank of the southeast Himalayas. There are also 42 villages as rural areas, structurally weak rural areas.

The neighbouring town Darjeeling is around two and a half hours away by car. It has a population of more than 120,000 and is literally fully developed for tourism; an overrun with all kinds of kitsch and fast food, completely overpriced compared to the surrounding area, which you wouldn't expect from the 'Darjeeling myth'.

In the chaos of all kinds of vehicles and pedestrians, you often can't tell who is going in which direction. Traffic rules are not necessarily followed, and most of them are nonsensical. Sidewalks are rare, often interrupted or impassable due to subsidence. But everyone finds their way between honking and no honking; every second lorry has 'Please Honk' or 'Blow Horn' on the back so that the driver knows you want to overtake. On other lorries it says 'Stop Honking;' someone should understand that? But now that I've spent so much time in India, it's no longer annoying me. It's completely normal and serves everyone's safety. Pure chaos theory, because there are far fewer accidents compared to us and everything somehow sorts itself out in the end; and usually with a mutual friendly, typical Indian head shake.

Kalimpong is on the old trade route Tibet to Bhutan kingdom, that stretched unbelievably far from the serene Tibet to today's Bhutan for hundreds of years. In addition to the originally indigenous *Lepcha* population; here are many migrants from Tibet and Nepal following the annexation of Tibet by China.

The relatively pleasant climate, even for us, here in the south-eastern Lower Himalayas at this altitude has always made the region attractive. In addition to tea, rice and other typical agricultural produce, flowers such as gladioli and orchids as well as cacti are the main attractions. In addition to independent agriculture and an important army base, tourism is the main employer. The city of Kalimpong is also known far beyond West Bengal for its educational institutions and for preserving its traditional craftsmanship.

People are always friendly, I have never seen Indians arguing in public. And it's colourful in every respect. They like colourful clothes, house paints and, of course, decorations. Like the colourful garlands with the prayer flags, flowers and flower pots, all kinds of decorations of their Tibetan, Nepalese or Bhutanese origin and religion; peaceful and friendly coexistence and togetherness.

There are also historically significant temples with the thousands of years old artefacts from all religions; Jewish and Christian faiths as well as Buddhism and Islam are ultimately developments from Hinduism, which is many thousands of years old. They were passed on as the stories from one generation to the next via the network of trade routes over land and sea, later known as the Silk Road, and eventually written down.

The area is also currently being strongly developed as an important base for the Indian armed forces, and military skirmishes with China are continuing. The population welcomes this, because everyone is a bit afraid of China, and additionally the construction projects offer temporary paid work or the continued supply of the barracks permanent income opportunities.

If you talk to people about the region's aspirations for more autonomy from the federal state of West Bengal, they themselves know of course that regional autonomy is a rather impossible aspiration given the size of India with its many extremely diverse cultures. The country – better say continent – has now the world's largest population of 1.4 billion people. And to the state West Bengal it's just a small region, comparable to a neighbourhood of Delhi or Kolkata. But their calculation is to get Tribal People status as *Gurkhas,* that they can finally rest in peace. They all know, that the term *Gurkha* is actually just a collective term for Hill Tribes with different indigenous ethnicities, but then we get more subsidies, they laugh, shaking their heads.

A curiosity for me is *Bhutan House*, the outer residence of the King of Bhutan. The region historically belonged to the Kingdom of Bhutan for centuries, but at some point one of the kings felt it was too far away to control and protect. So he gave up the area and reserved a park with a few houses for himself; today it is a Bhutanese enclave on the out-skirts of Kalimpong, inside guarded inside by his guards and outside by Indian soldiers; they play cards together through the barred gate.

If you drive up to the top of the mountain or around it to the other side, you have an indescribable view of parts of the worldwide known Himalayan scenery with the outstanding peak *Kanchenjunga*. It can't be mentioned often enough, the people here are naturally particularly proud and it has an important spiritual significance. Here, of course, it is claimed to be the second highest peak, but who wants to argue about a few some metre of rocks or permanent ice at these heights?

Shortly before I leave for Kalimpong, I read about the controversy surrounding the world famous climber *Reinhold Messner* from the German speaking region *South Tyrol,* North Italy, who is also well known here. It seems funny that he wouldn't have been the first person to reach all the 14 summits of the so-called 8,000+m peaks without oxygen equipment, because he wouldn't have reached the top of one of them. His cool answer to this in the sense, 'then why don't you take it, I've got enough.' Of course I like that.

Kalimpong, problems and potential

In a culture, thousands of years old and extremely different even to-day, we are not entitled to patronising advice from outside. Not only in terms of language, religion, particular history, or the geopolitical situation. The British colonial rule still has an impact today, India only became an independent nation in 1947.

As I have been working with locals in development projects in various parts of India for many years, I am naturally asked about this.

So I can show examples of other regions that are still unknown. India as a nation is as culturally diverse as Europe; our apple growing in Norway is also different in northern Italy's *South Tyrol*, there again they are very different to their Italy's southern *Sicily* region.

Consequently, of course, I did not express some critics directly; it would be an irreparable *faux-pas*; criticism here is expressed indirectly and with the typical smiling head shaking in the sense, yes, we both would like to change it, but ...

There is an almost stoic tolerance for noise, for example when neighbours listen to loud music for hours on end, days of work on a building site nearby or chainsaws from forestry workers remind me of earplugs from the plane somewhere in my suitcase; and then I have my peace and quiet.

Despite the government's Clean India campaign, which is often effective in cities, almost everything is dropped after use here in the countryside, or worse, burnt on the roadside or in the undergrowth.

There are already successful pilot projects for plastics in large cities or on islands. To my hosts I had a Plastics Waste initiative in the river Ganges Delta *Sundarbans* and in a Kolkata suburb explained to them with photos of successful collection and environmental education projects together with schools. I was also able to show them waste collectors separating waste on rickshaws and a plastic recycling company. They had already heard about possible public support for something like this. But they couldn't imagine how it could be organised here in the mountains.

We are also discussing this for the small aluminium bags that line virtually all roads, even footpaths in the forest. They know that this not only kills animals, but burning also poisons their important farmland and thus the legacy for their children and grandchildren. My host *Giri* has set up collection bins himself at the school next door and at the taxi rank, and he knows that some people are quick to burn their household waste with the traditional ash fertiliser. But where to put the hazardous waste? You can already see the first Plastic Free Area signs or posters about using waste bins, but then where do they go, they ask; there is no waste collection service.

Naturally, they want to know how this is done here. They have seen mountains of yellow plastic waste bags from Europe in illegal landfill sites in Asian countries on TV. I prefer not to explain the German waste separations and recycling Yellow System, but instead describe to them how we collect plastic bottles and drinks cans for the relatively high deposit. This brings us back to the pilot projects on the islands in the Ganges Delta, for example.

We remember the city council's outdoor consultation hours in the preschool next door. In the evening, everything was littered with small plastic water bottles and aluminium snack bags. There is a poster and a collection bin on the street in front of the preschool ... but how are they supposed to learn and practise environmental protection here when the official administrators 25 m further on are showing them exactly the opposite – without any aware-ness of climate damage for future generations?

An important approach of the booming tourism is Green Tourism, because they don't want to end up like the city Darjeeling, slowly degenerating into a total kitsch market due to rapidly growing and uncontrolled tourism. Hence the close contact with the small neighbouring state of Sikkim and the Kingdom of Bhutan. The aim is to preserve culture and, in particular, nature.

Everything is actually available, potential of private guest rooms, organic kitchen gardens, traditional cooking with the hosts, rice, tea, spice and medicinal herb cultivation, spiritual places and experiences of all religions, indescribable landscapes with an almost unbelievable network of stair-like and natural trails on the mountain directly past the small house farms; often directly in-between. The people greet you cheerfully ... and invite you for a *Ciyâ*.

This then fits in with the Social Engineering approach (see chapters *Home away from Home* and *Goodbye, and see you again)* which includes social-entrepreneurship and -cultural Capacity Building in equal measure, to describe it in our western understanding. First programmes and initiatives are already emerging, such as training, promotion of economically, and of socio-cultural skills and start-ups in the form of cooperatives.

First impressions are also important. Organic, Himalayas, Darjeeling ... as product branding in combination with the Home Staying potential are already there. But when you get up in the morning, you'll see clouds of smoke from afar with the assumption that waste is also being burnt?

There is still a lot to be done to change the attitudes and behaviour of many people. But how are we to know that people in this traditionally very poor region toil from sunrise to sunset to survive and to make everyday life easier? And this is mostly done by hand, as the use of machines is less than limited in the mountains.

In organic gardening, the soil yields are lower in quantity, but the market yields are much higher. They realise that this market exists. We've come to the conclusion that long-term sustainable income security is a more effective motive than the social romanticism of tourism.

And then I reflect on our German Yellow System, how it was supposed to work and how, after decades, too many people are still throwing their waste in somewhere. To summarise, I remember a sentence from home ... 'Mom doesn't clean up'.

SHGs and the cooperative

Finally, around three weeks before my journey back home, I have the opportunity to talk to *Gobin*, NGO project manager for cooperatives in the area. He lives 20 km away from us, but in-between is Kalimpong town; even by motorbike it's almost an hour drive to us.

Most of his projects are much further away. Even if you look across the valley to the next mountain and recognise the roofs of houses, it takes him mostly one or two hours to get there, and the roads are often just better dirt tracks; our road up here is still one of the best developed roads. And of course it is always advisable to be back before dusk.

Our cooperative is spread over several villages; he calls it the Echhey Project. It started 20 years ago when *NABARD,* the National Bank for Agriculture and Rural Development. supported women SHGs.

I know this from other rural and structurally weak regions. For example, 10 women get together, each per month is saving 50 Rupees (55 Eurocents). If the group remains stable for two years, they all get the total amount saved doubled by the state and, as a group, are entitled to a low-interest loan, for example for agricultural equipment or to start their own business. The women help each other, for example by providing members in need, such as for school fees or illness, with temporary loans from their own funds at very low interest rates; a private bank would not give a loan for an illness or school fees. The SHG account receives interest, which is paid out to all their members; small amounts, but important as motivation and retention factor.

What began in 2004 with around 200 SHGs was consolidated in 2017 as District Kalimpong Rural Area Program with 70% of the population (excluding Kalimpong city). There are currently 120 SHGs in the region; not all of them worked at the beginning. And not everyone was prepared to save money each month on a permanent basis; but also, some dropped out due to an alternative income opportunity, for example, when the husband works abroad, or one gave up vegetable garden farming. Another typical social problem is that men are often sceptical at first and don't want her wife to have own money with a bank account or to go to SHG trainings. However, as soon as they see that household income stabilises and improves, their resistance usually changes, motto, 'can't you also take part in something like this?'

I know that from other countries too. It was the micro loan experience, an initiative of *Yunus Grameen,* Bangladesh; with his *Grameen Bank* he got the Nobel Peace Prize 2006 for their work, 'to create economic and social development from below.' Here, too, it is primarily women's SHGs that are supported; they are more serious about handling money, think about school for the children and loan repayments. This is why India has been supporting this approach massively for a long time, also in order to reduce migration from its rural areas.

In addition to this financial support for the SHGs – as well as direct financial support for women living below the poverty line (see chapter *Darjeeling Village Life too,* at *Sunday school* ...) – participating households are supported with training such as self-employment, handicrafts or gardening and bee-keeping as well as benefits in kind, for example a bee box, seeds or interest-free loans to buy a cow.

For many women in the mostly very traditional rural areas, having their own bank account is an enormously important step for personal development and social recognition. This reminds me of my parents' family register (married 1956), which stated 'the husband decides the keys.' I found that rather strange when I read it as a teenager.

The cooperative consists of 55 SHGs, each with 10 households, in average of five or six people in each household (parents, two children, grandparents); just under 3,000 people. It is already relatively advanced in its development and economically independency, with their sales channels via three markets in the region, where they sell not only the usual kitchen garden and field produce such as fruit and vegetables, herbs and cereals, but also handicrafts. And they have also recently started supplying organic chilli, honey, spices and medicinal herbs to Kolkata, 650 km away, for the well-off and discerning middle class clientele that is now established there; the markets' demand for their products is constantly growing.

When asked about social aspects, in addition to the purely financial start-up support, project manager *Gobin* explains, personal development should not be underestimated, regardless of economic success or even failure. The women are not only role models for their daughters and can help their children in the future, it also greatly promotes the level of education in the structurally weak region and reduces emigration. Birth rates have also fallen steadily to two or three children per household, leaving more space and time for socio-cultural interaction.

In remote and still underdeveloped regions, the birth rate is significantly higher. I am also familiar with this from other so-called Developing Countries in Asia or Africa; as soon as income stabilise and a school system covers all children, birth rates fall.

Gobin also considers joint social activities such as singing, dancing and neighbourhood help to be important for the Capacity Building of a society. The divorce rate in rural regions is also significantly lower than in the big cities, where it has increased enormously.

And the success of the SHGs and cooperatives then automatically leads to further support from the government. Asked about future prospects, he believes that a stable government is crucial. Experience shows that even successful programmes are not continued when governments change, because politicians want to make a name for themselves with something new and associated with their person.

However, sustainable promotion is important because mental attitudes only change in the long term and not through quick effects. He mentions the many new Home-staying adverts, for example in the middle of the city or alongside a busy and noisy street. For him, training is needed to analyse what customers want, how to find them, how to market yourself? 'Simply hanging a sign in the window won't attract customers,' he says. *Gobin* sees a lot potential in the region and knows that waste disposal and, for example, cataract surgery, very common here in the rural area, are under discussion. The topic is also close to his heart; his mother also suffers from this disease. And the non-profit organisation *SSDC*, for which he works (see next chapter *Darjeeling Village Life too,* at *SSDC visit*), wants to start a project for outpatient surgery here.

Years Follow-up Treatment

The smallest problem and first consultation

Who doesn't know the little drama of the urine test ... and it doesn't work. There's only one thing to do and the doctor gives me two large bottles of water, drink them now and come back in an hour. I then have as well an espresso in the visitors' café in-between.

When I try again, the nurse reminds me, 'think of the central line.' I know what she means, of course, because I've been on the ward long enough. But I can't help but make the remark, 'lengthwise or crosswise?' ... 'You see, it does work,' says the doctor, as she happens to be passing later by during the blood collection, 'next time please don't go to the WC in the morning and drink a lot in the evening and in the morning beforehand.'

So it quickly becomes routine for me. And if I forget, I remember it in the car on the journey there at the latest. Then I quickly grab two or three small bottles of water, which are always in the car for hiking.

Often the blood collection goes like clockwork. Stitch, and it's on. And it's usually the full programme, 16 tubes of different sizes with different colour rings have to be at least half-filled in the laboratory. But it also happens from time to time, they give up after two attempts on both forearms, even though I ask them to just keep trying. Because I wouldn't leave here without giving blood. Somehow they don't want to or aren't allowed to, and they call someone else, for example from the intensive care unit opposite. They probably have completely different problems ... and the blood is running.

Without the values from the laboratory, which are usually available after an hour, they cannot perform a bone marrow extraction. Or it does not make to talk to the professor or his doctor.

During five years of regular follow-up treatments, I also received at the beginning time additional blood transfusion, and the clinical study pill for the first two years. After that, I only had regular major blood and urine tests, ECGs, sonograms and consultations as well as bone marrow extractions ... the full programme; initially every three, later every six months.

I somehow feel like I belong to the hospital, but it is a sublime feeling to drive back home. On the way, I mostly stop at the cemetery to visit my friend *Rainer*, who passed away up here.

During my time in hospital, I had repeatedly searched for information about the probability of my survival – subconsciously it was probably more about the risk of death – knowing full well that at least half of the information on *Google, Wikipedia & co.* is wrong. Because anyone with half a clue can write anything on internet blogs and the supposed social media is even worse. Instead of social interaction, it's more gossip, spreading unchecked prejudices and hyped-up scare stories with the motto, 'have you heard that ...?' or exaggerated self-promotion.

But I was basically just looking for confirmation of a single index; and at some point I read about a 30% chance of survival. Well, I had guessed it. The search for confirmation started in my head. Who had I seen in patients so far? Who was unwell? Who had suddenly disappeared? And so on and so on ... and then there were the empty, sterile beds covered in foil in the corridor for new patients.

And also the horror stories among us patients, where did Mr *So-and-so*, who was in such a bad way last week, passed away? Thank God someone saw his wife at the admission control for the bone marrow transplant. Even with the last hope now, but at least he was still alive; relief. Then again, sad faces with a suitcase in their hands. Often during meal times, so as not to meet anyone, relatives collected the last of his personal belongings.

Of course, I couldn't let go of the 30% index. I kept looking for new information and found that new treatment methods have improved considerably in recent years. At some point, I realised that almost all such websites, blogs etc. mostly not include a date; this gives the false impression of so-called Up-to-Date Information.

I've asked my professor directly at the first consultation during the follow-up treatment. He seems to avoid me. So, I ask again and mention the 30%. He relativises: 'To whom should these indices apply? Women or men, old and young, with or without previous illness or after a so-called Alternative Therapy then at some point too late here with us? I'm just saying Mistletoe Therapy.' He draws an imaginary statistical curve on a white sheet: 'No matter which point you take on the curve, it says nothing about you individual. There is no 30% survival rate for you. At most, this is important for our planning of the capacities to be maintained in relation to our catchment area here. For you, there was only Yes or No.' Then, after some seconds he goes on, 'stop looking for an index on relapses. It's best to simply stop asking the doctor *Google*. If you keep searching, you'll have every disease in the world in no time. These forums are the worst thing for us, where patients and especially I've-Heard types exchange information. It's grossly negligent what they do there. But I also understand, people are desperate to find any kind of information.' I suddenly realise that I've done exactly what I con-sider to be a mistake with my students.

In the beginning, I also say: 'Hello,' at my former ward to the checkpoint, and if possible, I visit my frequent most roommate *Peter*. Sometimes I can only speak to him from the door because he's in the aplasia phase or unwell, so we can't talk.

And since my dear friend *Rainer* didn't survive his bone marrow transplant here, I've avoided the ward. I have to let go of it, even if in hindsight I see it as an important time in my life that I don't want to suppress. Because then I would be taking a part of my life away from myself.

Administration for the sixth time

When I go to the consultation with my former professor at the hospital, who continues to accompany me in my long-term follow-up treatment I usually see him with a computer and huge piles of paper on his desk, which is twice as big as my own; that's saying something.

In the hospital hierarchy, the professor always used to be at the top as a doctor, and in individual cases of treatment this is apparently still the case. In the meantime, however, so-called Business Optimisation is increasingly influencing the general scope for action. There is a joke: When a so-called Management Consultants such as from *McKinsey & co.* will analyse an orchestra, most of the instruments are gradually will be eliminated; that would be the end of culture.

As this is the case everywhere, hospitals are becoming increasingly over-loaded with regulations, forms and process descriptions; it's called Controlling. At the same time, staff on the wards, in laboratories etc. are being cut back. It's like in a university today or when I worked for a corporate group, more and more people are sitting at their computer screens filling out forms for a key index-based management; it's called Clinic- or Health Management, as I read a short time later (see also following paragraph ... *or administration for the seventh).*

Inwardly, I can't help but play a cynical word game with people, life and value. And the current AI hype, so-called Artificial Intelligence, where even its algorithm-supported graphics labelled AI art, won't stop at hospitals either. But like all technical progress potential, I hope that not everything that seems technically possible will be realised.

Some time ago, I read from a leading AI researcher that he likes to provoke those who seem too AI-loving or who think they can't live without a phone in their hands. He was one step ahead, he said, because God had already given him the left side of his brain at birth.

False alarm

In the years of my follow-up treatment examinations with the regular blood tests and bone marrow extractions, I receive the medical report after around two weeks; many pages of specialised medical texts and tables with blood and other values that I don't understand. There is information on the main and secondary diagnoses, study, therapy status and course, allergies, current reason for the examination and haematological-oncological therapy concept, medical history, and some with many sub-items on the physical examination findings, laboratory reports with tables of measured values as well as other findings and course.

In the beginning, when I was more or less back on my feet in hospital and at the start of my follow-up treatment, I read all of these reports. But with all the terms, *antigens* and *antibodies, CT, MRI & ECG, blasts, leukocytes* and *lymphomas, markers* and *contrast agents, stem* and *T-cells, receptors, enzymes, proteins* and *hormones, molecules, cytostatics, ...;* everything got mixed up in my head like in a big pot of soup.

Now I spare myself *Google,* because almost all of these are terms that I don't know or understand or would misinterpret anyway; even if there is a squiggle around a value, which can be an anomaly.

Once I read *'recurrence'* in one of the medical reports. I don't really notice it at first and scroll on. Then, what did it say? Back to page 7 ... *recurrence,* the term now screams at me like a red light. My hands start to shake and I feel faint. I close the report. My eyes go black, but I take a deep breath and regain my clarity.

I open the report again and look for the word Recurrence, I had already forgotten the page number. Yes, it's really there. I close my eyes. Now I've to decide. Do I want to go back to the hospital, chemotherapy cycles again, or the last option of a bone marrow transplant? If they ever find bone marrow for me? It's not stored like blood? First of all, someone has to be found and then be willing to donate, and, and, and ...

My friend *Rainer* passed away in the process. Can I lie there? Possibly in the same room or bed?

Again I read the report and I see a line from the copier at the top with another name below. When copying the report, a sheet from a previous copying process must have got stuck in the automatic feeder; it has probably slipped in-between my copies. Now I realise page 7 exists twice. False alarm, I am relieved. Immediately I think of the person for whom the page is now missing who is surely happy not to be relapsed. What will happen to the person and the family when getting the missing page now? Immediately I call the hospital. They already have a notification note there, 'please call urgently ... don't be alarmed, there's a sheet from another report in-between.'

Bone marrow extraction and Small talk

I know the doctor, she has often done my bone marrow extractions during my follow-up treatment and who also professionally steps in when she has time during seemingly unsuccessful blood collection attempts. She used to be a neighbour until she got children and moved into a bigger house nearby. Sometimes I meet the family at the market on Saturdays and we have a quick chat.

While I lie on her treatment couch, colourful children's drawings hang on the wall in front of me. Sometimes she has to pop over to the intensive care unit or up to my old ward. But she often sits at the computer before and after; I never imagined doctors spending so much time at the computer – except in research.

During the preparations for the bone marrow extraction, we make small talk because she naturally wants to know what's going on in her old neighbourhood. My objection at some point, 'you're just distracting me from what's about to happen to me,' she returns professionally: 'No, or yes, I do want to know what's going on with Ms or Mr *So-and-so*, but of course it also helps to distract you.' And then she pushes the thick needle into my pelvic bone. Sometimes it's very easy, but sometimes it takes longer and is painful, but it's bearable until it's through into the bone marrow. Once she says: 'It is often the case that one side of the pelvic bone is softer than the other.'

Then comes the Horrible 10 Seconds. For a long time now, I've been doing without a bite stick and playing the strong man; I don't really know why? I refuse a general anaesthetic, I'm hanging onto my now second life after all. She was the one who told me once: 'You have been given a second life, never forget that'.

Another time I asked her about the army officer, one roommate for three days, on whom she had performed a spinal cord puncture in the lumbar vertebrae area at the bed next to me. He was already trembling before it started, and later he screamed. I ask: 'Is it more painful with the spinal cord than with the bone marrow?' 'Yes, I remember him, who I once punctured next to you. No, it's definitely less painful. You also have to look at it psychologically, everyone feels pain differently. Members of the armed forces and police officers are often very tearful about something like that,' she answered. I immediately feel stronger again ... but only until the blood is taken from my bone marrow again using negative pressure.

Rehabilitation follow-up and Jose Carreras

Therapies are discussed and decided individually, I don't know all of them and some of them are only hearsay. I can make requests such as muscle relaxation (I knew positively) instead of autogenic training; I often used to fall asleep during this. And some things, such as measuring blood pressure or device-supported physiotherapy, you con-

tinue to do on your own after an individual introduction and then
have to record the progress.

After a rehabilitation day, I'm usually so exhausted in the evening that
I fall into bed tired straight after dinner ... and sleep through the night
more and more often, which was one of my goals.

A rehabilitation day, randomly copied from my weekly schedule:

*Daily before 07:30 a.m., measure blood pressure, blood oxygen, weigh,
Fridays, urine and blood sample (room ...)*

07:30 a.m.–08:30 Breakfast
08:30 a.m. Massage SNR
09:30 a.m. Lecture: Immune system, vaccinations
10:50 a.m. Brine inhalation
11:30 a.m.–12:30 Lunch
01:00 p.m. Individual physiotherapy spine
02:00 p.m. Lecture Sport, exercise and cancer
03:00 p.m. Walking, group 2
05:00 p.m. Individual psychological counselling
05:30 p.m.–06:30 Dinner

Evenings, (tbd.) rehabilitation lecture, film, reading, music ...

Other appointments on other days may include *doctor consultation, res-
piratory gymnastics, relaxation training, physiotherapy individual or group,
sleep training, walking and gymnastics, lecture,* for example *Dealing with
exhaustion and Fatigue,* and other often voluntary lectures after dinner,
for example, *Stress Management, Healthy Food & Cooking, Rehabilitation,
and then?*

In a physiotherapy on the machine or in group gymnastics, you
look at what the others are doing and try to be better; I know that also
from physiotherapy at home. It's nonsense, of course, because it's individual and sometimes depends on endurance and sometimes on
strength, but that seems to be typical for men.

At the first psychological group therapy session, the therapist repeatedly evades my questions on a so-called Fatigue Self Assessment
Index, I didn't want to disrupt the group or question her knowledge
of indices, so I cancelled the next appointments. On the contrary, despite my reservations, I was completely convinced by the individual

therapy with an experienced therapist who had actually already retired. I would have gladly continued with him.

I read the book from *Jose Carreras* during my rehabilitation follow-up treatment. When he was diagnosed with acute leukaemia end of the 1980s, virtually at the height of his career, it was like a verdict of imminent death. But he was one of the few people at the time who managed to survive with the help of medicine. He then founded the German *Jose Carreras Leukaemia Foundation* in line with his motto, 'Leukaemia must be curable, always, for everyone'. For many years, the foundation has contributed to the further development of bone marrow and stem cell transplantation worldwide. In addition to research projects, this also includes social support such as parents' homes and camps for children. This is because he and his colleagues recognised early on how important social support is, whether for survival or as End-of-Life care.

Because life is life, regardless of whether it's many more years, just a few months or even just a few days. That's what I adopted for myself back then and what I want to express with this book.

... and rehabilitation for the second time

My professor said in the last year of follow-up treatment that I would not need any further rehabilitation follow-up treatment, but if I absolutely insisted on it ..., but I don't want that. I don't feel like arguing with my health insurance company and subsidy.

So, I am registering as a private payer at the same rehabilitation centre as before, because it did me good there and also felt like it helped and, in particular, put my reservations about psycho-oncology into perspective. I see it as a holiday for me this time. Compared to a hotel plus the therapies, it's actually inexpensive, and my wine dealer of around 30 years is just a few vineyards away; but nobody needs to know that.

It's the same daily routines, the same friendly staff, the same beautiful view of a river valley, the same beautiful weather and, for the most part, the same treatments. I also know some of the therapists already and some of them know me too; is it because of my sometimes silly sayings? Unfortunately, the psychologist who previously had helped me very well – a reason for me to choose this centre again – he has now finally retired and moved away. The only noticeable difference this time is that there is no *Covid* time and there are four of us at the table for dinner. The table is set according to criteria I don't recognise. It's strange at first, but if you don't know it, it's understandable and good at the next meal.

On the one hand, different personalised nutrition plans are easier for the staff to manage and simpler to use. On the other hand, people open up more quickly in a recurring round table and it is also more fun because of a certain group dynamic. As the group takes turns each week, someone can sit at the table for just one week or the whole time.

We once had one at the table who always ticked with two small stones in his trouser pocket; mechanical sound. He once points out to a new waitress that this is a special step-maker because of his illness. Then it suddenly clicks faster. Oh, a *Saxon* – from a beautiful region in Germany with a strange dialect that people like to joke about – and turns his head towards the entrance ... and other heads follow him.

In my last week, a woman of a sect-like so-called Free Church sits at our table. It quickly becomes clear that she truly believes in the story of Adam & Eve created from his rib, etc.; I deliberately don't call it Creation Theory because otherwise it would give the impression of being scientific.

In response to my question as to why humanity has very different origin stories, why the majority of people do not believe in Christianity and why it has imposed itself on other peoples with extreme violence, she says (the both others at the table are also very sceptical): 'I'm now sitting at this table as a sign for us from God.' I return: 'Couldn't it be the other way round? It's a sign for you, because I could be a Buddhist or Hindu, for example?' She represses with other signs of her God to us, such as that we haven't died of cancer and that we need to find God through her in a rehabilitation centre. I then break it off for myself: 'If God created everything, including evil like the devil, he can't be good. I prefer to use my energy directly to do things that their creator obviously doesn't care about. Like for shelter and schooling for innocent children in a war zone, instead of self-centredly celebrating myself in a small sectarian religion until the revival or a new Son of God appearance together with others.' I immediately think, ouch, that's a bit too much. 'Look,' she repeats, 'another sign from God, he has chosen you to do this.' Well then, I think, I don't need a church or any other sect. 'Sorry, I have to go, the application is waiting.' This sentence can stop any conversation in a rehabilitation centre without being rude.

Later, I look for information about their cult leader, an alleged professor of technology. But there are only crude evangelical and partly homophobic texts. His title was a job title as director of a research institution; common and does not mean scientifically relevant research. So, he lets the title shine through to the outside world as an illusion of his crude evangelical views; psychologically known as Halo Effect; the over-radiation or glamour effect is often used as a business model for example in marketing or greenwashing. But if the people who follow it and donate and dance and sing and laugh ... are happy, then that's good. Isn't that what we all often do, simply enjoy something without questioning it?

Individual psychological counselling (1 hour), room 730, Ms DP ... on my treatment plan on Fridays. 'Not her again,' I think, I'd skipped further group appointments with her in the previous rehabilitation follow-up treatment because of her supposed incompetence and also because she had avoided my repeated questions. So I only go to the first one-to-one meeting to confirm my preconception; but it's completely different. After the three appointments, I would have go further on with her. She not only helped me personally, but also managed to ensure that I now fully support psycho-oncological counselling – as long as it is provided by genuinely trained, experienced therapists and not as self-proclaimed therapy, coaching and the like.

I have had pain in my lower lumbar vertebrae for six months when lying down and turning, standing up and bending down to tie my shoes. Two *MRIs* focussing on the puncture areas of the bone marrow extractions – which would somehow be obvious – revealed nothing.

So, during the admission interview, I also asked for a back massage with a special focus on the lumbar vertebrae.

Then, of course *SNR,* shoulder-neck-back, is a topic during the *massage* and the *individual spinal therapy.* A few weeks before the rehabilitation follow-up treatment, I heard the term Fascia for the very first time in my life. 'That's the summer slump word in physio-therapy, because it's always been a standard part of our joint and spinal treatments,' says a therapist while pressing a trigger point that I groan in pain. 'It just depends on how you deal with it,' he adds and goes on, 'also that you don't concentrate on it alone, working only on fascia doesn't solve the problem,' presseing on the trigger point again ... At another therapist, however, I learnt about less painful approach; in the end, both did me good. And with the recommended exercises, which I now continue to do for myself, my back is now feeling much better.

Clinic management' ... or administration, the seventh?

In the rehabilitation centre, I find a book reference on a notice board outside the psychotherapist's room. I order it and it arrives just one day later. There are 11 reports: Cancer in the Family. When I start reading part of the book while I'm still in rehabilitation, I realise why I wanted to retreat into solitude for three months.

With last text corrections now, I also know I am writing about my cancer and life here with so many similarities, points of reference for reflections and insights and (most important for me) the whole thing happens without distraction. That's why I unconsciously at first, and then more and more consciously, linked the two times in life together in parallel and kind of staggered timeline. Even it may remain unpublished, writing it down is important for me personally and especially for my children. But perhaps also for friends and people who had to experience me more closely during this time, to explain everything again, why I was sometimes not accessible and probably still often am not. Perhaps my reports and thoughts about cancer will help other people affected by life-threatening illnesses or their relatives.

The actual planned book project, about my experiences in university education and -administration, I've been preparing for over 10 years. Although I have scanned all the material I have collected and taken it with me, it will now have to wait. Evil tongues claim that it is not Public Service at all, but ever-increasing waterhead in complexity.

I read that 500,000 new cancer cases are diagnosed every year, half of which are curable and many of those affected can lead a long, carefree life afterwards. There are minute specifications for processes on the ward, on the patient, etc., because hospitals today are run by so-called managers without any specialist medical profession and experience of their own; often lawyers or business graduates. However, business is not management, but administration of a cost and service system.

Few years ago in a group of friends, the daughter of our hosts proudly told friends that she would soon be doing 'her MBA for becoming a Top Manager;' after all, she knew the term MBA, Master of Business Administration. Everyone nodded at her, her parents approvingly and almost admiringly. I didn't tell I am teaching in such programs for years worldwide, and what the term really meant if she couldn't translate it properly herself. And I didn't want to destroy her career dreams at the table in a family of lawyers; for them it was bad enough that her daughter didn't at minimum will study law.

Like employees nowadays are Human Resources, patients are now called Clients or Customers, and not those who need help and provide help. And everything is reduced to key indices. In administration, a part-timer is then called 0.5 *VAK* (half full-time working employee), which sounds a little more human again as an abbreviation for the term in personnel planning for full-time employees, but only a little. For example, *PriceWaterhouse,* a former auditing and consulting firm now calls itself International Consulting – by the way, they repeatedly appear in financial scandals – gives in their analysis and consulting reports process statements such as '13 minutes per patient in the ambulance.' Does it mean, from 14th or 15th minute onward, the doctor or nurse should then ask themselves whether helping from now on makes sense? The fact that they don't immediately calculate people in their individual parts as product values – 'they made soap from bones and melted down the gold teeth,' my grandmother's words about the German *Nazi* time resonate with me, in the spirit of Human Capital Index (HCI), a key index in Human Resources Management. Among other things, it is intended to indicate past and potential future performance in relation to, for example, Return on Investment which is also a strange indicator for investment in further training.

The German term *Humankapital* (human resources) is coyly concealed, as it evokes bad memories for the older people because of *Hitler*, the *Nazis* (National Socialists) and *Holocaust* (genocide of 2,7 million Jewish people). So, HCI sounds more chic and as supposedly modern management in the consulting world ... but then again, it's just copied from *Gauthier's* 19th century texts, *l'homme en est venu à traiter l'humanité comme une matière* (loosely translated, man has come so far as to treat humanity as a raw material).

Shortly before I left for India, I read an article on Mass-produced Goods, regarding the publishing companies. Of course I was interested, because after all, I've been writing and publishing for years myself. The global corporation *Bertelsmann Penguin Random House,* the world biggest publisher with 365 publishing subsidiaries and brands with around 16,000 new publications mass-produced goods each year.

Where publishers used to discuss matters directly with authors, today it is the so-called Literary Agents who calculate the optimisation visions of the *McKinsey* world together with the financial investor and a salaried program manager. A business sense for quantity is replacing an aesthetic sense for quality. Publishers and editors have more to do with administrative and management tasks than with authors ... a rogue who thinks of hospitals.

Psycho-oncology

My personal first experience is suddenly standing next to my bed as the visible second chemotherapy cycle drips into me. The young man wants to talk to me. At first I think a young modern priest without the usual, recognisable religious-spiritual insignia to offer me confession or Last Rites? But he introduces himself as someone from the hospital's Psychological Service.

I haven't thought much of it so far, along the lines of, if you study psychology, you have problems yourself, or you talk yourself into it as a young person, or because it sounds chic or because it's *en vogue* at the moment? But I don't want to stress about it either, because I already feel that I'm in the right hospital and I can somehow manage it.

After an hour, I know more about this young man than he knows about me; he has just finished his Master's degree at the university.

The same applies to a clown. I see her sometimes on our ward, dressed in costume and equipped with a guitar and, for example, a singing bowl. She is certainly experienced in dealing with long-term patients. But I feel it's better for me to make my way back to our lounge room with my laptop and my infusions plugged in; '*Emil*, say goodbye to her.' She laughs and replies: 'Good idea, I'll have to remember that.'

It's not really my thing, but I know some of my fellow patients enjoy this kind of variety, including *Peter*, my frequent long roommate. He particularly liked the singing bowl. He's very open-minded about everything anyway, despite his age; that's not a given.

I'm more concerned with my self-organisation and work goals as well as my daily medical and nursing routine. And I'm also probably still unconsciously suffering from the consequences of the shock. Or is it just an escape because I don't want to open up emotionally?

Today, writing here and living with the people in the mountains, I am also experiencing for myself that singing and making music together brings relaxation and mental balance.

Psycho-oncology is a relatively new direction in the care of patients, relatives and other connected people; and it is therefore also a scientific field of research. My first expectations or experiences were initially confirmed prejudices. I didn't even know the word beforehand, and it didn't come up in the first conversation at the hospital. And I wasn't prepared to open up to questions like, what is the goal, what can we do next?

The subsequent follow-up treatment, which included oncological treatment, had in the meantime been replaced by a new provider (investor?) in a different market segment. And in the second rehabilitation follow-up treatment after another two years, the group therapy was a failure for me. On the other hand, the one-to-one sessions were helpful, as they slowly introduced me to the subject.

After a small talk, it starts in the classic way. What feelings and opinions do I perceive? What feelings does this generate in me? This is my ego, the way I perceive myself, I am told. And in the next step, I learn to reflect together with the psychologist. For example, why is it like that? Does it come from my upbringing? Or from my professional and family socialisation? As a result, the type of cultural and individual programming dictates my feelings and emotions.

This then leads me to deal with it further. For example, through discussions at the next rehabilitation centre, research and experience reports such as the '11reports' in the book mentioned above.

Nowadays I know that typical consequences such as a burn-out or, worse, permanent depression, post-traumatic stress disorder and persistent fatigue can lead to suicidal thoughts.

Help begins to reflect with: 'Why?' And, a therapist is more helpful than self-therapy, -medication or -proclaimed pseudo-therapists.

There are so many long-term consequences that ultimately affect not only the patient themselves, but also their relatives, friends and colleagues. They may actually need psycho-oncology even more than the person affected, who automatically has more knowledge about the disease than their private environment.

And then the circle closes, because you don't necessarily want to talk to relatives about the topics that are really important for patients, so as not to shock them or burden them further. This is where a rather neutral psycho-oncologist who knows about the disease and has experience with patients can help.

A wide red folder stands diagonally opposite of my desk on the shelf in my home office with all the documents that I have received from the hospital over the years:

- Reports from the *MRI* radiology department of the university hospital,
- countless *Excel* tables with medical laboratory values,
- an *Excel* spreadsheet I keep with the invoice amounts (around 175,000 Euro to date, now in its sixth year, at the end of the follow-up treatment as part of the clinical study),
- medical reports from admission to follow-up treatment (initially every four weeks, after discharge every three to six months),
- including pathological-anatomical values and expert reports,
- including haematology laboratory, *ECGs* and in-between a long-term *ECG* with a cardiologist, laboratory cytology and molecular diagnostics, molecular-genetic findings, mutation analysis ... I can't even spell some of the words correctly, as well as the
- study, randomised phase III to evaluate intensive chemotherapy with/ without ...

I only touch the folder to file new medical reports with lots of tables of medical values that I still don't understand, and to enter the new costs of my leukaemia follow-up treatment in an *Excel* spreadsheet that is now pages long.

And the last time before I go back to Kalimpong to write, to scan a few selected documents as reminders. And then again later, after my return from Kalimpong, because they say we need the final blood and bone mar-row values for the study ..., 'grrr.'

Back to work

To be honest, despite all my hopes of being able to lead a normal life again right from the start, after the long hospitalisation and the follow-up treatment I can no longer mentally find my way back to my job and the university as a place to work.

Firstly, from an external perspective, there is professional re-integration according a specific work re-integration model after such long period of incapacity for work due to illness. For me, it initially means only working half time together with a temporary severe disability. After that, I can continue to reduce my working hours by half until I retire by consistently reducing overtime. But a lecture is a lecture and a seminar is a seminar, you can't just do half or two-thirds. And why should the students be at a disadvantage because of my personal illness?

So the *Covid* lockdown basically suits me; purely in terms of organisation, of course. The long hospitalisation has trained me to work in lockdown, so to speak. At first, I didn't really want to switch to virtual lectures and seminars. But once I've converted at least one course to virtual – I think at least once – I suddenly can't switch everything to virtual fast enough.

And as if without a transition, in our region the great river *Ahr* valley flood comes; the more than heavy rain also hits our university campus hard, and so it continues virtually. But my conscience is burdened, so much happiness with so much misfortune for so many other people?

And then I'll retire and have all the time in the world to do the things I've been doing for years and can now concentrate on.

So much for the perceived plan. But of course things turn out differently. 'You can't replace him that easily,' my former dean said in a slightly ironic undertone. Of course I agree to two compulsory lectures. And again for the next semester ... and then again ... and ...? My advantage now is that I say how I'm going to do it and enjoy my fool's freedom.

Firstly, the crux of the matter is that although my retirement has been a foregone conclusion since I became a civil servant, it's now far too late to advertise my position. Secondly, it's a bit of a joke, because I specialise in personnel planning; in the broadest sense of human resources management.

The saying, 'a prophet is worthless in his own house,' is especially true for universities. This brings me back to hospitals and institutions under public law. Management here means administration after all. Of course, there is no such thing as succession planning, a deputy system, personnel risks, etc., which every student of economics learns in their first semester. Instead, there are around 100 project groups, commissions and offices with and with-out exemption from teaching etc. for anything and everything.

I would be interested to know how many people were involved in the workload full costs – personnel and ancillary costs, allocated over-head- plus opportunity costs for direct business processes not carried out at the time – and for the papers on gender-equitable language. Experience has shown that in such a large organisation, the results of such working groups are thrown into familiar large bins anyway, regardless of their socio-cultural importance in the current trend. But, salary on the first of the month comes ... yes, from and through whom and for what?

But of course I continue to support individual students in a targeted way, which also helps me to stay young at heart. And this even beyond their studies. I have also been working for years on projects in quality management and certification in international development cooperation as well as in the accreditation of study programmes at universities – increasingly also abroad. And two foundations and advisory boards that I need time for, and of course private interests ... so it remains exciting.

Interestingly, as I have often heard, when you retire, the number of enquiries increases by leaps and bounds. We're still looking, we'd like to work with you, could you imagine ...?

But, I also realise, I am no longer as resilient. The frequent tiredness has remained and so has the consequence of no longer taking in every-thing that presents itself. Or is it the other way round, that I no longer find a lot of things interesting, because basically it's the same thing over and over again, and that's why it's tiring or not motivating. I realise, I can spend hours working on texts and research. I've already turned my back on a lot of things and feel liberated. It's similar to leaving school or university behind, or the first years of work and then changing jobs and locations. Or the children are suddenly standing on their own feet or have left home – they are in their mid to late 30s and have been on their own interesting paths in life for a long time. Or a long marriage comes to an end and something new begins; I don't talk about my relationship – in this current social media wave of sharing as much as possible with everyone, usually in an exaggerated way; something should also remain private.

Cancer ennobles ... but annoying!

Often someone says, you or they had such a bad illness, and I'm somehow treated specially or as someone entitled to pity. Or behind my back I sense a whisper, 'you must know, he had a leukaemia.'

Of course I like to talk to someone who has been through chemotherapy themselves, for example. That sounds a bit macabre – because I wouldn't wish it on anyone – but it's so important for you as a sufferer. It's just that there aren't that many people with leukaemia who know about it. And the people I got to know at the hospital are either deceased or there is no contact. Of course, a hospital doesn't give out names, telephone numbers or addresses as protected patient data; I wouldn't want that either.

When you're in hospital, you don't have time to think about the after-math or ask people for their telephone number. It's all about survival and daily blood values.

It was similar in the rehabilitation follow-up treatment, although it would actually have been the right time. But I was also afraid to talk openly about my illness there, except in therapy. And to speak to others directly and ask questions? And what if the answer is that I've had my breast amputated and have a stoma ... that also seems too intimate to me.

During the years follow-up treatment, I read the book: You must Change your Life (by *Peter Sloterdijk*, currently considered, one of the most German influential, scientifically sound thinkers). Drawing on

Nietzsche (19th century world known philosopher), he uses relevant sources to expose a society that sees disabled people as beings who need to get ahead. Because this is the only way they can achieve recognition. Known at the time as Cripple Anthropology, the spectrum ranged from 'putting oneself on show' in a circus to disabled art, up to 'I take myself in my own hands, I made myself well again'. Nowadays, achievements of disabled athletes are particularly emphasised, with the focus being on the disability rather than the performance. Or the astrophysicist *Stephen Hawking* († 2018), severely disabled in a wheelchair unable to look after himself. Everyone looked up with fascination when something about him was in the media; he was regarded as the explainer of the universe. Hardly anyone ever paid attention to what he really discovered and wrote. I confess, neither have I; physics has always been incomprehensible to me.

Was I mentally incapacitated in hospital because of the shock? Two years later, a leukaemia patient is still 100% disabled. Am I allowed to think differently (even strangely) from my fellow human beings?

Back to, 'you must know he had leukaemia'. Okey, I'm not poor, my arms are still there, even if they're a bit bruised from infusions and blood sample-years. But, disabled means somehow 'poor' in my language, no matter what else you do. Can I therefore anthropologically justify my aversion to pity? Or do I consider it an assault on myself if I am indirectly forced to say thank you for pity in accordance with convention?

Writing down my thoughts at the time, I am now '60% severely disabled.' What percentage or what is the actual distinction between disabled, severely disabled, and most severely? I'm going to *google* it myself: in Germany it's defined as, 'having a functional impairment from da degree of 20% disability;' whatever it means? Is it purely physical or also mental? As far as I know, the intelligence index as so-called An IQ is measured on the basis of very different intelligence models and methods, without the users of such tests even being aware of the differences in intelligence theories.

Personally, however, I don't even feel that severely handicapped. Quite the opposite, even if it sounds macabre or even cynical to some people? I feel stronger, even more mentally and physically liberated than in the living and career conventions I lived in before. In the US, a country with a much longer tradition of anti-discrimination, they say, 'challenged people.' I like, accepting and overcoming challenges.

Merry Christmas to me

It's probably the best Christmas of my life. Of course, it was always nice as a child, if only because of presents and sweets. Later, as a teenager, you would always meet up with childhood friends now in training or studying somewhere else after a parental compulsory Christmas Eve exercise at home. And of course it was also nice as a family with children; although for parents of three children, including visiting grandparents; at the end as enriching including parallel stress.

This time it's completely different. I want to be alone, I insist on it. And I remember reading I have read *Jose Carreras'* biography in my second rehabilitation time, where tears came to my eyes in many places; from sadness or happiness, I can't remember. I then bought a *CD* of him, which I put on this Christmas Eve and googled something about him. Then, suddenly there's the annual Christmas Gala on *YouTube*. I don't really like such kind of a pompous self-congratulatory event. And I don't know what year it's from; it doesn't matter. I got completely stuck on it and actually cried the whole time. From happiness or was it also the second glass of red wine ... but that's not really why I'm crying.

The Truth remains   ... Darjeeling Village Life too

It was a tragic incident, but like any tragedy, it cleanses the mind and only brings out the positive in the course of time ... He made it possible for me to find myself because I realised how much I was frozen in habits, in routine, how little I had used my mind; how much I had almost set myself up for a spontaneous visit from the Grim Reaper.

Peter Ustinov, in: Monsieur Renè

The Truth remains

Psycho-oncology for the second time

During the second rehabilitation I read a book – a recommendation of my psychotherapist – about cancer in the different perspectives like from the point of view of relatives, friends or colleagues at work. Together with my own reflections in therapy, I finally realized much too late that all these people around me are often more psychologically burdened than the patient himself.

Especially during the chemotherapy cycles, and all personal and electronic monitoring, side effects, days or weeks of a initially feverish and trance-like aplasia phase, there is hardly any time to think about what was, what is and what will be? Then there is the daily routine of examinations and measurements, blood samples, infusions, catheter changes, electronic beeping, care services and, and, ... and of course, you also share in the fate of your roommate. I can't remember having slept a single night. After falling asleep sometime after midnight, you are woken up at 6 a.m. at the latest and are at the centre of this routine ... while relatives and friends wake up every morning and wondering how he is, whether he is still alive, whether he will survive?

For me, the emotional crashes came unexpectedly in spurts, usually at night. It was a constant alternation between deep guilt and inner reproachful lack of understanding. On the one hand, the children and best friends feel ostracized, possibly offended, or in worst case, rejected if they are not immediately informed. And on the other hand, I'm mentally unable to cope with this demand in this personal situation and environment. So in addition to the new and very problematic circumstances for everyone, you may also lose the chance to strengthen or confirm the relationship and friendship. For the children, and so for their partners, it is even worse and often an ongoing problem, possibly associated with a deeper loss of trust. This is almost the same as dying without having taken them into your confidence beforehand.

Conversely, I also have to slow them down myself or set limits on their feeling that they have to take care of everything and anything on a daily basis, because they have their own lives with partners, families and jobs. Taking time out and regularly taking a deep breath are just as important for them. And you yourself often need distance, peace, quiet and the feeling of not being completely dependent.

The devices connected to my body and the infusions pumped into, so to speak, and the orchestra of medication swallowed, as well as the (surely sensible) instructions from the medical and nursing staff are quite enough. This total loss of control is (at least for me) logically impossible to get a grip on; it can only be managed, for example, through distractions such as work or with the help of the little red wonder pills ... and I sleep.

Today I know that you firstly have to accept cancer and learn to live with it, and secondly you also have to share it. Being terminally ill is also just a shell, an invisible glass ball into which you place yourself; and which you don't always consciously realise.

Sure, as soon you move, stand up, are questioned about it or read an audit report, you are immediately confronted with it again, physically and mentally. And, of course, there are sleepless nights in which you cry or tremble endlessly. And, as I now realise, the closer you are to your family and friends, the more you have to think about it.

Couldn't I have done it the night I was admitted, or the next morning after my escape, or after the first bone marrow extraction, or on the way to the intensive care unit, or, or, or, ...?

In any case, from the point of view of my family, it was far too late. I only found the mental strength to inform them after the first acute danger phase back on the (normal?) ward. Now I realise that it was definitely too late.

The feeling that I have to deal with this on my own, I want to protect them, etc., is certainly understandable for many people. Just like children don't find out everything from their parents and, conversely, children don't tell them everything either. But in this case, what would have happened if I hadn't woken up? You would wake up again and again for many years and ask yourself questions such as, did he have so little trust in us? And dreams and even nightmares could remain.

And, what's particularly bad, even if you go on living, they now always have to have the feeling whether it's really true when I say, 'all is fine.' This leads to anxiety and, in the worst case, perhaps even depression in people for whom you are jointly responsible, regardless of whether you have died or survived. I had to experience for myself how a relative slipped into a burn-out with her own extreme professional and private challenges. Then, in the middle of it all, I was suddenly struck by my long and serious illness; a strong, if not triggering factor?

At some point in the years follow-up treatment and -care, it's a sentence that really gets to me and reminds of this conflict in the family.

I downloaded a multi-part movie for a week in the evenings; I can watch the short 50-minute movies without a break. The old father of the researcher has a cancer relapse and it's about a new chemotherapy treatment. But he doesn't want it anymore, he can't take it anymore. Everyone around him tells him, 'do it again, it's not just about you, it's about us.' Short memory sequences about glances, short conversations and remarks run through all parts of the series. But I'm no longer interested in the actual content, only in the father-daughter relationship. At some point toward the end, he says: 'Listen, about the chemo,' … but the daughter interrupts him. It remains unclear if he still refuses or if he wants to do it for her. 'No,' she says, 'we'll do whatever you want. I just want us to be together and use this time for us.'

Months in hospital, weeks in rehabilitation centres, years of follow-up treatment ... if I had known this beforehand, would I have embarked on this ordeal?

Today I know, during the first spontaneous escape already after the first few hours in hospital, the first few days back, then intensive care and back on the ward, I was completely in shock, despite thinking being supposedly rationally aware; even later in phases.

After a good two and a half years, the professor tells me during a follow-up treatment, I have good news and bad news for you: 'Don't worry, the cancer is physically gone, you are now considered fully recovered,' he explains. I immediately ask him: 'And what is about the bad news?' 'If you choose to, you will have to have your blood tested regularly for the rest of your life. And you will never be the same again, never again. You will, if you haven't already realised it yourself, be a different person. Yes, you had cancer, a leukaemia. *AML* leucaemia is one of the most dangerous incisions in a life, both physically and mentally. Precisely because it forces you to take extreme action at very short notice. But then again, the good news is that if you accept this and don't try to suppress this fact and the memory of it, but allow it, then you will also allow yourself to live again. Otherwise you are taking an important part of your life away from yourself. These intense moments, weeks, months and now for years, the new hope, the joy of new goals. And the positive attitude and enthusiasm that we particularly noticed in you during your treatment at the hospital,' he motivates me.

I now know that memories, not only of beautiful things, but also of important and not so beautiful things, are part of life. You have to learn to bear these memories too. This is the only way to recognise the everyday as having true value in life, to become cheerful again in bad phases and to enjoy new things. And this is also how you keep your life before and during cancer, which is also real life, which is finite and therefore unique.

The cancer is gone, you are now in full remission, they say. But it remains a constant companion in my head, takes me to the theatre and shopping, sits with me on my bike and by the big river when I look across the water to the mountains with their deep green forests. That sounds bad at first, as if you're under psychological strain.

For me, it's also a good thing. I perceive things differently, my life, the days, seasons, children and friends, everything is more intense; I'm more relaxed. Maybe that's why it's more intense, even if I seem more serious and thoughtful on the outside, but inside I'm jumping with joy, I could scream with happiness. And I have finally managed to free myself from material accumulation of More, Newer, Fashion, Bigger, More Expensive etc.

But of course I also fulfil my dreams. From many people's point of view, the five sinfully expensive whiskies such as *Brora, Port Ellen,* that have long been secretly coveted are nonsensical. of Scottish distilleries that have not existed for decades; I have seen the ruined foundations of two of them on one of my many trips to Scotland.

On the other hand, I am giving money away to those who need it more. I am parting with an inherited share portfolio, which had never interested me anyway, as the basis for a foundation that looks after street children in one of the most dangerous areas of the world. Children caught between hostile terrorist groups, enslaved and/or often abused; so much for the topic of Human Resources. And that's despite the fact that I was once a so-called Human Resource Manager for a long time before I started working at a university, and then also represented the subject academically for around 20 years. Here, too, my illness has shown me that there are more important things than adorning yourself with company cars, titles and business cards.

Adaptation training?

What I read at some point and found again shortly before this book went to press, on the Art of the Human Being fits in well with this, 'everything is an adaptation training,' (freely translated from: You must Change Your Life, by *Peter Sloterdijk,* 2011).

Symbolically, whether in predominantly Christian Europe, Communist China or Hindu India ..., in schools, universities or companies, in state organisations or even in NGOs through certificates, titles, levels achieved or dress codes, medals, labels and even plastic cosmetic surgery, everything looks like spare parts for the still supposed semi-finished product towards the end product of a successful person.

Even so-called Dropouts use symbols – usually not really understanding the meaning – such as *Rasta* curls or Hindu *Tikas,* or proudly postulate, they have already reached the Third Degree of some esotericism or found their Christian Divine illumination. Ultimately, they are (un-) consciously, just looking for a recognised role in a new system. And if they don't manage it in their own cultural context, then in another, in order to stand out as something special in the own culture.

Personality falls by the wayside, advancement and recognition are only achieved by adapting to one of such systems. He now lives in London, according to a former colleague, previously so-called Management Consultant. Later it was Switzerland etc.; of course he didn't really live there, it was just for the image and/or to save taxes.

A rogue who, looking back and forward, is now thinking, what has the author been drinking? And who knows me, did he finally manage to open the wall cabinet?

The whisky cabinet and a map

Now, it was the fifth anniversary of my hospital discharge, and I want to do 'something good' for myself on that day.

Five bottles of very rare Single Malt whiskies (I mentioned above) in an Art Nouveau wall cabinet. I only ever drink them with friends because you'll never have the same experience again – at least not you, I always smile – or on a day like this. And it doesn't matter if it tastes good; old and expensive does not mean it tastes good.

But on my very Personal Celebration of that day, exactly the same thing happens that happened 25 years ago. Because I always hide the key to this cupboard somewhat theatrically, but now I can't remember where I've put it months ago. Back then, I went from one locksmith to another with my ward-robe and nobody could help me. I finally ended up with a retired furniture locksmith in the backyard. His secret was to work the lock through the furniture via the hinges.

Just like back then, I only find the key by chance days later. So, the bottle hasn't been opened; I'm waiting for the next special day.

In addition to my annual donation to the *Leukämie-Initiative* on the occasion of my discharge date from hospital, I am writing a few lines and greetings to the current patients in their weekly patient café; they were such a great mental help for us, no matter how bad we were feeling. Weeks later, I receive a card, '... how happy you made us and the patients at the ward here, thank you so much, five years have passed since your time here, we are so pleased that you look back with such gratitude.'

South Kivu, my personal thanks to life

Having worked there for international NGOs for many years, I have to organise my personal commitment to the street children in such a way that it will be sustainable without me. I now know first-hand that life can quickly become finite.

After the first chemotherapy cycle, I feel like, 'time is running out and I've got to get things done', as they say. Initially together with my children and a lawyer, I can sort out my financial affairs virtually at my bedside; and with help of *ChildFund Germany*, an internationally active NGO with which I have been working for some time, set up a foundation for homeless street kids in Africa (*www.meierStiftung.de*).

My earlier individual donations, for example, school supplies and toys for 40 abandoned children, have now become regular and independent of my life. Together with a rapidly growing circle of donors – THANK YOU to all of you at this point – we have also been able to achieve, for example, solar energy, a septic tank for sewage disposal, new mattresses and furniture.

Eastern Congo, 'the worst place to be a child,' according the *UN*, characterised by terror on an almost daily basis, in the border region with Burundi, Rwanda, Uganda. Some may have heard of the genocide against the *Tutsi* tribe in the 1990s; a total of almost 1 million people were killed. This war continues subliminally to this day.

If someone asks me how many children I have, I say: '43,' and the people look up in amazement; after a short pause for breath ... 'three with my former wife and I don't know any of the other mums.' The amazement continues, and at one point someone slips out, 'are you a sperm donor?' No, it's like a sponsored children's home for street children. Like other children, they also have the right to dream for the future. No, of course we won't be able to save the world ... but we can make some little starfish happy (see story below). And even if it were only for a while, we would want to make that possible.

Yes, it's street children somewhere. Yes, terror and misery seems to be unstoppable. Yes, we hear that a lot of money is disappearing into the pockets of corrupt politicians. Yes, there are also many people in need of help here with us ... and, yes, it's just a drop in the ocean.

I hear these comments again and again, more or less directly or see it in their eyes. Mostly from those who fill their lives with ever new consumption; the new covers for the branded patio chairs are currently the biggest problem to be solved, I think pityingly. But then I can't resist a response with the <u>Metaphor of the Girl and the Starfish</u> (from the film *The Guru*, US 1998).

> *A man saw a girl walking up and down the beach, seemingly always picking something up and throwing it away. He walked towards the beach and saw that the storm had washed countless starfish onto the beach during the night with its roaring waves. They were now lying there on the black shingle, starfish as far as you could see. The girl kept picking up a starfish and throwing it back into the sea. The man went up to the girl and asked her: 'Why are you doing this? There are so many starfish lying around here. It doesn't matter how hard you try, you'll never be able to cope.' The girl paused for a moment and looked at the man thoughtfully. 'Maybe what you say is true,' she replied to him, and she picked up another starfish. 'But for this one now, it's good that I'm putting him back in the sea.' And she threw the starfish as far back into the sea as she could.*

My illness has already become relative for me again.

Often the only difference in a problem or misfortune is how we judge it? Not why it is there, or who is to blame? Because you often have no control over that and it doesn't help to find a solution. But you have the choice of how to deal with it now? That is responsibility for your own life, how you see it, evaluate it and react to it.

During his visit to me in Darjeeling, my son showed me a book he was reading. I photographed a chapter from it on the subject of misfortune and took an example from it: If you are mugged, you're not to blame, but you are responsible for how you deal with it. For example, you can panic or fight, freeze and or wait, call the police, treat it as an accident or deny that it ever happened ... Many people react in the sense that there is nothing I can do, I have no choice. But you always have a choice (from: You are always choosing, in *Mark Manson:* The Subtle Art Of Not Giving A F*ck).

After the shock of leukaemia, I initially decided to make the most of my (supposedly) remaining time. And not simply submit to the illness, especially not in lethargy or self-torture. And not complaining via *WhatsApp* & co. – I didn't anyway – and not hiding behind the bed-integrated swivelling arm with TV screen; there's no at home either. As soon as possible, I did things that I had been putting off for a long time and that I wanted to do – in a supposedly short remainder of my life – such as reading art, history and science, and do some writing.

In oncological psychotherapy, I later learnt to reflect on the fact, I'd often unconsciously reacted in this way in my life. Now I can say that I have learned more from the misfortune of this leukaemia than from many other situations or problems before. My personal conclusion, problems are also challenges to learn and develop in a short life.

The cancer is gone, but one feeling remains

I now know that cancer is not a one-off illness that you either don't survive or, if it is successfully treated, is gone forever. In addition to a more or less high risk of relapse, you can never escape it psychologically.

Except, of course, for a short time through drugs such as alcohol. I also had phases like that, where a bottle of wine would quickly run out in the evening, followed by a whisky or sometimes another one. Sometimes that would go on for two or three days. I wasn't entirely comfortable with that and then I rigorously stopped.

No symptom, no complaint, no change is ever normal or can be explained in any way without involving the cancer ... a cancer patient, however, cannot categorise any symptom as normal or harmless. It could always be a complication that leads to the cancellation of treatment, or even a harbinger of the end. Whether it's a persistent fever, cough, dizziness, headache, a pulling sensation in the back or tingling in the fingers ... these can be the usual minor complaints or new signs of a relapse. From the point of view of the former cancer patient, it always feels like a Sword of Damocles over him, which puts a permanent psychological strain on him. Because back then, at the time of the truth, it only started with a little dizziness, and ...; this is also how an oncologist who was affected by cancer himself describes it.

Although I have a vague feeling of shame or guilt – I have repeatedly addressed it in psychotherapy during the rehabilitation follow-up treatment and also systematically reflected on it looking for solutions in books and brochures – it remains.

So I have the feeling of being looked at by relatives and friends of the deceased in the sense of, why did he and our relative not survive? It wasn't just at three funerals or some grave visits, but suddenly completely unprepared in-between.

For example, I went to the car park after an follow-up treatment at the hospital. An older and a younger woman got into the lift with me; I assume mother and daughter. 'You've made it now for going home,' was my friendly comment. 'No, this is from my husband, he can no longer come home to us,' one replied. That was a shock. I offer my condolences and am glad that the lift door opens at that moment and they get out. And again I have this feeling, why did I survive and her husband and father had to die?

The last (preliminary) Bone Marrow extraction ...

When I return from my extended stay in India for writing this book in mid-January, I find a message on the answering machine about a new bone marrow extraction. I call and find out that another one has to be done as part of the scientific study.

I'm going to take it sportingly now. At the same time, I resolve to ask the professor, the doctor and the receptionist if I can mention their names in my acknowledgements? I also have half a page of a very medical text that I would like to have proofread, because I don't want to make a complete fool of myself with the naive medical knowledge I heard and read at the hospital.

... Darjeeling Village Life too

Harvest rice

In the morning, as well as preparing a large *Roti* dough, they always cooked a big pot rice. For them as two people, they calculate 1 kg per day. More rice was then eaten for parties and visitors such as the son in his semester holidays, relatives, guests, the project manager, the beggar monks and often the day labourers as well as myself.

As in the whole of India and many Asian countries, rice is the daily basis. Of course, I could write something similar about potatoes or noodles for other cultures. The two brothers cultivate their few small cultivation terraces together, so that their parts are ripe for harvesting one after the other and they can help each other. Each of them has an area roughly the size of a football pitch. The area available for drying after cutting is limited; anything that grows upwards, such as wheat or rice, needs relatively more space to lie and dry. This means, other garden areas that are lying fallow at the time are used, for example for potatoes or the terraces around the house, etc.

Each household produces just under 400 kg of rice. However, this is not enough for their own needs and they have to buy additional rice, three to four of 50 kg each per year.

I had resolved to eat more rice at home and have now got used to it. So, back at home, I look at my stock of rice; a good cup of leftover white rice, a packet of black rice and an open packet of red rice.

I'll make sure I buy Basmati quality in future, even if I have no idea what that means; my mum would have said now, 'but we still do'.

While the white rice simmers, I remember our November rice harvest and look at photos. Neighbours and day labourers help; it had to be quick and dry quickly before it was threshed.

Cutting with a small hand sickle in a strenuous stooped posture in bundles and folded behind him into larger bundles, laid apart again to dry for a few days, threshing out again in bundles by hand on large plastic tarpaulins. The brother has the stalks ploughed under.

Those who can afford it get someone to do it with their motorised hand plough; 60 Rupees (66 Eurocents) an hour. Soil is then slurred and mustard seed, for example, spread as a natural nitrogen fertiliser. The rapid growth keeps back weeds and prevents soil compaction, I learn.

Giri cuts a bamboo trunks at the edge of his property, which also includes a small mixed forest; they often above 10 m long and as thick as an arm. There are also larger bamboo trunks in the area that are well 25 m long up to 25 cm in diameter; used in furniture making, as kitchen utensils, tins or waist-high for churning ghee like a butter churn.

With a day labourer he quickly build a scaffold on the slope below the shelter for the cattle, on which the rice straw can be stored, covered with a tarpaulin to protect it from rain but ventilated from below. It also serves as supplementary fodder in winter or as bedding for cattle.

While the rice is laid out to dry, thick clouds gather one morning. Haze had been hanging over the whole valley since the morning and only a nearby mountain could be vaguely recognised. Under no circumstances should it rain or remain this foggy. If the rice doesn't dry so that it can be threshed, half the year's harvest will be gone; it would be a minor disaster.

The brother only manages to thresh out part of it, and the rest is piled up in bundles as a pyramid-like around dome 3–4 m in diameter a good 4 m high. The outer thatch acts like a thatched roof and rain and night-time dew run off. Finally, a bouquet of flowers is placed on top, which is traditional and also looks beautiful.

Two weeks later, the weather is stable, sunny and dry all day. I'm invited to take photos at breakfast, so I'm glad I wasn't invited to help. I certainly wouldn't be able to do that physically in the blazing sun and at this altitude.

Two oxen have already arrived early in the morning. The pyramid of rice straw is now taken down by hand in layers in bundles and lightly threshed out. It is then scattered under the oxen in the path around a thick bamboo pole driven into the ground and threshed according to tradition. In the end, this results in roughly the same amount as previously threshed by hand.

The bamboo pole and the oxen are decorated with a flower arrangement. The only important thing is that they don't do their business in-between. But he has his tricks for that, laughs the oxen contractor in response to my question, who spends half or full days travelling from farm to farm.

Rice flour, Dal and spices

Rice flour is used, for example, to make the sweetened fried *Sel Roti* for special occasions. The rice can be milled nearby at a small family grain mill.

Traditionally, rice is pounded like an oversized mortar with an oversized wooden hammer operated by the feet and then ground with a hand-operated plate-sized millstone. Some of the neighbours still use these old hand-operated machines, and of course, the old people still swear by them.

There are also people who make *rice noodles*, but they don't know how to do it. They prefer to buy our type of noodles because it is something special from a different culture and, of course, it is less work.

Manju has also eaten *rice oil* elsewhere from time to time; it is probably relatively expensive; mustard oil is standard here anyway.

They've also heard of *Rice milk.* 'Why should we bother, the cow gives us 4 litres of milk twice a day,' says *Giri.* However, *Rice pudding,* made from their own home-grown rice and cow's milk is very popular. But, that's not really my thing, because my grandmother used to torture me with it when it was warm, sweet and with cinnamon, I think. Here, it is often eaten as a dessert with sultanas, nuts etc., just like sweet cereals here, which I really liked.

Rice with fresh milk is also the sole dish for our *Mr Tiger,* Basmati quality of course; when he's around. Lately he's often gone for days at a time. I wonder if there's a nice, pretty cat somewhere that he has his eye on?

I have cooked a lot of *Dal* in the past, the traditional – for us supposed – lentil soup in many variations. Here I am learning how to do it properly. From a rather strongly flavoured hot broth with relatively few lentils in the morning to a thick soup or stew in the evening, which is usually also enriched with vegetables. The variety of lentils in India is similar to our variety of bread; both are confusing, at least for me. But *Dal* here also means all other pulses such as peas and chickpeas, mung and other types of beans.

The main purpose of the large bowl of *Dal* in the morning and evening is to make the rice smoother and more flavoursome; I have never experienced a *Dal* simply eaten as a soup, as we do here, in many visits to India in the past and during my long stay in the country. Various vegetables – always at least two – are added to rice or *Roti patties.*

I also use more typical spices and *Masala,* spice blends for cooking vegetables, or fish, etc., and more often fresh coriander; goes very well with potato soup ... and chilli is a must.

Many people later use the mustard seeds scattered on the harvested rice fields to make home-made chutney and pickle, for example. The ingredients and spices are actually equally variable, the difference is more in the consistency and flavour, ranging from sweet and sour to extremely mustardy or vinegary. All are used for soups and as a condiment for vegetables; and also as an addition to the spiritual offering plate.

Mustard oil, household standard, is not worth making yourself because of the small amount of mustard seeds spread. They buy their household requirements of well over a litre a week in 2-litre bottles and 15-litre canisters. At spiritual festivals they need considerably more; mustard oil with a wick in small clay bowls burns like candles and also repels mosquitoes. At *Diwali* festival I counted around 60 bowls in and around the house.

Giri buys the dried molasses left over from grinding the mustard oil – which looks like pieces of charcoal – in 10-kg bags directly from a small mustard mill owned by a local family or from a trader. It is dried and added to the animal feed.

Theoretically I knew, there are two fundamentally different Indian culinary traditions in the North and the South of India. In a hotel in Rajasthan I stayed a few years ago, my Indian colleagues laughed when I came from the extensive breakfast buffet and my plate was full of norther and southern Indian food; whatever I thought tasted good or seemed interesting to try. Indians never would do that; okey, pork knuckle and fish in Germany don't necessarily go together on a plate either.

The fact that food becomes increasingly spicy and hot towards the south has developed climatically over the millennia. On the one hand, a higher humidity needs more antiseptic food, and what could be more obvious than hot spices? But the food here is also much spicier compared to Europe, partly also due to hygiene, as there is often no sewage system.

Drinking water is always boiled here; the fairy tale of the clear source of the Himalayas mountain stream has been a thing of the past at the latest since unbridled tourism, which people are now trying to limit. Even the so-called Alternative Backpackers were and are still not necessarily environmentally friendly, even though they have been in search of enlightenment since the 1970s. The amount of plastic and other waste that can now be found under the melting snow and ice fields in the Himalayas due to climate change is almost immeasurable.

Rice harvest for the second time

Suddenly it gets much cooler around noon and clouds gather, It'll probably rain. People from the neighbourhood hurry up the hill to the couple of day labourers who also have a few rice terraces. I don't want to stand on the sidelines and follow them. I arrive at the top quite out of breath and slightly dizzy. The others are tying rice straw that has already been laid out to dry into large bundles.

I help, of course; how would it have looked if I had just taken only photos? We work from top to bottom. After a few failed attempts at bundling and tying into a large bundle with thin bamboo bark, much to everyone's amusement, I manage to do quite well; not their speed, of course. Two men, bent over with headbands, carry up to four of the large bundles on their backs, first from a terrace to a lower one and then down on footpaths where a large pile is stacked and covered with tarpaulins.

I had previously only climbed up the steep trail with difficulty, and often holding on to something. Although it's already relatively windy and cool, I'm soaking wet after a short time and have to catch my breath after around 5–7 seven bundles. And there are so many small, branching, half-height terraces that there seems to be no end to them.

To break up the constant bending, I try to pick up two of the large bundles and try to carry them down. I have to drop the bundles as soon as I reach the first edge of the terrace. It's too heavy, I feel dizzy and I'm afraid of stumbling on the steep trail with the load.

Everyone is in a good mood, they laugh a lot and are surprised that I'm helping out, which for me is natural. I hope I'm not disrupting the proceedings too much. In the end, it starts to drizzle, so we form a chain and throw the bundles down the terraces one step at a time. In the dark and when it starts to rain properly, we're done; and I'm especially done. But it's a great experience. Tomorrow I'll try to count the terraces from below, preferably enlarged on a photo; I'm not going to climb up there again voluntarily.

Being in India or writing about India cannot leave out the topic of child labour. Of course it exists, but there are just as many misconceptions about it here.

Child labour is just as prohibited by law in India as it is here. The *UN* defines it up to the age of 13, but it says nothing about life expectancy and generously allows exceptions even in our western countries today. Even in Germany, such an exception is now referred to in labour law, for example, for children and young people working in their parents' business; Contributing Family Members,' they say.

Child labour was an invention of the up to now so-called Industrialised Nations. Who is not familiar with the novelist *Dickens*, who indirectly described it in the era of emerging industrialisation in England. Child labour in Europe was only banned in the mid-1950s. Not primarily based on ethics, but on military. In World War II the military did not have enough physically mature young men as soldiers.

With widespread production outsourcing to low-wage countries in the following decades, child labour emerged in places where there were no schools or where parents could not afford the school fees.

Today, companies engage in *Greenwashing*, do not feel responsible or in a position to take responsibility for the entire process chain from raw mate-rial to product and disposal. Instead, they adorn themselves with certificates Fair, Social, Green ... but knowing full well that child labour is used for their products, even as underpaid women and day labourers without social security are employed through subcontracting. It is naive to believe that there is a T-shirt for 3 USD or any phone without child labour.

Now, as I'm doing the final proofreading of this book text, I'm reading press reports such as, 'Too Expensive Control of Child Labour: Companies rant against Supply Chain Law,' or, 'Expensive Control of Supply Chains: Every German employs 30 to 50 Slaves.' All international and local NGOs too in such low-wage countries could show these Board members and Production managers and their Human Resource managers where children produce their preliminary and end products under slave-like conditions for our consumption. Everyone involved knows it, but prefers to be like the Three Wise Monkeys: See no evil. Hear no evil. Speak no evil. Cynically, it occurs to me why they don't actually show their partners and children on site what daddy works with?

As I'm searching and writing this, I've seen a new version, Four Wise Monkeys; the fourth one is sort of bowed in social media. But the gag contains the new truth, 'I am very busy in the new reality.'

Which parents would force their children for hard labour? Only those who would otherwise not be able to survive and have no schools. Then it makes sense for children to at least learn how to survive in some way, but provided that their physical and mental development corresponds to the effort they put in. Or should they fall into 'wrong hands' in the street or starve to death?

The children in these so-called Collective Cultures are often proud to be able to contribute to the family's livelihood. Sensationalist journalism with poorly dressed children – sponsored with 2 USD a quasi-set – only leads to the children going back to work the next day a block or a farm away. Instead of simply denouncing child labour and demanding bans, alternatives must be offered at the same time.

Dear readers, as you can see, this topic is close to my heart. I have been working on it for decades and learning has proven to be truly sustainable. For example, agreeing with the local entrepreneur to reduce working hours and sponsor a teacher so that the children can learn to read, write and do maths, that they can get out of this unspeakable cycle; there are many successful examples worldwide. Just as there are very simple and efficient examples of checking your supply chains, no matter how far away and convoluted they may be; why not working together with local NGOs, they know what's on.

In relative terms, the number of child labourers has been falling steadily for two decades, but it is increasing in absolute terms due to population growth. The rapidly, for example in India but as well in other developing countries, slowly growing lower middle class due to education and basic income is leading to a broad-based decline in birth rates, income security and school attendance; for children in such countries, school is the greatest thing of all.

In India, for example, the average household among the hill tribes has only two children, while in metropolises such as Kolkata, Mumbi, Delhi, there are often only one or two children from lower middle class upwards. The current population growth is only due to the large number of girls born in the past.

SSDC visit

A brief look back; it's mid-November and I've been here in Darjeeling for a month. *Manju* announces a visit from Kolkata over breakfast. First I think of the organisation of my friends who have done entrepreneurship training and consulting here for the SHGs and now organising the sale of products to the market in Kolkata *(www.soceo.de* or *www.symagine.org)*.

The year before, I briefly visited an eye-care hospital with them in the *Sundarbans*, the Ganges Delta islands and peninsulas, where they supervise or advise, for example, agricultural NGO-funded projects. At the same time, they themselves always support something else in the region, because such funded projects creates envy in the neighbourhood along the lines of, why do they get support and we don't?

We had collected donations in our private circle for expensive eye lenses from *Zeiss Jena* Germany (20 Euro/each) and were able to hand over 2,000 Euro months later we received a list with photos and names of those who had undergone surgery.

Suddenly the *SSDC* director, a project and a finance manager are standing here. We immediately embrace like old friends; my hosts are surprised.

Sundarbans Social Development Centre (www.ssdcindia.org.in), a large aid organisation that focuses on cataract surgery, among other things. A relatively simple outpatient operation can protect the people from blindness who would otherwise lose their last means of survival.

The plan here for *SSDC*, to travel from house to house within a two hours catchment area for outpatient diagnosis. If surgery is necessary, it's with 3-day Home-staying in the cooperatives' households. Everything is done voluntarily and as doctors' unpaid overtime. Patients have to pay their own travel costs to and from the hospital. This contribution – often a day labourer's daily wage – is important for their self-esteem. At present, the women have to travel to the city and spend the night there, which is relatively expensive for them in addition to the surgery costs; those who can afford it have the surgery done in neighbouring Nepal.

After visiting the relatively large house of my hosts in a favourable location and the neighbouring households of the cooperative with their organic kitchen gardens, the *SSDC* director quickly decides to start with a room for out-patient surgery here. *Giri* immediately made the room available for use until the next step of a hospital is realised.

So, patients can see the principle and potential of the now very successful cooperative, which helps to spread the vision of Kalimpong Green Tourism in the region. They don't want to end up like neighbouring Darjeeling town in overpriced mass tourism organized by international travel corporations. The local population or seasonal labourers work there for a pittance of 150-250 Rupees per day (1.80–3 USD).

Ambulant eye-care or hospital are not available in the region, but are urgently needed both medically and socially. In addition to preserving the eyesight of the many ageing people, it is also a small step towards a healthier diet and learning from the model of a secure basic and additional income for the SHGs and the cooperative with its agricultural and artisanal products.

After an early dinner together, the director and his two employees discuss the next steps with *Giri* and some neighbours who have joined them in the meantime. The rapid, initially outpatient implementation is intended to quickly show the people the successes before possible blindness. *Giri*, well connected politically, will look for a suitable plot of land for the hospital. According to the director, he has a donor who will buy the land and donate it to the *SSDC*.

As they say goodbye in the early evening, many people are there for the weekly sing-along. The *SSDC* director takes the opportunity once again to inform the neighbourhood about the upcoming project, he listens to their opinions and answers their questions.

The employees keep pointing at their watches, the schedule has probably gone off the rails, and driving to the next town in the dark is not without danger for them in this relatively impassable area. But he listens to the singing for a while and claps along to the beat. Finally, he says: 'Well, we're with the right people here, a hospital and patients need culture too. It would fit in very well with the cooperative with home-staying and organic gardening and its approach to this social interaction and cultural cultivation.'

Sunday school and the 'Papal-sir'

Now the time has come for me to attend Sunday School at Christmas. I started it at the very beginning in the first few days here below me in the prayer room. And about three weeks ago, with the enthusiastic support of around 20 children, *Manju* invited me to take over during her absence. Because Christmas Day this year is a Monday, I quickly moved the Sunday School to Monday; Christmas Eve is not known from a Hindu perspective. Jesus is like Mohammed, for example, just a prophet among many others before them.

Christmas Day, on the other hand, is known because the Christians here celebrate, and Nepalis, for sure, take every opportunity to celebrate together anyway. Basically, we do the same, simply adopting the festivals of other cultures as a party without their background.

My preparation is with limited resources, but there is enough paper and crayons, and some children bring their own crayons. I improvise the rest, using the scissors from my pocket knife to cut out the sun, moon, stars, circles as balls etc. for colouring and thin strips of plastic bag as hangers. *Giri* helps me with the wooden frame tree with freshly cut bamboo from the garden. Then I add three large plates with biscuits, cream sweets and pieces of cake. I draw four large paper strips: *Frohe Weihnacht* (German), *Merry Christmas*, मेरी क्रिसमस (Nepali), and as it is pronounced: *Mêrî Krisamasa*. Two sheets of my writing paper stuck together as a small poster with the programme:

- *We will do now.*
- *The story of Mini-Monkey.*
- *Singing with a Computer chorus.*
- *Christmas with my young children.*
- *Paint Christmas tree hangings,*
- *... and hang them + surprise (?).*

I forgot all about Christmas Eve because I was so busy preparing, and I did not go into the kitchen during my announced Christmas Eve fasting, it's suddenly night. I fall to bed 9 p.m. in the evening, dead tired.

We had said 10 a.m. for the next day, we already calculated Indian Time; by 11 a.m. 20 children were there. The weather is normal for Christmas Eve; bright blue skies, 22°C and a slightly cool breeze. We sit on the floor of the covered terrace and my strange contortions and grimaces during the *Mini-monkey* story at the beginning break the ice. When I pull out the bamboo Christmas tree construction from behind the curtain, the children can't stop colouring sun, moon and stars. In-between I tell them how we used to celebrate Christmas with our children and funny things that happened.

There are no arguments. Of course, a cream candy while painting works wonders. I then run out of things to hang on to and have to improvise; a break to move around and collect candy wrappers and the like with the story of the *Starfish* retold in plastic and aluminium bags. Each child is allowed to take something from the Christmas plates after collecting it. Did the adults watching understand this hint?

Giri and a neighbour, who translates me into Nepali, take photos and at the end a video of everyone singing the *Merry Christmas* song together. And all the children were excited to click on the interactive moose choir on my laptop. Each child quickly found their favourite moose, and they even tried to imitate its movements and sound on the terrace. Afterwards, the keyboard was completely covered in children's hands. But what is a sticky plastic keyboard compared to the laughing, shining eyes of children?

As soon as we have dismantled the Christmas scenario in the afternoon, the always dirty little 3-year-old boy from the day labourer's family, arrives and cleverly asks: '*Papal,* sir?' He then fights his way down the stairs free-handed with both biscuit and sweet in his hands; the loot is more important at the moment than his trousers, which are hanging down at the back of his knees.

We then wrap the Christmas tree with an LED garland from the festival of lights; in the evening it lights up in the entrance to the house on the street. A woman comes by and gives me a small dark red jewellery bag, symbolically filled with medicinal herbs. It is an invitation to New Year's Eve during the day; after the festival is before the festival.

Next morning, I'm still sitting at my desk before breakfast, writing down yesterday's news, when the little boy – as if he'd been playing in the mud at night or early in the morning – comes in looking for sweets; he asks again: '*Papal, sir?*' Luckily I still have some leftovers; and then he comes at least once a day, already calling out to me from downstairs; now I'm the Papal-sir.

I wake up at night to dogs barking and howling. I dream of my former partner who gave me a second chance and I blew it again. What happened to her and her children and her sick parents? But I can't turn back time.

A loner is howling under my balcony with the motto 'I'm a dog and I'm one of this street gang.' Annoyed, I quickly empty my half-full water bottle over him; he runs off howling. A few minutes later, I can still hear him howling, just from a corner further away. But here, nothing can really shake me anymore. I stoically accept things as they are.

Next day, little boy *Kunal* - I had asked *Manju* for his name – disappeared. Where is he, where could he have gone? I'm worried too, I realize the little boy and his '*Papal,* sir?' have somehow grown close to my heart.

In the evening, I learn that he walked to the next village. Someone recognised him there and brought him back. This reminds me of my running away once when I was three or four years old; I was found playing with the egg carbons at the coal merchant's; back then, without a telephone, it was (supposedly) normal for the coal merchant, I often played there when my father was in his neighbourhood with a work colleague.

A day later, as I'm writing late in the afternoon, looking out at the slowly setting sun, *Kunal* walks in on me. Again as dirty as ever, he drops a bag of wet clothes, looks at me questioningly. Then I say to him directly: '*Papal,* sir,' and shaking my head Indian style; he laughs.

As I try to guide him out of the room and downstairs, I see what he was doing before. All I have to do is follow the dirty, wet footprints on the tiled veranda and I end up outside by the washbasin. He must have been playing laundry. Well, I smile to myself, at least his feet got some water again.

New Year's Eve was also

In the morning *Giri* told me, we wanted to walk 2 km up-hill. I've been here long enough to know that time and distance are very, very vague here. Indian Time and a difference in altitude of 100 m or more on the serpentine road; that doesn't seem so easy, even for locals. We were invited to a (supposed) New Year's Eve event during the day.

Half past 11 a.m. I'm asked whether I want to take stairs and footpaths as a shortcut straight up or would I rather go along the road? I ask if it's as far as the house with the vet and the fish pond at the beginning of my stay here? I don't have the courage to go that far.

Yes, that would be about half the height. A friendly, 'yes,' in the affirmative, but without any substantive meaning, I now realise. But somehow I have the feeling that the question is a joke, because one neighbour is already slowly walking up the road. So we take the road, and after three or four serpentine-like curves with a bit of a climb, it's back to small talk. The driver of the village taxi lives here. He shows us his brand new car, and we are joined by two others that I also know.

Then he says, 'goodbye,' and drives off uphill. 'Holy sh ...,' I think to myself, 'what's this all about?' My companions had been laughing in Nepali the whole time, and somehow I had the feeling it was about me too. Because the brand new taxi – still without a licence plate – is parked two curves further on and we get in.

Me in the front seat of course, leather seats, plenty of legroom. My companions, four full-sized adults, squeeze into the back seat, staggered forwards and backwards. I take my revenge: 'May I offer you this comfortable seat, I'll make you a good price.' The taxi driver likes the idea after someone has laughingly translated for him. He wants to think about making this more comfortable front seat more expensive.

The festival is on New Year's Eve, but it is a religious Brahman-Hindu event of the upper caste. The daughter of the house gets her First *Sari*; now, she is an adult woman, my companions explain to me. But they are *Gurkhas*, casteless, something of their own, but there is very good food here, they laugh.

I learn later, this traditional puberty ceremony follows the lunar calendar and happens to be on New Year's Eve this year. It reminds me of confirmation or youth consecration with rituals; here with praying, blessing, incense candles and horn blowing, chanting and shouting dance around a decorated ritual mark. At the same time, the now young woman is decorated by women, including *Tika* and painting, and she receives many gifts. A monk goes round 3-times with a porter to all the visitors asking for fruits of the field; rice, flowers and money have become common, because they are the easiest to store, I learn.

Monks and priests work on a quasi-freelance basis. Here it's someone from the extended neighbourhood who also regularly plays the harmonium in our singing group. Otherwise, he is a farmer with a family, like everyone else. He is booked and paid for his religious services or remunerated with donations. So he knows the challenges and worries, people live with here.

The buffet, from a cook & catering service, is of course vegetarian and very varied and delicious. I estimate there are around 200 people of us. The house, with its small rice terraces, garden and small park-like rest areas, is some-what secluded from the road; I would have loved to live here too.

In the evening, there seem to be New Year's Eve celebrations going on somewhere. You can hear various music and drums coming up from the valley. A house nearby, where music is often played loudly anyway, also seems to be gearing up. My host meant, I shouldn't be frightened, they're sure to let off firecrackers at night. It can't get any worse than dogs howling under a full moon, I think. And because both happen to coincide, I've saved one, I laugh. I do hear the occasional firecracker later on, but I didn't notice anything about midnight.

It is unusually cool at 14°C in New Year's morning when the sun tries to fight its way through a few veil clouds. And the temple and the Hindu, or is it the Buddhist, monastery compete with each other with traditional sounds; drums, singing, flute playing … just as you would imagine it here.

My last days in Darjeeling

After New Year's Eve, the mood feels more depressing for me. Or is it my mood because I'm experiencing everything here for the last time? I sort out books for later guests and wash clothes that I want to leave here for the poor day labourer family. And I think about whether I have everything I want to take with me as memories and whether it will fit in terms of weight.

For a few days now, there have been precisely forged grilles on the kitchen house, which the neighbour's boy is now priming and painting; his mother, who cooked for us while *Manju* was away, is helping him. He has just turned 17 years old and is saving up for a second-hand scooter; the be-all and end-all for all young people here on the mountain. During the current 2-month winter holidays, he takes any job he can get; threshing rice, felling bamboo trees, working in the fields. He is only allowed to drive the scooter when he is turns 18, so he can't take it into town, he laughs, but there are no police here in the mountains.

I'm going to give him something as a parting gift, along the lines of a tank of petrol, and in return: 'So, I'll get a free ride to Kalimpong on my next visit.'

Window-grilles in the kitchen house have become necessary since regular income with some prosperity have been achieved. Gas hobs, TV, music systems are popular and can be quickly turned into money, which also increases crime. They used to have their houses open all the time, whether they were at home or not, but now it's different.

In the afternoon, *Giri*'s phone rings; it's for me. My Kolkata friends are calling from Germany and want to know if everything is okey for the return journey and whether they should send a driver? 'No, it's not necessary, someone from the village here is driving me who has just set up his own transport service; he's also cheaper than the ones from the big city,' I answer. They will be back at their Kolkata home a day after me; and I'll got a job.

In three days, the evening before I leave for Germany, there will be a reading in their new restaurant in Bengali from a book about the German *Weimar Republik* (time after World War I from 1918–33 with rise of the *Nazis* and *Hitler*), and I'm supposed to moderate it. In English, which everyone understands; there are also some who understand German.

They have already sent the book electronically to project manager *Gobin*, he will bring it to me on a USB stick; once again my electronic media diet is a hindrance, but what diet isn't?

Great, I think sarcastically, now I have to read the book in a few days and prepare a presentation with people I don't even know. I basically only have four days until the reading and am waiting for the book. The very next day at lunchtime, *Gobin* came with a USB stick containing the book for me; he also takes the opportunity to say goodbye to me.

I then read it, *Geschichte eines Deutschen* (Defying Hitler: A Memoir, by *Sebastian Haffner*) over two evenings and half the night in one sitting. I was immediately captivated by the story and looked forward to the reading and presentation, as I suddenly learnt more about my own father's childhood from the author of the book.

Late afternoon we are delighted when *Manju* returns from the workshop in Bangalore, only six hours late on a 2,600 km and 3-day train ride, wow. She naturally has a lot to tell and shows us photos as we all sit together in the evening. The neighbour has cooked for the last time, a big meal for us, her family and other neighbours.

Next day, the day before my departure, *Giri* has cut tendrils of a rare variety of *Dal*. *Manju* and I pick them, then they are dried on a traditional round tray made of bamboo netting the size of an arm until noon. I then toss them up again and again to sort out any leftover pods or straw, as seen in pictures from smallholder regions around the world.

But it is monotonous and never-ending work. But I can think and calculate: 1-sqm of ground, two or three growing poles or a simple wooden frame, cultivating and sowing, weeding, regular watering, harvesting, winnowing, sorting, drying and now throwing and sorting for a long time … the result is just under 2 kg. Is it worth the effort? 'Yes,' says *Manju*, 'it's organic, there's nowhere better,' … and after a moment's thought she adds, 'that's our tradition.' She probably thinks to herself, why do you always have to charge for everything you do?

After the lunchtime snack, I make a tea masala spice blend under *Manju*'s guidance; basically the in-house blend of cardamom, cloves, black pepper. Everything was briefly roasted before-hand to remove the last traces of moisture and make it easier to grind.

And then the monkeys give a farewell performance, as if they had known it was coming. This time it's intense, I've never seen so many at once in my life. Lots of monkey mothers with their babies clutched in their fur and the monkey kids jumping up and down the rice terraces. Even some dogs are impressed and keep their distance, barking. They also ignore tone throwing and simply duck away for a moment. I assume they can hear the stones flying towards them from the sound in the air.

Eventually I give up, exhausted but satisfied, and think that you have to be able to lose. The only thing I see as a planned provocation to me in this situation is that two of them are having sex in the middle of everyone, completely unimpressed, so to speak, producing even more offspring. Before I turn round, I give them the Stinky Finger to say goodbye.

In the evening, *Manju* puts out my former coffee box full of our freshly cooked *Dal* for me to take away. And she has cooked the rest in a large pot as fresh *Dal*. I am thrilled and hide my burgeoning tears. *Giri* surprises me with a traditional grass broom, which he has tied for me during the day. Back in my room, I have to cry after all.

Farewell ... and off to Kolkata

In the morning it is 13°C, the sun is just coming out from behind the mountain opposite and there is relatively little haze in the valley; so it will probably be another beautiful, sunny and blue day.

Manju sweeps the terrace, because two guests from Kolkata are coming today around noon. I suspect they are two Germans who I will also see in Kolkata the day after tomorrow.

Manju and *Giri* are very sad. Since their two children left home, no one has lived here with them for so long. They will probably have to get used to the fact that guests will be travelling away again; after all, offering Home-staying is their future goal.

Giri told me yesterday that he wants to set up four guest rooms. We then laughed and talked about what guests expect, and we came to some key requirements. If there isn't a normal wedding in the area, one has to be set up for tourists. He will team up with other Home-staying houses in the area, he smiles. And then definitely there should be a trained herd of monkeys and if necessary, a pair of peacocks as an emergency solution if the monkeys demand limited working hours and holidays, he laughs. I wonder if deer would work? Red deer can be tethered if necessary and they can't fly away.

Then he says that he and the neighbour across the road are going to the airport. I spontaneously want to joke that they just want to make sure I'm really away, but I don't. It's a nice day trip for them too, because they can't leave here that often.

After all, my 'goodbye' is not that easy. Luckily, the two German day visitors arrive at the same time. *Manju* is a little distracted and I don't miss the opportunity to serve everyone and myself a last *Ciyâ*.

I've already made my rounds to the immediate neighbours, to the grandmother, brother and sister-in-law next door and across the road to the neighbours.

A relative from nearby drives us. He set up his own business some time ago with his new car – he washes and polishes it spotless every day – and specialises in longer (and he emphasises) VIP trips. Like *Giri* and his brother, he is also Ex-Army. It's even written on the back of the rear window, and it seems to have some significance here.

We don't talk much because we're all a bit depressed. I promise that I'll bring the neighbour a garden gnome next time too. But that doesn't really lighten the general mood in the car. Then *Prashant* calls and wants to confirm my flight number again. He wants to be at the airport this evening when I arrive, as he's staying nearby during his internship in Kolkata.

The journey takes longer than planned, as we have to fight our way through two eternally long roadworks. The flood damage from over three months ago has still not been repaired. Shortly before Bagdogra airport near Shiliguri, we are waved out by the police. We were forced into the opposite lane by a coach that suddenly emerged from a hotel driveway. Not really a problem in India, you just drive slowly with hazard warning lights along the centre barrier against the traffic until you can turn back into your lane.

The driver gets out and back to the policeman. 'Everyone is considerate, except the police,' says *Giri*, 'they can earn some extra money now.' When the driver enters back into the car he says laughingly and sarcastic, 'everything is okey,' shaking his head in the Indian way. Did Ex-Army on the window help or rather a long handshake with a few banknotes help?

At the airport, things have to move quickly. As soon as you get out of the car, the driver is asked to leave. It makes no sense for my companions to get out, because they can't go into the airport building without a flight ticket; like everywhere else in India, it's guarded by soldiers. And they force us to get the car away. So, the farewell is short and we all try to hide our tears.

I have 5 kg spices in my cabin luggage for the restaurant in Kolkata, including 2 kg turmeric. After my checked baggage and boarding pass were done, I go on to the security check with my cabin baggage. They notice a metal object in my backpack. I open it and give the female soldier my toiletry bag, which she puts back in the radiation. "No problem, sir," she says as she hands it back to me, 'it's the stabilizing metal bar.' I put the toiletry bag back in my open backpack. Then she says, 'I smell something, what's it?' 'Oh, yes, that's just Turmeric for my friends in Kolkata,' I reply. 'Sorry, sir, such kind of spices are not allowed.' All my pleas and explanations bounce off her, of course. I understand that she has her instructions, for example, chili powder is not entirely safe. But she is kind and has a solution. I still have enough time and should go back to the check-in.

After my explanation, they call back my checked baggage and half an hour later I have repacked it. The new security check is then no problem and I'm sitting at the boarding gate. Then I remember that there's another half a kg of spice samples deep down in my backpack ... yeah, that works.

Back in Kolkata

On the flight, I flick bored through the airline's English-language magazine. At the front of the editorial is a short reflection on a travel term from another culture. The current issue, by chance, with a short article on German *Wanderlust* (historic German word for the joy of hiking and traveling). Later, back home, I search. The English language uses the German (above) term as a so-called Borrowed Word.

It reminds me of a visit to Colombia around 20 years ago. Over the Sunday coffee, we exchanged memories of our typical Sunday afternoons. I talked about such long hikes through nature with picnic or stop at a café. An uncle there says: 'Yes I've heard about this. But for me, I couldn't imagine just walking through woods and fields.' There was no suitable word in Spanish either. He preferred to watch TV, walking across his fields is for him almost every day. On special days, he likes being well-dressed in the city park. I remember that from my grandparents; see-and-be-seen, and according to informal rules regarding dress, address, etc.

Manju and *Giri* also want to see faraway countries, then again they don't. 'Who will look after the animals, the garden and fields?' Everyone around them is busy with their own daily chores at the same time; the animals and plants have no free time, weekends or even holidays. 'I've seen many other areas as a soldier,' says *Giri*, 'for me a forest is a forest, and a lonely lake is just a lonely lake.' And he decides for himself quite practically that we have everything here from top to bottom and from right to left. And for what is more they bought a TV some time ago.

Will my feeling of having to experience the whole world still remain? I have travelled a lot throughout my life, both professionally and privately, and almost on every continent. I can't imagine my life without it, even though in recent years I've been discovering more and more of my immediate surroundings at home and realise how little of it I know. And I know how good it feels to stay in one place for longer, like here.

Ultimately, however, I agree with *Giri* inwardly, because a church is a church; mosque, temple, etc. included, just places of peace and contemplation, no matter what. And everyone in the world now has shopping streets anyway, they all have the same shop systems and brands with, at best, culturally adapted trinkets; they are correspondingly uninteresting.

Later, I think about where else I want to go? Yes, I have *Wanderlust*, but it doesn't hurt me, it feels good. Unlike so many other people in the world, I personally am lucky enough to have these opportunities.

When I step out of the airport building in the dark, *Prashant* is already there. He has not missed the opportunity to welcome me; he has his internship here in Kolkata exam the next day, then he'll travel home. He has already been in contact with my friends' driver and everything is sorted.

But after just 15 minutes he has to get off the bus; he now has to go in a different direction to his hostel. We promise to stay in touch and will make an online appointment with Manu and *Giri* soon.

My bed in my friends' house in Kolkata is ready. Just a quick small talk with mum *Suniti*; I have to sleep. They return from Stuttgart next morning. They also have to sleep and, like me, adapt to the rapid change in climate. And the next day, their two German friends, who I was able to greet briefly when I left the highlands, also return. In the evening, we enjoy the finest traditional Bengali cuisine under the gui-dance of the chef in my friend's exquisite table restaurant. The next day, I withdraw from the others and pre-pare to present the reading the following day.

I have devoured the book in the last few days. It describes the time, now hundred years ago with the rise of the *Nazis* with *Hitler* from a child's and teenager's perspective. I read sentences as I experienced them as a boy and rebellious teenager in my own father-son conflict. I was politicised in a total different way, the opening to the European East in the 1970s and the left-wing terrorism, I had no idea about the *Weimar* period between the two world wars. And therefore not really about the socio-political situation of my father's childhood and youth. I only knew his rascal stories, and about his mother's early death ... now I realise some things.

In the evening, I briefly meet the translator and reader, a nice and like-able, quirky 85-year-old lady. We both briefly agree on what she would like to read and what I will take up as key words. The next morning, I go through everything again and think to myself that everything will go well.

We meet shortly before the reading. Of course, she has reconside-red, wants to leave something out and read something else instead.

The coordination gets complicated, her Bengali version, the English version and my German version don't match in terms of pages and the paragraphs ... , 'grrr.' In the end, the restaurant is full – the audience and us few Germans see many parallels in both India and Germany at the moment – and everything goes well.

Afterwards, we eat together at the Calcutta Rowing Club, just like when I left for Darjeeling three months ago. And actually as we have always done for over 12 years now; sometimes twice a year.

Some people know me there now and I recognise faces. If only it wasn't for the hot and humid climate, I would feel at home; sometimes a little bit of 'bourgeois' is nice too. And we meet an old friend, a film professor, whom I was able to invite to Germany nearly 10 years ago. Of course, there's a lot to talk about.

I notice the physical strain, now heat and high humidity again, almost 2,000 m difference in altitude in one day, so many people and cars in this mega-city. I'm short of breath and feel slightly dizzy, which then prompts my friend to call his driver for a some hundred meters distance to a restaurant.

So, I'm glad to be travelling to the airport very early the next morning; hopefully everything with the by themselves named *Star Alliance* with *Air India–Lufthansa* will go according to plan this time.

From 'Wanderlust' back to a new journey 'home'

Of course not, nothing is going according to plan. Flights have been postponed indefinitely due to fog in Delhi. I stay calm, I have a 6-hour time buffer there. In the end, I barely make the flight Delhi–Frankfurt, and I can even switch to a free seat in the emergency exit row with more legroom.

An icy cold weather awaits me in Frankfurt, but I savour it. Considering that I've just come from the Himalayas, I smile proudly to myself. But my joy is already gone on the rail platform, nothing works at first. Many northbound trains are cancelled, snow, roadworks, track closures. Then I enter train on the to next platform to a town near my home town, that should have left an hour ago ... at some point it actually sets off. But it stops at a suburban station on the other side of the river *Rhein*. I can see the central station across the river. Queues at the information desks. I give up when they tell me: 'Take a regional train back to another city and then continue by tram to my hometown.' But will it run? They don't know. It can't get any worse, I think.

Then I laugh at myself. I was supposed to be born in this town here. My mother, heavily pregnant, travelled by bus in the snow exactly in this month now to my father in the countryside, who had found a job there after being a prisoner of war. And almost exactly 67 years ago, she couldn't get back home to this town here in time due heavy snow-fall; so I had to be born somewhere in the middle of nowhere on this side of the river; this was a lifelong disaster from grandparents' s point of view.

The sarcasm is gone at the latest in the icy wind on the Cathedral Bridge – you walk exactly straight onto Cologne Cathedral next to the main station – with two 23-kg bags and a heavy backpack. My son and his girl friend had left a big travel bag with their Nepal hiking equip-ment in Kolkata, which they didn't need on their way to South East Asia, and I was now taking it back for them.

Even if I'm not the physically strongest, sometimes I can be persis-tently stubborn. Instead of possibly taking a taxi, when something is not working in the area, I have to fight my way with a full backpack and two heavy travel bags across a bridge after three months, while sweating like a ...

Completely exhausted and soaked in sweat, I'm then later standing in the underground at the central station and, as ordered, tram no. 16 arrives on time and practically pulls up to my door in my home town. That works, I think, and sit happily in the tram.

And so I see strange figures on the train at the night. Diagonally opposite me, someone seems to be proudly showing off his weed use to everyone by making few joints in an affected, artificial celebration.

A mountain of letters and e-mails, a full answering machine and a totally cold flat await me at home. Of course, I'm still too wound up and can't sleep. So I sit down to deal with the old and new communication technologies.

Having just somehow survived Deutsche Bahn's (German Railway) nocturnal information policy, I'm now skimming over a rejected objection notice from 2007 (!), which was delivered to me now 15 years later. I'm in Germany, a file number is processed, no matter how long it takes ... wow. A university circular e-mail has a 7-page document on Gender Appropriate Language attached ... but why Germany, we are only 1% of the world population. Why not start directly with English, so half of the world's population is reached straight away ... it would be much more effective to remove every single Man and all Men together from Woman and Women? Then I see the headline of a government party: Companies against the new Supply Chain Law, and I add in my thought, ... but for Child Labour. I realise, I'm really back home; irony up to even cynicism are still good fun for me.

I lie down in a hot bath; what a pleasure. Even if things back home are often complicated, incomprehensible, narrow-minded, opinionated ... quasi *Kafkaesque* in the finest mood, it's still nice here. The socially romanticised Ideal World only exists in fairy tales.

Honey

At the end of January 2024, I open the honey that my hosts have given me as a gift for breakfast. It's their first home-made honey from their own kitchen garden. I was naturally delighted to see two bee boxes in the garden when I arrived. Unfortunately, one of them was empty; 'fled,' laughed *Manju*.

At the beginning of December, I was there when they harvested their own Darjeeling Organic Garden Honey for the first time. They think it's a good idea, but they haven't thought about marketing it yet, as the quantity isn't yet sufficient. *Manju* learnt beekeeping in a workshop run by an aid organisation for the cooperative and had previously taken part with a friend.

Both, *Manju* and *Giri* wear typical beekeeping nets as head protection. They work without gloves and with a rather pitiful incense lamp. Of course, I keep a safe distance in my own interest. While *Giri* repeatedly and ultimately unsuccessfully relights the incense burner and searches for the problem, *Manju* continues to work calmly and carefully pulls the honeycomb frames out of the top of the hive with his bare hands. 'The important thing is to keep quiet, I'm not doing anything to them, they get sugar water from us too', she smiles ... and continues very quietly, 'I'm only stealing their honey, but they don't realise that until later because they're so happy about the sugar water.'

Everything goes into a large bowl, including parts of the combs. Then the bee box is closed again and both of them squat around this and another bowl and let the honeycombs drip off first; some of the honey really runs out. *Manju* removes individual bees sitting or stikking to the honey-comb with his fingers and carefully sets them aside. In-between, we all took teaspoon as a honey test, divine. The honey is much darker in colour than our honey. And all without being stung even once. *Manju* has often calmly caught a bee that has strayed into the kitchen – or strategically spied on it – with bare hand and brought it back outside. In the end, the quantity results in three full 0.75-litre bottles, which equates to 3 kg of honey.

With the one bee colony, they have twice this amount per year. They don't want to sell any honey yet, although the market for such cooperative organic Himalayas honey in Kolkata, for example, is crying out for it. They would like to revive the second hive soon.

One of my favourite breakfasts in Germany is a poppy seed roll with honey, which I once told them during small talk at dinner when we were comparing eating habits. I got it from my grandfather, who also had bee colonies. Unfortunately, most of our honey is now artificially extended. My Darjeeling hosts have heard that too, and that it's better to make honey yourself if you have a kitchen garden. As bread and bread rolls are unknown here, they baked me *Roti* with poppy seeds in the pan a few days later – an absolutely lovely gesture.

Tears well up in my eyes as I drip honey onto the bread roll. This reminds me of how *Manju* and the neighbour's wife later asked me again and again when, in their opinion, I ate too little. So, it became here in Lower Echhey my nickname *One more-sir?*

... and a word afterwards

अवसरहरू आउँछन्, तर टिक्दैनन्। *(Avasaraharū ā'um̐chan, tara ṭikdainan)*
Opportunities come, but they don't linger.

Nepalese proverb

These true events in the places described could also have been in any other hospital or retreat, far or near. It's always a question of what you decide to do while you're still in hospital, whether it's only days or months away.

It wasn't until later that I accepted how important it is to communicate, especially with my family and close friends; I suppressed it too often. Many people are also confronted with cancer in their own social environment. And even now I'm still dodging some questions and playing them down a bit.

In psychotherapy, I learnt that the people around me have a right to the truth. That's another reason for this book, even if it's a bit of an attempt to communicate openly for the most part, but only indirectly. Because I don't just have physical fears that it will all come back, but also feelings, of course. Which brings me back to the beginning. I can't and don't want to say every-thing, but I hope I have opened up a little more.

After I've totalled up the medical bills I've collected (in sum around 175,000 Euro so far), I put the Red Folder back on the shelf, but now far to the back so that it's no longer in my field of vision.

And I've more or less finished the book now. Does this now mean that leukaemia is over for me? And am I now cured? Or am I only free of cancer for an indefinite short or long time?

In a book by a doctor who survived his own cancer, I read that you are never cured; you were only cured if you have died of another disease or a natural death. Yes, leukaemia is a closed topic for me and somehow never again ... but now with a good feeling.

These parallel records, independent yet somehow interwoven, they complete the circle for me between the months spent in hospital in

286

quasi-quarantine and the spartan surroundings of a small farm in Darjeeling. The longer I spent away from the hospital and back in the company of others, as in my previous everyday life, the more I found myself longing for the solitude of a confined space.

The time in the hospital, ultimately being left to my own devices in a limited living space, was therefore also an important part of my life. Of course, it wasn't just medical, social and scenic – basically, the hospital ward was also a kind of landscape around me – documentary observations. I often digressed according to my nature, such as into socio-cultural and -political topics; that is my emotional side. I am a human being, subjective, emotional ... and I'm happy about that.

Just before I left for Darjeeling, I read short stories Attention! Prejudices by *Peter Ustinov,* he wrote shortly before he passed away as a kind of retrospective of his life. One sentence has been etched in my mind ever since: 'There is much to suggest that in an empty head, prejudice flourishes.' How true, I immediately thought at the time.

As I now was writing, I kept thinking of this sentence and how to incorporate it into the book ... there it is.

All my experiences and feelings, even new to me, are shared by many of us. They have always existed in humanity, ergo, it's Part of Life.

You always hear people saying that life is so short. I see their efforts everywhere, but they also try to organise it in the same way. They simply don't know how to organise and use their time. They complain that everything goes by so quickly, and yet at the same time it is always not fast enough for them. Always striving for a goal, always regretting in-between that it will be so long before they reach it. If only it were tomorrow and another, if only it were next month, next year ... Nobody wants to live today, they are never satisfied with the present moment. They would gladly give their all if they could speed things up until they reach their goal.

Loosely based on Jan-Jaques Rousseau (1712-1778)